MARY LAY

THE PRICE OF COAL

MARY LAY

First published in Great Britain in 2022
Mary Lay Stories

A CIP Catalogue of this book is available
from the British Library

ISBN: 978-1-7396653-3-3 (Paperback)

First e-book edition September 2022
ISBN: 978-1-7396653-2-6

Cover and layout design by Chandler Book Design
www.chandlerbookdesign.com

Self-published by Mary Lay Stories
www.marylaystories.com

Printed in Great Britain by
TJ Books, Padstow, Cornwall

For Lily

CONTENTS

1

THE FUNERAL

The 17:20 train to Cheltenham left Oxford station in a swirl of steam and determined snowflakes. Caroline Munhead pulled her knitted scarf up over her mouth and tried to shrink into the corner of the carriage seat she shared with a pair of businessmen in dark suits and bowler hats. Three similarly dressed men sat opposite, each reading a folded newspaper and disinterested in their fellow passengers.

The carriage was cold, even for January. 1926 had begun with the usual winter weather expected in the south of England. Snow, ice, wind and fog clung to woollen clothes and crept through crevices. Caroline had been thankful that her visit to Oxford had been a largely indoor affair. She had been met at Oxford station that morning by Luke Frampton, newly-qualified doctor and brother of Caroline's old school friend Midge. They had arranged to tour the Pitt Rivers and Ashmolean museums after Caroline had shown an interest in Luke's knowledge of history. Though a doctor of medicine, he could have studied history had he wanted to.

Caroline thought back over the day. She liked Luke but had a feeling he was rather keener on her than she was on him. There had been times where she had felt more lectured than spoken to as they had moved from exhibit to exhibit, when she had been quite able to read the information on the exhibit labels herself. The shrunken heads of the Pitt Rivers and the mummy of the priest Djed-djehuty-iuef-ankh that lay in his inner coffin at the Ashmolean's Egyptian hall had been her favourite items, and she wished she could have spent more time looking at them. The throng of visitors had been three-deep however, and she found herself uncomfortably pressed up against other people until Luke had stepped back and allowed her some more space.

When Luke suggested the outing while Caroline stayed at the Frampton's vicarage in Pangbourne before Christmas, she hadn't been sure that she would be able to meet him. Between her job at the Sunningend engineering works where she sewed canvas onto frames that were eventually assembled into aeroplanes, and her mother Elizabeth's illness, her time was less her own now than it had been the previous year. She had wanted to work, though she did not need to. She had not wanted to become nurse or companion again to her mother, and she was thankful that this time her father George had employed a professional in Nurse Alexander. It had been so different, she mused, when her older brother Freddie had been killed in the last days of the Great War.

Elizabeth had taken the news of Freddie's death badly. She was inconsolable and became mute for several weeks. Prescribed laudanum, which brought its own issues, Elizabeth had taken a long time to regain her former self and Caroline had become central to her world. Their relationship was tense rather than close. George Munhead eventually asserted his authority and Elizabeth agreed to at least let Caroline occasionally out of her sight, if not out on her own. It had meant that Caroline had missed out on the social events that a girl could expect in Cheltenham in the early 1920s, with only an occasional trip to the cinema when her neighbour Florence was home from the finishing school she had been sent to.

The carriage jolted and rocked along, the businessmen taking turns to unfold and refold their newspapers. Caroline wondered who they were, where they worked, if they had families. She was interested in people of all kinds and, much to her mother's annoyance, had started to make friends across the social classes over the previous year. A small allowance from her father had enabled Caroline to begin accepting invitations, and 1925 had been a year of new experiences for her. As she started to doze in her corner, Caroline wondered what 1926 had in store.

When Caroline arrived home the curtains were drawn and the trees in Glencairn Road were swaying with the cold breeze. She was hungry and chilled, and hoped that Annie their maid had left some dinner on the stove for her. Caroline had grown up at number twenty, arriving with her parents and brother when she was two years old, and Freddie was eight. It was a substantial family home built in 1905, furnished in a heavy Victorian style which had developed a patina over the years with constant rubbing of hands and scuffing of feet. Her father had bought the house from the builder at a very reasonable price, assisted by a small mortgage from the Cheltenham and Gloucester Benefits Building Society where he worked as a senior accountant. That mortgage was now paid, and the family lived comfortably though not extravagantly.

The house and those of its fellows in the curved street off Queens Road backed on to the railway embankment. The gardens were large enough for vegetable and flower beds. Number twenty had a pair of apple trees and was separated from the next-door properties by low brick walls. Growing up, Caroline had spent many hours sitting on the curved top of the wall with the twins Florence and Timothy who lived at number twenty-two and were the same age as Caroline. They had shared a governess for a short while before Caroline had begun as a weekly boarder at Mrs Pendersen's School at Pittville on the other side of town. It was unusual for a local girl to board at the school, but George foresaw a lack of playmates for his daughter as he and his wife had no siblings and therefore no cousins for Caroline to socialise with. As Freddie was considerably older, his social circle had been very different.

Caroline had adored Freddie, as had most people who knew him. He was happy, energetic, friendly and curious about everything. He loved music and played the piano and sung in the choir. He played chess and was good at mathematics and sports at school. He would have gone to university, or to a technical school, had the Great War not entranced his generation and ultimately captured and devoured him. He died just a few days after his twenty-first birthday in France, crossing a canal under enemy fire, and only days before the Armistice.

As Caroline hung up her coat in the hallway and placed her bag, gloves and hat on the side table, she noticed the house was silent. On Saturday evenings, her father had taken to playing her mother music from the old phonograph which he had carried upstairs to her room. That evening there was no music. Caroline went along the hallway to the kitchen. Annie was not there, but the scene was of domestic pride, with every surface scrubbed and a covered plate on the stovetop which Caroline gratefully moved to the table and began to eat from.

There were only two years in age difference between Caroline and their maid Annie, and the young women had much less of a mistress and servant relationship than would normally have existed. While Annie always addressed Caroline as Miss, Caroline thought of Annie as a surrogate sister and their conversations were often intimate and unguarded. Annie would be married soon to her long-time boyfriend Jacob Jenks, whose father had a coal yard next to the railway station. She hoped to stay in the Munhead's employment until the couple were expecting their first child. Annie had begun as a maid of all work, but since the family's cook Mrs Monger had retired, Annie had taken on those duties as well. She slept in the attic room during the week, going home to her parents and sisters on Saturday afternoon and returning after church on Sunday.

The house had a routine. George asked very little of Annie, being generally uncomfortable with the master-servant relationship himself. Elizabeth was more at home with giving instructions but as Annie proved her worth, and needed less supervision, the household had settled down together. Caroline had begun to learn some simple dishes from Annie over the past year, with the understanding that eventually she would need to be able to feed herself, and at some point, perhaps a husband and family too.

As Caroline finished the mashed potato, carrots and slice of steak and onion pie that had been left for her, her father appeared in the kitchen doorway.

"I thought I'd heard you come home," he looked drawn, tired; his eyes red-rimmed.

"I was about to make some tea. Would you like a cup?" Caroline got up and moved to pick up the black kettle.

"Caroline, please, stop for a moment. Your mother… she passed away this afternoon."

They stood, looking at each other across the kitchen table. In the bottom of the stove, the fire shifted as the coal burnt. George moved first and sat down on the chair nearest to the door. Caroline replaced the kettle and sat down again.

"I'm sorry I wasn't here."

"I am glad that you were not. She has been in such pain, and now… she is not. Nurse Alexander has taken care of everything."

"Can I see her?" it felt the right thing to say, even though Caroline did not want to. She had never seen a dead person before.

"Of course. Shall I go with you, or would you rather be alone?"

Looking at her father's haggard face, Caroline recognised that he needed time to himself.

"I'll go by myself. Would you make some tea for us please and we can have it in the parlour when I come down?"

Elizabeth's bedroom smelled of soap. Nurse Alexander was an advocate of Wright's Coal Tar, and the smell would from then on always be associated with this moment in Caroline's mind. Elizabeth had been washed and redressed in a clean nightgown and laid out under a single sheet on her bed. Her long hair, now thin, grey and wavy, spread out on her pillow framing her face. Caroline thought how small she looked. She realised how little her mother had eaten over the weeks since first being taken to the hospital after admitting to the lump in her side. Caroline shivered; the fire was of course not lit, and the only light came from the bedside lamp.

The chair her father had been sitting on all afternoon was next to the bed. Caroline perched on it and reached out to touch with the tips of her fingers her mother's hand which lay on top of the sheet. She imagined George had been holding it, cold against his own warm skin. Caroline did not take her mother's hand. She could not remember the last time she had touched her mother's skin. Elizabeth had not been one to demonstrate her feelings for her children with hugs or kisses.

Caroline wondered if this event would cause a radical change in her life, or if things would carry on much as they had over the past year. She had begun to venture further from home on her own and with the friends she was making. Would her father now expect her to spend more time at home with him? Could Elizabeth's death clip Caroline's wings just as she was learning to fly on her own? If he insisted, she would give up her job and take on the running of the home. A sudden wave of defiance rose up inside her; she would not give up her new-found freedoms and step back in time. Freddie would never have been expected to do so, and she was determined to go on living on his behalf.

Elizabeth's death was not a surprise. After ten minutes, Caroline decided that tears would not come and went back downstairs to find George in the parlour, the tea pot, cups and saucers on the table. She went to him, placed her hands on his shoulders from behind and kissed the top of his head. He patted her hand. They had always been closer, particularly since Freddie's death. George did not live vicariously through Caroline but wished her to have the opportunities and freedoms that he understood were now expected by young girls of her age. He met many people in his position as branch manager, from all walks of life, and had a genuine interest in them all. This position of privilege had allowed him to gradually understand how much Caroline had been made to sacrifice in looking after Elizabeth, even as Caroline had not known it at the time. He had encouraged Caroline's interest in history and art, and they had often spent Saturday afternoons in his study looking at maps, reading newspapers and periodicals, and discussing current affairs.

As Caroline took up the teapot, George cleared his throat, "Just the two of us now, my dear."

"Yes, Father," she handed him his cup.

"Did you enjoy your visit to Oxford?"

Caroline sat down again opposite her father, "I did, thank you. Luke is so full of information. I rather think I preferred the Pitt Rivers, with its strange collection. Have you heard of the shrunken heads?"

"I have heard of them, yes, but never seen them."

"They are grotesque, doll-like, and yet fascinating at the same time. Luke says some people consider them to be mementos of their loved ones…," she paused, her cheeks blushed red, "I'm sorry, that was insensitive of me."

"Not at all my dear. Your animation is a relief from the weight of today," he tried to smile.

Caroline continued to describe some of the objects she had seen for a few moments. As she talked, she also developed a second train of thought; she did not know what society expected when a person died at home. There had been no funeral for Freddie, no grave to attend. As her voice trailed off, George appeared to read her mind.

"The undertaker will be here in the morning before we go to church. They will take your mother to their premises. I did not want her laid out in here."

Caroline nodded.

"I will speak to the Reverend Canon in the morning," George continued, "and arrange the funeral. The ground is not frozen so I would expect it to be held next week.

You should know, your mother and I purchased a plot in the cemetery some time ago."

He sipped his tea, "People will expect to congregate here afterwards. Annie will need to prepare light refreshments, small sandwiches and the like. I wonder, should we obtain a coffee pot? People seem to prefer coffee these days."

Caroline was surprised at the question. She had noticed over the past year that many people did indeed prefer coffee, but at home they only had tea and occasionally hot chocolate or Ovaltine.

"I don't think we need to purchase a coffee pot. Mother would not have wanted it."

"Yes, you are right. Would you call in at Curzon's when we have a date confirmed and arrange the flowers? Some for the church, a small arrangement for here, and a small basket for the grave," the last word caught in his throat, and he took another sip of tea, "I shall place an announcement in the *Chronicle* and order some appropriate stationery for afterwards. One attends funerals of course, but one rarely needs to consider the mechanics of them."

"I have never been to a funeral, have I? Did I when I was very young?"

"No, I don't believe so. Your grandparents died before you were born, except your mother's mother who died when you were a few months old. And of course, we were spared the scourge of the influenza, and then Freddie…"

Caroline and her father spoke to the Reverend Canon after the morning service at Christ Church and arranged for the funeral to be held on Thursday of the following week. On their walk home Caroline called in to Curzon's Exotic Plant Nursery which inhabited approximately five acres across both sides of Queens Road. She expected to find

Josiah Curzon in his home behind the glasshouses but there was no sign of his motorcar. The majority of his employees were attending services at St Mark's, Christ Church and the Methodist Chapel on Gloucester Road and the only worker Caroline could find was a young boy who was engaged in washing used plant pots in a bucket. A black and white cat lay on its back nearby and watched the boy attentively. Caroline gave the boy a penny and instructed him to ask Mr Curzon to call that afternoon.

Annie was in the kitchen when Caroline returned home, mixing batter for Yorkshire puddings. She had assisted Nurse Alexander the afternoon before and had hurried back to Glencairn Road as soon as the service at St Mark's Church had ended that morning rather than lingering with Jacob. Caroline sat at the kitchen table as she had so often done over the years with Annie bustling around her.

"The funeral will be Thursday at one o'clock. Father says he has some papers to attend to this afternoon and should not be disturbed. I am expecting Mr Curzon to call about flowers. Hopefully he will not be late as I also want to visit Mary and Philip."

Philip Rose was the young curate assisting the soon-to-retire vicar at St Mark's. Caroline had become good friends with both Philip and his wife Mary since they moved to the parish in the autumn of 1924. Philip expected to become the vicar of St Mark's in the coming months, and was well liked by the parishioners, although some were still to be won round on account of Mary's Caribbean heritage. Caroline had needed no such encouragement; she and Mary had hit it off immediately and their friendship had been the first real test of Caroline's resolve against her mother's wishes to make new friends of her own. Mary had been born in Trinidad but had arrived in Bristol with her mother Celestine as a

two-year-old. Her father was with the British Army in Africa
and had been for many years; Celestine still lived in Bristol.
Caroline had unexpectedly assisted with the birth of Philip
and Mary's daughter Angelica the previous summer and was
now the little girl's godmother.

"You'll be having the wake here afterwards?" Annie asked.

"Yes, you and I should go through the requirements after
lunch. Father does not want any extravagance. Do you think
potted meat and fish sandwiches would be acceptable?"

"Yes Miss, and fruit cake. I'll make one this afternoon
with a drop of sherry in it. How many are we expecting?"

"Do you know, I have no idea. Mother was known at
church of course but wasn't very sociable beyond that.
Perhaps twenty people? I will ask Father, but we need to
take as much of the decision-making from his shoulders as
we can."

Josiah Curzon called at Glencairn Road as Caroline and
George were eating dessert and Caroline received him in the
parlour. The floral arrangements were quickly agreed, and
invitations extended to Josiah and his fiancé (and Caroline's
next-door neighbour) Florence. Once lunch was finished,
Caroline set out to visit Mary Rose. A light rain was falling,
occasionally turning to sleet. The fifteen-minute walk to
the small end-of-terraced house that the Church rented
on Philip and Mary's behalf was enough to chill Caroline
and she hoped that her friends would be at home when
she arrived.

Philip welcomed her in and showed her through to the
small kitchen at the rear of the house with its brick floor and
big black range. Mary was sitting on a chair by the side of
the range, Angelica sleeping in the crook of her arm. Washed
nappies were hung from a length of string tied to each end

of a shelf, and the small window that looked out on to the back yard was steamed up with condensation. Philip left the women to talk, and Mary explained quietly that Angelica was teething and had only just gone to sleep after being awake since four that morning. The baby turned her dark head at Mary's voice and the women held their breath until they were sure she was still asleep.

Caroline asked quietly if there was anything she could do. Under Mary's direction she turned the drying clean nappies on the makeshift washing line and put the kettle on the hotplate to boil for tea. Caroline noticed that the coal scuttle was almost empty and asked if she should fill it from the bunker in the yard. Mary said she mustn't spoil her clothes and that Philip would do it later. The women talked about Caroline's visit to Oxford and about her mother. Philip appeared again at the sound of the kettle boiling and Caroline was able to ask him more questions about funerals and their administration. She wanted to understand as much as possible so that she could assist her father. Philip offered to mention Elizabeth in the service that evening and include her in their prayers, which Caroline thanked him for.

Caroline usually visited the Rose family on a Wednesday after she finished work, and more often than not had her dinner with them before returning home. Today she declined their offer to stay to tea and agreed that she would not visit again that Wednesday but would see them all after the funeral on Thursday at Glencairn Road. Philip asked Caroline several times if she and her father would be alright. She reassured him that with Annie still engaged as their domestic, they would all manage.

It was sleeting more determinedly when Caroline left the Rose's home. Philip returned to the kitchen and added more hot water to the teapot.

"She is holding up very well."

Mary yawned, then answered in her lilting musical voice, "She would be more upset if it was her father laid out."

"Yes, I rather got that impression. Elizabeth's passing does at least end her suffering. We should thank God that it was not prolonged."

"It may yet be a blessing," Mary said with her eyes closed.

Mrs Betty Chandler, supervisor of the day shift sewing room and dope room at Sunningend engineering works, agreed to Caroline's request for the afternoon off for Thursday. She would leave work at midday when the girls stopped for their lunch and forfeit the afternoon's pay. Caroline's friend Lottie was very concerned to hear of Elizabeth's death, and equally concerned that Caroline did not appear to be upset by it all. They had their lunch in the cloakroom, which was less crowded now that a small café had opened opposite the railway station and offered a range of cheap lunches to the workers of Gloucester Road. Caroline tried to explain her relationship with her mother.

"I am sad of course, but not distraught. It was not a shock; more a question of when and not if."

"I would be terribly upset if my mother died. Or Father. Or anyone I knew."

"I can't explain it Lottie, I feel sad but also relieved that she is no longer in pain. I haven't cried. I don't feel like the tears are there. Perhaps I will on Thursday. Perhaps then it will become more real."

The service at Christ Church was simple, despite the church's status as High Anglican. There were over thirty people in attendance, and most followed the cortege through the streets to the town cemetery on the edge of Prestbury.

George said very little, and Caroline stayed by his side, her arm through his. The day was grey and still, and everyone was thankful that the sleet and rain had passed.

Caroline and George caught the tram home and had only just removed their coats when the first of the visitors arrived to pay their respects and consume the sandwiches and cake that Annie had prepared. Extra kettles and teapots had been borrowed for a steady supply of hot water and tea to warm the guests. The parlour filled, people lingered in the dining room and the hallway. George stayed in the parlour while Caroline helped Annie keep the tea flowing. Philip Rose stayed briefly, offered a few words of comfort to George and Caroline and explained that Angelica had had another sleepless night causing Mary to remain at home with her. It was almost half past four and the house at its capacity for comfort when Josiah Curzon arrived with Florence. Caroline and George thanked him for the flowers, for which Josiah had refused payment. Florence drew Caroline to one side while the men talked.

"I need to tell you we have set a date for our wedding. Saturday the twentieth of February at the Methodist chapel on Gloucester Road. Naturally there will be written invitations, but I wanted to tell you as soon as we had it confirmed. And look!"

She thrust her left hand towards Caroline. Josiah had already purchased an engagement ring before Christmas for his intended, but Florence now had what she called an eternity ring to accompany it. It was a thin gold band, set with tiny stones whose initials Florence explained spelled out 'dearest'. Caroline thought it gaudy but smiled and congratulated her neighbour. There had been a time when Elizabeth had hoped for Caroline to be in Florence's shoes, and Caroline felt relieved that she was not. Josiah had been widowed after only a few years of marriage to his first wife and had not expected to find another.

Florence was enticed by the opportunity that selling a portion of the nursery site to a builder had presented to Josiah. Their age difference did not appear to trouble her, she had expected to eventually marry an older man who would have established himself in some business or other. Florence's parents, both teachers who had attended Elizabeth's funeral but declined the refreshments afterwards, were consenting although her wealthy great aunt was less happy about the situation and referred to Josiah as 'the tradesman'.

"Caroline, would you be my Maid of Honour? I really have no one else to ask. It's a simple job really, just help me dress, carry my bouquet, that sort of thing."

Caroline was used to Florence's inconsiderate timing and streak of selfishness, and in some ways was grateful for the change from being offered condolences. She agreed and hugged Florence before excusing herself once again to the kitchen.

As the last few mourners finished off the tea and the final sandwich triangle, there was one more caller at Glencairn Road. It was almost six o'clock and Caroline and George were both feeling wrung out after so much restrained socialising. Annie had been instructed to make no more sandwiches or tea at half past five in an attempt to bring the proceedings to a close. Caroline was standing just inside the parlour doorway when Annie quietly informed her that Lottie's brother, Bob Lewis, was in the hallway and didn't want to come any further on account of still being in his work clothes. He would have waited on the doorstep had it not been too cold to leave the door open.

Caroline went out to meet him. He was standing awkwardly, cap in hand.

"Thank you for coming, Bob. Would you like something to eat or drink?"

"No, thank you, I won't linger. I just wanted to pay my respects and see how you were faring," the genuine look of concern on his face drew a sad smile from Caroline. He wanted to put his arms around her, but found his feet welded to the floor. It would have been inappropriate in any case, he thought.

"It was expected, as you know. And there has been so much to arrange, one doesn't realise until it happens. This has come in useful though," she produced the handkerchief that Bob had given her at Christmas, with her initial embroidered on one corner by his sister.

Bob nodded without smiling, "I never meant for you to have to use it like this. Caroline, this Sunday might be too soon, but if you would like to take a walk around Montpellier gardens next Sunday for an hour or so, I would be happy to walk with you."

He had rehearsed the lines on his way there, sitting on the tram as it chimed its way along Gloucester Road, but having said them out loud now he thought it sounded a crass invitation.

Caroline could see his discomfort. She stepped forward and placed her hand on his arm.

"I think I should like that, thank you. If the weather is fine, would you call for me at half past two?"

"I will do. Now I won't stay, I've to be getting back as there's a meeting this evening about changes in the gas supply if anything happens with the miners. I'll call for you, half past two."

He hesitated, desperate to kiss her cheek as he'd seen other men do with their girlfriends but couldn't quite bring himself to do so there in her hallway. He sniffed, turned and let himself out through the front door as George was accompanying their last visitors into the hall for their coats and hats. He looked enquiringly at his daughter; she was looking at the closed door and unaware of his gaze.

12 January 1926
Budleigh Salterton, Devon
Darling Caro,

My sincere condolences of course on your mother's passing. I sympathise totally as you'll remember I lost my dear sister Sophia only three years ago. Ones' parents always seem so robust, and yet death stalks us all.

Should you feel the need to get away, we are completely at your disposal. In fact, Tommy insists that you come down as soon as you are able. He is in his element here, there has been a change in him since we moved in, and he took up his painting again in earnest. That's not to say we no longer have occasional nocturnal visitors of course, but he is more focused, even more determined to create than ever before. It is quite refreshing and keeps him occupied.

I too have been busy ingratiating myself in Budleigh Salterton's lofty circles. I have joined the Women's Institute and have my sights on the parish council. You'll note from the return address above, we have taken a house on the main street in the village. A stout little place with a footbridge over the stream that also runs along the main street here. We have a daily, and Tommy is negotiating the use of a shed to store his beloved car at the bottom of our tiny garden. You would love it here, truly. Do say you'll come down. We can meet you at the station here in Budleigh and we have ample room. Stay as long as you like, or as long as your Mrs Chandler will permit!

I insist you write and let me know which train you will be arriving on – or telephone us, we are Budleigh 125.

Yours sympathetically
Helen

Helen Postgate, school friend of Caroline and now wife of Tommy Gersen-Fisch, had written as soon as she received Caroline's short note with the news of Elizabeth's death. Caroline had written a similar note to Midge, dropping both into the red post-box in Queens Road on her way to work. Helen's letter arrived on the day of the funeral and Caroline read it before she went to sleep that evening.

She had been a witness to Helen and Tommy's unconventional wedding in Blackpool a few months before. Helen and Tommy had no romantic or sexual interest in each other (both were attracted to their own sex) but for convenience and respectability's sake they had decided to get married and rent a house in south Devon together where they could live as they chose without familial interference. Caroline had always been slightly in awe of Helen, her more sophisticated friend. Tommy, she had warmed to immediately when they first met, and she was pleased to hear that their arrangement appeared to be working as they had planned.

It was too soon to abandon her father and run off to Devon, Caroline decided. But she would see her friends again after a suitable period of mourning and Florence's wedding had taken place. Budleigh Salterton, what a curious name.

2

THE WEDDING

While Caroline was thankful for the money and the distraction that her job provided, she found she had an increase in activity to keep her occupied once her mother's funeral was over. Florence became a more regular visitor, now using the kitchen door as her entry and exit, and preparations for the wedding consumed much of their spare time. Florence was having difficulty reconciling her wish for a lavish event with Josiah's personal Methodist sense of restraint. Josiah was willing to pay for whatever Florence wanted, but at the same time instructed her on what would be acceptable to his fellow congregation members and minister. The sale of land had been completed and the couple were viewing houses in Cheltenham's respectable Tivoli and Montpelier areas, Florence standing firm that she would not move into the squat, brick house that sat amongst the glasshouses of the Curzon empire.

Bob had called on what had become the last dry day that year so far. They walked through Lansdown to the Montpellier public gardens and drank tea in the pavilion before walking back again. Caroline had felt conspicuous in her mourning black and resolved to banish it to the back of her wardrobe once the outfit had been laundered. Two weeks had passed since her mother's death, and she felt that should be a sufficiently respectful period. Over their tea Caroline confided in Bob that she was concerned about her father. He had been spending long hours in his study and she had had to sometimes persuade him to leave his papers and take meals with her.

To change the subject, she asked about the meeting that Bob had had to hasten back to on the evening of the funeral.

"There is talk of a miners' strike. Surely you will have read about it in the newspaper? Father has been keeping his ear to the ground and says it's likely they'll go out sooner or later. They say it'll be all mines, even the ones in the Forest which is where most of our coal comes from here. The meeting was to discuss whether we could cope with any increased demand for gas if it happens. The management wanted some figures and to understand the peak times now. They seemed happy enough with what we told them, but I don't mind telling you Caroline, it will be a nasty business if the miners do strike. It'll only be a day or so before people start running low on coal and other things. The prices will go up, fires will go out. We've got supplies in reserve of course at the gas works, but they won't last long. No bread to be had, and no tea!" He drained his cup, "There's even talk of a General Strike, but I don't think it will come to that."

Caroline tried to imagine a life without coal. It was unthinkable. So many depended on it for their heat, cooking, laundry, how would anyone cope for long without it? She thought of Annie's fiancé Jacob and his father's coal yard. How long would they manage with no deliveries?

"The miners must know they would be doing great damage to the country if they did strike. It seems rather selfish."

"Of course they do, that's the point. They have no other recourse, Caroline. It's not like living in a town or city, there are no other jobs to be had around the mines. Whole families are employed in the same place, so all suffer if the wages are cut, or the hours extended. We could say they should find work elsewhere, but where? They won't take action lightly, they know they will lose pay and could be locked out, but what else can they do to bring their conditions to the attention of those who could do something to assist them?"

"Would you ever strike?"

"I pray I never need to. It's a last resort for desperate men. They deserve a fair wage and to see daylight now and then, not to be kept down underground for twelve, thirteen, fourteen hours a day for three pounds a week. But it's the agitators that are egging them on, you see. Father says the unions are tied up with the communists."

"And you aren't a member of a union?"

"No. I can see the benefit of them, the Gas Workers and General Labourers union was one of the first to be formed and there are quite a few who've joined them recently, but this 'one out all out' at the blast of a whistle doesn't seem to me to be the best way to improve conditions. To be honest with you, we're alright at the gas works. Pay is reasonable and most of us work five and a half days a week. We even get our summer outing, though there was no Christmas box this year. No, I'm in no hurry to join the union. I shall keep working and so will Father and maybe a quarter of everyone at the works if there's a General Strike. We'll keep it going for as long as we have coal, and then we need to make sure it's safe, you can't just walk out on a fire. They will call us scabs, but safety is important."

It was the most Caroline had heard Bob say on any subject and she warmed to his understanding and pragmatism. There was a passion there, though he rarely showed it. Bob caught the attention of the waitress and asked for the bill and changed the subject again to ask Caroline if she had done any more paintings recently.

February began with heavier rain across the south of England. Areas began to flood after a week of unrelenting downpours. Roads became rutted, muddy tracks; vehicles became stuck or else slid off the roadways entirely. When Caroline picked up the letter addressed to her from the hallway table, the writing was streaked, and the ink had run with rain drops. Still, she recognised who it was from and took it into the parlour to read.

5 February 1926
Pangbourne, Berkshire
Dear Caroline,

So sorry to hear about your mother. Everyone here sends their condolences and mother says you are to come and stay if you feel the need to get away.

Matthew and Kate are praying for this rain to stop. They'll be married next week and at this rate will need to borrow a boat to get to church rather than a car! The Thames is virtually lapping at our front gate this morning. Matthew's cottage is coming along, he has the extension wall up to about four feet now. We are keeping some furniture here for them until it is completed, so that it doesn't become damaged by the rain. I'm embroidering a tablecloth as a wedding present, with different flowers on each corner representing the four seasons. I haven't sewed much since school and it's not as neat as I'd imagined it in my head, or up to your standard, but I think they will like it. Do you remember those horrid thread-work blouses we all made at school?

Mark is settled in Tanganyika, in a place called Kigoma. He says it is rather hot, and there is a large lake there, almost an inland sea, and the compound where he is staying is near the railway. He sounds very happy there, making plenty of friends and working to provide mechanical training for the local men. I have examinations in March and then I will be able to apply for a teaching position out there with him if I want to. I think I shall. I'll be staying with Helen in Devon for the Easter week to either celebrate or commiserate. She said she had asked you along too. It would be good fun for the three of us to be reunited again, don't you think?

Did you hear the broadcast on the radio in January that people thought was a real riot? A Catholic priest, I think his name was Father Knox, presented "Broadcasting from the Barricades". It was satire, totally made up, but a lot of people thought it was real. You might have seen reports of it in the newspapers.

Luke was here yesterday and wanted me to let you know that the University Charter dinner will be on 17 March at the Town Hall. He would like you to accompany him, though understands if your period of mourning prevents it. I am very jealous! I've never been to a grand occasion with Mayors and Chancellors like that. Will you go? It's on a Wednesday so I assume you'd need to take some time off work and stay over as it will finish rather late in the evening. It's probably better to let him know directly, he is at 12 Wantage Road if you remember. If you don't go, I shall insist he takes me instead (though I have absolutely nothing posh enough to wear!).

I do hope you are bearing up alright old thing. It must
be awful to lose a parent, however infuriating they might
be at times.
    Yours
    Midge

Caroline wondered how she could continue to work at
Sunningend when she seemed to regularly need to ask for
time off. She knew it was inconvenient for the other girls, as
they all worked in pairs and when one was left by themselves
then a girl from the dope room had to be brought in. That
naturally slowed down the production as the pair would
need to find their rhythm and the dope room girl would
not necessarily be as skilled. Caroline had wanted to work,
and enjoyed it, despite the wear on her hands.

Learning that Midge would be staying with Helen helped
to make up Caroline's mind to accept that invitation. Midge
was right, it would be good fun to be together as a three
again. Caroline decided to hand in her notice at Sunningend
either if she decided to take up Luke's offer or just before
travelling to Devon. That would give her another month's pay
to help keep her ticking over until something else turned up.

Caroline's twenty-second birthday was on February 18
and was overshadowed by the wedding of her neighbours two
days later. Still it rained and Florence repeatedly complained
that her shoes, bought new for the occasion and made of
cream silk, would be ruined the minute she stepped outside.
After much deliberation, George had agreed to be Josiah's
Best Man, and was holding an umbrella over both he and
Josiah as they walked to the chapel.

"Very good of you, George," Josiah said for the fourth
time since they had left the Exotic Plant Nursery which was

diminished in size since the recent sale of two acres on the eastern side of Queens Road.

George took the repeat as evidence of nerves. They could not exactly be said to be friends, but acquaintances seemed too light an association. Josiah had wanted someone of good standing by his side, and as George also knew Florence and her parents, he was a suitable choice. Florence's parents had gone on ahead and were already in the chapel, with Florence's twin brother Timothy who had arranged some time off from his employment as a shipping clerk at one of the warehouses at Gloucester Docks. Florence always referred to her brother as working in imports and exports, which while true, was an elevation of his current duties. Florence's great aunt had declined the invitation to the chapel and the reception afterwards, the former because she did not hold with Methodists and the latter because it was to be held inside one of the glasshouses.

The men reached the chapel and went inside. Kitchen and dining room chairs had been rounded up from all corners of the congregation as normally they stood for the services. There were two small arrangements of flowers at the front of the chapel, a special consideration to Josiah as it was his business, and much to the annoyance of Florence that there could not have been more. The preacher greeted the men and made small talk, every so often looking at his pocket watch. The bride was late.

Caroline was at that moment doing her best to hold an umbrella over herself and Florence, while also holding a corner of Florence's dress up off the ground and trying not to drop the two small flower posies that had been delivered earlier that morning. The very best orchids, white with pink centres, and some forsythia and narcissus.

As they crossed the bridge over the railway tracks, an engine belched a cloud of steam and smuts and Florence let out a shriek.

"Don't stop!" Caroline kept walking, tugging her friend's dress, "The quicker we get to the chapel the better."

"I don't understand why one of his men couldn't have driven us there," Florence sulked.

"It's less than half a mile! Really Florence, please keep up or else I'm going to drop either the flowers or your dress, I can't hold them all much longer."

They waddled onwards, stared at by a group of young children playing by the entrance to the railway station. They would not be concerned about smuts thought Caroline, glancing at their wet grey clothes, mostly either too short or too long for the bodies currently inhabiting them. Finally, the pair arrived at the red-brick chapel.

Florence suddenly burst into tears. Caroline was astonished. For weeks she had heard of nothing else but this day, Florence had become a first rate bore about it, and now on the very cusp of matrimony, tears?

"Whatever is wrong now?" she asked, incredulous.

"I'm scared. I don't know these people. I don't want to know these people. This is not the kind of wedding day I ever dreamed of Caroline!" she took the handkerchief Caroline offered her as they stood in the rain beneath the umbrella at the chapel door.

"But I thought you wanted to marry Josiah? You have a lovely new home, and you'll be mistress of it with your own maid. Away from the railway too!"

"That's not what scares me. It's… it's tonight that I'm scared of. Josiah insisted we share a bedroom when I was all for having separate rooms. He keeps talking about children and I don't know what to do…" she sobbed again.

Caroline tried to muster some sympathy. It was difficult. Florence had taken the initiative, encouraged Josiah when at the time he was being considered a suitor for Caroline by her own mother, and had practically lured him into selling his land to fund their new nuptial home on the promise of living happily ever after with her. Florence had quite literally made her bed and as far as Caroline could see had very little alternative but to lie in it.

"Surely it won't be that horrid. It's what people who love each other do. We wouldn't be standing here otherwise. Come along now, dry your eyes and do let's get in out of the rain."

Florence sniffed. She knew as well as Caroline that this was a situation of her own making. She did not love Josiah; she knew that in her heart. But she would swallow that pill and make the best of it, and of his income. She nodded her head in ascent and Caroline opened the door into the small lobby of the chapel.

Two hours later, Josiah got to his feet and tapped his knife against his wine glass. The gathering hushed. He looked out at the faces of his friends, colleagues, workers, neighbours and a few distant relations who had been merrily consuming the wedding breakfast he had provided and smiled benevolently. They were seated in one of the glasshouses that had been cleared and scrubbed for the purpose. The staging removed and trestle tables set in an elongated U shape, covered with white cotton bedsheets, and chairs hired from the Town Hall which had been brought up by horse and cart the previous day. The scent of flowers was heady; the warmth of the bodies gently steaming as they dried out from the rain and the arrangements that Florence wished could have been in the chapel mingled in the air.

"Friends! Just a few words, friends, and then I will let you get back to your luncheon. As many of you know, this is my second marriage. I never imagined that God would favour me with another woman so bright and vivacious as Florrie here, after my Emma was taken back into his arms. But here I stand before you, the luckiest, happiest man on earth today." He looked down at Florence who blushed. There were smiles and nods of agreement from his audience.

"As you also know, there are changes afoot. You'll have seen the glasshouses being dismantled across the road as you arrived. I am not an old man, but I have worked hard, and I plan to take the next few years at my leisure. Now, I have no desire to sell any more land, let me be clear about that. Curzon's Exotic Plant Nurseries will be here for many years to come, God willing! But I have an announcement to make, and if I make it now, I shan't have to repeat it over and over to some of you individually.

"Last year I took on young Jim Cox there, as my office assistant. No, no need to stand up lad. As my good wife and I will be moving to our new home in Tivoli, where of course you are all warmly invited to call on us once we are settled, the house I have lived in here will be vacant. Jim, I would very much like you and your wife Hannah to move in. We can discuss it later, but I wanted everyone to know that we owe a debt of gratitude to you and your generation, and this is my small way of saying thank you. Thank you to you and all who served, some of whom never came home for us to thank."

He paused, and his yard foreman raised a glass to propose a toast 'to those who served!' which was echoed around the company. George looked up at Josiah and nodded his appreciation of the mention of those who did not return.

"Now then. One last thing, and I promise you can all go back to enjoying the party. I want to thank my neighbours here, George Munhead and his daughter Caroline. They have fulfilled their duties as Best Man and Maid of Honour today admirably, despite this weather. I know they have had a difficult time of it lately, but I truly appreciate how they have looked after me and Florrie today. I dare say it can't have been easy but thank you both.

"It only remains for me to say that I hope you all enjoy this afternoon. We have a band coming along shortly so we can have a bit of dancing when we've all finished eating, for those of you who wish to. Thank you very much everyone."

Once again, the yard foreman raised his glass and proposed a toast this time to the bride and groom. Caroline glanced at Hannah and Jim Cox who were sitting opposite her a little way down the table. They were beaming from ear to ear, clearly excited to be offered a new home where Jim would not have to walk far to work on his shattered leg. Caroline wondered if the move would mean Hannah could finally have the baby she craved and give up her sewing room duties at Sunningend engineering works. Then Caroline looked at Florence whom she was sat next to. The girl was looking down at her plate, her hands in her lap as if praying.

"Is everything alright Florence?" Caroline whispered.

Florence didn't trust herself to speak, she just nodded her head once to say yes.

The yard foreman took charge of rearranging the tables and chairs to the outer reaches of the glasshouse when the band arrived. It had stopped raining briefly, so the doors were left open to get the air moving, and the band struck up a jolly waltz for those who wished to work off some of their luncheon. The bride and groom took a tour of the room, greeting everyone in person and thanking many for the gifts that had been laid out on another table near the entrance. As people milled about, and more arrived to wish the couple well, Caroline noticed a familiar face in the crowd making their way towards Josiah and Florence.

Caroline turned her back for a moment and looked for her father. George had seen the same person at the same time and was making his way to Caroline.

"What is he doing here?" Caroline whispered.

"Josiah is considered a local dignitary; this is an important social event. You have no need to hide yourself, my dear. I rather think we are 'old news' to Mr Shaw now."

Arthur, or Artie as he preferred to be called, Shaw was a reporter working for the *Chronicle*. He had arrived with his photographer, with the hope of being able to sneak a plate of food as well as getting a few lines of copy to use. Money was always tight with Artie, his gambling habit saw to that, and food was an occasional luxury. He surveyed the table of gifts jealously, waiting for the bride and groom to reach it so that they could be photographed with their guests in the background. He had just noticed a small box of silver cake forks displayed with their lid open when Josiah clapped his hand on Artie's shoulder.

"Mr Shaw! Good of you to come! Meet my wife, Florrie, this is Mr Shaw of the *Chronicle*. He is going to write a column on our nuptials, and I see he has brought his photographer along too. Where would you like us, sir?"

Florence was immediately interested in this new development. She lifted her head and smiled as brightly as she could, meeting Artie's gaze square on.

"Good afternoon, Mr Curzon, yes always obliged to record the most prestigious events in our town's calendar. And the new Mrs Curzon, it's a pleasure to meet you," what a corker, he thought, how did old Curzon manage to bag this little beauty? "Now, if you could both stand about there, that's it. Does the bride have her bouquet?"

Florence turned to look for Caroline.

George had been watching while Caroline remained with her back to the group.

"Caroline, I think Florence is in need of you. I shall keep watch, don't worry."

As Caroline turned, a small girl came trotting over and announced that 'the party lady wants her flowers'. Caroline reached across the table, picked up the posy and with a deep breath crossed the glasshouse to the waiting bride.

"Caroline! Well fancy seeing you here. I hope you are well. I was sorry to hear about your mother of course. Such a generous lady."

"Good afternoon, Mr Shaw, and thank you. Here you are, Florence."

"Are you the Maid of Honour Caroline? Well let's have you in the photograph as well then! Is there a Best Man also Mr Curzon?"

"Of course, where is George, we should include him too," Josiah turned and bellowed over the noise of the band, "George! Come along and have your photograph taken with us!"

Artie frowned. He had not expected it to be a family affair. At least the old woman wouldn't turn up and make it any more awkward. She had driven a hard bargain when he had attempted to explain to her how Caroline's friendship with the photographer Elsa House could lead people to suspect Caroline herself could be engaged in undesirable activities. She had used the ugly word blackmail, though Artie had considered it more a payment for a good deed in warning Elizabeth what might appear in the *Chronicle* if Caroline and Elsa had attended the Gold Cup horse race

meeting together. Five pounds in his hand as he left their
house in Glencairn Road, and another five pounds a month
later after not publishing any suggestive copy, had gone some
way to clearing his debts at the time. If only he could be
paid for not publishing anything on a more regular basis.
It had been a trick he'd used a few times in the past, but in
a place such as Cheltenham word would soon get round if
he tried it too often or with the wrong people, and he had
almost been undone with George being on good terms with
the bankers in the town. His lines of credit had all but dried
up, despite keeping his end of the bargain and he suspected
George had been instrumental in that.

Still, he had a job to do. He arranged the group for their
photograph and took out his notebook for a few words from
Josiah as Caroline and George moved away again. He found
himself constantly losing track of the conversation while
looking at Florence, she was truly captivating. And now a
woman of means, perhaps she would be worth developing
an acquaintance with, he thought. After a few minutes he
shook Josiah's hand and they bid each other a good day. The
bride and groom resumed their tour of the guests, the band
played on, and Artie slipped the box of cake forks into his
jacket unseen before taking his leave.

The following Monday it was Hannah Cox's turn to
ask their supervisor Mrs Chandler for some time off work.
Caroline had decided to accept the invitation from Luke to
attend the University Charter dinner and was about to speak
to Mrs Chandler when Hannah called out to her first. The
women moved to the side of the room as the others took up
their positions either side of the wooden frames that would
have sheets of canvas sewn onto them. Caroline watched the
conversation without being able to hear any of it until her

partner at the frame Gwen tapped her hand to get Caroline's attention back on their job. Gwen was non-verbal, no one really knew why, but was nimble fingered and one of the best workers in the sewing room. She frowned at Caroline disapprovingly, as if to scold her for eves-dropping. After almost a year of working together, Caroline understood Gwen's many facial expressions.

"I wasn't being nosey Gwen I know what Hannah is asking Mrs Chandler. I was just wanting to have a word with her myself."

Gwen nodded but didn't give any indication that she wanted to know any more detail.

Caroline waited until the lunch bell sounded before asking Mrs Chandler for the Wednesday and Thursday in mid-March as holiday.

"I thought for a moment you were going to say this week, and I'd have had to say no as Hannah won't be here. I think it should be alright. Doing anything interesting with your time?"

"I have been invited to a rather posh dinner in Reading. The University is getting a Charter, though I'm not entirely sure what that means."

"It means they are becoming a university in their own right. I read about it, and that the Technical College there might be swallowed up by it. That would be a mistake in my opinion, we shall always need skilled engineers."

Betty Chandler was not against academic thought; she was well versed in politics having been involved in the suffrage movement some years before but was fully supportive of giving a man (or woman) the tools to learn a trade by which they could then support themselves and their families. She read the *Daily Herald* when she could obtain a copy and was well respected by the women in the sewing and dope rooms who she supervised on the day shift. No one dared gossip about her friendship with the general manager Mr Cambridge.

Caroline joined Lottie in the cloakroom where the girls continued to have their lunches when the weather was too poor to sit outside. They had become firm friends; Lottie was the niece of Mrs Chandler as well as being sister to Bob. She often passed messages between Caroline and Bob, as neither home had yet acquired a telephone.

"This cheese is a bit smelly, sorry girls!" Lottie chuckled as she took a bite of her sandwich.

"Lottie, I have just told Mrs Chandler that I will be leaving at Easter."

"Leaving where? Here? Oh Caroline, I thought you liked working here."

"I do, I have, but I can't keep taking time off and disrupting everyone's routines. Your aunt has been very good about it up to now, but I feel as if I am taking advantage of her, and I want to spend some time with my father and with Mary and Angelica."

"So, you're not leaving to work somewhere else?"

"No. I mean I will get another position eventually I'm sure, but that's not why I'm leaving here."

Lottie chewed her sandwich thoughtfully for a moment, "You're very lucky to be able to do that. Mother and Father wouldn't hear of me wanting to stay home and not work. What will you do all day?"

"I think Annie will be leaving us soon, so really, I should learn to cook properly before she goes. And running the house of course the way mother did," she stopped herself then. What had her mother done exactly that was running the house?

"Perhaps you should learn to cook before you get married," Lottie looked at Caroline with a cheeky smile. She was referring to her brother Bob of course. He had taken a strong liking to Caroline over the past year. They had been out to dances, to the cinema and for tea and walks around the various parks and gardens that Cheltenham hid like gems between the houses and workshops.

Caroline shook her head, "No, Lottie. I won't be learning to cook for any future husband, I need to do it for myself and for Father. And I won't be here for two days on March seventeenth and eighteenth, I am going to Reading for a very important dinner."

"Lummy, you do get around! What's this for then?"

"It's to celebrate the new university. My friend's brother has invited me to join him there. Luke is a doctor, he graduated last year."

"Should I tell Bob?"

Caroline considered the question as she finished her own sandwich. She remembered Bob's reaction before Christmas when her friend James had visited Cheltenham for the evening on his way to Bristol. Bob had been upset, thinking that he and Caroline had an exclusive understanding. It had been a surprise to Caroline who before then had not realised the strength of his feelings. She had explained that she was trying to make friends and find new experiences, to catch up with what everyone else seemed to have been doing while she had stayed at home with her mother.

For his part, after his initial upset, Bob had taken the news stoically. He knew he wanted to marry Caroline, but he also knew she needed to spread her wings and get all this wandering out of her system. He would not change his plans; he was saving his money to eventually get a small house in Prestbury with a garden where he could keep chickens and grow vegetables. He would wait until Caroline was ready.

Caroline didn't want to upset Bob unnecessarily, "Perhaps it would be better if he didn't know. I shall only be away for one night. Don't look so horrified, I shall be staying in a hotel by myself."

"I won't say anything. But Caroline you should consider your reputation you know. If you keep going away with men people will talk."

"I don't keep going away with men!"

"You had dinner with that James the film maker, and then you went off with those two with the car. If Bob should hear you've been out with another one, well I don't imagine he'd be happy about it."

"Those two with the car are now married to each other, remember? Lottie, I shall tell Bob when I get back."

23 February 1926
Florence, Italy
Dear Caroline

As you will have seen from the postage on this letter's envelope, I decided on Italy! I have taken a small house here in Florence for six months to see if I can get my foot in the door of the industry here. There is quite a community of English people around the city, the property is ridiculously cheap, and I am living on wine, bread, sausage and cheese. It is beautiful, the fountains are incredible, and everything is so clean and well cared for. I believe you would love it here.

I have some film and theatre contacts who are making enquiries on my behalf. Of course, the language could be a barrier, but I have a few words of French under my belt, and I hope to get by on those until I can learn more Italian. Tomorrow I am having luncheon with a fellow director. Meals here last for hours, there is much talk and gesticulation and the wine flows, yet no one appears to become intoxicated.

There are a young couple living next door to me, they have a small boy Gianni. I am teaching him English in

return for eggs from their hens and milk from their goat.
Have you ever tasted goat's milk? It is rather different to
cow's milk, I thought it was sour the first time I tasted it,
but I have grown to like it as a balance to wine.

Now that you have my address here, I should very much
like to hear from you.

Fondest regards

James

The letter was waiting for Caroline when she arrived
home after work that day as if Lottie's mention of James had
summoned his presence. Six months in Italy was something
far beyond Caroline's ability to imagine. She had read about
Rome at school, and to her it was populated by gladiators
and people in white togas. But surely, they wore more
conventional clothes now, she thought. She would need
to find Florence on one of her father's maps, and she went
to find him in his study while Annie laid the dining room
table for dinner.

"Father, do you remember James who I helped make the
film last year? He has gone to Florence in Italy; I suppose to
seek his fortune. Can you show me where that is please?"

George had been reading through more documents at
his desk and took off his spectacles for a moment to rub his
eyes. He was an intelligent man who had worked his way
up to manage the Cheltenham branch of the Cheltenham
and Gloucester Benefits Building Society as their senior
accountant. He was slim with dark hair now greying at the
sides, and a generally expressionless face when working
that softened when he was at home. He and Caroline had
always been close; now it was just the two of them he was
determined to ensure a comfortable future for her as best
he could.

"Fetch the map of Europe, it's where you left it when we were looking at Prussia the other day. Florence, you say?"

They unrolled the map and used books to weigh down the corners to stop it curling back up again.

"Now, Florence is in the region of Tuscany, here in the north of Italy."

They both peered at the map and Caroline found the city with her finger. She noted it was further from the sea than Rome and asked how far apart the two cities were.

"I have no idea. But look, the distance appears to be similar to that from Bristol to London, so perhaps it is a hundred and fifty miles?"

Annie put her head around the door, "Excuse me Sir, Miss, but dinner is ready."

"Thank you, Annie, we shall be through in a minute. If you can serve without it spoiling, please do so."

Annie withdrew and pulled the door closed.

"Caroline, I have something I wish to tell you, sit down for a moment."

Caroline sat on one side of the desk and George retook his seat nearest the wall.

"Since your mother died, I have been reviewing all of our finances. She had an insurance policy, and also some investments which provided her income. I do not think we have ever discussed your grandparents in much detail, and I do not propose to do so now – though if you are interested then of course we can over dinner. But the long and short of it is, the monies they left to your mother and I when they died were invested to provide us with some security while you and Freddie were small, and I was still a young accountant," he smiled to himself, "it helped us to purchase this house, and we are fortunate to have done so and to not be continually paying rent like so many others.

"But this house was built for a family, and I think, at least I hope you will agree, that it is too large for just you and I. Caroline you are starting to make your own way in the world, and I do not want to be encumbered with the upkeep of a home where I use only two or three rooms. Therefore, I have decided to sell it."

Caroline was shocked. She knew her father to be a pragmatic man who would not have reached this decision without careful consideration. It explained his long evenings here in the study with piles of papers spread out on the desk.

"But where shall we live? Father, isn't it a little soon to be making this kind of decision?" she asked.

George stood up and indicated they should go through to the dining room, "There are some new apartments that are almost complete on the other side of the Park. I thought we might arrange to view them on Saturday, unless you have other plans of course."

Over dinner they talked of Caroline's grandparents, conscious that Annie should not be alarmed at the decision to sell. George's father was a Postmaster in Gloucester who had lived frugally and saved a few pennies each week. Elizabeth's father was a butcher who owned a shop in Upton St Leonards and had done the same. Both George and Elizabeth were only children, unusual at the time, and had been introduced at the wedding of a mutual acquaintance of both families.

After dinner, George retrieved a photograph from his study that showed a young man in Royal Mail uniform. Caroline held it in her hand and looked into the young man's eyes. She could see her father, and her brother. She wondered what his voice had sounded like and handed the photograph back to George.

"Shall I put some more coal on the fire?"

"Only if you are cold my dear. Jenks have increased their price per hundredweight again and I should like to not have to order any extra next month. That was another consideration I have taken into account with the new apartments. They have a central heating system powered by gas."

"Have you been to see them already?"

"No, I wanted to wait until I had broached the subject with you. However, I have seen the plans, as we are assisting the builder. Two of the six apartments have already been reserved."

"It must be your decision, Father. I do understand what you said about this being a family home. A family with young children and more than the two of us. By the way, I gave notice to Mrs Chandler today."

"Then the other piece of news I have for you should be more welcome. I felt it was prudent to review all of the investments we have, given the current discord in the country. As I suspected, we had a number in industries that are not performing as well as before and some that clearly will continue to decline. I have made some changes to the portfolio and have set aside a particular group of shares and stocks that will provide you with a small annual income. Mostly they are in a young company called National Benzole who produce petroleum. I'm afraid I could not stretch to the fifty pounds you had last year and this, but at current rates they should yield approximately thirty pounds a year."

Caroline sat back in her chair and ran her hands through her hair. This was an evening of surprises, and she needed a moment to take this new information in. She had assumed she would always have to work in some manner to have an income, it had never occurred to her that she might have stocks or shares to generate that income for her. It was independence, for as long as the investments performed.

George was happy that he had been able to surprise his daughter. It gave him pleasure to be generous.

"One more small thing that I hope won't affect you for some time yet. I have redrawn my will. There are one or two small bequests, but everything else will come to you in time. It is held by our solicitors in town, Embry and Burton. You might also consider making a will now that you have something to bequeath."

There was something that had been troubling Caroline over dinner and now she had to ask, "Father, what about Annie? Are these apartments serviced? Will we still need her? She will be terribly upset if we have to let her go, she was hoping to stay until after she and Jacob are married."

George of course had considered Annie's future. This would be his best surprise of the evening and he could not suppress a smile, "I have placed an order for two bicycles. One for you, as I thought you might need it to travel to Sunningend but of course you can use it around town. The other will be for Annie to use if she decides to stay in our employment."

"Bicycles! Oh Father, what a clever idea!"

"Well, yes I rather thought so too," he chuckled, "but there will be some changes for Annie. I propose that she comes each afternoon during the week to clean and prepare our evening meal, and to be available after church on Sundays to prepare both luncheon and dinner unless we make other arrangements. I do not think we need her on Saturdays; I am happy to take dinner elsewhere and I am sure you will often be otherwise engaged. She will be responsible for the laundry arrangements, and with your supervision, our groceries and other accounts. I know she has been more than just a maid to you over the years, I do not want to damage the relationship that you and she have. I feel it has provided many benefits and may yet contribute to your stability."

"You have planned all of this meticulously. I think it will work. When do we tell her?"

"I think we should view the apartments first. You might feel they are too far from town or the railway station for your needs. You also might not like their style. I am told they are very modern and not at all like this house," he leaned forward, "Caroline, please do not think I am having some sort of crisis or that I want to banish every memory of your mother by doing this. No one will ever replace her, and if anything, this house embodies her and our years together. I feel if I am to carry on without her, then I need to do so in a place where everything is new. Perhaps that is difficult for you to understand?"

"It still feels a little soon, but I do understand. I know some people choose not to disturb the bedroom of a son who never returned from the war, as a kind of shrine. I've always thought that a little distasteful and really quite impractical. I was meaning to ask you when we would go through Mother's things, and if you wanted to do it, or if I should. I suppose this now means we could wait until we decide on somewhere new to live?"

"I was thinking along the same lines, yes. I was also thinking of not taking very much of our existing furniture with us. Josiah, Mr Curzon, told me he had been considering what he called a 'dispersal sale' on his house contents before he decided to leave the majority for the Coxes to use. We would take things that are dear to us of course, but it would be impossible to fit the contents of this house into a smaller more modern home."

"You mean we would just decide what we wanted to take from each room, and leave the rest to be sold? And we could use the money to purchase new items that better suited wherever we move to?"

"I anticipate it would be an auction. We need not even be here when it happens. The agent would take care of it all for us."

"Let's see what the apartments are like before we make any firm decisions. Though a dispersal sale does seem like a most simple answer."

When she went to bed that evening, Caroline's head was still swimming with the changes her father had put to her. She pulled out her keepsake box from under her bed and opened the lid. She had spent the previous year collecting mementos of the places she had been and wanted to add James' letter because the postage stamp was so different to the English stamps with the King's head on that she was used to. The one on James' envelope was grey and showed Saint Francis of Assisi. There were two dates on it and Caroline could see it was to commemorate an anniversary of some kind, perhaps his birth and death. She placed the envelope on top of the other objects, closed the lid and put the box back in its home.

Home. She had thought last year about how she might one day have her own home and where it might be. She could see now that this for her would be a temporary move, from her childhood home to a new location but not by herself. She would have her father to show her what needed to be done and guide her through it. She was excited, and relieved, to have this half-way step offered to her so unexpectedly.

The next few days dragged for Caroline. She struggled to keep secret her news from Lottie; she wanted to tell her friend so much but at the same time wanted to be sure that the apartments would be right for her and her father before she announced anything. Lottie was able to fill any silences over lunch with her news from around the town, gleaned from her mother's job at the telephone exchange. She also had some news of her own; the young man she had been courting for a few months, Eric from the gas works, had suggested that they might get married if he was successful in gaining the promotion he was hoping for. Caroline was thrilled for Lottie, and the girls talked a lot about how Florence's wedding had gone and what Lottie might want for her own.

George arranged to view the apartments at eleven o'clock the following Saturday morning. They caught the tram to the Norwood Triangle terminus and then walked toward The Park. It was one of several parks and green public spaces around Cheltenham but had always been known as The Park or Park Gardens. One hundred years earlier there had been a proposal to create botanical gardens with an ornamental pond and a variety of caged animals in the twenty-acre teardrop-shaped site. Subscriptions were raised, and at the same time a second proposal for zoological gardens was gaining interest to the north of the town. Neither venture was realised. The Park was given over to activities such as archery and golf, and the houses that had been built around the perimeter were finished and sold. It was one of those original houses that had been demolished to make way for a new building containing six apartments, now called Norwood Court.

Caroline had rarely been to the southern end of the town. She thought the houses there resembled those at Pittville where she had gone to school, and the villa Helen's parents had on the outskirts of Plymouth. The heyday of the Spa was long behind them now and many were looking rather shabby and in need of fresh paint. The trees were still mostly bare, but she could imagine how the street might look in the summer with the shade and the birds that would be attracted.

They arrived at Norwood Court and met the agent, Mr Scott. He was a small, busy man with a facial tick that caused him to blink continually. He carried a sheaf of papers and began the viewing by pointing out the row of six garages on one side of the drive that would serve all of the apartments in the building. There was a semi-circle of grass, neatly clipped, that separated the gravel drive from the road. The building itself had a wide entrance with semi-circular steps up to the doors which had full glass panels and curved brass handles that resembled two blades of grass.

Mr Scott explained that the apartments were arranged three on either side of the central stairs, two on each floor. The two on the ground floor were finished and ready for occupation. The other four were due to be finished over the following weeks and could also be inspected if George and Caroline wished. The entrance lobby reminded Caroline of Lady Victoria's apartment in London though on a much-reduced scale. There was a small porter's hatch, and the staircase spiralled upwards from the centre of the space. Behind it was access to the rear gardens which were laid mostly to lawn with a few shrubs and a small seating area with wooden benches that would be in the shade for much of the day.

They began on the ground floor. Mr Scott unlocked the front door to apartment number two and showed them into an entrance hall off which were a lounge to the front, two bedrooms, a bathroom, a separate toilet, all facing to the rear, and a kitchen with an archway through to a dining area facing to the side and front of the property. The floors were of wooden parquet in a checker-board pattern and highly polished. The walls were painted white, and the windows were large with rectangular panes of glass held in black metal frames that curved at one end to follow the line of

the building and create a narrow bay. They filled the rooms
with light and Caroline was again reminded of how bright
the lounge room in Lady Victoria's apartment was. That had
looked out onto a garden square with six-storey residential
buildings on three sides. The lounge in this apartment looked
out across the entrance drive to the Park on the opposite
side of the road, but the view that day was predominantly
of green-painted railings.

Caroline was very satisfied with the bathroom with its
sleek enclosed bath and pale green, white and black tiles.
The separate toilet was tiled in the same fashion. The kitchen
was a revelation. It too was painted white but had two eye-
level cupboards and a white and beige modern enamel gas
cooker with gas burners on one side and a large and small
oven on the other. Both oven doors had the maker's name,
Stoves, in silver-plate lettering. Mr Scott demonstrated how
it worked and George commented on the safety of the gas
supply which had greatly improved in the town over the
previous decade. The white Belfast sink had a small gas
boiler above it that provided almost instant hot water, and
a grooved board was fixed to one side at a slight slope to
use as a drainer for clean crockery. While the men talked,
Caroline ran her hand along the edge of the kitchen sink
and draining board and looked into the dining area which
was again painted white with a smaller window.

They asked to see an apartment on the top floor, and Mr
Scott showed them number five, so that they could see the
layout in reverse. When George and Caroline looked out of
the lounge window there, they could see through the trees
to the Park beyond. It would be a little obscured when the
trees were in full leaf, but there was a gap where the lake
could be glimpsed. They looked at each other as they stood
there and knew they would take it.

Caroline had written to Luke and asked him to reserve a moderately-priced room on her behalf for one night in a hotel not too far from the Town Hall where they would be spending the evening. He replied with the details and Caroline caught an afternoon train to Reading with her long dark blue evening dress and overnight things safely packed into her carpet bag. She was to make her way to the George Hotel on Kings Street and Luke would collect her at seven that evening.

During the journey she ruminated over the events of the past two weeks. Her father had expressed their interest in apartment number five at Norwood Court and had arranged for a small deposit to be paid in order to secure it. They had told Annie and explained her new terms, and she had taken a day to consider them (and the bicycle) before accepting. She had been quieter than usual, even before she heard their news, and Caroline was concerned that something had happened between her and Jacob. George had begun to make enquiries to arrange an auction of their unwanted furniture, and to transport the items they were going to keep to the new apartment. It was expected to be finished and ready for them to move in just after Easter which that year fell at the beginning of April. As Caroline was due to be in Devon for that weekend, it had been agreed that the auction would take place while she was away, and George had arranged to have a few days off work to settle in. With the exception of Elizabeth's funeral, it was the first week off he had taken as holiday in six years.

Caroline had begun to tie labels on to objects around the house, and to make lists of smaller items that they would keep. Having seen the size of the rooms at Norwood

Court it had become clear that much of their furniture would be too heavy, large and dark to take. George had requested catalogues from Gerrard's department store in Gloucester and Cavendish House in Cheltenham, and they spent evenings picking out new items and keeping a tally of the costs. Caroline was still a little concerned that her father was taking on too much change so soon after her mother's death, particularly as the costs rose. He reassured her that he had adequately budgeted, and she was not to worry. She tried not to.

Reading railway station was bathed in sunlight as Caroline arrived. She remembered the route she and Midge had walked on her previous visit, and Luke had said that the hotel was a large old building that would be difficult to miss. He was correct, not least because of the green bunting that had been hung across the outside of the hotel to mark Saint Patrick's Day. Caroline was installed in her room less than half an hour after stepping off the train. After hanging up her dress, she decided to take a walk along the main shopping street before getting ready for the evening. She also thought she might find something light to eat. If Luke was meeting her at seven, they would be unlikely to start dinner until eight thirty or even nine o'clock.

Broad Street, to which Kings Street joined, certainly lived up to its name. Trams continually rumbled along in both directions, and the buildings on each side were mostly of red brick with intricate patterns in white bricks and carved stone lintels above the windows. They were very tall, with an occasional smaller, older building sandwiched between them. As her previous visit to Reading had only covered the eastern end of the town centre, Caroline was surprised to find a much larger department store than Jacksons which she and Midge had visited previously. It was called Heelas and was bigger even than Cavendish House in Cheltenham or Gerrard's in Gloucester.

Caroline wandered along the south side of Broad Street as far as the intersection with St Mary's Butts, then crossed the road and made her way back along the northern side. She looked in the windows of assorted shoe, book, tobacco, chemist, outfitters and grocery shops until she reached a Lyon's tea shop. While waiting for her cup of tea and egg and cress sandwich, Caroline listened to the voices of the other customers. They had a noticeable accent, of which Midge and Luke had only a slight hint when they spoke. It sounded similar to the voices she had heard in London; not as harsh on the vowel sounds but still with the lack of a pronounced 't' in the middle of any word containing one. She also identified several Irish accents, as Reading had a considerable community of Irish who lived mostly to the west of the railway station and around the cattle market.

Caroline thought back to the accents she had heard in Bristol when she visited Mary's mother, and the sing-song tones of the Trinidadian that mixed with the much softer native Bristol speech. And then to Blackpool, where the inhabitants could have been talking a completely different language with very different vowel sounds. Caroline wondered how she sounded to all of the people she had met over the previous year. She didn't consider herself to have any kind of accent, but now realised that she did, just the one she was most familiar with. She was middle class and her accent said so. Her mother had been worried that she would become working class by taking the position at Sunningend, but as far as Caroline could tell, she had not.

At five minutes to seven that evening Caroline sat in the hotel lounge, conspicuously over-dressed for that establishment, waiting for Luke. It was much cooler now the sun had set, and she was thankful to have brought her coat. At ten minutes past seven, Caroline reminded herself that Luke's job was not one he could just leave in the middle of treating someone, but he would surely not be too much longer. He surely would not have forgotten that he was meant to collect her. At twenty minutes past seven Caroline was about to take off her coat and order a pot of tea when Luke appeared in the doorway. As usual he was out of breath and full of apologies. He had run most of the way from his digs near the hospital after going home to change into his dinner suit.

They walked at a brisk pace to the Town Hall, where Caroline was relieved of her hat and coat. They were shown into a large reception room that was already full of people. It was noisy and warm, the gas lamps giving off heat as well as light. Luke offered Caroline his arm and they made their way towards a small group of men and women that Luke introduced as his 'school chums'. Caroline quickly realised with some relief that none of the women had studied at the university college. After a few minutes a loud voice rang out over the general hum of chatter to announce that the company should take their seats for dinner.

The dining hall was laid out with four long tables perpendicular to a fifth at the far end of the room for the guests of honour. Caroline sat next to Luke with another young man on her right who Luke had introduced as Charlie Crisp. Drawing on everything she could remember from deportment lessons at Mrs Pendersen's school, Caroline managed to negotiate the neat rows of cutlery and different size crystal glasses and bone china plates in the correct order. There were to be five courses with speeches after the first and fourth. The atmosphere was jovial, everyone assembled was delighted that Reading should have its own university, and many felt it would only be a matter of time before the town was granted city status by His Majesty.

As social events went, Caroline decided that it was enjoyable and not nearly as stressful as having to be pleasant to a smaller group that one didn't know but everyone else seemed to. All she really had to do was eat, drink, and applaud in the appropriate intervals. Luke and Charlie kept up a steady stream of chatter while they ate, to which she really only needed to nod along to and ask occasional questions to keep the conversation going. She learned that Charlie and Luke had been top in their year, but that Charlie would be joining his father's practice in Northampton after a short holiday in Scotland. Luke was very interested in all that Caroline could tell him about Cheltenham's hospital. She found herself agreeing to provide Luke with Dr Riley's contact details in case there were any opportunities for Luke there.

As they walked back to the hotel at a little after midnight, much slower than they had walked earlier that evening, Luke was in good spirits. He chattered on about a patient he had been treating who had a badly broken arm from getting it caught in some machinery. Luke had operated on the man's arm, and it seemed now to be responding well to treatment with some feeling returning to his fingers. Caroline was interested but was also feeling rather sleepy having drunk and eaten more than she had in a long while.

"What time is your train home tomorrow?"

"Just after ten o'clock. I shall ask to be woken for breakfast when I go in, or else I fear I shall miss it!"

"I've very much enjoyed this evening, Caroline; I hope you have too."

"Yes, very, it's not something one gets the chance to do every week. Thank you for inviting me."

"It's not something I make a habit of either, but I hope one day… perhaps when I am established in a hospital somewhere, there will be more opportunities for evenings like this."

"There are always fund-raising events. Hospitals seem to require an awful lot of money to keep them going. Well, here we are."

"Caroline, I won't be able to see you in the morning, but could I see you again soon?"

Caroline felt she really wanted to go and lie down now and didn't catch the sincerity in Luke's voice.

"Oh, I'm sure we will. It all depends on your schedule really, doesn't it? I won't be so inconvenienced by work after Easter, so yes, as the days get longer, I can come for the day if it suits you. Midge will have our new address."

"Yes. Thank you. Well, goodnight, Caroline," he kissed her cheek, but she stepped back again quickly preventing anything more. Luke was disappointed but could see she was trying not to yawn and let it pass.

THE LABELS

Caroline worked her last day at Sunningend on Friday 26 March 1926, so that she would have the following week free to organise the last of the packing and then set off to Devon on Maundy Thursday. Midge would be there already; she was spending a full two weeks with Helen and Tommy as she had not seen her friend for several years and Caroline was happy to give them some time together before she completed the party.

The Saturday after her last day at work had not gone exactly as Caroline had planned. After attempting to bake a fruit cake in the morning and burning the top, she had taken the tram into town to see her friend Elsa House. Elsa owned a photography business. Some years earlier she had been connected to a salacious affair involving a wealthy local businessman and some young men. It had been Artie Shaw who had brought the connection to Caroline's mother's attention. Elizabeth and George had forbidden Caroline to remain working for Elsa in the shop.

However, Caroline had not been forbidden from seeing Elsa as an acquaintance. Elsa would have liked nothing more to have Caroline back, as an assistant or more. The sudden infatuation that Elsa had experienced towards Caroline had taken Elsa by surprise, despite her preference for female lovers. It had been a strange relief to Elsa that Caroline had been forced to give up her job in the shop, but Elsa had since engaged a young man called Peter to help her. Caroline had not seen Elsa since just before Christmas when Elsa delivered a cheque to Glencairn Road. Caroline and Florence had been models for a charity evening fashion show at Gerrard's department store in Gloucester and Elsa had been the official photographer. Florence had thoroughly enjoyed herself and there had been talk of her becoming the store's face of 1926, but nothing more had come of it.

Arriving at the photography shop, Caroline greeted Peter and confirming that Elsa was not with a customer, she went through to the rear of the shop to the kitchenette and put the kettle on the small stove. The cramped room was familiar to her, with its piles of newspapers, letters and other paperwork scattered on every surface and empty tin mugs and china cups balanced on top. The ashtray was as usual overflowing and there was no sugar in the caddy. She made the tea, waited a few moments, and then poured it into the two cleanest cups. She decided not to risk the half bottle of milk on the windowsill, and carefully carried the cups up the narrow staircase to the studio on the first floor.

Elsa was at a small table at the window, bent over a photograph looking through a magnifying glass.

"Can you stop for a drink?"

"Caroline! Oh, how wonderful to see you! Here, let me take those, pull up that chair. You're looking well," she looked at the contents of the cups with a frown.

"Thank you. It's only tea, you don't have any coffee or sugar and I rather think the milk has turned solid in the bottle."

They sat opposite each other in the light from the window and smiled. Caroline was very fond of Elsa; she had enjoyed learning about the photography techniques from her and that knowledge had been the catalyst to James asking her to accompany him on his film set in Dorset the year before. Caroline also enjoyed the way Elsa spoke, so matter of fact yet understated. Though Elsa was a few years older than Caroline, they had always treated each other as equals and Caroline appreciated that.

"I'm sorry I haven't been to see you for so long. What with my work and everything else I seem to hardly have had a moment to myself since Christmas."

"I got your note about your mother. I'm sorry Caroline, that must have been a blow to you."

They spent the next hour catching up. Elsa had seen the photograph of Josiah and Florence in the newspaper and had wondered why Caroline had not been smiling for it. Learning that Artie Shaw had been there explained all.

"I've hardly been here myself if truth be told. You'll remember I went to stay with my aunt in London over the new year? I looked up some old friends and spent some time dragging those fashion prints around. One thing led to another, and I got a couple of commissions out of it, so I've been back a few times since."

"That's wonderful Elsa! Well done you!"

"Thank you. I would never have imagined that fashion photography would go down as well as it seems to be. And I have another reason for returning to London again in a couple of weeks. I have met someone."

It took a moment for Caroline to understand Elsa's meaning. When she did, she was surprised at her own reaction, "You mean, a lover?"

"We're not quite at that stage yet, but yes, we very much enjoy each other's company and I think she could be as serious about it as I feel. Her name is Roberta, but everyone calls her Bobby."

Caroline stayed another half an hour and then made her excuses, saved in part by the arrival of a young man enquiring about some photographs of his dogs. Once outside the shop, Caroline looked around for somewhere to sit for a moment and gather her thoughts. The weather was dry, and all of the benches were occupied, so she walked along the Promenade to the fountain of Neptune at the far end and leaned for a moment on the stone wall that surrounded it.

She watched the water in the fountain create circular ripples and contemplated that one singular action could cause similar ripples through a group of people, or even for one person throughout their life. Elsa's involvement with the photographs that caused the scandal would haunt her for years to come, Caroline was sure of that. She could see why her parents had insisted she no longer work for Elsa. Had she herself caused any ripples? Had her desire to live actively to honour her brother Freddie's memory been the cause of her mother's illness and eventual death? Caroline had suggested that the miners would be selfish to strike, but she considered now that she too might have been selfish in her pursuit of freedom. Bob had said, the miners had no choice. What choice had she had?

As she stood in contemplation, she did not notice a familiar figure stop and lean on the wall beside her.

"Penny for them?"

"Bob! Goodness I was just thinking about you! Well, something you said at least. Are you on your way to the football?"

"No, they're playing away today. I need some more boot polish, so I thought I'd take a walk into town and get some. Would you like to walk with me… or should I leave you to your thoughts?"

Caroline had not seen Bob since her visit to Reading and knew she should tell him about it.

"I shall walk with you," she said as she turned away from the fountain and took his arm.

They made their way back up the Promenade and into the High Street where Bob made his purchase. They talked about how well Cheltenham Town were doing in the football league, about the difficulties of deciding which books to keep and which to let go, and about the weather which seemed to have finally turned its face towards spring. Anything except Caroline's trip to Reading.

This won't do, she thought. I have to tell him, else he will think I have something to hide, which I do not.

"Bob, did Lottie tell you about my little trip to Reading the other week?"

"No, should she have? What did you go there for?"

They had arrived at the gates of Sandford Park and Bob nodded to two young men he knew as they went in.

"I was invited to a dinner. It was rather grand, at the Town Hall. It was in aid of the University getting a charter."

Bob did not want to ask who the invitation had been from, but Caroline had left the question hanging between them and he felt he had no choice, "Do you know someone at the University then?"

"Not exactly. I know someone who was studying there until recently," just say it she told herself. "Midge's brother Luke. He passed his exams to be a doctor, top of his class which is how he obtained the invitations."

Bob said nothing more for a moment. He did not think Caroline was deliberately provoking him, he did not believe she was that kind of girl. Still, he felt stung that she had once again been enjoying the company of another man. As if a film maker hadn't been bad enough, this one was a doctor;

Bob could not compete with that in any way. Caroline had told him last year that she would have male friends and he was to think nothing serious of it, but it was so difficult when he wanted to be the only man in her life. He realised the silence was dragging on.

"Was the dinner a good one? What did you eat?" If in doubt, ask about food he thought.

"It didn't start until eight thirty, I was famished by then and honestly would have eaten bread and dripping if it had been put in front of me, but thankfully it was not. There was mushroom soup, then salmon, jellied tongue, a peach sorbet, roasted pheasant and then dessert was a pink blancmange and some fruit. It was all rather rich, but the wine was very good."

"Sounds like it would feed us for a week at least!"

"It was a special occasion. Everyone was very happy that they are getting their own university. There were speeches too, though I couldn't really follow what they were saying. Lots of 'distinguished gentlemen' and 'honourable ladies' and thanking lots of people I'd never heard of."

"Did you enjoy it?"

"It was a pleasant experience, yes. I don't think I should like to go to one every week."

"I doubt I shall ever be invited to anything so grand as that sounds," Bob took comfort in Caroline's disinterest in making a habit of such outings.

"I think I prefer smaller dinner parties rather than grand affairs. I like to hear what people are saying to each other and the Town Hall was so big, all I could hear was the scraping of cutlery on plates."

Bob saw an opportunity, "Would you like to have some dinner this evening somewhere? We could go to the Orchard, they do a good game pie there, Father says."

The Orchard was a small restaurant at the west end of the High Street between St James railway station and the gas works. It was popular with the working men and women of the town, offering food that they recognised, and of slightly better quality than they could produce in their own homes.

Caroline looked at her watch. It was getting on for four and she was starting to feel hungry as lunch had been bread, cheese and a pickled egg while she had waited for the fruit cake to bake.

"What time do they open?"

"I believe at six o'clock. Don't feel as if you need to dress up for it. What you are wearing now is alright," he paused, a thought occurring to him, "why not come and meet Mother and Father, and then we can go on to the Orchard from there?"

Caroline hesitated. She enjoyed being with Bob, he was a good, stable chap. But she was conscious that he could assume she was more serious about him than she actually felt, and she really didn't want to lead him on. They had completed a circuit of Sandford Park and exited through the ornate iron gates.

"I should like to meet your parents Bob, and to have dinner with you, but please don't think any more of it than that will you? You are a good man and I do enjoy being with you. I just am not ready to be serious about anyone still. Do you understand?" she said it as gently as she could as they walked, her arm still through his.

"I understand. I understand that you need to keep trying new things until you find something, or someone, who fits. But do you understand that I think you fit with me? I like you very much Caroline. Part of why I like you is because you are so interesting, and part of that is because of the things you do. They are so different to the things I'm used to. I won't pretend I'm happy that you go about with other men, but I hope one day you'll get tired of them and find your fit with me."

"Would you ever be happy with me? Truly, Bob?"

"I think I would be. It's more a question if you'd be happy with me. I think you would in time. I can wait."

"Dear Bob. If some other girl should catch your eye, promise me you won't hesitate to sweep her off her feet. Do you promise?" Caroline was smiling and trying to be light-hearted.

Bob shook his head, "I promise, but it won't happen."

Bob and Lottie's parents rented a small, terraced house with three bedrooms in a side street near to the gas works. Robert Lewis senior was a foreman at the gas works with a keen sense of responsibility for the welfare of the workers under him. Jane Lewis had secured a position at the recently opened telephone exchange and didn't like to gossip but often couldn't help herself. The house was sparsely furnished but clean, or as clean as it could be being sandwiched between the gas works and its coal fires, and the rail line to St James' station. There was a small square yard at the rear with a privy and a handpump for water shared with the neighbours. The front door opened directly onto the street.

Saturday afternoons would usually find Robert and Jane at home. Lottie would often spend it with her boyfriend Eric, and Charles (the youngest surviving child at 14) had moved to Filton near Bristol to take up an apprenticeship at the airfield. He longed to be a pilot but was training to be an engineer.

Bob opened the front door with his key and called out to his parents to let them know he was home. Although larger than the house Philip and Mary Rose occupied, the Lewis' home felt much smaller to Caroline. The front door opened directly into a living area with a fireplace surrounded by four upholstered chairs in various styles and states of deterioration. A worn rug was spread on the wooden floor and a small table stood at the window with a large plant blocking some of the light. A mirror hung on the chimney breast and the mantelpiece was cluttered with odds and ends, letters, a box of matches and a small, framed photograph showing Robert and Jane taken several years earlier.

Through a door opposite the front door was the kitchen with stairs leading up to the three small bedrooms. The kitchen was almost the same size as the living room with some cupboards for food and utensils, a scrubbed table and wooden chairs, a Belfast sink, a dresser and a large black range. Robert and Jane had been sitting at the table with the back door open onto the yard. The newspaper was spread out on the table and some knitting placed next to it. They had got to their feet as they heard Bob tell Caroline to follow him through.

Bob was much taller than his parents. He introduced Caroline, which set Jane fluttering around the kitchen pulling out a chair and passing the kettle from the range to Robert to go out and fill. Cake was offered, and although Caroline would have liked to accept, she declined thinking that she might be taking the last morsel from the family's mouths. She sat self-consciously in the chair offered to her and waited for the tea that would follow.

"Lottie will be sad she missed you," Jane said taking down cups and saucers from the dresser.

"Is she out with Eric?" Bob had introduced his sister to his workmate a few months earlier and they had quickly fallen for each other.

"No love, she's down the street taking a turn to mind Mrs White's baby."

Bob explained that Mrs White had had a difficult birth and Mr White was serving six months in Gloucester prison for stealing a sack of coal from the Railway Inn's yard. The women in the street took turns to care for the baby and do housework for Mrs White while she sat in their back yard and stared into the near distance.

"How terrible," Caroline said, thinking of Mary and her spotless little house.

"It's not her fault she married a wrong 'un," said Robert as he returned with the full kettle.

"Oh no, I didn't mean… it's sad that she is not able to manage on her own."

Silence fell as they waited for the water to boil. Bob shifted self-consciously in his seat.

"We're going to have dinner at the Orchard. Made sense to stop here on the way instead of Caroline going all the way home and then all the way back again."

"And you live near Sunningend?" Jane spooned a small amount of tea into the teapot. Caroline noticed a chip in the lid.

"Yes, at the moment. We're moving to Norwood Court shortly. That's over near the Park."

"There are some grand houses over that way," Robert knocked his pipe on the stove and began filling the bowl again with tobacco.

"We've taken a new apartment. Father felt our house needed a young family and seems to rather like the idea of a new start. And the apartment is fabulously light and airy, we're selling a lot of our old furniture as it simply won't fit," Caroline stopped, suddenly aware that she might appear insensitive to the Lewis' lack of ornamentation in their home.

"Just you and your father, is it?" asked Jane.

"Yes, though we'll be keeping Annie on as well which I am very happy about," again, Caroline realised her hosts might find her somewhat patronising. This was all rather awkward, she thought.

"Well, I shall have some cake, Mother. Are you sure you don't want any Caroline?"

She accepted the lifeline, "Perhaps a small piece then."

The kettle seemed to take forever to boil, and then of course there was the wait for the tea to brew. The cake, a madeira, was dry and after finding the first bite clung to the roof of her mouth Caroline nibbled in the hope of eventually having some liquid to wash it down. When the tea arrived, it was half a cup of milky warm water. Caroline was thankful none the less.

Their dinner at the Orchard was a far more relaxed affair. It was busy and Bob worried that they might not get a table. They were squeezed in and enjoyed a meal of game pie with potatoes, cabbage and gravy, followed by helpings of apple crumble with custard. There was an upright piano near the counter and a young man began playing a jolly tune as Caroline and Bob were just finishing their dessert. Some of the other patrons began to sing along, the atmosphere becoming more like a public house. Bob paid the bill, sucking on his teeth as he counted out his shillings, and then escorted Caroline out into the cool evening.

As they waited for her tram at the junction of Gloucester Road and Tewkesbury Road, Caroline felt pleasantly full.

"It was nice to meet your parents today," she said, trying to hide a yawn.

"Most of Cheltenham will know about it by tomorrow morning, no doubt."

"Really? But how?"

"Didn't you see the faces at the windows as we left? And the two old girls on their doorstep across the road? Gossip will run like wildfire."

"But what is there to gossip about?"

"Me bringing a pretty girl home to meet my parents of course. They'll have us married off by the end of next week! Oh, don't look like that, I know what we said earlier. I'll not push you to make a decision that you're not ready for Caroline. Just know that when you do make it, I'll be waiting for you. That's a promise I can make."

So having burnt her own cake, been saddened by the news that her friend was leaving town, and fearing she had left a poor impression on Bob's parents, Caroline retired to bed that evening feeling more ready than ever to start a new adventure with new people and new surroundings.

Number twenty Glencairn Road had become a collection of piles to keep and piles to dispose of. In every room objects were labelled and arranged so that no mistakes could be made. Items were often moved from one pile to the other, and back again, as space was assessed and reassessed. The dining room had become a repository for a number of large wooden packing crates that were slowly filling and some hessian sacks to tie around vulnerable chair legs and lamps.

George had offered Annie the chance to select one or two pieces of furniture from those with sale labels on as a gift, which could be stored in the garage at the apartment until she had her own home. Annie had burst into tears, not with gratitude as George first thought. On calming the girl down, he learned that Annie and Jacob's future looked much less rosy than it had previously due to the growing unease of the coal miners across the land at their reduced wages and increased hours. The price of coal had gone up again only that week, yet Mr Jenks senior dared not increase his prices for his domestic customers. Many were already in arrears, and Jacob had told Annie that some were becoming abusive when he called to collect payments. She worried he would be hurt, but worried more that their wedding would have to be delayed which in turn would mean they might miss out on one of the new houses being built by the town council to the north of St Mark's church. She had her heart set on one and was reluctant to move in with the Jenks however temporary it would be.

"Do you intend to buy or rent the house, should you be offered one?"

"Jacob was hoping to get a mortgage so we could buy one, Sir. We've got some money saved but not enough to buy outright."

"I see. Tell Jacob to come into the office after Easter would you, and we'll see what might be available to him. We have arranged two or three mortgages on the most recent release of properties in Tennyson Road, and I am satisfied with their quality. You have a sponsor for your application?"

"Mr Rose, sir."

"Ahh yes. Good. Well, no more tears now, eh? Try not to let the future become too daunting Annie. We shall keep whatever furniture you would like for as long as necessary."

Annie eventually chose a small side table from the parlour and a collection of older pieces of crockery that were often used as serving and resting plates. George meanwhile added a label to the wardrobe and dressing table in Elizabeth's room with Annie's name on.

"Annie, do you have the string?"

Caroline was holding a parcel of three books wrapped in brown paper closed with one hand and didn't want to let go.

"Here, Miss, how much do you need? This much?" she drew out a length and Caroline nodded.

The books were for Philip Rose and were from George's study. Caroline would be taking them when she visited Mary and Angelica that afternoon. George had decided to save two bookcases for the apartment and had then to cull his small library. There were now two piles of books in the study, one to pack into the moving crates and the other to give away or leave for the auction on Monday 12 April.

The weather was warming up as Caroline walked over the railway bridge and on towards St Mark's church. She carried the books wrapped in brown paper and hummed a little tune to herself. She was very much looking forward to her trip to Devon in a couple of days, to leave the chaos of her home behind, knowing that when she returned, she would be going straight to the new apartment, and everything would have been organised between her father and Annie in her absence.

Caroline found Mary and Angelica in the little square of garden behind their house. She had heard her Goddaughter's laughter as she approached and had gone through the side gate instead of knocking on the front door. Mary was pegging out washing on a line stretched across the garden from the house to the far end where it was attached to a tall concrete post. Angelica sat on a blanket on the small patch of grass, holding a towelling nappy which she repeatedly put over her head and then removed when Mary asked, "Where's Angelica?".

"Hello you two! That sounds like a fun game!"

"Miss Caroline! What a nice surprise. Let me just get this hung out and we can go inside."

"I don't want to disturb Angelica's game, so don't hurry on my account, please."

Mary spied the parcel. Always direct, she asked, "What do you have there?"

"A present for Philip. Some of Father's books on economics. He thought Philip might be interested in them."

"He might, he might," Mary said with a peg in her mouth which she then removed and put over a sheet folded in half, "and you are a lady of leisure now?"

Caroline smiled, she loved listening to Mary's lilting voice and how she usually went straight to the point of whatever they were talking about.

"Yes, I suppose I am. But I shall be so very busy this week before I go down to Devon, and then when I come home, well, home will be at Norwood Court."

Angelica let out a screech, affronted at being ignored, and both women said in unison "Where's Angelica?" even though she was not this time hidden by the cloth.

"Shall I bring her in?" Caroline asked.

"Yes, she can go in her highchair while we have a cup of tea."

Caroline picked the girl up, surprised at how heavy she had become, and took her into the kitchen behind Mary. The highchair was to one side of the small table and Caroline sat Angelica in and fastened the leather belt that was designed to stop the child slipping or toppling out of the seat. Angelica's chubby brown legs showed between her pink dress and the pink socks on her feet. Mary made tea while Caroline told her all about the packing, sorting and labelling, and Angelica contentedly squished small squares of bread between her fingers. As Mary poured the tea, she tried to disguise a yawn and failed.

"Is she keeping you up at night still?"

"No, not anymore. But her brother or sister will be in a few months," she smiled a small smile.

"Another baby! Mary that's wonderful news! Does Philip know?"

"Yes, now that I've had one, I have no need to check with my mother. What people say about not getting pregnant before the first baby is weaned is not true. But this one feels different all the same. I was tired before with Angelica, but I feel I could sleep for a week now."

"When will it be due?"

"I think the end of October. Perhaps this one will be a boy."

"I shall have time to knit another little jacket for him or her. And with my new bicycle I'll be able to still visit and help you as the time gets nearer, if you'd like me to, of course."

"I would very much like you to, Miss Caroline. It is good to have another woman around. And we shall have to ask the Church to find us a larger house."

"Do you think the Reverend Lloyd might move out of the vicarage to somewhere a little smaller when he retires?" A thought occurred to Caroline, "Perhaps you could swap homes with him!"

"Well, that is a fine idea. This house is small, but would suit an older man, and it would mean we were nearer the church. I shall ask Philip."

On her way home later, Caroline wondered if Mary was truly well. She had moved slowly around the kitchen with a strained expression but reassured Caroline that she would be alright after a good night's sleep.

Maundy Thursday dawned bright and clear. George carried Caroline's case down to the railway station and waited with her on the platform.

"Are you sure you will be alright?" Caroline asked again.

"Of course, my dear, you really mustn't worry. Everything is arranged, the removal men will be here on Saturday to take the items we are keeping, and the auctioneer will take care of everything we leave behind."

"And he will auction the house at the end of the sale?"

"That's correct. He felt it would be prudent to clear the property first. Now all you need to do is enjoy yourself with your friends and remember to come to the apartment when you return!"

"I shan't forget. I expect I will take a taxi as it will be rather late when I get back here."

"I shall wait up for you. And I will have a new key cut for you while you are away. Now, here's your train. Have a wonderful time by the sea!"

4

THE REUNION

The water sparkled. Caroline sat forward on her seat to gaze at it through the carriage window. She had the second-class compartment to herself, a luxury she had enjoyed all the way from Exeter where she had changed trains. The river Exe opened out into Exmouth Bay as Caroline travelled towards her destination. She reached up and pulled the window down, breathing in deeply to capture as much salty air as she could. Her excitement was growing, not only to be with her friends again but also to be near the sea. The summer before she had spent a month near Swanage with James Baker and his company of actors while they filmed a moving picture. She had thoroughly enjoyed herself, particularly the last few days after the rest of the company had departed and she had been alone with James and the housekeeper. She had regularly longed to go back to the sea ever since.

It had been a long journey and she had broken it at Exeter not only to change trains but also to have some lunch in the little station café. Once again, she enjoyed listening to the different accents as she ate her meal. Here, as in Dorset, the accent was much softer than she was used to, and the natives were slower in speech than those in Bristol. As she left the café, she gave a shilling to a young man who sat with a tin mug in his hand. He had no legs from half-way down his thighs and had two prosthetic legs propped up beside him on the bench along with a pair of wooden crutches. Their eyes had not met; he stared rigidly ahead despite thanking her in his west-country drawl.

Caroline had not told Helen which train she would be arriving on. She planned to make her own way to Helen and Tommy's house, assuming that Budleigh Salterton's High Street would be easy to find. She would ask at the station when she arrived, and if the porter thought it would be too far to walk, she would take a taxi. She felt confident and chuckled to herself that she was becoming an experienced traveller. The Guard was calling 'Exmouth! Next station Exmouth!' as he walked along the length of the train. Caroline could see many boats in the bay and wondered if she might be able to go out on the water this time.

Forty minutes later Caroline stepped out of the taxi in front of a substantial villa style house in Budleigh Salterton's High Street. As Helen had described, a brook ran alongside the street and each house had a stone footbridge from the road into the front garden. The taxi driver followed Caroline across the bridge carrying her case and carpet bag and she tipped him sixpence before facing the black painted front door and pulling the bell cord. After a moment the door flew open, and the next few minutes were full of hugs and laughter and 'so good to see you!' and a few tears of joy.

Caroline's coat was taken from her by Midge and hung on one of the pegs in the hallway. Helen explained that Tommy was out painting. He was expected home around dusk. She showed Caroline up to a bedroom with a single bed underneath a pink candlewick bedspread and with walls covered with a faded wisteria pattern wallpaper. There was a small dressing table in the window bay and a slim gentleman's wardrobe completed the room's furnishings.

"It's small I'm afraid, but first come first served and all that. Midge bagged the better spare room. This one has a glorious view of the houses opposite; you'll be able to wave good night to Mrs Deakin. Make it your own, dear, and come down to the garden room when you are ready."

Caroline washed her face and unpacked her things. She would be staying until the following Tuesday and had packed for all weathers and occasions. This included her bathing suit; she was hoping to have time to swim in the sea. She had also brought her small box of paints and brushes and a sketch book, hoping Tommy wouldn't mind her company on one of his painting excursions.

The house was around twenty years old and had an indoor bathroom on the first floor along with four bedrooms. Descending the dogleg staircase Caroline passed through the wide hallway with its black and white tiled floor, past the front parlour and into the rear sitting room. Through another door she could see the garden room Helen had spoken of. It was a conservatory with cane chairs and tables and tall palms and ferns in large terracotta pots.

Midge was sitting with her feet tucked underneath her in a cane chair with a green seat cushion. Her dark hair was shorter than Caroline remembered it and she wondered if Midge had been subjected to the same make-over that Helen had treated Caroline to in Plymouth the year before. Beside Midge was a small trolley with a bottle of gin and another of tonic water and a bucket of ice. Helen reclined on a chaise longue which was also covered in a green fabric. Her shoes were on the floor and her stockinged toes were flexing to some rhythm playing in her head. The doors of the conservatory were open, and Caroline could hear the birds singing in the garden. Hardly 'tiny', she thought; it was bordered by hedges and mature trees with flower beds and a lawn leading to a rougher area with fruit trees in blossom beyond.

Helen looked at the trolley, "Drat! Caro darling, there should be a bottle of brandy in the sideboard back there, do bring it out and help yourself. I know you dislike gin, yet I forgot to bring it through."

When Caroline returned and was pouring a small measure into a glass tumbler, Helen continued.

"Now you are to treat this place as your own, Caro. I've told Midge the same. We won't be standing on ceremony here. Come and go just as you please, sleep in 'til midday or get up with the dawn and go to bed whenever you feel tired. The wonderful Mrs Daniel will be along shortly to make us some dinner. Probably fish, it usually is. Midge, have we had anything other than fish since you've been here?"

"We had sausages on Tuesday evening, but there does seem to be a lot of fish."

"It's all they eat here. Mrs Daniel is a treasure. I am so pleased to have found her so quickly. And Tommy has found the most handsome gardener to take care of all things outdoors for us. Midge was quite excited when I described Ralph to her, weren't you dear?" Helen had a mischievous smile.

"Yes, until he arrived on Wednesday morning, and I discovered he is seventy years old at least!"

"Midge exaggerates. Ralph is no more than forty. I believe the term is 'weathered' to describe him."

"Storm battered I should say!"

The girls laughed, and Caroline took a seat on a cane chair near to the open double doors.

"Now, although I have just told you to come and go as you please," Helen continued, "we do have some entertainment planned. Tomorrow we shall go down to the beach whenever we are all up and ready. The shops will be closed of course, but I find that is the best time to go shopping here, one hardly spends any money at all. But shopping we will do on Saturday in Exeter. Tommy will drive us as I'm sure you have both had enough of trains. We'll visit the cathedral and have luncheon or afternoon tea, whichever is appropriate. And on Saturday evening the Major is showing a double bill of moving pictures at the Drill Hall which I thought we might take a stroll to and see. Sunday of course we shall be in church for the morning service. One must make an effort if one is to get on in a small town such as Budleigh. Beyond that, I have not given much thought. Midge will be leaving us on Monday unless we can convince her to stay longer."

"Helen, we've been around this several times now, I must go on Monday. Caroline, I have an interview with the missionary group that sent Mark to Africa. It is in Reading on Tuesday so you see I must be back for that."

"Goodness, so soon?"

"There will be several rounds of interviews if it is anything like Mark went through. I shan't know for sure if I've been accepted for a few months yet. Probably won't get out to Africa until at least September I shouldn't think, even if I am successful."

"I assume they want to make sure you really want to go. Though I cannot for the life of me see the attraction, Midge dear," Helen swung her legs round and got up to make another gin and tonic. She caught Caroline's frown.

"Darling, it's practically all tonic, look," she held up her glass so that Caroline could see how much tonic was in it and then topped it up with a small amount of gin, "I have it under control," she said, as much to herself as her guests.

Mrs Daniel appeared, wheeling her bicycle over the gravel path that led from the front of the house, past the conservatory and to the kitchen door. She had a bundle wrapped in newspaper in the basket and what looked like a bottle of milk.

The three friends chattered on, sipping their drinks politely as the sun dipped below the roof tops and bats began to swoop across the garden. Caroline asked about the telephone she had spotted in the hallway and Helen said both girls could make calls home if they needed to. It was still a novelty in many houses, and Caroline said she hoped her father would have one installed in the apartment once they had settled in. Tommy arrived carrying his easel and canvas, and a kitbag with his paints and brushes slung over his shoulder. His hair had grown longer, and he now looked every inch the artist with the sleeves of his collarless shirt rolled up and his waistcoat dabbed with paint. He greeted Caroline warmly then went off to change for dinner. Helen insisted the girls would not be changing. She was enjoying the bohemian atmosphere she had decided to create in the home she shared with Tommy, despite the respectable outward persona she was cultivating with the locals.

Mrs Daniel served them leek and potato soup with fresh bread rolls and butter, red mullet, and a dessert of chocolate sponge pudding and cream. Afterwards they took coffee in the front parlour and listened to the radio for a while. It was Tommy's pride and joy, just as dear to him as his temperamental car. Caroline found her eyes closing and made her excuses to go up to bed shortly after nine. Before getting into bed, she opened the sash window a little so that the sounds of the town could creep into her room as she slept.

How strange, she thought as she drifted off, it really did feel like home.

"What do you have in that bag?" Midge, Helen and Tommy were waiting for Caroline in the hallway as she descended the stairs.

"My bathing suit and a towel."

"Good Lord are you mad?! The sea will be terribly cold!" Midge screwed up her nose at the thought.

"Then I shall just have to swim fast," replied Caroline. She was itching to get down to the beach and into the water.

Tommy picked up his kit bag containing charcoal and a sketch book in case the mood should take him to create, "Shall we go then?"

It was a short walk of around five minutes before they could see the sea, and the smell found them much sooner. Rough laughing calls of the gulls filled the air. Midge had already spent some time walking along the seashore with Helen and sometimes Tommy, but she had no complaints about going again and again. There were a few people around, on the pebbles and walking along the road that ran next to the beach, but there was no activity around the boats. Good Friday was not for working and many of the inhabitants of Budleigh would be at church or chapel that morning. The sun shone encouragingly with just one or two whisps of white cloud against the blue. The breeze was stronger than Caroline had expected, but it was not unwelcome.

The beach curved around a small bay. On one side the red Devonian rock rose up in a ragged cliff. On the other, the landscape echoed the curves with a soft rise and fall of scrubland and a few blown and stunted trees on top of a lower red rock peninsula. The houses and businesses of the little town crowded mostly around two or three streets, with the railway slicing through it parallel to the sea front. The land swept up and away northwards from the town in wooded hills and farmland.

Tommy took up the role of tour guide. He explained to his companions that the red sandstone was the result of the area being covered in a great desert during the Triassic geological period, and that many fossils could be found as the cliffs gave way with each winter storm. There was no harbour at Budleigh, only a few small fishing boats pulled high out of the water and resting on their sides. Midge was interested in the boats and what they caught, noticing some lobster pots stacked up against one boat. Tommy suggested they take the car round to Sidmouth that afternoon to see the boats there. Though there was no harbour there either, at high tide pleasure steamers could dock alongside the sea wall and there were more fishing craft than at Budleigh.

They walked about a mile along the shore until Caroline could wait no longer. She had hoped for a convenient beach hut to be available, but there were none. Instead, she asked Helen, being the taller of the friends, to hold a towel around her while she quickly undressed and pulled on her woollen bathing suit. Midge folded Caroline's clothes back into her bag to help, and then sat on the pebbles with Tommy who was studiously looking out to sea.

"Are you sure about this old thing?" Tommy was still concerned about the temperature of the water, and the lack of locals on the beach, should Caroline require rescuing.

"Quite sure, thank you. I have been waiting for this for such a long time. If it is too cold, I shall come back out, have no fear!"

She left them sitting on the beach with her bag and towel and ran down over the pebbles to the soft red sand at the water's edge. The tide was some way out and not another soul was at the waterline. Caroline felt gloriously alone and for a moment savoured the expanse of water before her. Then she marched into the sea, the tiny waves tickling her ankles as the first shock of cold flashed through her.

"Better get right in and start swimming," she shivered.

Once in the water and moving, she swam as strongly as she could and tried to stay close to the shore. It was hard work as the tide was still on its way out.

"She's a good swimmer, don't worry," Midge tried to reassure Tommy, who had got to his feet in order to see Caroline better, "she won a medal for it at school, didn't she Helen?"

"I have no doubt about that, but the tide can take a man out without him knowing how far," Tommy was squinting to keep track of Caroline in the water.

Helen leaned back with her hands behind her, face lifted to the sun, eyes closed, "A brass button on a blue ribbon if I remember correctly and coveted by half the class. Now she is free of her mother, I fully expect Caro to do all kinds of ridiculous things such as this."

"Helen! How could you be so callous! It must have been ghastly to lose a parent that way, and to watch her decline over the weeks and months too. Have you forgotten so soon how Sophia was at the end?"

"Of course not, Sophia had been consumptive for years and we all knew how it would end eventually. I do not think losing a frail sister is at all the same as losing a parent. But let's be honest about the thing, Caroline's mother is the reason we had not seen Caroline for so long after we all left school. All of the things we did, the parties, the holidays, the socialising, she never had the opportunity to do. Now that she can, she wants to do it all. I don't blame her one bit, but she is still rather naïve."

"I suppose you're right," Midge conceded, "mind you, I never had that many parties or holidays to go to."

"But darling, you had that grotesque pile at Basildon House to ramble over, and those dear service men. You saw some life, is what I am saying. I certainly saw plenty of life. Caroline saw only the inside of her home and a very occasional visit to a friend of her mother's not more than a few streets away. That is not life. And life is what she needs now. She craves it, I can tell. And I wouldn't be at all surprised if she announces she is off to Italy either."

"Italy? Why ever would she go there? Helen, are you teasing me?"

"Not at all. You remember the young film director I told you about, James Baker?"

"The one Caroline went to Dorset with last year?"

"The very same. He has taken a house in Florence and intends to further his career there. If ever there were a couple meant to be together in this world it is James and Caroline, don't you think Tommy?"

"It doesn't matter what you or I think about it, neither of them seems inclined to do anything about it despite our efforts."

"Then perhaps they don't feel as strongly as you think they do," Midge dug a shell out of the pebbles and then discarded it as it had a broken edge.

"Oh, but they do. They simply are too concerned with themselves to see they would be perfect together."

"She's coming out, better get that towel ready."

"My brother Luke has taken quite a shine to Caroline as well, you know."

"Really? And there is a young man in Cheltenham too I believe. Who would have thought Caro would be the one fending off suitors!"

"Helen, now you really are teasing me. It was never likely to be you, was it?!"

Helen smiled and flicked another shell at Midge, "I always thought you would be the first of us married with a brood of noisy children at your feet."

Caroline had found the tide a match for her strength and had fought hard to be able to touch her feet on the sea bottom again. It was invigorating, exhilarating, and very hard work. Having proved her point, she decided not to prolong her exercise and waded out of the shallow surf back towards her friends. Her skin was red and tingling with the cold, and her teeth began to chatter. Helen handed her the towel and she quickly rubbed herself before handing the towel back to Helen so she could hold it up while Caroline wriggled out of the sopping bathing suit again. It was a tricky manoeuvre to get back into her underclothes while standing on the pebbles, though she was thankful there was no sand.

"There's no one about, so I shan't bother with my stockings unless we are going on to somewhere else."

"Goodness what a brazen trollop you have become!" laughed Helen.

"I think if God was offended by my swimming on Good Friday, he would have already struck me down, don't you?" Caroline pulled her sweater over her vest and reached for her shoes.

"Midge, you are our official religious arbiter, what say you?"

"I say we shouldn't push our luck. Particularly if you want to be considered an upstanding member of the community Helen."

"Oh dear, have I disgraced you already?" Caroline rubbed the ends of her hair with the towel and pulled her hairbrush from her bag.

Tommy chuckled, "Helen walks a tightrope between respectability and scandal, don't you, dear heart?"

"It is one's burden to carry. I am determined to obtain a seat on the parish council at the next elections. It doesn't do to complain about a place if one is not going to take control of improving it," she put her arm around Caroline's shoulders, "and if anyone should mention it, I shall simply say you are a friend of my husband's."

After lunch, Tommy and Midge took the car to Sidmouth and Helen and Caroline sat in the conservatory, this time with a pot of tea on the drinks trolley between them. It was warm behind the glass and Caroline had changed into a blouse when she had returned from the beach. Both women had novels to read, and it was almost an hour before Helen put hers down and spoke.

"Have you heard from James recently?"

Caroline put her bookmark between the pages, "He wrote a few weeks ago to say he was in Italy. I was surprised, I thought he would have gone to America as they make so many more films there."

"It's all about contacts I imagine. I seem to remember there being an Italian chap in James' circle for a while two or three years ago. They say money makes the world go round Caro, but *è chi conosci*."

"What does that mean?"

"It's who you know. Of course, money helps though. I hear you can take a rather large villa for just a few pounds in many places on the Continent."

"I should like to go one day."

Well, my dear, you do now have a contact, you could take the opportunity."

"You mean simply invite myself to stay with James?

Oh no, I couldn't possibly do that. He is there to work, and I don't speak a word of Italian."

"The language you could learn easily enough, and surely James will take a day off occasionally."

Caroline considered Helen's suggestion. It would be an incredibly long train journey of several days, but people did it all the time she assumed. Could she?

As if Helen was reading her mind she said, "I should make sure my passport was in order if I were you. Just in case."

"I don't think I should like to go so far on my own."

"You wouldn't be on your own when you got there."

"No, but there would be so many different countries to pass through. I should feel more confident if I had someone with me."

"Midge will be travelling to Africa by herself if she gets accepted onto that missionary thing."

"Most of that would be by ship though, at least to somewhere near Kenya, and then inland. I looked it up the other day, Tanganyika is almost in the centre of Africa."

"Yes, but still by herself. And I should think that journey would be a lot more dangerous than a train practically non-stop across Europe."

"You've been to Italy, haven't you?"

"Twice, yes, but many years ago. One has so rarely the opportunity to speak the language now I can hardly remember any other words. Mother took Sophia and I once and then a very distant cousin invited me to stay the summer we all finished school."

"Yes, I remember you wrote about how blue the sea was."

"Naples is the most beautiful city, truly," Helen looked off into the distance, remembering very hot days dressed in white linen, in fields full of wildflowers and a girl with black hair named Bianca. Then she shook herself, "All I am saying is, you shouldn't let the fact that James has been engaged before put you off pursuing him if you have feelings for him, which I know you do."

"Helen! The very idea..."

"You see, you do. He may well be busy with his work, but what he needs is a good woman to share his success with when it happens, and I have no doubt that it eventually will. He is not the kind of man who would expect you to stay home and raise a gaggle of babies either, not unless you wanted to of course and then I am sure he would be the perfect father."

"Helen, really, James and I are friends, and only friends. I am not going to chase across Europe after him, or anyone else come to that."

"Oh? Is there someone else in Europe you are holding a candle for?" Helen sat forward in her chair.

"No! Oh, you are incorrigible! There is no one anywhere who I would consider marrying at the moment."

"At the moment...."

"Helen, please. Alright, if you want to know how I honestly feel, then I do like James. But I also like Midge's brother Luke, and Lottie's brother Bob, and marrying any one of them would mean I would soon be raising at least one baby and not able to simply come and go as I please. There would be expectations of me that I am not ready to fulfil just yet. I enjoy the company of men, but I enjoy my own company just as much. I do not wish to become attached to any man before I have fully become my own woman."

Helen smiled. So, this Bob was the other player in the game; she would have to investigate that angle some other day. She was pleased to see some passion in Caroline, pleased that she seemed to be filling out like a loaf rising as the yeast fermented, and she respected her friend's decision. It would not do to push too hard to bring James and Caroline together again, but if she could find an opportunity, she would give them another gentle nudge.

"Shall we have some more tea? I think the pot is cold now."

Tommy and Midge returned carrying two large crabs in a sack, the claws bound with string. Mrs Daniel arrived just a few minutes after them with a cooked ham but agreed to deal with the crustaceans. Midge explained they had got talking to an old fisherman who was not at all inclined to give up a day on his boat for God and had shown them how to drop a line into the water with a small piece of bait and catch crabs. They had gone out a little way in his boat as the tide had come in, and they all agreed that the results would make a change from fish.

Saturday dawned overcast, and after a leisurely breakfast the four friends got into Tommy's car and drove to Exeter. They each had their own curiosity to satisfy with different aspects of the old city. Midge had particularly wanted to visit the cathedral and they began their visit by parking the car on the edge of the lawn surrounding it. Caroline had been to Gloucester cathedral some years before, Cheltenham being a town and not having a cathedral of its own. Exeter's she soon realised was on a much grander scale.

Helen naturally wanted to visit Walton's department store. Tommy needed to restock with some painting supplies and Caroline decided to tag along with him rather than have the embarrassment of Helen's generosity imposed on her again. Tommy left the car in Sidwell Street in the care of the Amberley Brother's garage so that they could adjust the steering; he was never happy with how his car was running. Helen and Midge headed off to Walton's and Tommy and

Caroline walked along the High Street and into Bedford Street where a small artist's equipment and picture framer's shop was situated. Caroline was soon clutching a box of charcoal and a book of stiff card sheets to draw on.

When Tommy had finished his order and they had both paid for their purchases, they stepped back out into the street as a tram rumbled past.

"Is there any other shopping you'd like to do?" Tommy asked as they crossed the street behind the tram.

"No, none, these were simply an impulsive indulgence."

"I really don't need anything else either, Budleigh has everything one needs. I say, why don't we take a walk down to the docks and see if there are any ships in?"

Caroline agreed. They walked downhill and along streets that gradually changed from commercial to residential, and then to warehouses along the riverside. The river Exe was wide as it cut through the city and had long been the source of communications and provisions. Caroline noticed the houses became narrower and taller as they moved away from the city centre. Some leaned precariously over the street below and many had windows with broken glass stuffed with rags. Dirty children stood in doorways and sat on the curb edge poking rubbish with sticks in the hope of uncovering something of interest.

"I thought cities would bring in good fortune for all who lived in them, but that's not the case is it?" Caroline said quietly as they passed a public house with the scent of beer and pipe smoke lingering in the entrance.

"Goodness, no. Poverty is everywhere Caroline. In some ways I would say it's worse in the cities, it seems to spill out onto the pavements like overflowing sewers. There are just so many people who can't seem to get a step up. And of course, they breed so."

"But why, if there is wealth here, doesn't it find everyone? I don't imagine it would do so equally, but it seems to miss so many of them completely. I thought wealth created jobs."

"It does to an extent, but you must remember, wealth is based on the exploitation of labour. For example, if I have a factory and I need people to make paintbrushes, I need to make sure I pay those people less overall than I make from selling the brushes. I need a lot of people, so I have to divide the amount available for wages between them. I, of course, also want to make a profit. I cannot pay my workers too much, otherwise I won't make any money for myself. And many people are not suited to the positions that I need to fill. Unfortunately, there seem to be many people in cities who are unsuitable for anything but the most menial employment. And some for nothing at all."

Caroline thought back to how Bob had explained the lot of the coal miners in the Forest of Dean. They had no option but to work for the mines because that was the only employer in the area. But here, there must be many more employers, yet even more people would be unsuited to any of the opportunities on offer.

"Tommy, your father owned a factory, didn't he?"

"He still does, yes, though he leaves the running of it to his managers these days. What of it?"

"Would you work there?"

"In the factory? Good Lord, no! I'm not in the least good with accounts, despite my heritage. It provides me with an income, and I stay out of the way."

"What work do you think you would be suited to, if you had to work?"

Tommy was silent for a few moments. They had reached a bridge across the river and were leaning on the parapet looking out at the array of vessels along the quay.

"I rather hope I am suited to being an artist. Of course, it's not something my father considers to be a profession, but if I can develop my style, I know a few places in London that might take one or two of my canvases."

"Could I see them when we get back to the house?"

"You've seen a couple already. The one above the fireplace in the front sitting room, and the other on the landing. Both are mine."

"Yours? I thought Helen had bought them. Tommy they are very striking, I like them a lot. I really would like to see more."

"You are kind, dear heart. There is no need to humour a friend though," he smiled yet his eyes showed disbelief and doubt.

"Don't be a donkey. If I didn't like them, I would have said so."

Both works were bold and angular in style. They were landscapes but painted with thick paint and a palette knife using only two or three colours. The one in the sitting room had stark black lines as part of the composition. They were not in any traditional style and Caroline was intrigued by them. She could see influences of the art she and Lady Victoria had viewed in London the year before.

They retraced their steps back to the commercial district of the city, and then along South Street. They had arranged to meet Helen and Midge at The Old Chevalier Inn, one of the many Tudor-style buildings that crowded along the main shopping streets with blackened timbers and square bay windows in the upper floors with small leaded glass panes. Caroline was not used to public houses. In many, women would not be served unless accompanied by a man, but this was an Inn with rooms to rent and the lounge was open to non-residents. Tommy steered her to an empty table near the entrance to the lounge bar and went to buy their drinks. Caroline took off her hat and gloves, noticing that she was the only woman in the bar but that after an initial glance, none of the men paid her any further attention.

Tommy returned with two half pints of bitter.

"Bottoms up!" he said as he placed the glass in front of her and took a seat facing the door.

Caroline took an apprehensive sip. It was indeed bitter, with a tang that stayed in her mouth after she had swallowed, but it was not unpleasant.

"They asked if we wanted to eat but I said no. I hope that's alright. I have no idea how long the girls will be, and we can stop on the way home if everyone is hungry. There's a nice place just after Exmouth Helen and I ate at the other week."

"I'm not hungry yet, your breakfasts are more than I would normally eat, all that bacon and eggs!"

"Mrs Daniel keeps us well supplied. We just need to find a reliable charwoman and then everything will be domestic bliss."

"Tommy, Helen said she had nothing planned for entertainment on Monday. I should very much like to go painting with you, if you wouldn't mind?"

"Not at all. What subject would you prefer, landscape, seascape, buildings or people?"

"I think land and sea if that's possible?"

"Yes, I think we can find somewhere. I warn you though, once I get going, I rely on the sun to tell me when to stop. We'll be out all day."

They discussed possible locations for a while until Helen and Midge arrived. Midge carried a stiff paper bag containing a cream-coloured blouse that had a scarf-like tie at the neck and some smaller items such as face powder and a small mascara block with a tiny brush for application. Helen was smiling contentedly over a lamp she had purchased which, she said, would look stunning in the sitting room and would be delivered on Monday. They all agreed that they would drive back to Exmouth for lunch; Caroline managed to drink half of her half pint, Tommy finished his, and they set off.

The car was waiting for them outside the garage, freshly washed and ready to go. The younger Amberley brother assured Tommy the steering was now perfectly aligned and suggested an oil change the next time he was in town. Midge chattered on about the interior of the cathedral until they pulled up outside the Sea Bird Café. A hearty lunch, called a Fisherman's Platter on the menu, was enjoyed by all. Crusty bread rolls, potted crab, small silver pickled onions that skated around their plates like marbles, watercress and chopped egg salad, washed down with a large pot of tea. The sun shone down from an azure blue sky with just the feintest whisp of cloud. They sat outside on a terrace and lingered over their tea to watch the Exmouth inhabitants go about their Saturday afternoon activities.

Helen suggested they have ice cream before they left Exmouth and led them along the main street to a small parlour that also sold fudge and chocolates made on the premises. Midge was beside herself as the small glass dish was placed in front of her. Two small scoops of vanilla ice cream with raspberry sauce drizzled on top and a sweet fan-shaped wafer stuck in like a warning sign that eating too much could make you feel decidedly queasy! They ate using teaspoons to savour the treat for longer. Midge had only had ice cream once before when visiting Luke in Reading but declared it would be the one thing she would miss the most from England while being out in Africa, should she secure her place there.

"I don't believe I would miss anything about England if I were in another country," Helen had finished her ice cream (just one scoop in her bowl, no sauce, no fan wafer) and lit a cigarette.

"I would miss our puddings," Tommy nibbled his wafer which he had saved until last.

"But they do have superior food abroad, dear."

"It's not like ours. I couldn't find a decent jam roly-poly with custard anywhere in France. And the portions are miniscule."

"What would you miss, Caroline?" Midge asked.

"I'm not sure. I know when I was in Dorset last year, I missed my own room at home the most. But once everyone else had gone, I really didn't miss anything at all."

As she said it, she was surprised by it. She really hadn't missed anything from her home in those last few days with James in Dorset. If anything, she would have liked to stay for longer, but she knew that was impossible as the house had only been taken for a month. She hadn't missed her parents or Annie, or the familiar sights and sounds of Cheltenham. She hadn't even missed attending church, which until that year had been an expectation every Sunday. How quickly all her routines had changed with a change in location.

Back in Budleigh they spent the afternoon pottering about the house, reading, dozing and chatting. They were served an early dinner of the ham that Mrs Daniel had brought the day before, and then dressed to go out to the Drill Hall to watch the Major's moving picture offering for the evening. Caroline had been more excited about this than visiting Exeter; any excuse to watch a film was one she gladly took advantage of. The Drill Hall was next to St Peter's primary school and was a long single story building painted white on the outside with muddy brown woodwork. It was rather similar to the village hall in Pangbourne, Midge remarked. Folding chairs were set out in rows with a gap down the middle of the hall. A large white sheet had been fixed to the far end. The heavy red curtains, a feature of many village halls across the land, had been drawn across the windows to keep out the daylight which was now fading.

The seats were around three quarters taken when the doors were closed, and the hall plunged into near darkness. A hush descended on the audience as the Major's film equipment whirred and clunked into life. Midge had brought a bag of toffees and passed them among her friends. They all tried not to make too much noise rummaging for the sweets and then unwrapping them.

The evening show consisted of two British-made films from several years earlier. The first, a comedy called *The Double Event*, starred Mary Odette as the daughter of a country vicar who had lost his fortune. The daughter then set about recovering it by becoming the partner of a bookmaker. The second film, *The Breed of the Treshams*, also starred Mary Odette and was a drama set in the Civil War where the Royalists discovered a Roundhead spy. Caroline was surprised at the rowdiness of the rest of the audience. They cheered and jeered in equal measure and no attention was paid to anyone truly wanting to become engrossed in either storyline. At the end of the show, everyone stood and gave a rousing chorus of *God Save The King*.

As the four walked back through the town in the dark, Midge asked Caroline if her experience of film making produced anything like what they had just seen.

"Do you know I have no idea at all! I have never seen the final cut as they call it. James took the reels back to London to do the editing and I believe the film was distributed in Germany rather than here."

"And it took a whole month to film it all?" Midge was trying to understand how a month could produce a film of just an hour in length.

"Yes, but we had to shoot the same scenes several times before James was happy with them. It's very tiring Midge and not at all glamourous."

As they reached the house, Tommy announced he was not a bit tired and would be taking another stroll around the town. He didn't linger to hear the good nights offered to him from the women. Caroline and Helen exchanged glances as Midge led the way across the footbridge and up to the front door. Once inside Midge went to make cocoa for them and Helen and Caroline sat in the front sitting room with just the light from two table lamps illuminating them.

"He has a special friend," Helen announced, as if they had been discussing Tommy since they entered the room.

"Here in Budleigh?"

"Yes, Stoneborough, near the gas works."

Caroline didn't know where that was exactly, but was concerned for her friend, "Isn't that taking an awful risk, someone so close to home?"

"He is discretion itself; we have a small gate at the end of the garden, no one will see him return at whatever ungodly hour it might be. There is no habit besides the habit itself, no one could predict and follow him there."

Caroline nodded, cautiously satisfied.

The next morning, Easter Sunday, the sun streamed through the windows and birdsong woke Caroline at a little after six. She lay in bed for a while listening to the sounds around her, picking out each bird from its competitors.

She recognised some from her own bedroom dawns and added black backed gulls to her mental list. A cart rumbled past in the street outside, she assumed taking milk to the station. Some things did not stop for holy days. She stretched, wiggling her toes under the sheet and blankets, and then wondered when or if Tommy had returned during the night. The nature of his activities intrigued her, the mechanics and the emotions, but she dared not ask the numerous questions she had.

Caroline heard the bathroom door open and close across the landing and realised she would have to wait now until it was vacant again. Her mind wandered to the new home waiting for her back in Gloucestershire with its sleek lines and enamel bath with hot water on demand. She resolved that taking a bath would be the first thing she would do when she got home. A long hot bath. The bathroom door opened and closed again while the plumbing gurgled, and Caroline got out of bed.

Tommy was absent from the breakfast table. Helen smoked her cigarette and poured coffee, apparently unconcerned at her husband's lack of appearance. He would often sleep until lunchtime on Sundays, she reassured her friends. Midge had taken charge of the meal, with Mrs Daniels not expected until the following morning. They had bacon and eggs, thick slices of bread thinly spread with butter, mushrooms and tomatoes from tins Midge had discovered in a cupboard.

A relatively new church, St Peter's was only 30 years old but built in a Gothic style. Its narrow stained-glass windows glowed in the sunlight and the vicar stood in his cassock at the door, welcoming his parishioners like a galleon in full sail. Helen introduced her friends, and he shook their hands warmly, promising Midge to talk to her after the service about her plans for Africa. Though warm outside, the pews were chilly, and Caroline was thankful for her gloves and coat. The service itself was as long as she had expected, and she was glad of the hearty breakfast Midge had prepared for them. Afterwards, while Midge chatted to the vicar, Helen and Caroline moved away from the main rivulet of people leaving the church and stood admiring the crocuses on the lawn that gave the area its name.

"I do wish she would buck up; I'm gasping for a smoke!"

"Midge gets along with everyone, she always has."

"She's a darling really, I know, I just can't very well light up on the lawn if I want to make a good impression with the ladies of the town... Good morning, Mrs Clarke, lovely weather, isn't it? You must tell me where you purchased your hat, it's simply divine!"

After a moment of pleasantries Mrs Clarke moved on and Helen turned again to Caroline.

"President of the WI, has been for years, so I'm told. Ghastly woman but one must ingratiate oneself wherever possible if one wants to get on."

"You really want to get involved with the politics of the town?"

"Indeed I do. If we are to make our home in Budleigh, then I want to have some say over what happens here. I see it as a challenge to climb my way as high as I can to the giddy heights of the town's nobility. Mrs Astor has blazed her trail and I intend to do the same in my own small way."

Back at the house having shed their hats, gloves and coats, the women discovered Tommy in the conservatory, coffee in one hand and cigarette in the other. His mop of black hair was unbrushed and his shirt open at the neck. He wore no jacket and Caroline noticed his socks did not match as he crossed his legs. He did, however, appear supremely relaxed and quietly happy with the world.

Helen kissed the top of his head lightly as she passed him to take a cane chair nearby.

"Have you made lunch, darling?" she asked.

"There is a chicken roasting and vegetables waiting to boil. Mrs D has left us rather a lot of cheese, I think we should have that for dessert unless anyone objects?"

"You make a wonderful wife," Helen teased.

"How was the service?"

"Long. Reverend Enderby does drone on once he gets into his stride. I suppose one should expect it today. Midge made a friend of him, as we might have predicted."

"He was interested in the mission; I could hardly ignore him."

"I complemented Mrs Clarke on her head ware."

"Nicely, I hope!"

"Of course! As I told Caro, one must make an effort if one is to become Queen of Budleigh."

"Today the WI, tomorrow the world," Tommy chuckled.

After lunch, safe in the knowledge that the end of the garden was not overlooked due to the mature trees along the borders with the neighbours, the three women took a rug, cushions and lemonade out on to the lawn. It needed mowing Helen said, loud enough for Tommy to wave his hand dismissively and say Ralph would have his instructions on Wednesday as usual to give it a trim. The sun was hot, and they had all removed their stockings and shoes so as to walk barefoot on the grass.

"I haven't done this for years," Helen announced as she settled down on her back with a cushion under her head.

She had changed into what Caroline had first thought to be a night dress, but which Helen assured her was a sun dress in very fine cotton that came to just below her knees. Caroline was wearing her favourite peach dress as it had no sleeves, and Midge, inspired by Helen's frock, had stripped down to her vest and pulled on a pair of long knickerbockers her mother had given her for bathing in the sea should she wish to. Midge said she wouldn't be seen dead wearing them outside of the house and garden, but they were light and cool and comfortable for an afternoon's lazing.

"Do you remember we used to lay on the grass in Pittville Park and watch the clouds?" Caroline was feeling drowsy after their meal.

Midge laid down with her head near to Helen's, "There aren't many clouds today, it's too hot. But that one looks rather like a blancmange."

Caroline joined the other two, their heads now all in the centre of the blanket on cushions and their legs pointing outwards making the corners of a triangle, "I'm glad we're all together again," she said.

"I'm glad we kept in touch all these years. Having brothers is so inconvenient."

"Surely you have some female friends, Midge?"

"Not really. There actually aren't many girls our age in the village. We have mostly young men, all desperate to either take over their family farms or leave for pastures new, and very young girls who are still in school and playing with dolls. Agatha Cawley and I have tea together occasionally, but she is a frightful bore, simply besotted with Richard the baker's son and hardly talks of anything else. And he has no idea, so how anything is meant to come of it, I don't know."

"But if a young woman is not meant to make the first move, how will any man ever know she is interested in him?" Caroline had been pondering this conundrum recently and was curious to hear her friends' thoughts on it. Not that she had anyone she wished to make the first move towards, she told herself stiffly.

Helen lit a cigarette, "It is not a situation I have ever had to concern myself with."

"Doesn't it work the same for women?" Caroline was even more intrigued.

"I would say, from observation, that it is all together easier. Women are naturally more intimate. Consider how we are now, the three of us in states of undress laying close together in nature. We can ignore Tommy for we know he ignores us in that way. Yet for any other man, the temptation, so I am told, would be far too great and they would either attempt to ravish us all or simply have to leave us so as not to disgrace themselves or us. Women hug, women hold hands, women touch each other's faces, and no one bats an eyelid. Really, we are the emancipated sex when it comes to opportunities for love. I feel sorry for our menfolk."

Caroline frowned, "But if women have the freedom to be more intimate as you describe, how does one know when that intimacy is more than just a touch or just a hug?"

"Is there some kind of signal?"

"Oh Midge, we are not spies. One does not wear a white carnation or a jaunty cap to broadcast our attractions. The real difference I believe is the speed of the courtship. The art is to take things very slowly, to measure the response and continue or not, accordingly. I do not believe men are capable of this, or even wish to be."

A robin sang from a tree nearby. Caroline closed her eyes to the sun, and for a moment was taken back by her memory to a path down to the river Tavy in Milton Abbot where she had been assaulted the year before. She had fought Harry Gregory hard and managed to scratch his face; in response he had slapped her and left her on the ground. Caroline had lost some of her naivety then but none of her virtue. Helen had been furious with the young man when she found out later at her father's new house in Tavistock. Helen remembered too; she reached out to her side and found Caroline's hand on the blanket. She gave it a squeeze of reassurance.

Midge was unaware of the shared history, "I think I would like a man to make himself clear. None of this dancing around each other."

The women were silent for a while, each with their own thoughts on the subject.

5

THE MOVE

Midge left Budleigh Salterton the following morning. Helen, Caroline and Tommy walked to the station with her and waved her off from the platform as the train made its way out and onward to Sidmouth and beyond. Caroline and Tommy had decided to take their art materials to the headland above Budleigh for the rest of the day, and Helen announced that she would attempt to bake a cake and wait for her new lamp to arrive while they were out.

"Helen is determined to make her mark on the Women's Institute, isn't she?" Caroline asked as she and Tommy set up their easels. The heat of the previous day had tempered, and a cool breeze blew in from the sea. Caroline had left her hat at the house and wore a thin sweater with her blouse and woollen skirt.

"Helen likes to feel in control of things. I have no doubt she would make a wonderful President, but the other ladies will need a little convincing of the fact, I think. Particularly if she is to oust Mrs Clarke."

"Perhaps that's why she is baking today. Brushing up her skills. She was never that good at cookery at school. Helen was always much better at deportment and languages."

"She was born to host. She certainly has the diplomatic skills required. Here, let me hold the canvas while you tighten the catch."

At Tommy's suggestion, Caroline had taken two canvases approximately eighteen inches by twelve. They were going to paint a view of the English Channel, and another of the sea front promenade of Budleigh below them. Caroline was a little intimidated by the size of the canvas, she was more used to her sketch book at a compact six inches by ten. Her paints and brushes felt too small for the expanse of white she had to fill, but after the first few light brush strokes where she sketched a few outlines and perspectives, she settled into her method. Tommy stood a few feet away and a little behind her. Skylarks warbled behind them in the rough scrubland, leaping into the air and singing as they parachuted down to the ground again. The sea was a calm green below like glass tumbled by its tempestuous state, and the sun glittered and sparkled on the surface.

After a couple of hours, they paused their labours to sit and have the sandwiches and lemonade that Helen had suggested they take with them. Caroline's depiction of the town was almost finished, and she was pleased with the perspective and detail she had captured. Tommy's style was angular and monochrome. It relied on shadow and light to create the buildings and contrast between sea, sand and sky. Caroline liked it but felt she did not have the confidence to attack the canvas in the same way. Tommy smiled as she told him, and said it was an outlet for his passions.

They turned their easels so that the sun would not be directly in their line of sight for the afternoon and concentrated on the seascape. Again, Caroline tried to capture the detail of the ripples of waves as they were lifted in the breeze and then faded again, transient and yet constant at the same time. When she decided she had finished, she turned around to find Tommy laying on his back behind his easel, a straw hat pulled over his face. She walked over and looked at his canvas.

"Is that me?" she gasped.

"I shall call it 'Girl at an easel'. What do you think? Honestly, now!" Tommy removed his hat and leaned on one elbow to face Caroline. She looked at it again. He had caught her in profile, her hair tucked behind her ear, her hand poised with the brush against her canvas. This painting was so different to his morning work, gone were the angles and shadows and in their place was fine brushwork and a kaleidoscope of colours.

"Tommy it is very good. The way you have caught the light. The delicacy of it. I love it!"

"That's alright then, it's yours."

"What do you mean?"

"I mean I'm giving it to you. If you don't feel you can take it on the train, I'll post it to your new place. I want you to have it."

"Thank you. I don't know what to say, it's such a generous gift. But Tommy you won't make a living as an artist if you give your work away."

"But in years to come dear heart, when I am famous, you'll be able to sell it to fund your dotage."

"I will never sell it, no matter how famous you become. Will you stay there, just as you are for a few moments? I want to sketch you too!" She was excited at the thought; she had rarely painted people preferring to focus on birds or still life compositions. But she felt inspired to capture

Tommy in his relaxed pose, and quickly got out her sketch book and a pencil.

"Have you tried using charcoal?" Tommy pushed his mop of hair out of his eyes. "There's some in my knapsack if you want it."

"I haven't, no," Caroline worked quickly with her soft pencil as she spoke, "it always seems so harsh."

"I suppose, it's certainly difficult to work over if you feel you've made a mistake. But I like using the smaller pieces, there is a fluidity you feel when working with it that I like when I'm sketching Chris... people." He looked down at his hat. Caroline could see him blushing.

"Is that your friend?"

"Christopher. Yes."

"Is he an artist too?"

"Good Lord no! He is an academic. He teaches chemistry at the school of science in Exeter. Can't bear to be in the city at weekends and took a house here to escape the politics of it all."

"And you draw him?"

"Often. He is exquisite."

His smile was broad as he spoke, and the blush had faded from his cheeks. Caroline smiled. She recognised his joy for what it was and was happy for him too. Love was complicated, she decided, but where one found it, this was how it should make one feel. After a few minutes she put down her pencil and sighed.

"Let me see," Tommy stood up and put the hat on his head.

Caroline turned her sketch book around, "I have never worked like that before. I'm not sure what came over me. I just felt a need to capture you as you lay there. It was as if the pencil did the work for me!"

Tommy took the sketch book from her and turned his back to the sun so that he didn't need to squint to look at the drawing. He nodded his head slowly, a smile creeping from his mouth to his eyes.

"I think you should work with more freedom more often Caro. This is very good, though I say so as the model. But it is. It looks how I feel."

"Darling, you look so relaxed!" Helen was holding Caroline's sketch that evening after dinner while they sat in the conservatory with their drinks, "You've captured his expression amazingly well, Caroline."

"I'm not sure I could do it again if I tried. It was a spur of the moment thing."

Helen handed the sketchbook back to her, "Then we should drink to the spur of the moment, and all the success it might bring! Cheers!"

As Caroline travelled inland and northwards to her new home the following day, the weather lost its pseudo-summer feel and gradually became grey and overcast. Tommy had tied the three canvases together, surrounded in hessian sacking, so that Caroline could take them all home with her. They were wedged in the luggage rack opposite her with her carpet bag resting on top to stop them sliding around or falling off.

Again, her compartment was empty, and had been since she had changed trains at Exeter. She stretched out her legs and raised her arms above her head. She had thoroughly enjoyed her visit to Devon, and so much more for having Midge there too. Caroline did not know when she might see Midge again; she felt sure Midge would secure the position with the mission in Tanganyika provided she passed her teaching exams. What adventures would that bring her friend?

Midge was so practical, so unflappable, and not someone to whom adventures would naturally happen. I never thought they would happen to me either, she mused, yet I feel like they are. If only everyone would stop assuming that I want to stop now and settle down with a man. Especially the men themselves!

The taxi pulled into the crescent driveway in front of the apartments and the driver left the engine running. He unloaded Caroline's luggage as her father came through the entrance door and opened his arms to embrace her. He had rarely done so before, she realised. He paid the taxi fare and then picked up her case and the sacking-wrapped canvases while Caroline took her carpet bag and followed him inside.

"I thought you might decide to stay on for a while longer in Devon, I heard on the wireless that the weather has been particularly fine on the south coast this weekend."

"I had a lovely time, but I wanted to come back, to come home."

They had stopped in the hallway of the apartment. Caroline took off her gloves and hat.

"Annie has helped get your room ready," George took in Caroline's slightly sun burnt face and the confidence she now displayed. His little girl was a young woman and he hoped she would not strike out on her own too soon but give him the pleasure of watching her grow even more.

"Have you eaten?" he asked.

"Not since lunch, no."

"Go and settle into your room and I will warm the soup Annie has left for us. It is oxtail, and there is ample bread and cheese. She has quite taken charge of the kitchen and gives me instructions as to how not to burn or spoil whatever meal she prepares."

Caroline looked at her father, "Are you quite alright? You seem, I don't know, somehow different. Lighter. Younger!"

George smiled, "I am just glad to have you home Caroline, and glad to have a new home for us that is better suited to our futures."

As Caroline picked up her carpet bag again and disappeared into her new bedroom, George went into the kitchen and turned on the gas stove to warm the pan of soup. He wondered if he could explain to Caroline the sense of liberation and freedom he felt in their new apartment, without her misunderstanding that his grief at losing Elizabeth had had been insincere, a pretence. It was far from those things. He felt the loss as keenly as he had that long afternoon he had wept at her bedside, her cold hand in his. He could not describe how silent the house had felt to him, how oppressive, carrying two ghosts inside it after being so many years with just the one of his son.

He had resolved the only way he could continue with his life would be to start afresh somewhere completely new. He had not been brave enough to move away from Cheltenham, though he had considered Oxford for a while. But he knew he could not continue to live in the house he had shared with Elizabeth and remain supportive and interested in Caroline's progress. Elizabeth's presence, or lack of, would have worn him down and turned him into an aging widower with few friends and years of solitude to look forward to.

This new apartment, this new start, would be his chance to continue living. He recognised it would not be fair to Caroline to do so vicariously through her. He would need to establish his own social life, his own entertainment and his own interests, so that they might remain companionable without relying completely on each other. He had allowed Elizabeth to lean too heavily on Caroline after Freddie's death and he was determined not to do so himself. He felt optimistic. He would not dwell in the past.

Caroline sat on her old bed in her new room and looked around at her familiar furniture. Annie had arranged things with care, directing the removal men to place the bed, dressing table, wardrobe and chest of drawers in a similar position to how they had been before. While she was happy to be amongst her things again, Caroline was struck by how they also looked out of place. Her father had been right when he had explained that their old furniture would not all suit their new home. It looked dark and heavy against the white walls and the brightness afforded by the large window. Seeking comfort, Caroline looked under her bed and found as she had hoped, her keepsake box. She had saved a wrapper from one of the toffees Midge had shared with her as her memento of the weekend, along with a slipper limpet shell from the beach that had a few grains of sand still inside.

Over their meal, George explained that the auction had gone well, with almost all of the items selling although some not achieving quite the amount he had hoped. He had instructed the auctioneer that there were to be no reserves so that as many things would be sold on the day as possible. Annie's items had been transported to the storage sheds at the coal yard on the Jenks' cart. George and Caroline were eating at the new table she had picked out from a catalogue from Cavendish House, and she began to spot other items she had circled with her pencil. The clock on the wall. A slender cabinet with marquetry doors displaying a star pattern.

"This room could do with some greenery, don't you think?" Caroline had been impressed with the conservatory at Budleigh and while the dining area of the apartment was not as large, it was bright enough to support more than the aspidistra that they had had for years at Glencairn Road.

"We should speak with Josiah Curzon perhaps?"

"Yes, I will call on Florence and see if he can suggest something suitable. It will be interesting to see their new home too."

"The house was also sold at the end of the auction. We are unencumbered now, and my calculations proved over-cautious. I intend to increase our investments and you could see your return as high as forty pounds. Still no fortune I'm afraid my dear, but sustainable I feel."

"Are you sure you have made sufficient provision for yourself?"

"Indeed. I have also made an appointment for us both with Embry and Burton, with Mr Burton, so that you can make a simple will and I can amend one or two things in mine. We are expected at midday on Thursday. You will need to give some thought as to whom you would leave your assets."

"I already have. I should like to leave everything to Annie, should I die unmarried of course. It is not a pleasant topic to discuss over dinner, but I appreciate it has to be done. Thank you for arranging it."

"I think Annie is an excellent choice, but would you not leave a portion to your godchild also?"

Caroline stopped mid-chew. How could she have forgotten Angelica? George rarely mentioned the little girl or her parents, yet he had remembered her responsibilities when she had not. She was ashamed.

"Of course, I must. Do you think perhaps one quarter to Angelica, and the rest to Annie?"

"I think that would be appropriate. That little girl may need more material assistance than the good Lord can provide as she gets older."

After dinner Caroline unwrapped her canvases to show her father. They carried them around the apartment, deciding which should hang where. The seascape was chosen for the hallway, the view of Budleigh for the dining area, and George requested Tommy's painting of Caroline for his own room, which she agreed to. Caroline had left her sketch of Tommy in Budleigh, on top of the dressing table with a note thanking him for his inspiration and an enjoyable weekend.

"And now, I should very much like to try out our new bath and go to bed. Travelling takes so much out of one."

After her appointment with the solicitor on Thursday, Caroline took the tram back out to the Tivoli area of the town, to the house Josiah Curzon had agreed to purchase for his new bride. It was a detached villa, built some fifty years before and recently modernised. Caroline wondered if she should take a gift but decided that flowers would be surplus to requirements in the Curzon household and nothing else offered in Cheltenham's shops would be to Florence's taste.

Caroline was shown into the parlour by a young maid, hardly out of school and dressed in a stiff black uniform with a starched white apron. After a few minutes Florence entered the room and Caroline stood up to hug her. Florence appeared to shrink momentarily at Caroline's embrace, and her smile was not echoed in her eyes that showed dark circles underneath.

"Are you quite well?" Caroline asked as they sat on over-padded Regency-style chairs.

"I am a little tired. Jones will bring tea shortly; you'll stay and have some?"

Caroline said she would love to. She explained the reason for her visit, apart from wanting to see her friend and ex-neighbour. Florence was not her usual talkative self. It was unusual for Caroline to have to make all the running in a conversation with Florence and once Jones the maid had brought the tea tray in and left them again, Caroline could not restrain her concern any longer.

"Florence, what is wrong? You are not yourself."

Florence's lip began to tremble, and a tear escaped from one eye before she could retrieve her handkerchief.

"It is as I'd feared on my wedding day," she managed to say before a great sob shook her.

"Oh my dear! Can it truly be so bad?" Caroline stood and moved to put her arm around Florence's shoulders as she cried into her handkerchief. After a few moments, Florence composed herself and dabbed her face.

"I am not ill-used; you must not think Josiah brutish in any way. He is generous and has provided me with everything I could wish for. But the intimacy. I...it is... Oh Caroline, I should not be talking of this. Please forgive me and forget I mentioned anything."

"I will not. If it is distressing you so, then you must tell me. I might not have experienced the married condition, but I am aware of the mechanics."

Florence smiled a little at that, "I rather think mechanical is an accurate description. I do not know if Josiah's ... needs are greater or less than any other man, but I find I am less enthusiastic than he wishes me to be. I really cannot say any more, Caroline, I feel I am betraying a confidence already. Please, don't press me on it. I shall endure it, and some accommodation will be made in time, I am sure. It is my bed, after all."

Caroline did not think that having to endure was really what marriage was about, but she accepted Florence's refusal to elaborate. Instead, she looked around the room to find something to complement and distract Florence's attention.

An hour later as Caroline walked back towards the Park, she was deep in thought about Florence's appearance and emotional state. She had left her with a request for a selection of house plants to be delivered to Norwood Court at Josiah's convenience, and an invitation to take tea one afternoon the following week. Caroline wasn't sure that Florence would take up the opportunity to socialise. It seemed that married life was a mix of ecstasy and agony for many people, and Caroline was more determined than ever to avoid its call, at least for the time being.

Annie was preparing to go home when Caroline returned to the apartment. The bicycles had been delivered and although Caroline had not yet tried hers out, Annie had embraced her new mode of transport enthusiastically.

"Beef stew in the oven for your tea, turn the potatoes on to boil about half an hour before you want to eat and when they are soft, drain them, add some butter and a drop of milk and mash them. They'll go to mush anyway if you leave them too long, them in that last bag are going a bit soft now."

"Thank you, Annie," Caroline lifted the lid on the smaller saucepan to find diced carrots in cold water.

"Those will only need 20 minutes."

Caroline nodded. She sensed that Annie was also not in her usual amenable state, "Is something wrong?"

Annie paused as she pulled on her coat, deciding whether to explain or brush off Caroline's concern.

She sighed, "It's looking like there will be a coal strike Miss, the newspapers are full of it, and I don't know what we'll do if there is."

By 'we', Annie meant her fiancé Jacob and his family. Jacob's father Matthew Jenks had been gradually allowing Jacob and his younger brothers to do more of the heavy

work as arthritis wore away his joints. The family lived in
a squat little house next to the yard, and any interruption
to the delivery of coal by train would cause them almost
immediate financial distress. Jacob had been saving up for his
and Annie's wedding and their hoped-for new house beyond
St Mark's church. A strike could seriously derail their plans.

Caroline put her hand on Annie's arm, "Is there anything
we can do to help?"

"Pray that it doesn't happen. There's nothing any of
us here can do, it's all between the mine owners and the
miners." She tied her coat belt and put her hat on, "Don't
forget to stir the stew in about an hour."

She closed the front door and left Caroline standing in
the hallway.

An hour later, Caroline had read through several of her
father's newspapers from the previous week and was much
better informed of the recommendations of the Samuel
Commission and of Prime Minister Baldwin's proposal
to accept them if the other political parties agreed. She
remembered Bob's explanation of how the mine owners
were pushing the miners to work longer hours for less
pay, and now she recognised that the reduction in pay
was significant; around 13 per-cent on already low wages
earned in dangerous conditions. Caroline was beginning to
understand not only the miner's predicament, but also the
impact that a strike would have on the nation. Everyone
depended on coal.

In their new apartment, the Munheads had a gas supply
for heating, cooking and hot water, and electricity for their
lighting and other appliances. However, the groceries they
consumed and the newspapers they read were transported
by trains that would not run without coal. Fresh food would
quickly run out. Towns and cities would be worst hit as

there would be no nearby farms to supply them with milk, butter, eggs or cheese.

Caroline had read two or three mentions of a 'General strike', which seemed to mean that workers who were not miners or directly involved in their dispute might also go on strike in sympathy with them. Everything could stop. Noticing the time, Caroline roused herself and went into the kitchen to turn on the flame under the potato saucepan. Thank goodness for gas, she thought, but what use would gas be if there were nothing to cook?

The following day, Caroline woke at six thirty which seemed to be her body's natural alarm call. She did not miss the early morning starts at the engineering works, but she was beginning to miss the chatter of the girls from the sewing room, particularly Lottie. A day without plans lay before her. The light behind the curtains did not seem to be particularly sunny; the false summer that had welcomed her in Budleigh Salterton had clearly remained there.

Caroline resolved to write some letters that morning. After lunch she would attempt to ride her new bicycle to visit Mary and Angelica and post her letters on the way. Then she would return in time to catch Lottie as she emerged from the Sunningend works at the end of her shift at six. Caroline breakfasted with her father, on toast and eggs that were definitely not runny-yoked. Still, they were edible, and she was improving slowly with her culinary efforts. At least the toast was only burnt on one side that morning.

It took Caroline some time to gather her thoughts into a narrative to commit to paper for each of her intended recipients. A short note to Midge, sending hopes that her interview had gone well and that she would hear very soon if she was to advance to the next round of selection. A longer letter to Helen, thanking her again for being an excellent host. In that letter she described the apartment and how green the trees looked across the road and at the rear of Norwood Court. It was still a novelty to live so high up, and Caroline spent long moments at the window in the lounge gazing out across the Park beyond.

She was about to begin the next to James when the postman delivered a letter addressed to Caroline with a postmark of Reading. She assumed it was from Midge and tore open the envelope, thinking she might need to re-write her own letter. It was not from Midge, though the handwriting had a similar distinctive hurried appearance.

18 April 1926
Reading, Berkshire
Dear Caroline

I do hope this finds you well, and that you have enjoyed your stay in Devon with my sister and your friends. I also hope you can forgive my presumption at writing to you, but I saw no other way to let you know my good news.

I have spoken to Dr Riley on several occasions over the past few weeks, and he has invited me to visit the Hospital in May. It seems he may have a vacancy for a Junior House Doctor, and I am seriously considering the opportunity. It would advance my career and provide me with experience of a less urban nature.

It could also mean that we have the opportunity to see more of each other. Again, I hope you don't find me too forward, but I did enjoy your company so much at the Charter dinner. I feel we have much in common and would very much like to spend more time in your company. If you feel the same way, do write to me here and let me know. I should hate to make a fool of myself, and I fear I may have

already done so, but one cannot help but grasp the nettle
and put forward my case to you Caroline.

I shall be staying with Dr Riley when I visit Cheltenham.
I am sure there will be time over the two days I plan to be
there for us to meet and take tea somewhere, if you would
consider it?

I look forward to hearing from you soon
Yours affectionately
Luke

Caroline sat at her father's desk which was now in the corner of the lounge. The only word that came to her was Lottie's favourite expression: Lummy! When she and Luke had talked about Dr Riley, she never considered Luke would take the initiative and orchestrate a potential relocation simply to be nearer to her. She shook her head, perhaps she was reading too much into it, perhaps he was really only trying to advance his career and it was coincidental that there was an opportunity at the hospital in her hometown. She read the letter again and felt a growing unease that she was not reading too much into it at all.

She put the letter back into its envelope, then put the envelope underneath a book so that it wouldn't distract her. She took out a clean sheet of paper and refilled her pen from her father's ink pot. For inspiration she looked out of the lounge window towards the Park and as she did a jackdaw landed awkwardly on the window ledge outside. It shook itself to settle its feathers, then paraded along the window ledge as if inspecting the view as Caroline had been. It turned and walked back towards Caroline, and for a moment their eyes met. The bird tilted its head, shook again and then took off and away out of Caroline's sight. She looked back at the paper and found a spot of ink had dropped from the pen, black as the jackdaw's feathers. '*Dear James,*' she wrote, '*I have just had a close encounter with a bird…*'

After lunch, Caroline asked Annie if she would help her with the bicycle. They went down together and unlocked the garage door, and Annie moved her bicycle to the opposite wall so that the other could be brought outside. Annie suggested that Caroline try sitting on it first before attempting to move off, as the gravel driveway was not suitable for cycling on but would help the bicycle remain upright. Caroline had chosen to wear a mid-calf A-line woollen skirt with a white cotton blouse, cognisant that a shorter skirt might ride up and reveal too much of her legs as she moved along. Annie had had to adjust the saddle height of her bicycle, being a good four inches shorter than Caroline. She stood with her hands on her hips to the side of Caroline who sat on her bicycle with her toes touching the gravel and pronounced that no alterations would be needed in this case.

"Now, see here these levers, you squeeze them to make the brakes work. Best not to go too fast and then you won't have to stop sudden."

Caroline squeezed and felt the resistance.

"I'll hold the frame, you put your feet on the pedals. See how they will go backwards? That helps you get them in the right place to start off. Hook your foot behind one and move it, that's right."

Caroline used her right foot to bring the right pedal up to the apex of its arc. She smiled at Annie and decided this was going to be an excellent method of transport.

Caroline dismounted and they walked the bicycle out into the street. The road around the Park sloped gently on the side where Norwood Court had been built but there was no traffic and Caroline was keen to start. Annie insisted on holding one end of the handlebars and the rear of the seat, walking slowly as Caroline moved the pedals. After a few minutes she stood back, and suggested Caroline try on her own. At first Caroline tried to start with both feet on the pedals, which caused her to topple frustratingly to one side and then the other. Annie stayed quiet, knowing Caroline would not want further comment, and after two more attempts Caroline left one foot on the ground and pushed off with the other on the pedal, and moved!

She had not expected the force required to keep the momentum going to be so great and after her feet had circled on the pedals once she started to topple to the side again and had to put her feet down. The sensation of overbalancing was new, she had never experienced anything like it before, but she was determined to master the machine. So many other women had bicycles around Cheltenham, it would surely just be a matter of perseverance and practice. She turned the bicycle around, waddling with her feet and legs catching the outside of the pedals and leaving a greasy mark on one stocking. Now facing Annie, she pushed off again, this time ready to exert more energy as each pedal rose to the top. She sailed past Annie who clasped her hands in pride and beamed a smile of encouragement. Caroline continued until she reached the junction with Moorend Park Road. She squeezed the brakes a little too fiercely and had to put her feet down on the ground as she felt herself this time toppling forwards. The outside of a pedal caught her ankle and she let out a cry. She took a moment to compose herself and blink away the tears that had sprung up with the sharp pain. Then she turned the bicycle around again and headed back to Annie.

This time she squeezed the brakes more gently and came to an elegant stop.

"You've got the hang of it alright now," Annie was still beaming.

"I think I should like to keep going up and down for a while to be certain. There's no need for you to supervise though."

The next hour was spent with Caroline getting progressively hotter but more confident in her ability to ride. She did several circuits of the Park, and even managed to wave at a young governess with her charge who were taking a walk to feed the ducks. Finally, Caroline got off and wheeled the bicycle over the gravel, propped it against the garage door, and went up to the apartment to wash her face, change her stockings, and collect her letters.

When Caroline arrived at Mary and Philip's house, she leaned the bicycle against the wall and went around the back as had become her custom. Washing hung limp on the line, there was very little breeze, and it was unlikely to dry, but at least it was out of the house. Caroline knocked on the kitchen door with a 'Hello!' and entered without waiting to be answered. The house was quiet but as the pram was still in the hallway Caroline knew Mary had not gone out. She put her head round the front parlour door, but that room was empty. She climbed the stairs, glanced into the rear bedroom and spotted Angelica, bottom sticking up, her knees tucked underneath her, fast asleep in her cot. Caroline turned to the front bedroom where the door was ajar. She knocked gently and said Mary's name before she went in.

Mary was laid on the bed, curled in a foetal position and wearing a thin nightdress. A tin basin was on the floor next to the bed, thankfully empty, but Mary was sweating profusely.

"Oh dear Mary, was it something you ate?"

"I think it's the baby. I think I am losing it Miss Caroline," she looked at her friend with fear and began to cry.

Once again Caroline found herself ill-equipped to handle the situation. She tried to stay calm, "Where is Philip?"

"In Gloucester with the Bishop. He won't be home until this evening."

"In that case I shall see if Mrs Brooks is at home and ask her to sit with you while I fetch a doctor. It's a good thing I have my new bicycle! Is there anything I can do before I go?"

Mary asked for a cup of water which Caroline brought to her. On her way down to rouse Mrs Brooks who lived next door, Caroline closed the door to the rear bedroom so that the comings and goings would be less likely to disturb Angelica. Mrs Brooks was a widow with two teenage sons, the second Godmother to Angelica and well versed in female medical matters. She instructed Caroline not to go to the doctor but to fetch the district nurse instead who lived along Gloucester Road. It was closer than the hospital or the doctor's house and the nurse would be more appropriate and would know whether a doctor was really required. Caroline accepted this advice and made off on her bicycle, not understanding the economy of summoning a nurse.

The nurse was not at home, but her neighbour opened an upstairs window and informed Caroline that she was on her rounds and would be home again sometime after three. Caroline's watch said two forty-five. She decided to wait and sat on the doorstep hugging her knees. Half an hour later the nurse arrived on her own bicycle and agreed to follow Caroline back to the Rose's house.

By that time Angelica had woken and Mrs Brooks was trying to feed her small squares of bread and jam on her lap while keeping an eye on Mary. Caroline took Angelica down to the kitchen, sat her in her highchair, and gave her a cup of milk which the little girl drank greedily. To distract herself as much as Angelica, Caroline carried the little girl into the garden while she took down the damp washing, then brought her back inside while she arranged it all on the clothes horse and the line strung across one corner of the kitchen. They went into the front parlour and played with a rag doll and some coloured wooden blocks for a while before Angelica started to whimper and her dark brown eyes filled with tears. Caroline picked her up and held her on her lap and rocked her while humming a simple tune that had no words. This seemed to calm Angelica. The little girl put two fingers into her mouth and laid her head against Caroline's shoulder.

They stayed like that for some time while Mrs Brooks and the nurse could be heard moving around above them in the bedroom. One of them came down the stairs, went into the kitchen, then went back up again without looking in on Caroline and Angelica. Caroline had never considered fully the perils of maternity before. Having no younger siblings and no cousins or even friends of the family with small children when she was growing up, pregnancy was rarely discussed at home. She had gathered all of her limited knowledge from the whisperings of her school friends and an occasional advertisement or article in a newspaper. Being present at Angelica's delivery had been a heady mix of instruction and amazement but had resulted in the normally happy little girl currently in her lap. Caroline knew of course that women often did not carry their babies to full term, and that unfortunately some women died in childbirth, as did their children. She had just never expected to be witness to either.

More footsteps on the stairs. This time Caroline heard the nurse tell Mrs Brooks she would arrange for a doctor to call the next day and to fetch her immediately if Mary took a turn for the worse. The front door opened and closed.

Mrs Brooks came into the front parlour a few moments later. She looked serious and concerned.

"She's lost it, poor mite."

"Is Mary alright?"

"The nurse thinks so, although there's still a risk of infection. We've to keep an eye on her 'til a doctor comes tomorrow."

"Yes, I heard. Could I see her or is she sleeping?"

"For a minute but she might not want to speak to anyone just now. Let me take missy here and you go and see."

They exchanged the little girl and Caroline went up to the front bedroom. The curtains were half closed, and a rectangle of light crossed the floor and divided the bed. Mary lay, again in a foetal position, her eyes open and glassy. Caroline noticed that the sheets had been changed and Mary now wore a yellow nightdress.

"Mrs Brooks has Angelica."

Mary did not answer.

"Would you like me to go?"

"No."

Mary moved her legs and Caroline perched on the edge of the bed.

"I do not like that nurse."

"Mrs Brooks recommended her rather than a doctor straight away."

"She talked about me as if I was not here. Not a person. I had a son. They took him from me."

Caroline did not know how to respond. Mary's anger was clear, and Caroline recognised the manner of professional distance that Mary described.

"Had you and Philip discussed names for him?"

"If Angelica had been a boy, we would have called him David. David Mark."

"That's a good strong, name," Caroline realised as soon as she had spoken that it might be insensitive given the circumstances, "I mean, in Biblical terms."

"Philip chose David. I suggested Mark, after the parish."

They stayed together in silence for a while. Caroline furtively glanced at her watch and found it was almost half past five.

"Did you say Philip will be home around seven?"

"Yes. He said he wouldn't stay for dinner."

"Shall I ask Mrs Brooks to keep Angelica until he returns?"

Mary closed her eyes, "Yes, if it's not too much trouble for her."

Outside the Sunningend works gates at five minutes to six, Caroline stood holding her bicycle. She felt tired, and sad, and had almost decided not to wait for Lottie but as she had to pass the gates in order to get home, she kept to her original plan. She was still working through the events of the afternoon in her mind. How a baby so small could already have imprinted itself, no, his self, on a family, only to then simply not be. She had learned from Mrs Brooks that the nurse had taken the evidence away with her, wrapped in newspaper and Mary's once white nightdress. There also seemed to be a suggestion from the nurse that it had somehow been Mary's fault, which Mrs Brooks hotly contested, so she had said to Caroline.

The workers for the night shift walked past Caroline, singly, in pairs and groups, men and women chatting in the cool evening. There was some excitement in the air after news of the birth of Princess Elizabeth had been announced that morning. Caroline was so lost in thought that she didn't see a familiar figure move through the crowd towards her.

"Caroline! This is a surprise."

She looked up to see Bob smiling at her. It was not an expression he wore very often, but he was genuinely pleased to see her. He read her face and his smile disappeared immediately, replaced by concern.

"What's the matter? Is it your father?" He reached out and put his hand on her upper arm.

"Oh Bob, no, Father is quite alright, thank you. It's Mary Rose. She lost her baby this afternoon. I've been with her, looking after Angelica, and it's so very sad," she felt herself close to tears.

This time Bob didn't hesitate to put his arm around her shoulders, and she leaned into him. Coming from a generally non-tactile family, she was surprised at how much comfort she drew from the simple gesture.

"I'm sorry to hear that. Very sorry for her, for them. And for you too."

Lottie had reached the gates and was looking for her brother in the crowd as he had said he would meet her if her fiancé Eric took a double shift at the gas works. She saw Bob's back, then recognised Caroline with him, and she held back. Only when Caroline stood up straight again did Lottie call out to them.

"Caroline, how lovely to see you!"

"I thought I would walk along Gloucester Road with you and cycle home through town."

"That's a fine new bicycle," Bob said as he positioned himself closest to the road with the bicycle between him and Caroline and Lottie. "Shall I wheel it along while you girls talk?"

Caroline relinquished her hold and smiled what she hoped was a sincere smile in return. Bob was nothing if not dependable, she thought.

Lottie put her arm through Caroline's as they walked, and fired many questions about the new apartment, and about her trip to Devon. It was a relief to have a distraction and to talk of nicer things. Bob listened attentively, particularly as Caroline described swimming in the sea and then her day spent painting with Tommy on the cliffs. Caroline had explained briefly the nature of Tommy and Helen's marriage to him a couple of times, yet still he had to contain his jealousy at the thought of another man enjoying time with Caroline alone. Bob did not paint. He could sketch a mechanical drawing with rough accuracy if required but was certainly not artistic. I can't compete, he told himself as they walked along, I just have to wait and hope.

Caroline declined Bob and Lottie's pleas to go all the way to their home. In turn she invited them to call on her one evening whenever they chose. She left them at the end of their street and mounted her bicycle again a little unsteadily for her ride home.

6

THE INVITATION

The owner of Norwood Court had originally intended to sell all six of the apartments and invest the profits into another development. Though the quality of the workmanship was not in question, the climate of uncertainty that spread across the country in the spring of 1926 led the owner to change his plans. He had succeeded in selling three of the apartments including the one George and Caroline Munhead now called home. The other three were put up for rent, for a weekly fee that would discourage any undesirables who might lower the tone of the property.

Edward Ferris considered himself lucky, yet completely suited to his new position as Doorman/Porter at Norwood Court. Having worked for many years in the Crescent Bakery near St James' station in the town, an accident with a sack of dried fruit and an awkward fall had left him with a bad back. He had been at a loss as to what employment could see him through to retirement, a state that was receding into the distance as his savings depleted in the present, when he saw the role advertised in the *Chronicle*. After a brief interview and the taking up of all three references he provided, Ferris was engaged. He thanked his good fortune in having a brother-in-law who was a police constable in Tewkesbury.

The early starts fell well within Ferris' usual routine. He arrived at Norwood Court each morning at half past five, to receive the newspapers, milk and other early deliveries. He checked the gas boiler and swept the communal entrance, stairs and landings, before taking a cloth and polish to the brass fittings and the glass entrance doors. He bid a good day to George Munhead, and Mr Rickard from number three as they left for work, Rickard being an optician in the town. On Mondays, Mr Monk from number two would leave at 6am for his position as trainer of aerial reconnaissance interpreters at RAF Bicester, returning usually on Thursday evenings. Mrs Monk would spend much of her time at the hospital while her husband was at work. As a trained nurse she now volunteered to sit with patients who were deemed 'difficult' by the managers.

Ferris would knock on the door of number one each morning around nine to make sure Miss Kettle, a retired schoolteacher from London was up and about. She was seventy-five years old and had moved to the Spa town for her health and away from the congestion of the city. Captain Robert McTimony at number five needed no such supervision. A veteran of campaigns in India and Africa, where he had invested in mining operations, he rose early and took a daily constitutional walk around the perimeter of the Park before breakfast.

The last resident of Norwood Court intrigued Ferris, though he would never dare to question the history of Mrs Bassett. He knew she was recently widowed, as she had arrived dressed in black with a large hat and veil. She rarely left her apartment before noon but would take in the bottle of milk he left outside her door almost immediately. She received a lot of letters, from local, national and international addresses, and Ferris wondered if she might be some kind of spy.

All the residents appreciated having a conscientious doorman at their disposal. To find their mail neatly stacked in the pigeon-holes in the entrance hall, have their milk placed outside their doors, and know that someone would be on hand to receive deliveries or visitors during the day was most convenient. Two or three of the residents considered him a necessity rather than a luxury. It was Ferris, then, who took delivery of a large bouquet of flowers one morning towards the end of April. The envelope accompanying the flowers was addressed to Miss C. Munhead, who Ferris knew to be at home.

Ferris liked Caroline. He liked George too, and felt of all the residents, they were the most amenable. Miss Kettle was by far the politest, but Caroline always had a smile for Ferris and the way she and George behaved with Annie struck him as being particularly genuine. Only Mr Rickard and the Monks had received visitors since all parties had moved in, and Ferris was curious as to the source of admiration which had prompted the floral gift. He took the bouquet up to number five and resolved to ask Annie casually about it the next time she stopped for a chat.

Caroline was also curious, and a little nervous to open the small envelope pinned to the bouquet's outer wrapping. Sending flowers was such an extravagance, the sort of thing Helen might do, but for no reason that Caroline could think of. The card inside the envelope had a simple message.

Meet me for dinner tonight at 7, Queens Hotel. Luke.

Caroline sighed. Annie raised an eyebrow while she darned one of George's socks over a wooden mushroom but waited to be told who the flowers were from.

"I shan't be at home for dinner this evening."

Annie continued to sew, "Yes, miss."

The scent from the freesias, roses and carnations was delicate but made Caroline smile in spite of herself. She sighed again.

"Annie, if a man was keen on you, but you were not as keen on him as he would like, what would you do to dissuade him?"

Annie wove the needle through the threads she had stitched across the thinned sock heel while she considered the question. There had been a young lad a few years ago who had started hanging around her family. Her father had asked her if she was interested in him, and when she said no, sent the young man off with a flea in his ear. She suggested this as an option.

"That sounds a bit drastic. And I don't want to upset Midge either."

Annie nodded, the picture becoming clearer, "Perhaps ask her to speak to him?"

"I could. I had hoped that he was just being friendly, but this does seem rather over the top! And dinner too. I thought he said he was staying with Dr Riley. Perhaps the doctor suggested Queens as a suitable place, their restaurant is very good."

Annie said she had heard so.

"Would it be wrong of me to go and then tell him directly that I am not as interested in pursuing the relationship as he seems to be?"

"It might if you left it until you said goodnight. If you got it out of the way as soon as you sat down, you could always leave if he took it badly. Having him pay for a posh dinner and then telling him seems rather rude to me, Miss."

Caroline had long understood that Annie's use of "Miss" when addressing her tended to be more prominent when she was disapproving of something.

"I could go, tell him how I feel, and then write to Midge and ask her to have a word with Luke too, couldn't I?"

"You could, yes. Do you really not want his attentions? A doctor is a very good catch."

"Annie, I am not looking to catch anyone or anything just at this moment. Or to be caught. I just wish men could be friendly without anything more. If men were all like Tommy, life would be so much simpler!"

Or Bob, she thought to herself, he seemed to have got the message alright. He certainly didn't presume to take things further when she had had a momentary need for comfort the other day. In fact, he was quite the gentleman about it all.

Having explained to her father that she did not know whether she would be home early or late, Caroline caught the seven o'clock tram to Imperial Gardens and walked on to the Queens Hotel. She did not want to appear keen, and so was fashionably twenty minutes late. Luke had been about to order a starter for himself, thinking that Caroline had not been at home to receive his message when he saw her being escorted across the dining room by the host. He stood up as she reached the table.

"Caroline, I'm so glad you could come. You look divine. Were the flowers to your liking?"

Caroline took her seat and poured herself a glass of water. This was not going to be easy, and the lines she had prepared on her journey suddenly seemed harsh or flippant. She sipped her water and began.

"Luke, the flowers were lovely, thank you, but so extravagant. A telegram would have sufficed, or even a note sent with an errand boy."

"Nonsense! I remembered you said you liked the table decorations at the Charter dinner, and I thought I know, she'll love a really big bouquet!"

The waiter came and before Caroline could glance at the menu, Luke had ordered for them both. She frowned.

"Luke, I really think I would have preferred the patè to start."

"Oh really? Shall I call the fellow back again? I'm sorry, just used to making the decisions, the chaps at my digs are so wishy-washy when it comes to food. I say, it's good to see you again. And good to be out of Riley's house for a while too!"

"Is he not a generous host?"

"Generous to a fault, but rather parochial in his ways shall we say. After mushroom soup for two nights, I rather fancied something more substantial. And to let you know I was here of course."

"I hadn't realised you were so keen to take a job here. I thought perhaps you might follow your brother and sister to Africa or some other far-flung outpost to do your good works."

"Funny you should say that. Father suggested joining up as an army surgeon too. I rather think I want to stay in England for now, and if I may be so bold, to stay as near to you as I can."

"Luke, really, there is something..."

The waiter arrived with their food. Caroline was hungry, and let Luke talk on about Dr Riley's hospitality while she ate. When she had finished, she tried again.

"Luke, I need you to understand something."

"What's that, old girl?"

"I am not interested in forming a romantic attachment to anyone at the moment." She bit her lip, it sounded so formal.

Luke put down his knife and fork and chewed the last of his starter. When he had swallowed, he took a sip of water, before responding.

"When you say, 'at the moment', does that mean you might in the future?"

"I don't know. I can't say. I expect I might eventually, but it is not something that I am looking for right now."

The waiter removed their plates and returned with the main course menu. This time Luke asked Caroline what she would have before the waiter returned. He then continued their conversation.

"I thought all young women wanted to settle down with a husband. The nurses at the Royal Berks certainly made it clear they were interested if you so much as sneezed in their direction."

"Midge doesn't want a husband yet either," she countered.

"Oh, but that's Midge, she's hardly in the same league as you."

"All the same, I think there are many women now who want more from life than just being married and having children," Caroline kept an image of her old sewing room supervisor Mrs Chandler in her mind as she spoke.

"My dear, what could be more important? A woman's body is designed to bear children, it is absolutely what she is made to do!"

Caroline was shocked by this statement, "If a woman is a mere vessel, why did God give us minds at all?"

Luke sensed he had hit a nerve and retreated slightly. "Of course, of course, women are intelligent creatures, mostly at any rate. But their caring nature is such that they are best suited to a life of devotion to their family."

"Luke, you are a doctor, do you not also have a caring nature?"

Now it was his turn to be surprised, "To a point, as a father might care about his children. But I am a scientist, and as a surgeon I hope to become an engineer of sorts also. To reconstruct, reattach, make good things which are broken, there is no requirement to care under those circumstances, only to succeed."

"We have strayed from the original subject. I simply wish you to understand that I am not to be courted. Ours is a friendship, and that is how I wish it to remain."

"For now."

"Yes, for now. For as long as I feel the way I do."

"And what is it that you feel, may I ask?"

"I feel I am an explorer in a strange land, or at least how I imagine they must feel. Some things are familiar, yet they behave differently to how one expects. Other things are completely new and exciting, and some things are dangerous or mysterious. I need to be free to explore all I can, if I am to decide my own future."

Their main course arrived. Luke waited while the wine was poured for him, sipped and then nodded. When the waiter had left them, he continued.

"Do you not think that attitude is a little selfish? Please don't be offended, I just wonder at dangerous element you alluded to just now. How might your father feel having lost a son and a wife, if he were then to lose a daughter as well?"

"My father encourages me in my explorations."

"Does he now? Perhaps in the hope that you might find some dashing adventurer to take you off his hands?"

"I do not think that is his reasoning. My father considers things from all aspects."

"And are you planning any escapades in the near future? Not joining up with a gang of Bolsheviks I hope!"

"None at the moment. My friend has just lost her baby and I should like to be supportive of her if I can be."

"I'm sorry to hear that. And of course, all this talk of striking miners could seriously curtail everyone's movements if it comes off. Well look, if I promise not to be so pushy, would you consider me as an interested party, and we'll leave it at that for now? I have things to sort out in any case, what with the junior house man's position here and a possible general practice opportunity in Newbury. Let's leave it all for now and just enjoy our meal, shall we?"

"I would like that very much, yes."

"Excellent. How is your salmon?"

On her way home, Caroline decided she had handled the situation with Luke as well as she could. His dismissive comments around the ability of women to be more than mothers and wives had grated on her. She was not at all sure she would be the kind of wife Luke might expect, regardless of any feelings she may have developed for him. She realised that mentally she was striking through his name on a fictional list of possible suitors. Caroline chuckled to herself, drawing glances from her fellow tram passengers. How conceited she was to think she would have a list of admirers to choose from!

George was in a contemplative mood when he returned home from work on Friday 30 April. As was his custom now on Fridays, he had left the office of the Building Society at four and taken the tram along the Bath Road to Norwood triangle before walking the remainder of the journey to Norwood Court. He met a lot of different people in his capacity as manager of the branch office and liked to think he had a good sense of what his fellow countrymen were feeling on the topics of the day. On that day there had been only one topic on everyone's lips; the impending miner's strike. Opinion was divided firmly along the expected social lines. The miners were work-shy ingrates who should know their station, with the mine owners simply trying to preserve the social order. Alternatively, the miners were social heroes fighting for their fellow workers' rights as well as their own against the tyranny of corporate greed and a class system it seemed was designed to crush any insurrection or challenge. Many felt it was their duty to join the General Strike in support.

George was not a man to take sides lightly. He understood the desperation of the miners; on paper he easily understood the disparity between a miner's wage and the price charged for a hundredweight of even the lowest grade coal. He understood the pride a man would take in being able to provide for his family, and the shame felt when he could not. But George was also able to take a long-range view of things. There were new industries that would appear to threaten the country's dependence on coal, new companies developing new technologies. Indeed, over the past few years so many more electrical appliances had become common-place, and one only had to look at the growing number of car owners around the town and the mushrooming of garages to house their vehicles to know that change was its own locomotive. He was satisfied that his investment on Caroline's behalf in National Benzole was a prudent one. All the same he knew that a General Strike, if it were to happen, could seriously damage everyone's short-term comfort.

Caroline was at home when George arrived. He had passed Annie on the stairs who informed him that Caroline was supervising their dinner that evening. When he had removed his coat and changed his shoes for some comfortable slippers, Caroline poured him a cup of tea and they sat together in the lounge looking out over the Park.

"Your friend Robert Lewis came into the branch today. He wanted to deposit some savings and discuss the current terms of our mortgages."

It took Caroline a moment to realise he was referring to Bob, "Really? He means to find a house in Prestbury, he told me so a while ago."

"Yes, I understand that is his plan. I'm afraid I tried to dissuade him, which I would not normally do. I fear that he may be over-committing himself at this present time."

"What do you mean?"

"We do not know which way this dispute with the miners may go. It is not an auspicious time to be committing to a mortgage. I told him if he possibly could, he should wait."

"And his response?" Caroline was curious, knowing how much it was Bob's dream.

"He thanked me for my advice and said he could wait until a more favourable time. I believe he will continue to save small amounts regularly and as such be in a stronger position when he comes to ask again."

Caroline nodded. Dependable Bob she thought.

"He also asked me if I might pass on a message to you. He would like you to join him at the cinema tomorrow as I understand Cheltenham Town football club are playing away at Yeovil. He requests your company at two o'clock outside the Daffodil theatre."

"Did you give him my answer?" Caroline smiled at her father.

"I would presume no such thing! Though I may have mentioned that you would probably enjoy Buster Keeton's *Go West* as I remembered seeing an advertisement for it. He seems a good man."

"Who, Buster Keeton?"

"No, my dear, Robert."

"He is dependable. I shall meet him at the Daffodil. Oh, and Mr Rickard has invited us to drinks tomorrow evening at seven. Should we go?"

"Rickard at number three? Yes, I should think so. Do you think he has invited all of the residents?"

"It will be interesting if he has. I've yet to see the woman in number six across the landing, though I hear her gramophone sometimes."

The film was one of Keeton's best and had already been a smash hit in America. Caroline and Bob laughed at Keeton's antics along with the others in the auditorium and the time flew by. It was an antidote to the seriousness of the situation in the country; a strike had been called to begin that morning by the miners. Caroline suggested that Bob accompany her back to Norwood Court as it was just after four when they emerged from the Daffodil, and after a slight hesitation, he agreed. The weather was again grey but dry and they walked rather than taking the tram. Annie had taken to baking on a Friday and Caroline knew there were scones and a Victoria sponge cake at home she could offer along with tea. She and her father still preferred tea to coffee and had not yet purchased a coffee pot.

They found George reading a novel in the lounge. Caroline left Bob and her father to discuss the looming strike while she brewed the tea and cut slices of sponge cake. She arranged tea plates, cups and saucers and napkins on a tray and took them through to the lounge.

"I don't think so, sir," Bob was leaning forward in his chair. It was clear the discussion was serious though not unfriendly.

"Bob says the gas supply will be safe as long as the strike is short."

"I thought it was only the miners striking," Caroline put down the tray and stirred the tea in the pot.

"At the moment, but wider support is growing quickly. The King is going to give an address this evening on the wireless set. The newspapers seem to suggest he is sympathetic to the strikers."

Bob shook his head, "How could he understand their plight? I believe the King simply wants the strike to last as short a time as possible. He will say whatever is necessary to bring that about. It will only be a few days before our coal runs out."

Caroline remembered what Luke had said over their dinner. "Without coal, the trains won't run, will they?"

Now her father shook his head, "No, it will be a matter of hours before the railways use up their existing supplies. Then it will start to affect the rest of the country. No food transported; some will spoil. No newspapers outside of the larger cities I should think. Of course, the gas and electricity are generated by burning huge amounts of coal, or in some cases oil. Some areas will lose their electricity supply after a few days, of that I am certain, and no doubt we will be advised to use it sparingly."

"Do we still have the oil lamps?"

"Yes, there are still four or five crates in the garage to be unpacked, and I believe they will be in there. We may not have any oil though."

"I shall find them in the morning. Oh, but I won't be able to buy any oil tomorrow, that will need to be my first task on Monday."

Bob sipped his tea, "It's a Bank Holiday on Monday."

"And everyone will be trying to obtain supplies of oil and candles on Tuesday," George took the slice of cake Caroline offered him.

Bob was now faced with the common dilemma of having to hold a cup and saucer, plus a small plate, and eat the cake and drink the tea, all at the same time. Caroline realised this and brought a small side table across from under the window.

Relieved, Bob put his cup and saucer down, "I expect we have some lamp oil I could bring you."

"That would be very kind of you Robert, thank you. But only do so if it won't leave your family without."

"We have plenty of candles. I bought a box only the other day just in case, and we only have the one lamp that uses oil."

Caroline had changed into her navy-blue dress with the peacock feather beaded belt and applied just a little of the make-up that Helen had given her. Then she and her father went down one flight of stairs and were admitted to apartment number three. George and Mr Rickard knew of each other, as the optician practiced his trade a few doors away from the Building Society office in the town. Caroline accepted a tiny glass of sherry from her host and hoped there might be port available afterwards. They were the first to arrive.

They stood in the lounge of Rickard's apartment and couldn't help but compare his style of furnishings to their own. Where George and Caroline had been adventurous and splashed out on a few pieces of modern furniture with sleek curves and stylised flower motifs, Vaughan Rickard had retained much of the furniture he had acquired for his previous smaller apartment in Fairview. It was dark, mostly walnut, and deeply polished. There was a small, rather worn sofa with two upholstered chairs positioned around a coffee table, a leather fireside chair by the window, a large dresser with glass doors and two large bookcases filled with books of all sizes and coloured spines. It was a well-used library and not a collection for show.

The next resident to arrive was Miss Kettle from number one. She had purposely wanted an apartment on the ground floor, she informed Caroline, as she was beginning to find stairs difficult. At seventy-five, Miss Kettle's eyes and ears were still alert, and Caroline felt she was back at school under the gaze of her old schoolmistresses. As it turned out, Miss Kettle had been a teacher at a girl's school in London. It seemed a natural topic to discuss, and Caroline was explaining how she had been a weekly boarder at Mrs Pendersen's school for girls at Pittville when a loud voice preceded its owner into the room. Captain McTimony had arrived.

Caroline and Miss Kettle moved to the sofa, but the room was too small to ignore McTimony, so the ladies gave up their conversation and listened to him instead. The Captain clapped Rickard on the shoulder heartily and shook George's hand as if it was a water pump. He declined a sherry, asking instead for scotch and soda which Rickard obliged him with before making his way to the door again. George was left with McTimony and smiled and nodded as the Captain gave his opinion on the construction of the apartments (favourable) and the miner's strike (less favourable towards the miners, and outraged at the prospect of Bolsheviks on every street corner). Rickard returned with Mr and Mrs Monk, who also both declined sherry in favour of scotch (his with soda, hers without). Mrs Monk looked towards Caroline and Miss Kettle with clear relief and immediately crossed the room to introduce herself.

Rebecca Monk wore a crepe drop-waisted dress in a deep plum colour. It suited her bobbed and curled dark hair and the plum-coloured lipstick she had applied. As both she and Miss Kettle were new to Cheltenham, Caroline found herself able to maintain the conversation by suggesting the best ladies' outfitters, cafés and grocers around the town. Rebecca Monk kept glancing towards her husband every few moments, as if to make sure he was still in the room. Captain McTimony had toned down his voice enough to enable the ladies to talk without shouting over him.

"Are we all here then Rickard?" he asked, draining his glass.

"I had invited Mrs Bassett; opposite you I believe George? Of course, she might not be at home."

"Have you met her?" McTimony asked George as Rickard refilled his glass.

"No, not yet. Neither has my daughter, Caroline."

Caroline looked up at the sound of her name. She excused herself from the sofa and went to stand next to her father. He introduced her to McTimony, and Michael Monk and she shook both their offered hands. McTimony's grip was strong and rather hot; Monk's was weaker, almost as if he had not wanted to touch her hand at all but was only doing so for convention's sake.

"We were wondering if any of us had met Mrs Bassett," McTimony barked.

"I have only heard her door on occasion, and her gramophone in the afternoons. I have no idea what she looks like, I'm afraid."

Rickard looked at his watch.

"Well, as its seven-thirty perhaps she won't be joining us after all. Such a shame, I had hoped to bring us all together as we are sharing the building and the gardens. I'm sure we will have another opportunity to meet the mysterious Mrs Bassett. Now, I have some canapés if you'll excuse me for a moment."

"I'll help you bring them through," Caroline offered and followed Rickard into the kitchen. She really only wanted to see how that room had been decorated, and to glance through to the dining area if she could.

The kitchen was typically male, with the same stove and cupboards as in Caroline and George's apartment but with far fewer pots, pans and pieces of crockery (which were all utilitarian and plain white). On the dining table, another heavy piece of mahogany with matching chairs, were oval plates with small morsels of food. They took a plate each and returned to the party. Caroline offered hers to the men first, and then took the plate to the ladies. She set it down on the coffee table and stood hovering with her now empty glass hoping Rickard would notice.

"Can I get you another drink?" He was a good host, and Caroline realised he was probably younger than she had first thought, perhaps in his early thirties. His spectacles required repeated pushing up his nose, which Caroline thought odd for someone in his profession.

"Do you have any port?"

"I do, one moment," he took her sherry glass and replaced it with a small tumbler with the rich dark liquid inside, "it's a ruby, I hope that's acceptable."

"Perfectly, thank you. Did you make the canapés yourself?"

"Gracious, no! Ferris recommended the tea shop on the Bath Road, and they delivered this afternoon. Most reasonable, most accommodating. Is it your maid I have seen here?"

"That must have been Annie, yes. She has been with us for years, though she is teaching me to cook as she won't be with us forever."

"Oh?"

Rickard was about to say something more when there was a knock on the door. He excused himself, and Caroline returned to the sofa with her port. As she sat down, the conversation faltered as Mrs Bassett entered the lounge.

Her bright red dress matched her lips and fingernails, though the latter were covered by long black silk gloves. She carried a black beaded evening bag on a silver chain, and on her head was a small black hat with a short black net veil pulled forward to cover her eyes and ended just above the tip of her nose. She assessed the ladies on the sofa expertly, smiled a tight smile of acknowledgement, and remained with the men near to the drinks tray.

As Miss Kettle and Rebecca chatted quietly about volunteering opportunities in the town, Caroline watched the behaviour of the men around the newcomer. If Captain McTimony's eyes could be any further from his head, she thought they might actually be sitting on Mrs Bassett's chest. His face had turned a florid red and he appeared to have lost his voice. This gave Rickard an opening which he took advantage of, offering alcohol (a sherry accepted) and canapés (declined with a small wave of the gloved hand), and making introductions. Caroline noticed the slight grimace on Mrs Bassett's face with her first sip of sherry, but she did not think any of the men had seen it. Her own father had taken a step backwards when Mrs Bassett had joined the group, as if to make his own appraisal. It occurred to Caroline that her father was a handsome man, and she wondered if he might ever consider taking another wife.

"...I hear she is a widow," Miss Kettle's voice interrupted Caroline's thoughts.

Rebecca glanced again at her husband, her face showing what Caroline thought with surprise was a look of fear.

"But she is very young," Rebecca whispered.

"Her husband was a little older, so I understand."

Caroline was intrigued, "Miss Kettle, did you know of Mrs Bassett before you came here?"

"Call me Agatha, my dear. I thought I recognised her name when Ferris mentioned her a few days ago. Her late husband was a face about town as they say, his death quite unexpected. A motor car accident. And to think she chose to move herself to Cheltenham. Interesting, don't you think?"

Caroline stood up again and moved towards the men. Michael Monk smiled at her, then turned and went to sit in the seat she had vacated near to his wife. Rebecca greeted him with a warm smile, but her eyes remained concerned.

"Mrs Bassett," George spoke up, "may I introduce my daughter, Caroline."

Mrs Bassett shook Caroline's hand: Caroline was surprised at the firmness of it, in comparison to Monk's and Rickard's handshakes earlier. The two women held each other's gaze for a moment until the older woman turned to George.

"Your only child?"

"My only living child, yes. My son, Frederick was killed in the War."

"Oh, I'm so sorry. I lost a brother. We must all hope it never happens again."

"I'm most certain it will, mark my words!" barked McTimony.

"Another canapé, Captain?" Rickard had realised that the Captain did not speak when he was eating and had mentally devoted an entire plate of hors d'oeuvres to that goal. He did not think he would be making a regular invitation to McTimony to enjoy his hospitality.

Michael and Rebecca Monk had risen and stood at Rickard's elbow.

"It's been super to meet you all, but I'm afraid Rebecca here has a headache, so we'll be taking our leave now. Excellent evening, Rickard," they shook hands, "do excuse our brevity."

The party said their goodbyes.

Rickard took his plate of food to Miss Kettle, leaving Caroline, George, McTimony and Mrs Bassett with their drinks.

"Do any of you play bridge?" McTimony helped himself to another scotch as he asked.

"I do a little. I'm rather a novice," replied Caroline.

George raised an eyebrow, "You do?"

"Well, yes, I learned when I was in Devon last year. I'm not sure if I remember the rules that well now, I haven't had a chance to play recently."

"Mrs Bassett?"

"I have played in the past, yes."

"George? Or is that too much risk for a banker?" he chuckled at his own joke.

George shook his head, "I'm afraid I never learned. Chess is my game these days, though I used to play cricket when I was very much younger."

It was Caroline's turn to raise an eyebrow.

"We'll need another for a four. Rickard, are you a bridge man?"

Rickard looked up from his conversation, "I play incredibly badly. Did I hear you say you play chess George?"

"You did indeed."

"Then we must have a game some time."

"I enjoy a hand of bridge, Captain," Miss Kettle had a distinct twinkle in her eye.

"Oh well, now, I don't know if I should be playing against three such young ladies!"

Miss Kettle smiled, "You have nothing to fear from me Captain, and perhaps the two girls would appreciate an older chaperone?"

"I suppose there won't be much else to do if this strike lasts more than a few days. Shall we have a game on Monday evening?" Caroline asked.

"Monday would suit me perfectly, let's say seven-thirty?"

Miss Kettle nodded, "I doubt we shall have to play by candlelight my dear, but seven-thirty is quite acceptable. Mrs Bassett, will you join us?"

Mrs Bassett hesitated enough for the ladies to notice but not long enough for McTimony or George. "Yes, I think I can play this Monday, although I might not be able to make it a regular thing."

"Excellent!" boomed McTimony.

"Indeed. And now I too shall take my leave Mr Rickard. It has been delightful to meet you all. I feel so much safer now that I know all of your faces," Agatha took Caroline's hand, "Would you see me down the stairs my dear? The sherry has gone straight to my head."

Caroline agreed.

As soon as they had pulled Rickard's door up behind them, dropping the latch to stop it locking Caroline out, and turned to descend the stairs, Miss Kettle straightened a little and reached for the banister.

"A little rouse, my dear, I'm afraid. I may be seventy-five, but I have no trouble digesting a little cheap sherry and dry biscuit."

Caroline smiled; she had suspected as much, "Did you want to say something to me privately Miss Kettle, I mean, Agatha?"

"I should like to let you in to a little secret. I am a rather competent bridge player, having won a few local tournaments when I lived in Bermondsey. I feel I should like you and I to make a pair on Monday, if you agree. I rather think the Captain needs an opportunity to either flatter or falter as far as Mrs Bassett is concerned."

"I am happy to be your pair if that's what you would like. Will you be alright going in?" They had reached Agatha Kettle's door and she pulled her key from a pocket in her cardigan.

"I shall be quite alright, thank you. It has been a most enlightening evening. Most enlightening. When the weather improves, I shall take tea in the garden in the afternoons at four. If you are free, I should be delighted if you would join me."

"I'll look out for you if I am at home, thank you. Good night, Miss… Agatha."

Caroline returned to the party, where all had moved to the sofa and chairs.

"Put the old girl to bed?" McTimony stood up to give Caroline his seat.

"Thank you, Captain. Miss Kettle is safely returned to her apartment, yes."

"We have been discussing this strike business," Rickard had put the plate of hors d'oeuvres on the coffee table and McTimony had left just three. Caroline helped herself to one.

"And what is your opinion, Mr Rickard?"

"One understands the cause, naturally, but it's going to be rather inconvenient for the rest of us. We are insulated somewhat here, so to speak, but I don't see how the country can manage for more than one or two days without a supply of coal."

George nodded his head, "We do have a first-class supply of gas in Cheltenham."

"If it spreads, they will have to bring in the army," McTimony drained his third scotch and put the glass a little heavily onto the table, "and quickly, before the agitators get out of hand. The socialists will run amuck, mark my words. Demanding workers' rights left, right and centre."

Caroline frowned, "Do you not feel that workers should have rights, Captain?"

McTimony drew in a breath as if to launch forth a long tirade. Rickard stepped in quickly.

"I think we all can agree that workers do, indeed must, have some rights, Miss Munhead. But the fact remains that workers should not be able to hold a country to ransom over their demands."

"Tell me, Mr Munhead, do you believe it will escalate to a national strike?" Mrs Bassett spoke quietly, as if it were only her and George in the room. Caroline noticed the Captain's face grow a deeper shade of red.

"I do think it might, unfortunately. Young men feel passionately that they must be allowed to support their families and their fellow workers. And many of them fought for us all to enjoy peace, let us not forget."

"Miners were exempt, Munhead." McTimony rumbled.

"When I was in Birmingham last year, there was a woman there speaking in the street about worker's rights and against capitalism. Helen knew her, what was her name now…. Maud, I think it was. She was certainly passionate in her cause."

"Maud Cassidy?" Mrs Bassett met Caroline's eyes again.

"It could have been, yes. A small woman with wild dark hair."

"She is making a name for herself in London as a firebrand. Something to do with Indian independence, Italian socialism, and I'm not sure what else. Tied up with the Irish too I believe. Quite neurotic."

"Troublemakers need taking down a peg or two," declared McTimony. "This strike could be just the thing to put some people back in their place."

George and Caroline returned from Christ Church the following morning to find Annie in tears over the roast dinner. The talks between Mr Baldwin's government and the Trades Union Congress had broken down and a national strike had been called to begin at one minute to midnight the following day. Despite Jacob's reassurances that everything would work itself out, Annie was convinced that the strike would ruin their plans for the future.

After lunch, Caroline cycled alongside Annie to Rowanfield where the older girl turned towards her home and Caroline went onwards to Philip and Mary's house. Caroline had not seen Mary since the miscarriage. Philip welcomed her into the little end-of-terrace house and explained that Mary had gone back to bed as soon as he had returned after giving the service that morning. Angelica was also sleeping, and the house was quiet.

"And how are you, Philip?"

"It's so very hard to say, Caroline. One moment I feel strong and in control and then the next, I could weep. I do not, of course. Mary needs me to be strong. But I grieve as much as anyone does at such a loss."

"It must be terribly difficult for you both."

"I came back from the Bishop's palace in such good cheer too. You see, he had agreed to what you had proposed to Mary some weeks ago, that we might swap residences with Reverend Lloyd so that we could have more space. The Reverend also agreed, he was very keen to have a much smaller garden to look after, he said. I'm really not sure if the offer is still good, now that... well..."

"Surely the Reverend's house is much more suited to you as a family. Do you really think the Bishop would rescind the offer in the circumstances?"

"I admit, I have been too afraid to ask. But now, talking it over with you, I feel I must bite the bullet as they say and write to him. God provides the opportunity; we must grasp it."

"That's the spirit! I won't trouble Mary if she is resting. Perhaps she would like Celestine to stay for a while to help with Angelica?"

"I wrote on Friday to ask the very same thing of my illustrious mother-in-law. Mrs Brooks has been an absolute Godsend, but we cannot keep imposing on her to have Angelica while I work. With any luck Celestine will be here on Tuesday or Wednesday."

"Let's hope the trains are still running to get her here."

The Monday evening bridge party was every bit the anticipated event. Caroline and Miss Kettle arrived at the Captain's door at the same time, to find Mrs Bassett already installed in his lounge with a glass of sherry slightly superior to the offering from Rickard. McTimony's apartment was a veritable flea market of items accumulated through his years in Africa and India. Maps and trunks, carved totems and taxidermy liberally decorated the lounge room. Caroline wondered if his bedroom had the bed of a Maharajah and then hastily pushed the thought of McTimony in any bedroom aside.

A table had been cleared and four chairs assembled one on each side for the card game to begin. Note paper and pencils were laid on the table, and everyone took their seats, bringing their drinks to the table with them. Each player drew a cross in the centre of their note paper and

marked the left and right sides with the characters E/W
and N/S to keep score. McTimony dealt the first round
of 13 cards each. Miss Kettle, once the cards were in her
hand, straightened her posture as Caroline had seen her
do when they left Rickard's the previous Saturday. Miss
Kettle meant business and Caroline could only hope she
would be able to keep up.

They started the bidding very cautiously with clubs
being trump and Miss Kettle at East winning the contract
at four clubs. Caroline looked at the three clubs in her hand,
knowing as a team they would need to win ten tricks, and
glanced at Miss Kettle who was smiling sweetly. Caroline
laid her hand on the table as the dummy hand and the game
began. She relied heavily on Miss Kettle to keep score and
focused on her own cards and her bidding when it became
her turn later on. By nine o'clock they had finished their
second match, with Caroline and Miss Kettle leading two
matches to none.

They all agreed to take a short break and then play one
more match.

Miss Kettle whispered to Caroline while McTimony was
pouring more drinks, "Let them win."

Caroline nodded and asked to deal the next hand. This
allowed Mrs Bassett to open the bidding and with Miss Kettle
passing, the Captain went for a grand slam. At ten minutes
to ten, Captain McTimony and Mrs Bassett had regained
some pride by winning the third match.

"A thoroughly entertaining evening Captain, thank you
so much for inviting us."

"It was a pleasure, Miss Kettle. Perhaps next time we
can make it a little more interesting, if you understand my
meaning?" he tapped the side of his nose with his finger
and winked.

"I believe I do, and I shall be delighted to wager a very small amount. Depending on the appetite of the other players of course."

Caroline and Mrs Bassett said their goodbyes and climbed the flight of stairs to the top floor of the apartment block together.

"Did you enjoy yourself this evening, Mrs Bassett?" Caroline asked as they reached their landing. There had not been much chatter between the ladies during the games with everyone focused on their cards. The older woman looked tired and took the last step as if it were a great climb. She paused and Caroline thought for a moment that she might fall backwards down the stairs.

"One should not like to make a habit of sitting in Captain McTimony's lounge with all of those animal eyes on one. The game itself was intriguing. I think Miss Kettle has been somewhat secretive of her bridge-playing experience, wouldn't you say?"

Caroline blushed, "She told me she had won a few tournaments when she lived in London."

Mrs Bassett stiffened. "She is newly from London?"

"I believe so."

"England is such a terribly small country. One really thought one would be able to escape the gossips here in Cheltenham."

"Oh, I don't think Miss Kettle is a gossip."

"Miss Munhead, all elderly women gossip. It is their chief pastime. One can only hope one does not reach an age at which it becomes expected."

Bob brought the promised lamp oil after work on Tuesday evening. He had to walk from the gas works as the trams had stopped running in the town. He stayed for a little while to listen with Caroline and George to the evening news broadcast on the radio. The BBC had increased their broadcasts to nine each day as the national and local newspapers reduced the frequency of production. He explained that the managers at the gas works had been requesting volunteers that afternoon to join the Organisation for the Maintenance of Supplies as special constables. Lottie's fiancé Eric had signed up, but Bob had declined. He foresaw conflict between the strikers and those doing the bidding of the government and wanted no part of it. George agreed and said he had released two of his office clerks that afternoon for the same purpose. He had brought home a copy each of the *British Gazette* and the *British Worker* newspapers, so that he could thoroughly read both sides of the debate that evening.

On Wednesday Annie announced that the Jenks' coal yard was down to less than three hundredweight of their roughest coal. There had been no delivery that day. Despite the trains now being operated by volunteers and strike breakers, there was little coal available due to the lockouts at the mines to keep the engines powered. They needed coal to deliver coal. Caroline noticed Annie had dark rings under her eyes as if she had not been sleeping well.

The atmosphere around the town was prickly. Small groups of people would gather in the street to discuss the latest news, from one side or the other. Scuffles had broken out at the coal yards, and grocery shops were starting to run out of provisions. The talk of strike-breakers grew, yet few were prepared to believe it. On Saturday the late afternoon news broadcast told of how lorries had broken through the picket lines at the London Docks and gone to Hyde Park where food was distributed to waiting crowds. The Army had been brought in to support the movement of the lorries, though they had not been armed. Churchill had been all for a display of arms, but Prime Minister Baldwin stood firm and refused.

Sunday morning, George and Caroline walked to Christ Church knowing that in Plymouth the day before, stones and other missiles had been thrown at trams in the city which had restarted, driven by volunteers. Feelings were running high there, as a football match between strikers and local police constables had resulted in a 2-0 win for the strikers. The thousands who had attended as spectators left a trail of destruction through Plymouth after the match.

George and Vaughan Rickard had played chess in George's lounge the evening before, as a distraction from the strike. Caroline had sat with them for a while, reading a novel by P. G. Wodehouse that Vaughan had brought to lend her. At a quarter to nine she had excused herself and went to her room. She opened her window and leaned on the sill. It was cool, and she could hear a light rain falling in the darkness outside, dripping through the leaves and settling on the flag stones that had been laid as a patio underneath her window. She realised there were no trains or trams, no voices. She wondered if the pubs were full in the town, or if, like Bob, most people had withdrawn to their homes. It would of course be difficult to dry wet clothes with no heat.

Monday the tenth of May was again damp and grey. It was unlike any May Caroline could remember, everything felt drab and depressed. She decided to take the bicycle to visit Mary. As Caroline rested the bicycle against the front of the house and walked around to the back yard, she could hear a voice singing. Celestine had arrived on one of the last trains from Bristol and in her usual manner had taken over from Mrs Brooks and the running of the home. She greeted Caroline with a shriek of happiness and a bone crushing hug.

Angelica, sat in her highchair, laughed heartily and raised her arms for Caroline to lift her out.

Mary came into the kitchen to see what the noise was about. Celestine shooed her and Caroline back into the front parlour with the promise of tea, and while Angelica was not impressed to be put back in her highchair, she was pacified with a wooden spoon to chew on. The front parlour was chilly and dark, no fire in the grate and there was little light filtering through the lace curtain at the window.

"My mother is in her element."

"It's lovely to see her again. She must be such a help to you."

Mary paused, "Yes. She is going to stay until we have moved. Philip used the telephone at the railway station and spoke to the Bishop. Reverend Lloyd wants to move here, and we are going to exchange homes as soon as this strike ends."

"That's wonderful news! It will be so much better for you to be in a bigger home, and Angelica will be able to play in the garden at the vicarage."

Mary looked out of the window and was quiet for a moment. Caroline wondered if she had said the wrong thing.

"Mary?"

"I always imagined I would have a big family, lots of children. The vicarage is a big house."

"In time, there will be more children, won't there?"

"Only God knows that." Mary kept her gaze towards the window as Celestine brought in the tea things on a tray.

"My girls, it is not right that I have nothing to cook! You have no fish here to salt, no pumpkin. I make brown stew for lunch Mary. There is nothing here, nothing!" she left the room shaking her head.

Mary stirred the tea pot, "She means we don't have the same food in Cheltenham as we eat in Bristol. Have you ever eaten mango?"

Caroline said she didn't think so. Mary explained how along with bananas, mango was prized whenever it arrived in Bristol. The Caribbean natives in the city would converge on the crates and scoop up any stray fruit no matter what condition it was in.

"And I cannot get the hot peppers here. I do not think Philip would like them if I could, but I miss the food of my home."

"When this strike has ended, why don't we take Angelica to Bristol, and you can show me these mangoes?"

"You would try hot peppers?"

"If you cook it for me, I will try it."

For the first time in many days, Mary smiled.

The strike ended on the twelfth of May. The Trades Union Council ordered its members to return to work and the miners were left to their own devices. It took a few days for the country to re-arrange itself to the level of convenience it had enjoyed before the strike. Trains were in the wrong places, food was rotting in warehouses, and the feelings of the country still ran high with anger against the miners of Nottingham who returned to work against the wishes of the Miner's Federation of Great Britain. However, within a few days, with great British predictability, most people's focus had returned to their own lives and the more general daily struggles of the classes.

7

THE GOSSIP

After her tears over Sunday lunch, Annie had become more and more withdrawn. The situation at the Jenks' coal yard was in the balance. They had run out of all coal, and as the price increased with the scarcity, the family had agreed to pool their funds. The savings Jacob had that were to go towards the wedding and the new house were spent on obtaining a delivery of coal as soon as it was available. Matthew Jenks negotiated hard but still needed the extra funds from Jacob and the small amount that Jacob's younger brother Colin had been able to donate. The family agreed that Colin and the youngest brother Peter would look for other employment so that the family would not be in such a vulnerable position again. It was a sad day for Matthew who had always wanted to build a business that all of his sons could benefit from.

At twenty-five, Annie was no older than many of the brides in England at the time, but she felt as if she was being held back. She and Jacob had known each other for several years and had been officially engaged for over a year. The only reason they were not yet married was, as far as Annie could see, money. She refused to move in with Jacob's parents at the coal yard; she wanted one of the new houses the borough council were building to the west of the town. Annie and Jacob would not be allocated one if they were not married.

Lottie and Eric were in a similar situation, except that Eric had been taken on as a volunteer during the strike and was now considering a new career as a police constable. His wages at the gas works were adequate to support himself and Lottie, but the opportunity for progression was minimal. Unlike Bob, he did not have an older relative at the works to assist with his promotion. Lottie had discussed things with her parents and Bob, and all had agreed that Eric could move in with the Lewis family when the couple were married. Now that the youngest Lewis offspring Charles was in Filton, Bob was willing to swap bedrooms with Lottie so that she and Eric could have a larger bed in the second bedroom. Charles would sleep at Betty Chandler's when he visited his family. Betty had offered her spare bedroom to Lottie and Eric, but as both worked in the west end of Cheltenham and Betty lived in the east, the young couple decided to stay closer to their employment.

Caroline's days were leisurely. She was becoming a passable cook, thanks to Annie's tutoring. She had discussed with her father the possibility of engaging a cleaner, but they had concluded that Caroline could manage to operate the carpet sweeper, and a cloth and polish. Most mornings she cycled to the parade of shops along the Bath Road and bought a few provisions for the evening meal.

Caroline had arranged with Mary to spend two nights with Celestine in Bristol at the end of May. Philip had been concerned at first that they would be taking Angelica with them and had insisted on them having tickets for a first-class carriage. The house swap with Reverend Lloyd had been accomplished with the help of several parishioners who found themselves out of work after striking. Philip was as generous as he could be to compensate them. Mrs Brooks had offered to cook for the Reverend every evening and to clean and manage his laundry. She said it would give her a new purpose now that her sons were getting older and less dependent on her.

The vicarage was not as bare as it might have been. Reverend Lloyd left several pieces of furniture that he could not have squeezed into the Rose's house. After a thorough clean, Mary made a list of the soft furnishings that she felt the house could do with. She decided that sewing and making their new home comfortable would help her dwell less on losing her baby. The trip to Bristol would be an opportunity to purchase some haberdashery.

Celestine welcomed them with her usual embrace, the kitchen filled with the smells of a spiced chicken and bean stew simmering on the range. She had borrowed a highchair and cot for Angelica from neighbours, and the women spent the first hour of their visit moving items out of Angelica's reach throughout the kitchen and parlour. It had been a difficult logistical feat to get Angelica's pram and other items on and off the train. The porters were helpful to a point, but still expected Mary to be able to carry much more than she could. Caroline didn't understand their attitude and chastised one unlucky young man at Temple Meads who watched as Mary struggled to get the pram from the bicycle carriage to the platform. It was a significant drop, and the pram was heavy and awkward. Having the pram also meant the women did not take a tram into the city centre and then up to Celestine's house. Instead, they walked, with some of their luggage stuffed into the parcel shelf under the pram body and tucked around Angelica's feet.

Having a full day in Bristol, and Celestine to babysit Angelica, the women decided to visit the zoological gardens in the morning. They marvelled at Rajah the elephant who was led around the enclosures on a chain by his keeper. The lions and other large animals were mostly asleep or pacing in their cages, but Mary particularly loved the exotic birds with their long tail feathers and colourful beaks. Caroline bought several postcards showing Rajah and wrote them over their lunch in a café near to the new University buildings.

The afternoon was spent shopping. Their haberdashery needs were met by a Belgian woman who owned a fabric and notions shop near St Nicholas market. All would be dispatched the following day so they would not be encumbered with heavy packages of linen. Caroline bought Angelica a new doll, and then the two women continued to the grocer that Mary had explained to Caroline would sell the exotic fruits and vegetables she craved. They spent some time sniffing boxes of spices inside the shop, and Caroline sampled small pieces of dried fruit and hot sauces. The grocer, Mr James Lord, a tall slim black man originally from Antigua, showed them his wares with pride. Mary slipped further and further into her Caribbean patois until Caroline found she understood very little of what was being said by either of them. She was amazed to find an hour had passed when they emerged from the shop with bags of dried mango and banana, coconut and peppers. Mr Lord had explained he would happily send supplies to Cheltenham on receipt of payment covering the postage, and Caroline was excited to share her new-found delicacies with her father and Annie.

Tired but happy, they returned to Celestine's house to find Tawny Antoine in the kitchen with her. A rum bottle stood open on the kitchen table with two mugs.

"Where is Angelica?" Mary demanded of her mother.

"She sleeping in her bed. Don't you go waking her now, she only been there some minutes."

"I shall check all the same. These are for you," she pushed a bag of groceries across the table to her mother and then went upstairs leaving Caroline feeling rather awkward under the gaze of Tawny.

"I remember you," he sprawled in his chair, his suit jacket draped over its back and his shirt darned and stained.

Celestine, despite appearances, had only had a sip of rum. She leaned across the table towards Tawny and jabbed her chubby finger at him as she spoke.

"We will have none of your wickedness in this house Tawny Antoine! Miss Caroline is a respectable young woman."

"Calm yourself, Celestine," he said slowly, his words dripping from his tongue. "I am resting me charms right now. But Miss Caroline, if you would ever care to share a bottle of rum with me, you come find me, you hear?" he chuckled to himself, seeing Caroline's discomfort.

Celestine moved the rum bottle to the sideboard, "You drink up now man and be on your way."

Tawny drained his mug, wiped his hand across his mouth and rested both hands on his knees.

Looking at Celestine he said, "Friday. I'll have your delivery."

He stood, put on his jacket and his hat that had been on the floor where Angelica had been playing with it before her nap.

He offered Caroline his hand, "Pleased to meet you again Miss Caroline. You take care now."

He winked at her, nodded in Celestine's direction and left.

At the sound of the front door closing, Mary returned to the kitchen. She had sniffed as close to Angelica's head as she could without waking the little girl and was satisfied that no alcohol had been used to induce sleep.

"I don't know why you still let Tawny in here."

"He bring me company. You want me alone all the time?" Celestine busied herself with the stew and spooned it into bowls.

"No, I do not want you alone all the time, but why you can't have your women friends here I don't know."

"Tawny is from home. These women here, from all places except Tobago. Did you go to Mr Lord?"

"We did. Your culantro is in that packet."

"Such a nice man, Mr Lord."

9 May 1926
Florence, Italy
Dear Caroline,

I can hardly believe that my six months here are almost at an end. I am thinking of extending the lease for another two months, which should enable me to finish the projects I have here. I can't say I have been particularly home sick, yet there are one or two things in England I have been missing recently.

I heard about the miners and the General Strike. No such issues here, the coal is in good supply and the markets are fully stocked with provisions after a particularly warm spring. Life here is more relaxed, I find most days that a shirt and trousers are all that are required, and the children are as brown as gypsies already. I have made a good friend in a fellow film enthusiast. His name is Pavel, and he comes from a town called Brno in Czechoslovakia. He may return to England with me, if his project completes at the same time. He has a romantic notion of London that I aim to disabuse him of!

Your new accommodation sounds very modern. Cheltenham, or what I saw of it, seems a pleasant town. Do you intend to remain there, content with your travels?

I won't bore you with my daily ongoings, suffice to say they are productive, and I am learning a great deal. Pavel is trying to teach me some of the Czech language but compared to Italian I must say it is difficult for my mouth to manage.

Helen wrote recently with an invitation to a wedding in September. Two of the young people that were in Devon where we first met, you might remember Lina and the dashing yet quiet Albert? The wedding is in Worcestershire, and I am to bring a plus one. If I am back in England by then, would you accompany me? I really don't think I can take Pavel, but as you know both bride and groom, what do you say?

As soon as I have a date to return, I shall let you know. I would very much like to see you once I'm settled in again Caroline. Your ears may have been on fire recently, I seem to mention you to Pavel rather a lot.

With fond regards
James

15 May 1926
The East Lawn Hotel,
Ilfracombe, Devon
Dearest Caro,

A short note as we are in some turmoil here. You will have noticed our address is no longer the delightful Budleigh. We have fled to Ilfracombe on the north coast, as a ghastly scene occurred last week between Tommy and Christopher. Tommy is distraught, hardly speaks, and I have no idea how to console him. Christopher's cleaner discovered the sketches that Tommy had left at the cottage, and you can imagine the uproar. Had it not been Tommy that our portly constable Harris had been investigating the poor man's discomfort would have been comical. As it was, it was excruciatingly uncomfortable for all involved. Christopher has taken digs in Exeter, and we immediately decamped to this awful place the following morning to avoid any further scandal. The cleaner has been assured of no impropriety, but Christopher's reputation would be in shreds had any of us remained.

My hard work at cultivating a position with the local dignitaries was wasted on them all but practice for myself. I do not think we will be in Ilfracombe for long, and wherever we land next, I shall resume my social activities with renewed vigour. For now, I must be a good wife and ensure Tommy is not left to walk the cliffs by himself or sink into whatever den of iniquity Ilfracombe possesses.

One other reason for writing, not that one is needed of course. You may remember Lina from our stay at Milton Abbot? I seem to recall you and she were on friendly terms when she was not entangled with Albert. They are to be married in Worcestershire in September and she expressly asked if I had your address, I presume to send you an invitation. I thought it best to ask first, and I include hers here for you so that you can make contact should you wish. I expect Harry and Charles Gregory will be invited, Albert was at school with them, and I wanted you to know that before you make your decision. Tommy and I shall go, wherever we may be residing by then.

I will write more when we have established a new residence. Have you heard from Midge about her interview? I am hoping that no news is good news on that front.

Let me know all your news, darling

Helen

Caroline had taken both letters into the rear garden at Norwood Court to read. As she sat engrossed on one of the benches, Ferris emerged through the apartment block rear doors carrying a tea tray, followed by Miss Kettle.

"May I join you my dear?" The older woman asked.

"Of course, please do!"

"Ferris, would you bring out a second cup and saucer from my kitchen please?"

"Right you are, Miss Kettle. Won't be a jiffy." He scuttled off and Agatha sat next to Caroline on the bench, the tray on the table to one side.

"So nice to have some sunshine, although I am glad this bench is in the shade in the afternoon."

Caroline put Helen's letter back into its envelope and placed it on top of James' on the bench between her and Agatha.

"It's a pretty garden. I'd quite forgotten about your invitation to take tea with you out here Agatha."

"We really haven't had the weather recently. But today, I thought, why not. Ferris is so helpful."

He returned with a cup, saucer, and teaspoon and then left them in peace.

"I spoke with Captain McTimony yesterday, he is keen to exact his revenge against our bridge pairing at our earliest convenience."

"You were rather naughty to pretend you could only play a little."

"Sometimes it pays to be a little bit naughty, my dear. I rather suspect he is still hoping to use it as an excuse to see more of Mrs Bassett, but whatever his reason, if you would like to improve your game then we could pair up again."

"I should like that Agatha, yes. Did the Captain say when?"

"He only said soon, but I got the impression that within the next few days would suit him. Do you have any prior engagements?"

"Not immediately. I spent rather a lot of last year visiting people and places, but this year despite having the means, I seem not to have the opportunity."

"But you and your father have a new home. One should try to make a home that one wants to spend time in, not run away from."

"That is very true. Except... no, it doesn't matter."

"Go on dear."

"Except it feels very much like Father's home still, even though we have a lot of new furniture and it's so very different from our old house. It just doesn't feel very much like my home. Does that sound strange?"

"Not at all. I spent many years in boarding houses and shared apartments when I was teaching. They were my home, but never really, truly mine. I have been fortunate to be able to take one of these new apartments now. It would have been well beyond my means had my dear sister not left me a small sum last year."

"Why did you choose to move to Cheltenham, Agatha? If you don't mind my asking," Caroline took the teacup offered to her.

"I had been here two or three times when I was younger, accompanying my sister to various spa treatments. She was somewhat neurotic and keen to try every new lotion, potion, purge and abrasion. I have always thought it a dignified town. Quite different to London of course."

"I went to London last year for the first time. It is so big!"

Agatha chuckled, "It must seem so if you are not used to it. What took you to London?"

"I stayed with some friends. Strangely, none of them are still there. In fact, soon none of us will be where we were last year at all."

"Young people do seem to spend such a lot of their energy moving around these days. But you do stay in touch with them?" Agatha had noticed the envelopes on the bench, particularly the corner of the Italian stamp that peeped out from underneath Helen's cream-coloured envelope on top. Caroline explained briefly about how she knew James and why he was in Italy, and about Helen and Tommy without going into any detail at all. She moved quickly on to Midge, feeling she was a safer subject.

"Four brothers you say?" There was a twinkle in Agatha's eye that Caroline recognised.

"Yes, Matthew the eldest is married to a nurse, Mark worked in a motor garage before he went to Africa, Luke is a doctor and John works on boats on the river Thames."

"Italy, Africa, would you like to travel abroad?"

"One day I should, yes. Florence, who used to be our neighbour, spent last summer in the south of France with her great aunt. But I think Florence was there more to be seen than to see, if you understand my meaning."

"I hear most people go to the south of France to be seen. Where would you like to travel to?"

Caroline considered the question as she sipped her tea.

"I really don't know. For a while I thought Egypt would be fascinating, but rather hot. There is so much of Britain I have yet to see, I feel I should explore more here first."

"A sensible approach. And your young man, is he the travelling type?"

It took Caroline a moment to understand who Agatha was referring to.

"Bob? Oh goodness no. I mean, he's not my young man, not really. He's a friend. I worked with his sister Lottie last year, that's how I know Bob."

"Forgive me, I assumed as he had been to visit, that he was significant to you."

Caroline placed her empty cup onto its saucer. Significant. The word was laden with meaning, not all of it inaccurate.

"Bob is not one to travel far. Bob is dependable."

"And James is in Italy," Agatha observed.

Caroline sighed, "Yes. And Luke may be here in Cheltenham soon too."

"And Mr Rickard?"

Caroline looked up sharply, "Mr Rickard? What about him?"

"I may be mistaken of course, but he was taking quite an interest in you the other evening. He has been asking Ferris about your movements also. I think perhaps he is on the verge of inviting you to a dance or dinner or whatever you young people do."

Caroline was lost for words. She realised her mouth was hanging open and promptly shut it. She thought back over the drinks party; had he been watching her? Now she thought about it, whenever she glanced up from her book when he and her father were playing chess, he had quickly averted his gaze.

"I may have been mistaken of course," Agatha poured more tea. Caroline suddenly remembered Mrs Bassett's words about how all elderly women gossiped. She would have to be on her guard.

Vaughan Rickard was at that moment standing at the window of his office, looking down at the passengers on the upper deck of the tram below. He often stood there, watching the people going about their lives up and down the High Street. Not that he wasn't busy; trade was steady particularly with mothers bringing their young sons to be fitted with spectacles. Mothers with daughters came less often he mused. He wondered, not for the first time, if Caroline would benefit from spectacles. She held her novel rather too close to her face when reading, he had noticed.

He was spending more and more time imagining Caroline's face, well aware that she almost certainly had no idea of the effect she had had on him. How could she? They had said barely ten words to each other since they had first met. Vaughan hoped that George would find their chess matches enjoyable enough to continue them regularly. He liked George, despite being several years younger than Caroline's father. Vaughan had so few real friends, though many acquaintances, it was nice to spend time with another man and not have to discuss their eyesight.

The tram moved away, and Vaughan turned as a drab woman in her forties propelled her son into the optician's office.

"Good afternoon, Mrs O'Shae, let's have Thomas in the chair here, shall we?"

The visit to Bristol seemed to have helped Mary shake off some of the grief that had weighed upon her. When the fabrics arrived, she set about them with scissors, pins and thread, and soon the vicarage was showing signs of her industry. Caroline was cheered by the apparent recovery of her friend and suggested that they might go back to their old routine of seeing each other on a Wednesday afternoon. Mary agreed only if Caroline stayed to dinner, which they ate usually at six so that Philip could return to St Mark's for the evening service at seven-thirty.

With one friend restored, Caroline's concern returned to Florence. She still did not fully understand Florence's reaction to married intimacy, but as she had not yet taken up Caroline's invitation to visit the apartment, Caroline decided to call on her again. The weather was beginning to warm up after a chilly beginning to May, but Caroline still needed a light coat as she walked from the Park to Tivoli. She stopped *en route* at the little parade of shops and bought two Chelsea buns, thinking they could have them with the inevitable pot of tea.

Arriving at the Curzon's house, Caroline was shown again into the front parlour with its gaudy, uncomfortable chairs. Jones the maid took the buns in their paper bag and said her mistress would be down presently. Caroline waited almost five minutes before Florence appeared. She still had a haunted look to her face, but seemed more collected this time. They sat and made small talk until Jones had returned with the tea things and the Chelsea buns on a plate. Florence did not seem to notice them.

"I picked up some buns on the way, I thought you might like one," Caroline offered.

"Thank you. Perhaps just a small piece. I have not been feeling well this week."

"Forgive me for saying, Florence, but you do look rather tired still."

"I do not sleep well. There is a considerable difference between a bed of one's own and sharing a bed with one's husband."

"I can imagine there is."

"I doubt you can." Florence said flatly.

"It must be odd, when one is used to throwing arms and legs around without anyone else in the way."

"If only that were the worst of it."

Caroline looked at her friend more directly, "Is there something wrong, Florence? You were upset last time we spoke, have things not improved?"

Florence looked out of the window, as if weighing up whether to confide in Caroline. Who else did she have? Her parents were happily married, so she assumed, and she had no close friends or relatives. Since her marriage she had become aware of just how lonely she was.

"I have found the physical nature of being a wife is most unpleasant. In fact, it disgusts me. The proximity of a man in that way, the sensations, the ..." she struggled to find a word, "...excretions! I apologise Caroline, but I do not know how much longer I will be able to tolerate what is expected of me."

Caroline was shocked, but not for the reasons Florence supposed. Caroline knew she did not have a comprehensive understanding of how sex occurred, but she had never heard anyone describe it in such a distasteful way before. Caroline had assumed it to normally be a romantic union, not one of tolerance and especially not in a marriage. She had a sudden flashback to Harry Gregory, his weight on her, his hands clawing at her clothes, her fear. She involuntarily shook her head; that was different, Florence was married.

"Have you spoken to Josiah of your feelings on it?"

"Impossible. He clearly enjoys what he does, else he would not continue. Indeed, he seems thoroughly satisfied after each event. He sleeps far more soundly than I."

A thought occurred to Caroline, "You say you've not felt well this week. Do you think you might be pregnant?"

The colour drained from Florence's face, "I had not, but now that you mention it, I think it might be possible. Oh Caroline, that is the very last thing that I want!"

"You have not taken precautions?" Caroline again wasn't completely sure what that meant herself, but she had heard the other women at Sunningend talk of precautions to avoid pregnancy and felt it was the right thing to ask.

"No! And I suppose I should have known it would happen eventually, but so soon! And I will grow fat and uncomfortable and I cannot think of anything I want less at this moment."

She began to cry, not in a dramatic wail (which Caroline might have expected from her friend) but silent tears that fell while Florence remained quite still, her hands clasped in her lap.

Caroline did not know what to say. She had never known a woman to not want a pregnancy or the following baby, or even babies. She thought of Mary and how distraught she had been after losing her baby, and a wave of anger rose in her that she fought back down. It was not Florence's fault that Mary's little boy had died.

Caroline tried another tack, "Think of all the pretty baby clothes and toys you'll need. And you will be able to decorate a nursery too."

Florence simply looked at her friend.

"I had hoped to model again for Mr Gerrard. He had some difficulties with stock in the spring and with the wedding I was too busy, but he has written and asked if I would consider modelling for him next month. We had such a fun time before Christmas, didn't we? And now I shall never be able to grace the runway again."

Caroline recalled that she had had a rather tiring time while Florence had been the star attraction modelling a collection for Gerrard's Department Store in Gloucester. She changed the subject, to the recent strike and the bridge party at Norwood Court, and Florence seemed to relax a little. When Caroline got up to leave an hour or so later,

Florence had fully recovered her composure, as if the tears had never fallen.

"Do call again, won't you?" she said as she opened the front door for Caroline.

"Really it's your turn to visit us you know."

"Yes, perhaps when I am feeling well again."

"I'm sure that won't be too long. Goodbye my dear."

Normally if Caroline had a question, she would ask Annie. As she walked home again from Tivoli Caroline decided it would be too embarrassing to ask Annie about matters of sexual intercourse. Indeed, she might get completely the wrong end of the stick and that would be most uncomfortable for both of them! She resolved to ask Lottie. She assumed that Lottie would know about such things, coming from a lower class and a more communal style of living. Had Helen lived nearer to Cheltenham, Caroline would have asked her, being a woman of infinitely wider knowledge than Caroline felt herself to be. Midge would have given her the most practical answers, but Caroline felt Midge would not understand the emotional aspect quite so well. Even had her mother still been alive, Caroline would never have been able to discuss the subject with her.

As the six o'clock bell rang at Sunningend engineering works that evening, Caroline was waiting at the gates for her friend to emerge. The first familiar face she saw in the stream of men and women was Gwen. Caroline waved and smiled at her, and Gwen gave a small wave in return. If Caroline missed anything about working in the sewing room at Sunningend, it was working in tandem with Gwen. Even though Gwen was mute and rarely expressive, the routine the girls had developed and the way they eventually matched each other in speed and accuracy had given Caroline a sense of pride in her work.

The next person she saw was Hannah Cox, who with her husband Jim had now moved into the house at Curzon's Exotic Plant Nursery. Hannah stopped to say hello and ask how Caroline was getting along, and while Caroline was saying how different it felt to live in an apartment than a house, she almost missed Lottie as she came through the crowd. She excused herself to Hannah and caught up with Lottie who gave a happy squeal to see her friend and linked arms with her immediately as they walked with Caroline pushing her bicycle.

"Are you coming to see Bob?"

"I rather wanted to speak to you, but if Bob is at home, then I could stay for a few minutes."

"He'd be sad if you didn't, but you know that. I have something to ask you too, but you go first."

Caroline looked around to make sure no one was too close to hear. They had walked past the queue for the tram and were now making their way along Gloucester Road towards St George's crossroads and were on their own.

"I need to ask you about pregnancy," It seemed the least uncomfortable word to use in a public space.

Lottie's head turned sharply to Caroline, "not you?!"

"No, no, not at all. No, a friend of mine thinks she might be pregnant, but she is very unhappy about it. The only person I have really known to have a baby is Mary, and of course I know how the end bit happens now, but I am still a little in the dark about the beginnings."

Lottie laughed, with more than a small amount of relief, "Lummy, you had me going there for a minute! Did your mother never explain about the birds and the bees?"

"Goodness no, it would have horrified her. I know women menstruate; I know the man must release his seed," Caroline could feel her face growing red, but she continued,

"But I wonder why some women seem never to become pregnant and others have child after child with no difficulty at all?"

"Those women who never seem to get pregnant probably know someone who helps them prevent it," Lottie said quietly.

"I've heard the girls talking about prevention."

"French letters and the like. Your friend isn't Catholic, is she? They aren't meant to use them. The Pope says so. You can still get unlucky and have one split. That's how Charlie came along, mother always says."

Caroline tried not to be shocked at Lottie's revelation and ploughed on.

"I don't think she is Catholic, no I'm sure she isn't. But am I right in thinking these French letters are no use if sex has already happened?"

"Shutting the stable door after the horse has bolted, yes. There are ways of ..." Lottie stopped herself.

"Ways of what?"

"Caroline you must promise not to say anything about this to anyone other than your friend, and she mustn't tell anyone either. Understood?"

Caroline nodded, uneasy at what she might be about to hear. Lottie was now the one to take a quick glance around to make sure they would not be overheard. Satisfied, she continued in a low voice.

"If a woman gets pregnant and doesn't want the baby, there are ways of getting rid of it. Some are old wives' tales of course, but others, so I have been told, do work. If you know the right people."

"You mean an abortion?"

"Shhhhhh! Yes, or ways to bring on a miscarriage."

"But Lottie that's illegal!"

Lottie looked at her friend for any trace of hostility and found only concern, "Yes, it is, but sometimes it's for the best."

"How can that be?"

Lottie sighed, "There's a woman in our street. She's got three young children already, one still on the breast. Her husband is a good for nothing drunk who is in and out of prison and beats her and the children all the time. She could not cope with another baby, she's away with the fairies herself most of the time. Better for her and the other three that another never comes along. If she can't stop him from getting her pregnant in the first place, then something has to be done when it happens."

"You said there were some methods, old wives' tales."

"Hot baths, gin, riding that bicycle of yours some people say can bring on a miscarriage," Lottie chuckled as Caroline frowned, "other ways, not so nice, like taking a potion or falling down some stairs."

"No one would do that deliberately though, surely?"

"It's extreme."

"And what if it didn't work but damaged the baby?"

"You know, babies are tough when they want to be born. All these things don't always work, and the baby comes out weighing ten pounds and singing the national anthem."

"Lottie, do you know where someone would go if they needed help like that? I understand if you don't want to tell me, and I cannot believe I am saying this myself, but is there someone in Cheltenham that would help my friend if she felt she really didn't want the baby?"

They had stopped walking "There is. Gwen's mother."

Caroline went to bed early that evening. She could not concentrate on conversations with her father, who then announced he was going to call on Rickard to see if he wanted to play chess again one evening. With Agatha's words jostling with Lottie's in Caroline's head, she did not want to be at home if the men decided to return to number five to play chess that particular evening.

She lay on her bed with her hands behind her head and let her mind ramble. Her talk with Lottie had taken an unexpected turn; she had only meant to clarify how babies began, not how to stop them from being born. She had left Lottie at the end of her street and asked her not to mention to Bob that they had seen each other. They had agreed to meet the following Saturday and go to the matinee film programme at the Daffodil together. The bicycle ride home had passed in seconds, and dinner had been eaten without registering taste or smell. George could see his daughter was preoccupied but did not press for an explanation.

Caroline thought of Gwen and wondered if her muteness was a result of a failed attempt to stop her being born. Surely if it had been, she thought, Gwen's mother would never have advised anyone again on how to stop a pregnancy. And then there was the fact that it was illegal. Not only for the person giving the assistance, but also for the pregnant woman herself. Caroline believed the punishment was life in prison, but she wasn't certain. Women could still be committed to asylums for even inquiring about things like that, she had read about a similar case in the newspaper only a few days ago. Would Florence be making the same investigations? Had she also read of the woman in the newspaper? She certainly seemed horrified at the prospect of being pregnant, and her whole attitude of disgust about the marital bed still confused Caroline.

There was a small part of Caroline that not for the first time whispered that Florence had made her bed and really should now lay in it. Florence had always been in pursuit of wealth; she had been raised to expect it as her ultimate destination in life. But to see her friend so distressed, over something that normally brought such joy, Caroline was worried about her. Rolling the situation around, Caroline next considered how she would behave if she ever had to face Florence's situation. It was difficult to imagine, for the first reason that Caroline did not intend to marry anyone simply for the financial security they could provide.

Ignoring that, could she, would she ever marry a man she did not feel attracted to? She thought not, although she conceded that the level of attraction was not necessarily a consistent one. But with an attraction, she felt the physical act of sex would surely not be as traumatic as Florence suggested it was. Another flashback of the weight of Harry on top of her in the lane down to the river Tavy in Devon came unbidden. She screwed her eyes tight shut and turned on to her side, a trick she had learned years before when waking from a nightmare.

Could she imagine having sex with anyone she knew? That was surely the next step in her mental explorations of the subject. Bob? She couldn't see how the opportunity might present itself. He was almost deferential in her company, reserved, dependable. That word again, she felt it described him perfectly yet also felt it was a little mean of her to think so. Who else? Luke? She liked his company, but she was not attracted to him. He seemed so young, though he was only a year younger than she was, so boyish. James? James was an enigma. Constantly telling her that he would not be a good husband, and yet there was something about him, and about the way she felt when she was near him, that she could not name. It seemed more than attraction, yet they were deliberately not acting on it. However, he was not even in the same country at the moment, and in being out of reach he should perhaps also be out of contention.

Caroline concluded that she could perhaps imagine being intimate with a man, even if it were not Bob or James. Could there be someone else out there who would sweep her off her feet as so often happened on the cinema screen? She drifted off to sleep with Ivor Novello's face smiling at her in black and white.

8

THE ESCAPE

Had Caroline known she was the subject of several conversations that evening, she might have adjusted her list of possible lovers accordingly.

Bob and his father were standing at the end of the saloon bar in the Rising Sun pub. Lottie and her mother and several other women from the street were in the Lewis' front parlour that evening knitting scarves, hats and gloves for the miners and their families who were still on strike. Despite it being June, the women had decided on simple patterns that would generate useful garments should the strike continue into the winter.

"Eric came to see me yesterday. Officially asked to marry Lottie. I said yes of course, seemed like I'd break her heart if I said no."

"Did he have a date in mind?"

"Mentioned the start of August. Seems a bit soon, hardly time to call the banns but I suppose they've been courting a year or so now."

"And they'll have our back room."

"Robert, we discussed this. You'll be in your new place soon enough, and they need to save a bit for their own."

"Oh, I know. I'd hoped to be able to buy that house on Mill Street, but I respect Mr Munhead's advice to wait a bit longer."

"And how are you and Caroline getting along?"

"I don't know dad. I'd like her to be my wife, but I don't think she'd say yes if I asked. She's as good as told me not to wait for her, but I'm not interested in anyone else."

"Your mother took some convincing too. I believe she was hoping for a better offer but settled for me in the end."

"I don't want Caroline to have to settle. If she doesn't want to be my wife, I'd rather she went off and married someone else. I'll just keep saving and when her father says it's the right time, I'll see if there is another house to buy and get some chickens."

"You've never forgiven me for putting them birds in the pot, have you? Look, you ask Caroline, straight out and no nonsense. And if she says no, wait a while and then ask again. If something's worth having, it's worth trying a bit harder for."

At number three Norwood Court, George Munhead and Vaughan Rickard were nearing the end of their chess game. George was winning, but Vaughan felt his game was improving with the practice. He had been hoping George might request another game, as he had something to ask him. He took George's white queen's castle with his next move.

"Sorry old chap, you left him rather without protection. I was wondering, does Caroline, your daughter, play chess?"

George did not look up from the game. He had anticipated that this kind of conversation would occur eventually.

"She does, on occasion. And bridge, and I believe Mah-jong also."

"Now there's a game I should like to try. Quite the rage in the country houses, so I hear."

"I believe that is where Caroline learned. Somewhere in Devon," he moved a white pawn.

Vaughan weighed this new information. He had not considered that Caroline might move in higher circles than those which would naturally include him. He decided to grasp the nettle.

"Does Caroline have anyone she is particularly fond of at the moment?"

"Several people I should think, but if you mean is she in a romantic relationship, then I do not think so. Although that is not to say there are no other suitors."

"Oh? Oh," Vaughan moved his bishop closer to George's white queen.

"Caroline is very keen on moving pictures. She even had a part in one last year, though it was distributed only on the continent as I understand. Perhaps you would like to ask her to accompany you one evening or to a matinee on Saturday, if that is to your taste also?"

"Well, I'm not a regular cinema-goer, but that would be enjoyable. Yes, how about next Tuesday? I have choir practice on Monday, but Tuesdays I am usually at home."

"I will ask her and suggest she leaves a note with her response with Ferris. Is that acceptable? And I believe that is check mate," he took Vaughan's remaining black knight with his queen.

Across town, Dr Riley was on the telephone with Luke Frampton.

"Yes, of course, excellent news!"

"Is the room still available? Until I can find my own digs of course."

"It is, though there are several small houses and apartments close to the hospital that you might be interested in, furnished as well as unfurnished. I'll have the papers here for you when you arrive."

"I shall come the Monday after next, as agreed. And thank you again for holding the opportunity open for me, I do appreciate it."

"Not at all my dear fellow, it would have been folly to let such a talented young doctor slip away to general practice!"

In a café on the outskirts of Florence, under an azure sky that was beginning to turn rose and gold with the setting sun, James and Pavel were at a table having supper. Their conversation, as usual conducted in a mixture of English, Czech and Italian, had been up to that point about their work. Pavel poured the last of a bottle of red wine into their glasses and then raised it to indicate to the waiter that another was required.

"Have I said today how much I miss Marta? When you return to England, you have a woman waiting for you?"

"There is someone, though she is not waiting for me. At least, I hope not."

"What? Come on, why would you not want her to be growing thin with missing you?"

"For the same reason Marta is not here with you. This is no business to sustain a relationship."

"But when we make our fortunes, then we will need a woman to enjoy it with, no?"

"You know I don't do this for the money."

"Ha! It is your art, I know this. But the money always helps."

James drank his wine. Was he being too hard on himself when it came to Caroline? Would she be content to spend time at home while he travelled on location with his work? Or perhaps she would want to travel with him but find other ways to occupy herself while he worked. He had liked the way they seemed to understand each other for those last few days in Dorset. They were comfortable in each other's company without imposing on one another's space. If he could be sure that would not change if they were to become officially in a relationship, he would go to Caroline as soon as he returned to England and ask her. Ask her what though? To marry him? To live with him? To visit him occasionally and he visit her? He found the young women of Europe rather more liberal in their views than those back at home. But he knew too that Caroline was also somehow more open in her outlook. Perhaps if Caroline agreed to accompany him to that wedding Helen had written about, he would have a chance to ask her directly what she might want to do about it all.

"You are thinking of her now, yes?"

James smiled at his friend; Pavel's directness was a stark contrast to the conversation of many Englishmen.

"Yes, I was thinking about Caroline."

"Whatever you were thinking, do it. Too many of our brothers did not live to see their sweethearts again, and I fear for what I hear in the coffee shops. I will marry Marta when I go home. And you will marry Caroline." He raised his glass to toast. James nodded and clinked his glass against Pavel's.

"I will ask her."

In the Cheltenham area known as Tivoli, Florence and Josiah Curzon were together in the rear sitting room of their house. Josiah was reading the newspaper and Florence had picked up some embroidery but was finding it difficult to see where to stitch in the fading light. She had eaten very little dinner, and Josiah had commented on her quietness. She had excused it as a headache, and his reply that he hoped it would be gone by bedtime, almost made her leave the table to vomit. Every night, without exception, regardless of her condition, it was her duty to accept him. He had announced that on their first night together and had kept his side of the arrangement since. Florence felt obliged, but no less unhappy about it with each passing night. She had been particularly distressed during her period, and shocked that Josiah had not declined his right. She could not reconcile herself to what was happening to her; he was not a cruel man, indeed in all other respects he treated her with the utmost generosity and kindness. It was that one thing between them which she found increasingly revolting. She decided that when they went to bed that evening, she would try to dissuade Josiah from doing his duty. He was, so she had said, a reasonable man.

9 June 1926
Cheltenham
Dear Helen,

I am so sorry to hear of Tommy's situation, and that it has caused such distress to you both. Hopefully everything will quiet down now that you are no longer in Budleigh and Christopher will not be cast out from his employment. Tommy must be, well, I was going to say heartbroken, but I don't know if that's the appropriate word for a man. I know you will look after him.

James had written to me as well about Lina and Albert's wedding. He has asked me to go with him, so I suppose I shall be protected from the Gregorys. It would be nice to hear from Lina if she has time, she must be so very busy with the preparations. I expect it will be a much grander affair than Florence's wedding last February. Will you and Tommy be staying at an hotel? Could I be a bore and ask you to reserve a room for me as well please? I have yet to work out how that might be done, you must help me understand it all when we meet. Father has been making enquiries to have a telephone installed, and of course that will help us with many arrangements. It's rather exciting!

Will you look for a house in Ilfracombe? I had to get one of Father's maps out to find it. He said we have some distant relations in north Devon, I wonder he didn't mention them before, but it seems they live in that particular area. Or it could possibly be north Cornwall, he wasn't exactly certain. They must be very distant, as he has never spoken about them before that I can remember.

So yes, do give Lina my address here please. And write as soon as you receive this with your news. I wish I could help you both, but I don't see how I could be of any assistance. Just know that I would if I had the means!

Love to Tommy,
Caroline

"Have you finished with the butter?"

George and Caroline were having breakfast at the small dining table, the sun streaming through the window and spotlighting a diagonal beam of dancing dust particles. Caroline passed the butter dish and bit into her own slice of toast.

"I suppose I should let Mr Rickard know if I will go to the cinema with him straight away."

It was Sunday morning and Caroline had already been to the Daffodil the afternoon before with Lottie. The programme of shows changed every Wednesday and Friday, so she could expect to see the same films by going again so soon.

"You have had enough time to consider it?"

"Yes. I think I shall. Now the weather has finally improved it will be nice to go out in the evening."

"Did you have any plans to be away over this summer?"

"At the moment, only to Lina and Albert's wedding in Worcester. That's not until September and I have asked Helen to reserve a room at whatever hotel they are staying at. I've hardly spent any of my allowance this year so I think I can afford a nice room for a few days. Have you ever been to Worcester?"

"No, though it has a cathedral, you may want to look around."

"More tea? I may need to spend rather a lot of my allowance on wedding gifts this year, what with Lina and Albert, Annie and Jacob, and also Lottie and Eric all tying the knot."

There was a heavy pause in the conversation. George decided to ask.

"And is there anyone you might consider tying your knot with?"

Caroline stopped mid-chew and stared at her father, who raised his hands as if to fend off an angry cat.

"I am in no hurry to see you leave here, my dear. This is your home for as long as you wish it. But with your friends all becoming wives, I wondered if the question of your own future had begun to crystalise in any way? It would be helpful to me if I knew your feelings on it."

"Midge isn't becoming anyone's wife, she is off to Africa, or at least she could be if she passes the next interview."

"Is Africa on your horizon also? Or perhaps Italy? I couldn't help but notice the postage stamp on your recent letter."

"From James. He says he'll be coming home although not quite as soon as he had expected. He'll be back in England by August. So no, I shall not be running off to Italy just yet."

After church, Caroline and her father stopped to talk to Dr Riley in the sunshine before he went to spend an hour at the hospital. Caroline tried valiantly to disguise her annoyance at the news that Luke would be taking up the position of Houseman at the hospital. Dr Riley even suggested she should show Luke around the town and help him settle in, knowing that they were acquainted with each other. Caroline was starting to wonder if Lottie had been right when she said to be cautious about the number of different men she was seen out with in Cheltenham. Someone was going to get the wrong idea if she wasn't careful, but she couldn't ignore Luke completely for fear of upsetting Midge and their family.

Annie was busy in the kitchen when Caroline and George returned home. Caroline changed her outfit and put on an apron before helping make the batter for Yorkshire puddings.

"Any news on your wedding?" She asked, the exertion of beating causing a fine sheen of sweat to emerge on her brow.

Annie was spooning hot fat over the roast potatoes. She put down her spoon for a moment and turned to Caroline.

"We're still going to do it, because if we don't, we won't get one of the new houses, but it will be just our two families. And you and your father of course, you've been like a second family to me all these years and I can't ever say how grateful I am for that. It won't be the big do I'd been hoping for, but Jacob and I will be man and wife and that's what really matters."

She turned back to the potatoes, so that Caroline wouldn't see her shut her eyes and wait for the threatening tears to recede. She had so wanted a full church and a big party afterwards, perhaps in the fields behind her father's little house if the farmer could be persuaded.

"Will that be at St Mark's?"

"Yes, first banns to be read on the fourteenth of August, and we'll be married on Saturday fourth of September at two in the afternoon, God willing."

"Lottie and Eric's wedding is on the seventh of August. Oh, September for yours?! I do hope Lina and Albert's is not on the same day. That would be terrible. I should have to decline their invitation of course, when it arrives. I've only actually been invited as a plus one at the moment anyway. But I shouldn't want to miss your wedding, Annie. Do you have a dress?"

"I do, just a simple crepe frock in white, but I have mother's veil."

"Will she be able to get to the church?" Annie's mother was crippled with arthritis and could only just move around their small house. She rarely went further than their tiny front garden.

"Father says he will carry her. Jacob says he'll use the coal cart, but he'll scrub it clean first!"

Lottie and Eric had decided to get married at the Registry Office in the town, much to the dismay of Lottie's mother Jane. She had hoped to see her daughter married in much the same style that Annie had wanted for herself, yet Lottie and Eric were determined to save every penny they could for a home of their own as quickly as possible and an extravagant wedding was a waste as far as they could see. Eric had applied to join the police force after his volunteer duties during the strike. He was only just tall enough to meet the regulations, but he was intelligent and had a strong sense of moral correctness, without an added layer of religious fervour. Indeed, neither he or Lottie had been inside a church for many years besides the occasional wedding, baptism or funeral. They had planned out their future; living with her parents while he completed his probation period as a trainee constable, and then moving to wherever the force required him to be, hopefully with a police house in which to raise a family.

Caroline dressed carefully for her evening at the cinema with Vaughan Rickard. She opted for a cream shift dress with a dropped waste, pleated from a band with a chevron pattern in green and orange. As it had no sleeves, she wore her light coat, finishing the ensemble with her plum-coloured cloche hat, brown shoes and a small evening bag. She decided not to wear any makeup, and the only jewellery she put on was the silver bracelet that Helen had bought for her in Birmingham the year before. Her note to Rickard had requested that he call for her at six-thirty so that they could be at the Daffodil for the seven o'clock show. At twenty-five past six, as Caroline was putting on her shoes, Rickard knocked on the apartment door and George admitted him to the hallway. Caroline hurried out of her room, and straight into a large bunch of flowers.

"These are for you. I hope you like them," Vaughan had bought several small bunches on his way home, not knowing which Caroline might prefer. In the end, he wrapped some brown paper around all four bunches together.

Caroline took them, sniffed them as was required in such circumstances, declared them to be 'lovely' and that he really shouldn't have, before looking helplessly at her father. George stepped in gallantly and took the flowers into the kitchen to stand in the sink until a vase or indeed vases could be found for them.

They walked to the Daffodil, Rickard keeping a respectful distance from Caroline at all times, and not presuming to offer her his arm. The evening was warm with the scent of buddleia and roses in the air, and children played out in the street with marbles, battered prams and skipping ropes. A group of girls had scratched a hop-scotch grid in the dirt outside the Baptist chapel and were taking turns to throw pebbles into each square, then hop and jump up and down the grid, picking up their pebble on the homeward leg.

"Did you ever play that as a young girl?"

"Of course, every girl does. I could still do it now, I think."

"A child's game?"

Caroline smiled at him and turned to the girls.

"Can I play, just one go?"

The girls giggled but one offered Caroline her pebble. Caroline passed her evening bag to Vaughan and tossed the pebble into a square about halfway up the grid. Then she was off, hopping and jumping alternately to the end, turning on one leg and wobbling enough to make the little girls shriek that she would fall over. Then back again, bobbing down to collect the pebble on the way. She handed it back to the owner with a big smile, retrieved her bag, and a little out of breath and red-cheeked continued towards the Daffodil as if nothing had happened.

Vaughan Rickard was enthralled. Such confidence, such disregard for social norms, such a grasp of life. How he longed to be able to throw off the shackles of respectability and return to childhood pastimes. Yet he had a business to consider, a reputation to protect and nurture. Oh, but to be in the company of such a lively young woman, he felt positively ten years younger! People often thought he was older than he really was, and at thirty-two he had done well to build his optician business up to a comfortable list of customers. He suspected that it was the spectacles that gave him an air of being more mature, that and the fact he had not been allowed to join the war effort because of his poor sight and a tendency towards asthma.

His experience with young women could have been written on a calling card. He had been raised mostly among men and the few women he saw were customers. It had not been his choice; it was simply how things had evolved. Vaughan was a romantic through lack of opportunity. There had been a girl who lived a few doors away in his street before his parents moved to Norfolk. Nellie had captured his heart from afar, they had never spoken, yet he still dreamed of her regularly. Now Caroline was starting to appear in his dreams.

Caroline was smiling to herself as she walked along. Why did childhood games suddenly become forbidden as one grew older? She remembered the skipping rope that she and Florence had played with in their back gardens, and the balls they would play catch with, chanting rhymes as they swapped the balls from hand to hand. She was so distracted by her memories that she was shocked when Vaughan suddenly grabbed her arm and pulled her back from an on-coming motor car as they came to where Painswick Road and Andover Road crossed.

"I'm sorry, are you alright?"

"I was miles away! Thank you, Mr Rickard, you saved my life."

"Call me Vaughan, please. I'm sorry if I hurt your arm."

"I'm sorry you had to; it was very silly of me not to look where I was going."

"Would you take my arm so that we can cross safely?"

She did. Vaughan felt himself swell with pride to have such a free spirit on his arm and hoped she would not let go when they reached the other side. She did not.

After the film, as the patrons spilled out into the twilight of a still warm evening, Vaughan suggested they purchase a bag of scraps to share on their walk home. Caroline agreed and added a pickled egg each to their order. They discussed the film as they walked to the chip shop, Vaughan enthralled with Caroline's knowledge of film production. In turn she asked him about his work. He started to explain how the eye behaves when exposed to too much light, but stopped, feeling self-conscious.

"I expect I'm boring you."

"Not at all, it sounds fascinating. If you'd rather talk about something else, tell me, have you travelled very much?"

"Abroad?"

"Yes, or in this country. Anywhere really."

"I spend a week each summer in Cromer in Norfolk. My parents moved there so that my father could write."

"Your father is an author?"

"No, he translates. He speaks Danish, Norwegian, Swedish and German."

"How wonderful! And do you speak those languages also?"

"A little German. I could probably make myself understood in Danish. Schoolboy French, but that's all. Do you?"

"No, Helen was always the star at languages."

She described briefly her schoolfriends' attributes, but carefully left out any details that could lead to uncomfortable questions. Vaughan was impressed that she was still in contact with women she had been at school with some eight years before. Truthfully, he was impressed with everything he learned about Caroline Munhead.

They bought their supper and sat on a street bench to eat. The heat of the day was evaporating on a rising breeze. An older couple passed by, and the woman frowned to see them eating out in the open. Caroline did not notice, but Vaughan did and blushed as he recognised one of his fellow choristers.

"I have never been to Cromer. What is it like there?" Caroline took a bite of her egg.

"Often it is cold, the fog rolls in from the North Sea even on sunny days. It is a small town, there is a long beach. Rather quiet and not many young people."

"Do people go there to paint?"

"Paint? You mean pictures? I have seen some men painting the boats, but I wouldn't say it was picturesque. Why?"

"I enjoy painting. I took my paints down to Budleigh Salterton when I went to visit Helen and spent a day painting on the hill above the town. You may have noticed the painting in the entrance hall of our apartment?"

"You did that? It's very good. I had no idea you were an artist."

"I'm not really anything at the moment. I was a frame stitcher at the Sunningend works for a while, and a photographer's assistant for a few weeks, as well as working on the film last year. I find the trouble with employment is that it rather gets in the way of the other things I am invited to do."

"Having my own business, I am able to manage my own leisure time should I wish to go anywhere." Though I only ever go to Cromer, he thought, suddenly ashamed.

Vaughan Rickard opened the glass door to Norwood Court and ushered Caroline inside. Ferris was locking the door to his room as they came in and wished them a good evening as he left for his own home.

"Decent chap, Ferris," Vaughan ushered Caroline to the stairs.

"Do you think so? He seems to look after Agatha, Miss Kettle."

"Very good for sorting out deliveries and the laundry van. It was one of the reasons I took the apartment here."

They reached Caroline's door on the top floor. The sound of Mrs Bassett's gramophone played gently around them.

"Well Goodnight, Vaughan. Thank you for a very nice evening."

"The pleasure was all mine, I assure you. Perhaps we might do it again, soon?"

"Perhaps. I promise to pay better attention to the roads next time," Caroline smiled, and Vaughan risked a kiss on her cheek.

"Goodnight."

George was waiting up for his daughter, reading in the sitting room by the light of a standard lamp beside his chair.

"Did you have a pleasant evening?"

"I played hopscotch, almost got run over by a motor car and ate a pickled egg on a bench in full view of the world."

"A very pleasant evening, then. Will it be repeated?"

"Perhaps," Caroline burped, "excuse me, without the egg."

As she was in need of wedding gifts, Caroline went into Cheltenham the following day. She called into Elsa's photography shop but was informed by the young but growing Peter that Miss House was in London for the week. She left a message, written on a scrap of paper and placed for Elsa in the kitchen underneath an ashtray which she emptied into what looked like a rubbish bin. Caroline hoped the sight of the empty ashtray would alert Elsa to the note, so unusual was it in the little back room. Caroline was disappointed not to see her friend and wondered if she was spending more time with her new companion. Rousing herself, Caroline muttered under her breath that it would not do to be jealous and marched into Cavendish House.

It was a large department store that filled the space between the Promenade and Regent Street, with just over twenty thousand square feet of floorspace. It had stood in that location for almost a hundred years and was the main reason many people visited the town – if they were not interested in the spa waters. The new electrical lighting gave off much less heat than the previous gas lamps had done and the building was a cool refuge on a warm day.

Caroline spent an enjoyable hour being shown crockery, cutlery, glassware and other interior adornments. After much indecision, she purchased a tea service with octagonal plates and soup bowls and a pretty pink rose design for Lottie and Eric. For Annie and Jacob, she picked out a set of six thick beer glasses that were presented in a box with a red satin lining. She had spent almost five minutes looking at a cocktail set before she realised Annie and Jacob would never use such a thing and she was actually craving it for herself. However, it would possibly be suitable for Lina and Albert, and she enquired if it could be put by for a month in case she could think of nothing else for them. She wondered then if James would be arranging a gift, from himself or perhaps from them both. She would have time to find out, she hoped. Two gifts in her name for people she had only met once seems rather extravagant.

After the cool of Cavendish House, she stepped out into the heat of the summer again. She bought a posy of sweet peas from a young girl on the Promenade and as she turned away almost knocked Miss Kettle over.

"I'm so sorry! Here, take my arm, are you alright?"

"Yes, yes, my dear, no harm done. I was about to tap your shoulder and you moved too quickly for me. Those are pretty."

"Aren't they, and they smell divine! We used to grow them at our old house, and I miss their scent. Are you off anywhere nice?"

"Only to the library. I thought I might learn a little about Cheltenham's history and the library is the best place to do that."

"I suppose it would be. If you are sure you are quite alright..."

"Yes, I shall be on my way. You should get those back into water as quickly as you can. Good afternoon."

Caroline did as Miss Kettle instructed, arranging the flowers in a small vase on the dining table. They were dwarfed by the large arrangement from Rickard, which Caroline moved onto the sitting room windowsill. It was hot in the apartment, though Annie had opened all of the windows and pulled the curtains to keep out the sun before she had finished for the day. Caroline took a glass of lemon barley water down to the garden to sit in the shade. She found Mrs Bassett on the bench. She was dressed in a yellow shift dress with red piping, and a string of red beads wrapped fashionably long around her pale, slender neck. Her hair was pushed back under a large red straw hat and dark glasses hid her eyes so that Caroline wasn't sure if she was asleep or awake. When Mrs Bassett invited her to sit down, she almost jumped and spilled her drink. Nonetheless she sat.

"This heat is tiresome," Mrs Bassett moved only her mouth, the rest of her was completely still.

"We are lucky to have this bench in the shade for the afternoons."

"One had not considered these apartments would become tropical greenhouses in the summer."

"Neither had I, but the light on a cool day is lovely. We had such a dark house before here."

"Our house in London faced north."

Caroline was desperate to ask a thousand questions of the mysterious lady, but manners held her back. Instead, she asked casually, "Would you like a drink? I could fetch you a glass of barley water if you like."

"I suppose it's a little early for a gin and tonic. Yes, a glass of barley water would be very nice, thank you."

She still did not move. Caroline put her own glass on the table and went up to her apartment. When she returned with the second glass, Mrs Bassett still had not moved an inch. Caroline marvelled at her composure; Caroline had often been told off for fidgeting when she was younger and even now preferred to have something to occupy her hands.

"Here you are. No ice I'm afraid. Father says we should consider getting an ice box but there doesn't seem to be much room for one."

"Your father is a sensible man," Mrs Basset said, with just a hint of warmth in her voice that Caroline wasn't entirely sure about.

"I hear your gramophone sometimes. Is it Mussorgsky?"

Slowly Mrs Bassett sat more upright and removed her sunglasses, "Clever girl. So, you know your composers?"

"I like his *Pictures at an Exhibition*. I like the way you can see the art through his music."

"And do you enjoy any other Russian composers? Borodin for example, or Rimsky-Korsakov?" She was looking at Caroline keenly now.

"Yes, yes, I do. There is much passion in the Russians' works, don't you think?"

Caroline was excited and a little surprised to meet another woman who enjoyed Russian classical works. They had always been frowned upon when Caroline was at school, and with news of the Bolshevik uprising any sympathy for their allyship against the Germans quickly melted away. England's musical tastes were now focused on the Americas, and on the home grown patriotic talent of Elgar, Holst and Vaughan Williams.

"There is much passion in Russia," Mrs Bassett sipped her drink.

"Mrs Bassett, do you mind my asking, have you ever been to Russia?" Caroline couldn't help herself.

A slow smile spread across the older woman's face. It showed the creases at her eyes and her slightly yellow but perfectly straight teeth.

"I am Russian. I was born in Smolensk, which is some two hundred miles west of Moscow. My father was a faceteer, he cut diamonds. He was very good, good enough to give me an education away from Russia. You detect no accent to my voice; I can see that."

Caroline blushed a little, aware that she had been trying to.

"I'm sorry. Do go on."

"There is little more to tell. I met my husband, Marius, in Amsterdam when I was 18 and we were married within weeks. We adored each other," she paused; Caroline waited.

"He was in the business, trading diamonds and other jewels. He made enemies. We moved around a lot, spent some time in South America – my dear, this is not hot compared to Havana. It was a glamourous, dangerous life. I loved it and I hated it in equal measure."

Caroline realised she was sitting on the edge of her seat. She tried to relax.

"Five months ago, five months, two weeks, three days to be exact, Marius was killed in a motorcar… accident. Everyone insists it *was* an accident."

"I'm so sorry," Caroline wanted to take the other woman's hand, so raw did the emotion feel in the air, but again she held back.

Mrs Bassett took out a cigarette and lit it with a dainty lighter. She did not offer Caroline one. She drew in deeply, then resumed, "You are wondering about my name."

"No, I, well, Bassett isn't Russian, is it, your husband, Marius, wasn't Russian?"

"His father was a Cornish mine engineer, his mother from Holland originally, although they met in Pretoria which is where Marius was born. Diamonds run, ran in both our blood."

"South Africa," whispered Caroline. The image of a world map filled her mind, with lines criss-crossing it from location to location in Mrs Bassett's history.

"An equally hot place. Filthy. You would not enjoy it there."

"My friend Midge is going to Tanganyika sometime this year, with a Mission."

"Yes, there are many missionary compounds in Africa. But you are not missionary-bound."

Caroline recognised it was a statement rather than a question.

"No. I don't really know what I will do with my life at the moment. Father says I don't have to decide just yet, but I rather fear if I don't, then I shall fall into a marriage and miss out on so much."

"Then you must find a husband who will not let you miss a single thing. Someone who shares your passions, your excitement. You do not look to me like a quiet housewife any more than a missionary."

Caroline absorbed Mrs Bassett's words.

The older woman continued, "Do not misunderstand me, you do not need money to share passions. Tell me, what do you enjoy?"

"Art. I love to paint. And the cinema, films. The sea. I enjoy visiting new places, though I have not yet been abroad. I'd like to."

"Then you will not be happy with anyone who does not enjoy those things also."

"Mrs Bassett, how did you come to live here in Cheltenham? Miss Kettle came here with her sister several times some years ago, but forgive me for saying, it does not seem the kind of place a woman like you would be happy in."

"It was your father's idea."

"What?!"

Mrs Bassett smiled to herself and drank some more from her glass.

"A friend of a friend recommended him as a trustworthy man. I needed to get out of London. I needed somewhere safe, where I was not known, and I could arrange my affairs. I contacted your father at his offices, and he suggested I take one of these apartments. I do not know how long I will stay."

Caroline was astounded. She had no idea that her father had any connections in London, and certainly not with international diamond traders! She thought back to the drinks party in Rickard's apartment and now understood how her father had withdrawn slightly from the group when Mrs Bassett arrived.

They stayed on the garden bench together for the rest of the afternoon. Mrs Bassett answered all of Caroline's questions, which flowed freely now that she felt the older woman was a family friend. They talked of different countries, customs, exotic foods and golden architecture. Mrs Bassett finally looked at her watch and declared it was a quarter to five. Caroline picked up the glasses from the table.

"Father will be home any moment. I should see what Annie has left us for dinner. It has been wonderful to talk to you this afternoon. Thank you."

"Thank you for the drink. Why not come to my apartment this evening and we can listen to Mussorgsky together for a while. Let's say eight o'clock."

"I should like that very much! Thank you, Mrs Bassett."

"Please, my name is Galina. Galina Ivanova Voronov."

As they entered the apartment block through the rear glass door, Ferris appeared at his door.

"Miss Caroline. There have been a couple of deliveries for you, I can help carry them upstairs if you'd like."

Galina went on to her apartment. Caroline put her head round the door to Ferris' little office. There in an enamelled bucket stood two large bouquets of flowers.

"Not your birthday, is it?"

"No Ferris, it is not. Is there a card?"

"Two, there on the desk."

Ferris carried the flowers in the bucket and Caroline carried the two small envelopes up to the apartment. When Ferris had left, with the bucket standing in the middle of the kitchen floor, Caroline opened the first envelope.

Dear Caroline

I have taken the position of House Doctor at Cheltenham Hospital and will be staying with Dr Riley until I find alternative rooms. Can I take you to dinner one evening soon? Let me know the day and I will arrange the rest.

Yours fondly
Luke

Caroline sighed. They were lovely flowers, but she wished Luke wouldn't be quite so extravagant. She opened the second envelope.

Dear Caroline
   I very much enjoyed our evening yesterday. Please accept these as a token of my affection and I very much hope we can see each other again soon.
   Yours Vaughan.

"Oh lummy, this is too much!" Caroline put the note back into the envelope as she heard her father's key in the door.

George was amused. "Are we to rival Curzon's now?"

"It's all a bit extravagant, isn't it? Did you ever send mother flowers like this?"

"I took her small posies once or twice, but never sent them. Vaughan Rickard is rather enamoured with your company it would appear."

"I don't know what to do Father, I tried to be just friendly and not encourage him, or Luke for that matter, too much. They are both jolly nice young men, I'm just not sure either are for me."

"Once upon a time, fathers would intervene in situations such as these," he watched his daughter as she bit her lip pensively.

"No. I shall sort it all out myself somehow. I'll have to do something – we only have one more empty vase!"

Caroline stayed for an hour with Galina that evening. The inside of her apartment was very sparsely furnished, Galina explained, because much of her London furniture was in storage for now. She had agreed to relocate to Cheltenham in order to clear her head, to mourn in her own way, and to decide the next chapter in her life. She did not know how long any of those things would take, but she had brought only the bare minimum of essential items with her. The gramophone was of course, an essential item. Caroline declined the gin and tonic offered to her but accepted a small brandy. The two women sat in a companionable silence as the notes of music arched and dipped around the sitting room. Galina swayed her head gently, eyes closed.

The next day the laundry van was the main focus of attention at Norwood Court. All of the apartments used the service and were afforded a discount negotiated by the owner of the apartments as an incentive to prospective tenants and purchasers alike. Caroline and Annie stripped the beds and rounded up the other items to be cleaned and took them down to the ground floor where Ferris had begun his logistical execution of the operation. Each apartment had a labelled calico bag to hold the soiled items, and they would be returned the following day, ironed and neatly folded into clean bags. Special arrangements could be made for suits and dresses of delicate material.

Ferris had a telephone in his room, though he was nervous about using it. He had no telephone at home, but he could see how his residents (as he liked to call them) would find it a great convenience. Knowing this, Caroline asked Ferris if he would make a telephone call to Dr Riley at the hospital and pass the message that she would meet Luke for dinner at seven that evening at the Queens Hotel restaurant. No point delaying the inevitable, she had told her father that morning. Ferris made the call, pleased to be trusted with it.

Caroline was getting ready to leave that evening when there was a knock on their apartment door. She opened it to find Bob just removing his hat. He looked her up and down and could see she was dressed to go out.

"I thought I would come by and ask if you would like to meet me in Montpelier Gardens on Saturday and we could hire chairs and listen to the band."

"That would be nice, yes I would like that, thank you."

George called from the sitting room, "Is that Bob?"

"Won't you come in? I'm on my way out to dinner with... a friend this evening but do say hello to Father."

He noticed the hesitation. He had wanted to speak to George as well, so he stepped inside the apartment, "Don't let me hold you up."

"Thank you, I really was just about to leave. Go on through and I will see you on Saturday, shall we say two o'clock?"

When Caroline had gone, Bob mustered all of the courage he could and asked George for Caroline's hand in marriage. George was quiet for a moment, understanding the gravity of the situation for both of the young people involved.

"Does Caroline know that you are asking me this?"

"No. I wanted to speak to you first. If you were to say no, then I'd not press it with her."

"You should be aware; Caroline is enjoying a certain amount of freedom at the moment that a little prudent investment of mine is enabling for her. She is going places, meeting new people. I think it is safe to say, Bob, that you are not the only admirer that she has."

"I'm aware of that Mr Munhead," He had seen the flowers on the table under the window and did not think Caroline would have bought them for herself.

"And yet, I have no objection to you as a potential son in law. You have a steady job, your family is respected in the community, and you have good prospects. The answer however must come from Caroline herself. I shall not seek to sway her in your favour or against you. There is one thing I will do, and I am glad that you are here as it makes it easier for me to arrange. If you would call into the office next week at your convenience, I believe we would be able to arrange a mortgage now if you have a property in mind. No greater sum than we had discussed previously, but with the strike ended and the markets a little less volatile I would be happy to advance you the amount we had spoken of. And that might be to your advantage."

Bob was shocked. He hadn't expected to hear this so soon after George had advised against a mortgage for the property in Mill Street.

"I'll need to see if there are any other properties for sale in Prestbury, I could do that Saturday before I meet Caroline. Thank you, Mr Munhead, thank you very much sir!"

Caroline did not enjoy her dinner. The hotel restaurant was stuffy with so many diners and the sun having poured through the windows all day. Luke was, as Caroline had been previously, twenty minutes late. He explained he had been showing a young nurse how to properly bandage a wound, which Caroline suspected was not the entire truth but let it go. The soup was too salty for her taste, the main course was not hot, and the dessert of rhubarb crumble had lumpy custard.

She could have tolerated the poor meal if the company had been more to her taste. However, she was becoming annoyed with Luke's assumptions of what she might eat or drink, as well as the flowers and the summons to dine with him as if she had nothing else planned. It didn't matter that she hadn't. Luke chattered on about the position in General Practice that he had declined in favour of the hospital, and how he had already begun to make improvements to the way his two wards were run. He had crossed swords with the matron and felt he had the measure of the woman now. He also said he would be dispensing with the legion of volunteers who seemed to congregate at the hospital daily. At this Caroline mentioned that she knew some to be trained nurses. Luke dismissed this, saying if they had been out of nursing for more than two or three years then they would not be up to date with the latest medical procedures and could do more harm than good.

For all Caroline's lack of input to the conversation, Luke enjoyed the evening immensely. He was so pleased with his new position, and felt he was about to make his mark on the profession. Dr Riley had given him almost a free hand to run the wards as he saw fit, and the other young Houseman, a doctor called Potter who had graduated the year before Luke, was keen to find digs that they might share. He sat back in his chair after finishing his crumble and lumpy custard, drained his wine glass and sighed contentedly.

"I believe that was an excellent meal. Did you enjoy yours too?"

"It was very nice, thank you," Caroline did not want to offend but had decided she must be blunt with Luke. "There must be several young nurses at the hospital, I'm sure they would love to show you more of Cheltenham."

"A lot of silly girls, yes. But easy on the eye. Potter has a fancy on the night shift."

"Luke, you do understand don't you that I am not anyone's fancy as you put it, and have no desire to be at the moment?"

"You told me that last time we met. I won't deny that I am somewhat disappointed that you still feel that way. Were it not for you, I wouldn't have had this opportunity to advance my career so soon after graduating. I will be eternally grateful to you for that."

"All I did was pass on Dr Riley's name; you have done all the rest. I accept your thanks but really Luke, I think it would be better if you made lots more friends here in Cheltenham. I might not be able to drop everything at a moment's notice and come to dinner with you every time you ask."

"Ahh, yes, perhaps I was a bit forthright there. But you're here so no harm done, eh?"

"And no more flowers, please. They are beautiful and I do like them, but they are so expensive and only last a few days."

"Would you prefer chocolates?"

Caroline thought to herself, how hard can this be to make him understand? "No, I would prefer no gifts, Luke. We are friends, there is no need for gifts."

"Oh. I see. Do you object to my paying the bill for our meal, or are you striking out for modern feminism and going to insist we go Dutch there too?" he asked with a smile, but Caroline could hear she had hurt him.

"I am happy to pay for my own meal, but if you would prefer to pay for both of us then please do. I'm sorry if I am being a feminist in your opinion to ask for no more gifts, but really Luke it is not necessary."

"Gifts are rarely necessary, that's rather the point. I do so enjoy talking to you Caroline, it's so refreshing after the case notes and illnesses one experiences every day. I think we would make a fine couple one day when you've got all of this out of your system."

When they left the hotel, Luke saw Caroline on to her tram and they parted amicably. As she travelled homewards, Caroline considered the word 'feminist' that Luke had used to describe her. Was she? It had not occurred to her before but thinking about it as she gazed out of the window perhaps that was what she had been trying to achieve without really knowing it had a name. At twenty-two, she still had three years before she would be able to vote. It wasn't about that kind of emancipation, but to be able to live her own life without the unwanted influence and expectations of men all the time, yes, that was what she wanted for herself.

On Friday evening, Vaughan Rickard came to the apartment to play chess again with George. To be polite, Caroline stayed in the sitting room with the men for a while, as she had done before, reading her book by the window. She had thanked Vaughan for the flowers and made sure his second bouquet was in the sitting room with Luke's in the dining area and so less likely for him to see. This time she was conscious of Vaughan looking at her. He had taken the chair directly opposite and had an unobstructed view of her profile. Yet he was concentrating on the game and did not speak to Caroline once she had picked up her book.

At nine o'clock, Caroline asked if the men would like a drink. They both accepted a brandy and Caroline poured three into their new goblet-shaped glasses with golden rims. As she handed Vaughan his glass their fingers briefly touched, and he looked up into her eyes, smiling. Caroline went back to her book. She felt uncomfortable, exposed, with Vaughan so close and in her home. He had every right to be there, invited by her father, yet she felt constrained again by etiquette, unable to excused herself too early for fear of seeming rude. She gulped her brandy in frustration and then wished she hadn't as it burned her throat and made her cough.

"Are you alright Caroline?" Vaughan made to stand up.

Caroline waved him away, "Just went down the wrong way. I'm fine."

Her eyes were watering, but Vaughan sat down again, frowning with concern. She stayed another half hour before theatrically yawning and stretching, and then excused herself.

Left alone, Vaughan broached the subject that had been on his mind all evening.

"George, this may sound incredibly presumptuous of me, but I do believe that Caroline would be an excellent wife. For me. One day."

George was again playing the white set of pieces, and he moved his knight towards Vaughan's king.

"She would of course make an excellent wife, Vaughan. I'm sure you would not expect me to say anything less."

Vaughan countered with his own knight, "I should be able to offer her a comfortable life. We need not stay in these apartments if she wished to move closer to town. And though I say so myself, I am in a line of business that does not fall prey to whims of the stock market. People will always need spectacles."

"Indeed, they will," he took Vaughan's advancing knight with his queen, "sorry old chap, you rather left that one open. I'm not entirely sure that Caroline is seeking a comfortable life at the moment."

"I'm not used to going out every night, but I can certainly make the effort to become more sociable. I quite enjoyed our little drinks party; I could host another. The cinema of course is Caroline's passion, and we could go weekly if she wanted. And perhaps to a performance at the theatre or the Town Hall. Cheltenham has a varied range of entertainments."

George waited while Vaughan made the next move, taking a pawn with another pawn. That again left him wide open and George was in two minds whether to mercilessly check mate which could be achieved in two moves or play a longer game. He sipped his brandy.

"Vaughan, are you asking for my daughter's hand in marriage?"

Vaughan blinked, nervously, "Yes sir, I believe I am."

"And have you spoken to Caroline about this?"

"No. But I believe I can win her round."

"It must be Caroline's decision. I will not attempt to sway her one way or another. But I would have no objection to having you as a son in law."

"Thank you, sir, that is most kind," he moved his king.

George moved a white castle.

"Check mate."

Caroline stood opposite the Rotunda at one end of Montpellier Gardens and waited for Bob. She had been to a new hair salon on the Bath Road that morning for a trim and set and had decided not to wear a hat despite the sun being in a cloudless sky. She wished she could take her stockings off and walk barefoot on the grass, perhaps even bathe her feet in the fountain to cool off a little. It was not something that a respectable young woman did in Cheltenham Spa. She was just pondering whether she could convince Lottie to go swimming with her one Saturday when Bob appeared, sweating somewhat under his hat and jacket.

"Hello, what have you got there?" she asked.

"Papers for houses for sale," they walked towards the bandstand, "would you like to sit in the shade?"

"Yes please, it is very warm again today."

Bob paid for two deckchairs. They sat down next to each other.

"Actually, do you mind if I take my jacket off? My shirt is clean."

"Of course I don't mind. I thought you must be awfully hot, have you walked up from town?"

"Yes, I wanted to call in to the agent on Oriel Street on the way and there seems no point getting a tram that little way up the hill afterwards."

"You are looking to purchase a house again? Has my father recommended it?"

"He did. He said if I could find a similar house to the one on Mill Street, he'll be willing to advance the mortgage."

"Oh Bob, that's exciting! A home of your own at last!"

"Well, yes, until I have a wife to join me."

They were both silent for a moment. Bob hadn't expected the conversation to get to that point quite so quickly, he wasn't ready.

"I'll be getting some chickens too," he finally announced.

Caroline smiled at him. She was very fond of Bob, but she was starting to feel that Mrs Bassett was right in her assertion that Caroline would need a husband who was passionate about all the things she was. Could she in turn be passionate about football and chickens?

"What breed of chickens will you get? Tell me all about them before the band begins."

They listened to the brass band until four o'clock. Bob bought two little pots of ice cream from the garden café, which had melted almost more quickly than they could eat them. They had talked quietly, so as not to disturb the other deckchair renters, of chickens, football, Lottie and Eric's wedding and how upset Bob's mother was with them for not going to church. As the band began to pack up their instruments and people vacated their chairs, Caroline asked to see the house papers. She had never looked at them before and was curious to see how they described the properties.

They looked at each one together, pointing out the pros and cons of each. Some they recognised as being in the town, and Bob dismissed them quickly as he was really only interested in purchasing a house in Prestbury. He was only going to do this once, and he wanted a home he could be proud of with a little work. There was one, an end of terrace house with three bedrooms on Blacksmith Lane in Prestbury. Bob passed the paper to Caroline without commenting, not wanting to influence her opinion of it.

"An end of terrace aspect with gardens to the side and rear," she read aloud, "a sound roof and indoor water supply to the kitchen."

"That's good. Better than mother and father have."

Caroline remembered the pump in the rear yard at Bob's parent's house, "Three conveniently sized bedrooms. Convenient for what, would you say?"

"A family I expect. What do you think of the price?"

"Compared to the others, it seems reasonable. That one with two bedrooms on the High Street was the same, wasn't it?"

"Near to the station, that's why. I think I might ask to see this one."

"It's not an auction, is it?"

"No, straight sale. Would you like to come with me?"

Caroline looked from the paper to Bob's face. She suddenly felt she could read his mind; she knew he wanted the house for both of them.

"I think," she said slowly, "that you should probably see it by yourself, or perhaps take your father or Eric along with you. I'm sure there will be things to measure, and I would only be in the way. And I might like it more than you, and then I wouldn't be able to forgive myself if you bought it because I said so." Her words picked up speed as they came to her lips.

Bob held her gaze. He wanted so much to ask her to marry him then and there, but that was not what he had decided to do after George had agreed the mortgage in principle. He was going to find a house, buy it, make it a place that Caroline would want to be, and then ask her. If she were still unattached by then. That was his decided course, and he would stick to it.

"If I like it, if as you say Father thinks it is sound in structure, would you see it afterwards?"

Caroline breathed out. Not a sigh; she hadn't realised she had been holding her breath.

"Yes. If you like it and you buy it, I will come and see it then."

Caroline and George were eating a simple Saturday evening dinner of chicken and leek pie, boiled potatoes and green beans. Caroline was particularly proud of the pie crust and had stood over it for a few moments before cutting spoiled its even golden colour. It was the first she had not burned.

"Bob thinks he might have found a house to purchase."

"In Prestbury?"

"Yes, Blacksmith Lane. I don't know it, do you?"

"I believe there are a few houses there in terraces, groups of four or five."

"This is an end of terrace."

"I shall expect to see him next week then."

"He's going to arrange to see it with his father."

"And what do you think of it? Will you be viewing it as well?"

"No," Caroline put down her knife and fork, "Father, I feel rather like a mouse in a farmyard with several cats. Each cat thinks they can catch me. I do not want to be caught."

George also rested his knife and fork on his plate.

"Caroline, I should tell you that two young men have asked me for your hand in marriage very recently. Now, don't get upset my dear, it is what young men should do, you know that."

"Who were they?"

"I am not going to tell you that. But I will tell you what I told them both; it must be your decision. I have no objection to either of them, and I suspect there may be more young men asking the same question before this year is out. But I am not going to choose for you Caroline. If you want advice, I will happily offer you counsel, but you must be the one to decide."

"Thank you. I think I will call on Mrs Bassett this evening. She is a very calming person, and perhaps she will let me listen to her gramophone again."

"She is a very colourful person. I did not tell you of our acquaintance because she asked for the utmost discretion. I am glad that you and she have found something in common."

Galina welcomed Caroline in and asked her to select a record for the gramophone while she poured them each a drink. Caroline chose Rimsky-Korsakov's Third Symphony, which turned out to be a rather scratchy recording by an Austrian orchestra. Caroline asked if she could look at the newspaper that was on the coffee table while the music played. She was leafing through the advertisements when she saw one that caught her attention.

ARTISTS' RESIDENTIAL SCHOOL
We are pleased to announce that vacancies
exist for weekly artist tuition, with full board, for
all weeks in August. Linen and food provided.
Artist materials must be purchased from the
establishment unless bringing your own.
Enjoy the Cornish sea air and views!
For terms, please enquire St Ives 48.

"Galina, do you paint?"

"No, I am not artistic in that way. I sing a little, that is all."

"See here, there is an artists' retreat. I think it might be just what I need, to get away from here for a few days and forget all these men."

"Why don't you telephone and find out the details? Here, let me get you a pencil to write down the number."

Ferris was only required to be in his office for two hours on a Sunday, and by the time Caroline had returned from St Mark's he had already locked his door and gone home. She fidgeted through lunch, then called on Miss Kettle for an hour to distract herself. Agatha had been back to the library for more books on the history of Cheltenham and its surroundings and was hoping to join the Women's Institute after seeing a poster in the library entrance. She thought she might be able to persuade Rebecca Monk to accompany her, now that her volunteering at the hospital seemed to be no longer required. Caroline said nothing about Luke's 'new broom' approach but was sad for Mrs Monk.

A shower of rain kept them inside rather than sitting in the garden. Agatha mentioned she had seen Caroline with Mrs Bassett on the bench. Caroline was again conscious of Galina's summary that all older women gossiped. She said they had discovered they shared an enjoyment of Russian composers and nothing more.

"And how was your evening with Mr Rickard?"

Caroline laughed, "You miss nothing! It was very pleasant, thank you."

Agatha blushed sightly, "One can't help but see who comes and goes, having my sitting room window facing out onto the drive. He seems a very pleasant young man."

"Is thirty young still?"

"It is when you are seventy-five, my dear."

After George had left for work the next morning, and Caroline had washed the breakfast things, dusted, read the morning newspaper and received a letter from James with details of his expected arrival back in England, Caroline finally took her scrap of paper down to Ferris and asked to use his telephone.

"I need to make two telephone calls, if that's all right? Could you show me how it works please?"

"Of course, miss. You lift this piece here and hold it to your ear, then you press this bit down three or four times to get the operator. Then you speak into this wide bit here. When you're done, put the earpiece back in its cradle."

"And I tell the operator the number I want to reach?"

"Yes, that's right, exchange and number. Let's see, what have you got... ahh yes, you'll say St Ives 48 please and you'll hear a click when they put you through."

"Thank you, Ferris. It's rather exciting, I've never used a telephone before."

"No miss," he smiled and went out to inspect the garages to give her some privacy.

After making arrangements to start a week's art course on Monday the ninth of August, travelling down the day before and being met at the station in St Ives, Caroline placed another call.

"Hello? Helen? It's Caroline here! How are you both?"

"Caro, darling, we are in transit. You have literally only just caught us, we are leaving this awful place this very afternoon, hopefully never to return, and taking up residence in Minehead."

"Where is that exactly?"

"Just over the Devon border into Somerset, on the coast. Tommy insisted on staying by the sea and I couldn't bear to heap more upset on his fragile shoulders, so Minehead it is. We have taken a house overlooking a park, not too far from the seafront. Goodness knows what the staff will be like, but all that matters at the moment is to get Tommy settled in. He has been beside himself darling, completely bereft. It is heart-breaking to watch."

"Look, I really can't talk for long, but will you write to me with your new address as quickly as you can please? I am going to Cornwall in a few days, and I'd love to see you on my way home if you can bare to have me?"

"Of course, Caro, Tommy would love that too! I shall write as soon as we hang up and post it as we leave this nasty little place. Arrive whenever you can, we're only a short walk from the railway station and I doubt we will be socialising straight away."

Caroline felt happy as she replaced the receiver in its cradle. Happier than she had in weeks, she realised. She was going back to the sea.

9

THE ARTISTS

Lottie and Eric's wedding was a simple affair. The bride wore a cream dress with a cream lace overlay and no veil, much to her mother's frustration. She had a very small posy of flowers, and her father, brothers (Charles had been able to travel up from Bristol for the day), father-in-law and new husband all wore their best suits with carnation buttonholes. Caroline was invited to the ceremony, and she sat in the front row of chairs between Bob and Betty Chandler. The vows were exchanged in just a few minutes, and then the party decamped to the upstairs rooms of the Rising Sun where a buffet lunch had been laid out and a couple of barrels of beer tapped.

Bob was quieter than usual. As Lottie prepared to throw her posy over her shoulder to the waiting group of young women and girls, he asked Caroline, "Are you going to try and catch it?"

"Oh no, I think that girl with the blue dress is determined it should be hers."

"She's too young to be the next married."

"And I have no desire to be," she changed the subject, "Did your father approve of the house?"

"He says the roof needs a few slates at the back around the chimney and the back bedroom window needs replacing, but nothing we can't do between us. I've made an offer on it, a bit less than the asking price, and I should hear next week if it's been accepted."

"You must be very excited."

"Nervous more than anything. But I suppose if they don't accept the offer, I can go up to the asking price. Your father has been very good about that."

"He wouldn't have approved you if he thought you would be a risk."

"Well, I am glad he doesn't think I am a risk."

They both knew he wasn't only referring to the mortgage.

Bob had offered to help Caroline take her luggage to the railway station the next morning, and she accepted with only a small protest that she could manage it herself. She had considered asking Ferris to arrange a taxi, but with Bob she could rely on the trams to get to St James station in town. Bob saw her onto the platform and waited with her for the train to arrive. It would be a long journey with three changes, and she had packed herself some sandwiches and an apple for lunch so that she would only need to purchase something to drink along the way.

"Father says St Ives is almost at the end of the land down in Cornwall. It seems an odd place to run a painting school."

"The light in Cornwall is famous. There is quite the artist community there, Galina was telling me."

Bob nodded to one of the porters who wished them a good morning, "And it's a husband and wife that run the school?"

"Yes, Mr and Mrs Bohenna. He teaches painting and she teaches ceramics and fabric arts. I shall be able to try lots of different materials while I'm there. Perhaps I will make a pot for your new house."

"I'd like that. And you've got enough money on you in case something happens?"

"Oh Bob, yes, but don't worry so. I'm only going to Cornwall for a week, not Siberia. Nothing will go wrong. I shall send you a postcard to let you know I have arrived safely. Would you like that?"

Bob blushed a little, "It seems a long way, that's all. You're used to travelling, I know. Here's your train now, I'll put your case on for you and then perhaps I'll see you when you come home?"

"Come for tea next Sunday and I will tell you all about it."

The change at Bristol Temple Meads was without incident. Caroline felt a pang of sorrow for Tommy as she passed through Exeter St David's station and hoped he would be able to put Christopher behind him and start again with Helen in Minehead. The next change of trains was at Plymouth, but as they approached Ivybridge the train slowed to a stop. After a couple of minutes, the guard opened the compartment door and informed Caroline and her fellow travellers that there were cows on the track, and they would be delayed for a short while until the farmer had collected them. Caroline was sharing the second-class carriage with a man in a well-tailored suit with a bowler hat and a moustache, and an elderly couple, all bound for Plymouth. The moustached gentleman huffed and sighed at the delay and kept looking at his pocket watch.

The train pulled into Plymouth twenty-five minutes late: Caroline missed the connection she had hoped to catch by five minutes. She would have to wait an hour for the next train and made herself comfortable in the small waiting room where tea and cakes were available to purchase through a small hatch. The station was quiet, being a Sunday lunchtime. Freight trains rumbled through on the outer tracks carrying china clay, fish and potatoes towards the rest of the country. Caroline lost herself in her new book, a murder mystery called *Whose Body?* by an author she had only just discovered, Dorothy L. Sayers.

The next train which Caroline hoped to catch was also delayed by five minutes. Leaving Plymouth almost an hour and a half behind schedule, Caroline realised she was now the furthest west she had ever been from home. Not the furthest overall, that had been Blackpool the previous year with Helen and Tommy, but the furthest west and soon also to be the furthest south. She hoped that her lateness wouldn't inconvenience her hosts. The train crossed the River Tamar on Brunel's impressive bridge and Caroline glanced out of the carriage window tentatively at the water below. The tracks seemed very close to the side of the bridge and Caroline decided to return to her seat and admire the small boats on the estuary side instead.

Back on land, after a stop in Saltash where Caroline was bid a welcome to Cornwall by the guard, the train rattled and chuffed through the countryside. Caroline felt that rolling was by far the best word to describe the landscape she could see when the train emerged occasionally from tunnels and rhododendron-covered deep cuttings. Fields of hay, wheat, corn and barley waved gently in the breeze. It was warm in the carriage and Caroline dozed between stops. Her book was safely stowed in her carpet bag so that it wouldn't drop to the carriage floor.

The final change came at St Erth, a very small station and platform, where Caroline had to make her way to the front carriages on the train to be able to alight, the guard following behind with her case. There was no waiting room here, only a small ticket office with two wooden chairs on either side of a small fireplace. Caroline chose to wait outside on a bench against the ticket office wall. When the train had departed, all was quiet. Not silent, she realised; grasshoppers chirruped, and bees and other flying insects inhabited the parched but pretty garden of the Station Master's house next to the railway tracks. Sparrows chattered in the hedge. In the distance, her first clue that she was nearing the sea, a seagull called its own welcome to Cornwall.

The St Ives train ran on a branch line, up and down from the mainline to the coast every hour between 6am and 9pm daily. The engine was painted in green livery, and its three carriages were all bright red with brass fittings. This was by far the shortest of the legs of Caroline's journey, only fifteen minutes from one end of the branch line to the other. She passed the saltings at Lelant, that day empty of workers but usually a mass of men and boys harvesting salt to preserve local fish. Then suddenly Carbis Bay appeared before her as the train approached St Ives. The almost white sand curved around the Atlantic Sea like an ermine collar on a turquoise silk coat. It was beautiful.

As instructed, Caroline had no difficulty in finding the little black car that served as a taxi from the station to the surrounding lanes of St Ives. She could hardly understand what the driver said to her, his accent was so soft and rolling just like the hills, but she smiled at him and that seemed to be enough to get the final stage of her journey underway. They drove through the town and up the hill beyond and pulled in at a large white house with green paintwork that stood a little way back from the road. As Caroline got out of the car, a woman with long wavy red hair burst from the front door of the house.

"Edgar dear, put the luggage in the hall please, we'll take it from there. You must be Miss Munhead? Phyllis Bohenna, Phyl to everyone."

She held out her hand with a broad smile and Caroline shook it.

"You must be exhausted and starving too I expect. Come on through and meet the others, we've six this week, a rum bunch but I'm sure you'll all rub down together in a day or two."

Phyl led the way into the house, through the main hallway which led off to rooms on either side and had a staircase set back from the main door. They went around the stairs and through a small passage which then opened into a large sitting room.

"Ed darling, Caroline Munhead has arrived."

"Welcome! My wife will show you around and we'll be sitting down to dinner in an hour or so. Can I get you anything before then? Tea? Some cheese and biscuits?" Edward Bohenna had risen from the comfortable armchair and came around the sofa to shake Caroline's hand.

"If it's no trouble, I would very much like a cup of tea and perhaps some cheese to keep me going until dinner."

"No trouble at all! Emily will bring a tray up to your room drek'ly as we say here," he smiled warmly and went off towards the kitchen.

Caroline and Phyl continued through another door to a second staircase at the side of the house which led to the five small guest bedrooms and a bathroom shared by them all.

"I've put you in the smallest, I hope you don't mind being on your own?"

"Not at all," Caroline was somewhat relieved to have the luxury of her own bedroom; she had expected to have to share as she had at Knapp House with the rest of the film crew.

She was shown into a pretty room with pale yellow flowers on the wallpaper and a window that was open and looked out onto the fields to the side of the house. It reminded her of the bedroom in Tavistock she had stayed in at Helen's father's house.

"Now then, we'll go through the week's schedule when we're all together for dinner this evening, but we take all our meals in the dining room which is on the left as you come in through the front door. Dinner is at seven, breakfast is from six until eight. If the weather holds, we shall want to be out as early as possible to capture the light. Lunches are packed, Emily is such a treasure, if there is anything in particular you don't eat, please let her know. Ah here she is!"

Emily, a girl of sixteen with a rash of freckles and bright blue eyes that sparkled like the sea, brought the tray into the room and placed it on the dressing table.

When Emily had gone, Phyl continued.

"Please don't feel you must stay in this room, you are welcome to use the sitting room where Ed was, the garden room and the garden itself. If you feel like doing a little weeding, I'd be grateful, I never seem to have enough time! We have several cats, you'll get to know them over the week, just shove them off any seat you want to sit on. You're not allergic, are you? No? Good show. We had a man here a few weeks ago, didn't stop sneezing and scratching the whole week, bless him. I should mention it in the advertisements really, but one doesn't want to put people off. Now, is there anything I can get you?"

"No, this is perfectly lovely thank you. I shall come down shortly to meet the others."

"Excellent, they are in the garden, it's such a lovely evening, seems a shame to hide away indoors. Come down when you're ready."

Caroline sat on the bed and sipped her tea. Emily had cut three fingers of cheese and laid them on a plate with a tomato cut in half. The cheese was tangy and had an unusual crunch to it. The tomato felt warm, and Caroline wondered if it had been freshly picked. After her snack, she washed her face and quickly unpacked her case. She had brought her short black dress just in case there was an opportunity that called for something glamourous, and also her bathing suit because she was determined to swim in the sea at some point during the week.

She considered Phyl; she was younger than Caroline had expected, around the same age as Galina, and wore peasant-style clothing that Caroline suspected she had made herself. Her white cotton blouse had hand-embroidered garlands of tiny flowers on the collar and on either side of the button placket, executed in exquisite detail. Her skirt had been red and full, gathered to the waist with a broad fabric belt, tied with the tasselled ends hanging to one side. It was an exotic style, and certainly not clothing Caroline was used to seeing in Cheltenham. It made her think of gypsies.

She found her fellow retreaters intent on improving their artistic ability in the garden as Phyl had said. They occupied a variety of chairs and benches scattered across a flagstone patio area outside of the garden room. On an iron table stood a pitcher of lemonade and several glasses. A ginger cat sprawled on the warm stone beside it, the tip of its tail occasionally twitching as it dreamed. Caroline took an upturned glass and poured herself a drink as the company introduced themselves, prompted by Ed.

"Everyone, this is Miss Caroline Munhead from Chester, no, forgive me, from Cheltenham. She is the final member of our group for this week. Shall we go clockwise and introduce ourselves? Mr and Mrs Fisher?"

A middle-aged man stood up and offered Caroline his hand, "Benjamin Fisher, and my wife Dorothy, or Dora, we're from Tiverton, almost next door." He chuckled at his own quip.

Next were two older sisters, in their fifties. "Ruth Liddell, very pleased to meet you Miss Munhead, and my little sister Agnes."

"Please, call me Caroline, all of you," she placed their accent somewhere around Sheffield.

A young woman stood up and came across the patio, "I'm Sarah, Sarah Hansson. And I'm glad to have someone else my age here!" she beamed at Caroline, who couldn't help but return the smile.

The last member of the group got awkwardly to his feet, and Caroline could see that he did not use his left hand to steady himself. He wore his hair short, but even so it took a moment for Caroline to realise that he had no ear on the left side of his head. She tried not to stare and looked instead directly into his dark eyes before looking away.

Holding out his right hand, he said, "Max Bird."

"Nice to meet you, Max," the words felt thick in her mouth which was suddenly dry. She took a sip of her drink.

Sarah had returned to the bench and patted the space next to her, "Come and sit here Caroline and tell me all about yourself."

Caroline let go of Max's warm hand, but inexplicably felt she was still touching him. His eyes had been deep circles of brown flecked with amber, honey and gold. There were scars on the left of his face, hidden partially by a day's growth of beard. She had wanted to touch them. As she sat with Sarah, she felt Max looking at her, or so she thought. Sarah chattered on about how she had come to expand her embroidery skills having heard of Phyl through her Women's Institute in Winchester.

Over dinner the group learned that they would be spending each morning under Ed's tuition, painting various subjects in a range of media. Each afternoon Phyl would lead them in a craft of their choice, from a list she produced and handed round for them all to see. The list included linocut, embroidery, pottery and small sculpture, ceramic tile design, mosaic, and basketry. She suggested they pick one or two crafts so that their projects could be completed during their stay. At their own cost, their projects and artwork could be packed and sent to their homes at the end of the week, and all materials used would be billed to them within thirty days. These terms had been explained to each of them over the telephone when they had booked their place on the course, but Phyl always felt it best to remind everyone before they got started.

After dinner the sisters and the Fishers returned to their rooms for an early night. Caroline and Sarah chatted for a while on one of the sofas in the sitting room. Caroline found her very easy to talk to, as if they had known each other for years. They had several things in common. Sarah's older brother Graham had also been killed in the Great War, though at the beginning of hostilities rather than at the end like Freddie. Her mother and grandmother had died of the influenza, and her aunt, her father's sister, had moved in with them to look after the remaining family. It was this aunt who had introduced Sarah to the Women's Institute and Sarah had found comfort in the routine of the meetings and the solidarity of the women.

When Phyl returned from the kitchen, Sarah asked her about the embroidery projects she might think would be suitable, and Caroline decided to take a few minutes in the evening air before retiring to bed. She never ceased to be surprised at how tiring travelling could be, even though one did not physically do anything. Outside on the patio as dusk turned to night, Caroline could hear the sea faintly on the breeze. The air was cool, but the heat of the day had roused the scent of the flowers in Phyl's garden, and the perfume of the roses in particular was still strong.

Max was sitting on the same chair he had occupied that afternoon, smoking. The tip of his cigarette glowed in the dark with every draw he made on it. Caroline hesitated for a moment in the doorway; she felt a strong physical attraction to Max, despite his disfigurements, that she had never experienced before. She had read about 'love at first sight' and had occasionally wondered if it really existed but then dismissed the idea as one strictly confined to romance novels. Still, as she looked at Max across the darkening courtyard, she couldn't so easily dismiss how she felt. Taking her courage in hand, Caroline walked to the chair nearest to him and sat down.

"Isn't it quiet," she said.

Max turned his head, "I'm sorry, you'll have to speak up if you're on my left."

"Oh Goodness, I'm sorry. I said it's quiet here. Let me sit on the other side of you." She got out of the chair and almost tripped over Max's left foot in the dark, seeing it just in time. She sat on the chair to his right instead. It was closer to him.

"Can you hear me better now?"

"I can. And yes, it is quiet here. It's what I wanted."

"Oh, would you prefer me to leave you in peace?"

"No."

They sat in silence for a moment. Again, Caroline felt a desire to touch Max's face. She was shocked at herself.

"Thank you for not staring earlier. My appearance is horrific to some people."

"That would have been rude," and I couldn't have stopped myself blushing if I had, she thought. "What craft do you think you'll do with Phyl?"

"I think my choice may be limited. Perhaps the tiles. How about you?"

"I rather like the idea of what Phyl calls free-hand embroidery, but yes perhaps the tiles also. If you are." She hadn't thought about it, just said it as it came to her, "I really came for the painting though."

"Yes. I came because my doctor recommended it. He feels artistic expression will aid my recovery," he stubbed out his cigarette on the flagstones with his right foot.

A light was switched on at a window above them, presumably the bathroom Caroline thought. She could see Max in profile now, his right ear intact, and again she was shocked at her own reaction. Max turned his head slowly to face her. They looked at each other. Neither of them smiled, that would have been too frivolous an action for what they both felt in that moment. Eventually Max spoke, his voice sounding dry.

"You must be tired. We've an early start."

"Yes. I should go to bed."

"Yes. Sleep well."

Max stayed in his chair as Caroline went back into the house. He had thought until that moment that nothing would shock him in life after experiencing the horrors of the trenches and then the brutality of the surgery and hospital wards. Yet here was a young woman who unlike his wife did not seem nauseated by his appearance. And unlike the two prostitutes he had visited over the recent months, she seemed attracted to him without needing any financial inducement. She was, to Max, beautiful. He looked at the stars in the velvet sky above and waited for his heart to beat slower before attempting to get up from the chair and go to his own bed.

After breakfast, the group gathered on the patio which had been set up with easels and paper on boards around the iron table. On the table stood a white ceramic jug filled with flowers from the garden that Phyl had picked. Ed explained that they would be using the same subject that morning but that he would be setting them specific challenges to complete. The first was a 3-minute sketch to get them all loose and warmed up. They could use pencils, chalks or charcoal, but no paint. Caroline chose an easel opposite Max and next to Sarah on one side and Agnes Liddell on the other. All three women were nervous about making the first mark on the paper, as this was not a style they were familiar with at all.

Ed started his time count. Caroline could see the two men's arms moving freely across their easels, and the women were all much more hesitant. She looked at the jug of flowers, then at Max's concentrated face above his easel, then back to the flowers. Ed declared that a minute had already passed, and Caroline was yet to make any mark at all on her paper. She gripped the stick of charcoal and began. She felt the glide of the charcoal across the paper as she drew the outline of the jug. Instinctively she understood that it was the indication of the flowers that was required here and not the detail. Her hand moved quicker, building the layers of petals and foliage, the Hollyhock spike emerging last from behind a pair of roses just as Ed called, "Stop!"

They wiped their hands as Ed told them they would look at each of their efforts in turn and give a critical or emotional response.

"We are all friends here," he said, "so by critical, I of course mean constructively critical. Ben, shall we start with yours? Could you all gather round Ben's work please?"

Ed did eventually allow them to pick up paint brushes. The Liddell sisters were much more comfortable with their watercolour boxes open, and Caroline followed their lead. By lunchtime they had all produced three sketches and a work in their own preferred medium and were chatting together about each other's styles and abilities.

Caroline had been wondering where the afternoon sessions would be held. The house didn't seem to have any appropriate rooms for glazing ceramic tiles or throwing clay pots. What she had not realised was that the garden fell away steeply beyond the bank around the patio area. It was terraced with a path that wound down the hillside and led to a large stone barn. This was Phyl's workshop. It had no windows facing the hill, but on the seaward side large expanses of glass let in the extraordinary light. Beyond the workshop the path continued to a small private beach with white-gold sand and rocks erupting from the ground filled with pools of limpets, crabs and sumptuous red anemones.

The main area of the workshop was an open space with three trestle tables set out with embroidery materials, and small squares of lino with cutting tools. On one side of the tables, long stems of willow were stacked against the wall. On the other, with a door through to the kiln room, were shelves of glaze and tiles, clay wrapped in sacking and two potter's wheels. At the rear of the workshop an area was set aside to store the easels and painting equipment that

Ed used. A white cat with one ginger ear and the bluest eyes Caroline had ever seen sat washing its paw next to a bundle of willow stems.

The company assembled themselves around the activities they had chosen. The Liddell sisters and Dora wanted to make baskets with the willow. Sarah and Caroline sat at the embroidery table. Ben Fisher was keen to try the linocut, and Max dragged a chair to the table nearest the shelves of glaze and tiles. The afternoon passed quickly with Phyl moving from table to table, dispensing advice and praise. The atmosphere was relaxed and cheerful, and no one was in any hurry to race along with their project.

Sarah and Caroline decided to work on embroidery that reflected the landscape of Cornwall. They were encouraged by Phyl to simply stitch on the cotton squares without any drawing or guide, and to vary their stitches to build up an almost three-dimensional representation. The sewing store contained threads of many different fibres, from silk to flax, thread made from bamboo and wool, and some with metallic filaments. It was the only craft, Caroline realised, that had no rules. That was liberating to know, yet she was intrigued by the linocut that Ben was working on and how it would be used to print with. The rule there was to cut away sections of the design that would not transfer ink later.

The older women chatted companionably as they worked with the willow withies. The rule for them was that the willow had to be freshly cut, with the sap still flowing, so that the withies would bend rather than snap when woven. Max's rules were the strictest, because with the wrong glaze mixture, the tiles would not produce the desired colours and patterns. Caroline watched him occasionally and saw how he used his weaker left hand to steady the tile while painting or dragging a pointed tool through the glaze with his right hand. He was working on small bisque tiles, roughly three inches by three inches. They would be fired over-night in the kiln room.

As they walked back to the house for their supper, Caroline asked Sarah if she had brought a bathing costume with her.

"Yes, although I haven't worn it yet. I hope it doesn't stretch too much when I get it wet."

"Shall we go for a swim later? It looked like the tide was coming in."

"Yes, lets! It would be a shame to waste having our own beach so close to the house."

They asked the other ladies if they would like to join them. The Liddell sisters had not brought any bathing things, but Dora had and agreed to go with them. Ben said he would sit on the beach and watch just in case anyone got into difficulties.

"Will you come, Max?" Sarah asked.

"I will, though the path down might take me longer than you."

"I say, Phyl, could we have a small campfire on the beach? Would that be alright?" Sarah called to the teacher.

"Of course. There is driftwood at the top of the beach, help yourselves. If you're going to swim, might I suggest you have only a light supper and then take some cake and biscuits down with you for when you dry off."

"What a wonderful idea! We'd better take something to drink as well."

They left the Liddell sisters to work on crosswords in the sitting room and carried a basket with the food and drink down to the beach with their towels and a blanket. The men were left to start the fire while the women ran into the sea which was completely calm and splashed and swam for half an hour or so. Dora's bathing suit was of an older fashion with knickers down to her knees. Sarah's did indeed stretch, which caused much laughter as she emerged from the water and tried to wring out as much liquid as possible before making her way up to the fire to dry off. Caroline felt a freedom that only came when she was in the water, using her whole body to move, roll, dive and float as she had learned while at school.

They stayed by the fire as the sun sank below the water and left a rose-golden stain across the sky. Caroline deliberately kept Sarah between her and Max, conscious of the company and not wanting to be thought of as shameless or inappropriate. Max noticed, said nothing but quietly watched Caroline as he smoked and drank a bottle of beer. They kicked sand over the fire before it got too dark to see the path back to the house and walked happy and contented to their beds.

And so, the week continued. Caroline grew more experimental with the sketching exercises Ed set the group, much preferring charcoal to the chalks or pencils the others used. On the Wednesday, Phyl was their life model. At breakfast, Ed and Phyl asked the group how they felt about drawing a nude, and after some hesitation on Dora's part, all agreed that they would be willing. They had, of course, all seen a naked woman before. It occurred to Caroline that she had not seen a naked man and she wondered if Sarah had. They decided to swim at lunchtime that day and Caroline asked Sarah as they floated together in the sea.

"Yes, several times."

"Your brother?"

"Once, but also a chap I had a brief affair with last year. Billy was doing some work on the house next door to ours, pointing the brickwork or something like that. He was beautiful, if that's the correct word to use for a man."

Caroline processed this information. She had to ask, "So how did you come to see him naked?"

"We had sex. My aunt would have kittens if she knew. She was out, it was the maid's afternoon off, Billy's gaffer had gone to fetch more supplies. I took him a cold drink and we ended up having sex."

Caroline couldn't make the mental leap between the two actions, "I don't understand."

Sarah had been floating away; she turned on her stomach and swam back to Caroline, then floated on her back again.

"It was all rather quick the first time. We kissed, then we embraced, and when he lifted my skirt, I decided not to stop him. It was exciting and dangerous of course, but I wanted to. It wasn't very comfortable though; I was squashed against the wall of the house. The next time I was alone, I brought him indoors and that was better."

"Weren't you scared you might get pregnant?"

"I didn't think about it the first time. After that, we took precautions."

That word again, Caroline thought, "But your reputation..." she realised it sounded very old fashioned as she said the words.

"Oh Caroline, no one knows except you and my friend Olive, and she is sworn to secrecy. Billy was only around for a few weeks, I shan't ever see him again, and I don't care. I didn't love him or anything like that. It was just an affair."

Caroline was a little in awe of Sarah. To be so self-assured, so uncomplicated, to do as one pleased and hang the consequences. Except there didn't seem to be any consequences here, each party were satisfied with the outcome, or at least it appeared that way. If Sarah were lying then she was extremely convincing, and Caroline decided she was not.

"We should ask Ed to model for us tomorrow," Sarah said as she floated past Caroline again.

"Sarah!"

"What? It would be only fair, as the men have seen his wife, for us to see all of him, don't you think? He is rather handsome."

"Do you think he would?"

"I don't know. I might ask him at dinner."

"Sarah, you are brazen!" They both laughed and began to swim back to the beach.

"Can you imagine the Liddell sisters' reaction if he did?" Caroline was still laughing as she swam.

Their reaction at dinner that evening when Sarah asked Ed as she passed him a bowl of new potatoes was not what Caroline had expected.

"Would you really, Mr Bohenna? One has so little experience of drawing the male physique," Agnes was enthusiastic, and Ruth nodded her head as she finished her mouthful of pork chop.

"I don't mind at all, it's very flattering to be asked, I must say."

Dora was less happy at the suggestion, "I really don't think I could. I'm sorry Mr Bohenna, but I really would prefer not to," she looked worriedly at her husband.

"I certainly won't force you, Dora. You could perhaps draw Ed from behind?"

"But… I should still see…"

"I could sit on a chair, with my legs crossed. Would that help you, Dora?"

"I really don't know," she was blushing profusely and looked as if she might cry.

"See how you feel in the morning," said Ed, smiling at Sarah.

"And you don't mind, Phyl?" Caroline had noticed the woman had not spoken.

"I could hardly object," she kept her eyes on her plate as she answered, and Caroline felt she was being noble rather than enthusiastic.

There was some tension there. It suddenly occurred to Caroline that Ed and Phyl might not have the kind of traditional, happy married union that they had so far presented. Caroline looked at Sarah and Ed again, and back to Phyl who was resolutely not looking at her husband.

In the sitting room that evening, Caroline found herself alone with Max. The sisters had gone for a walk to the beach, Dora and Ben were on the patio, and Sarah had excused herself to her room after dinner. Max sat on a sofa, a tumbler of whiskey in his right hand. Caroline poured a small glass of port, as she'd been told to help herself by Phyl, and sat on Max's right, nudging a thin black cat out of the way, then turned herself to face him.

"How are your tiles coming along?"

"Good, I think. I have the hang of the effect I was trying to produce now. It's rather like icing a cake in some ways. And your embroidery?"

"It's an interesting technique, I would never have thought of it by myself. I prefer the art though. Do you ice many cakes?"

Max smiled, "None. But I have watched others and the technique seems similar."

"Your sketch of Phyl this morning was very good."

"Thank you." He drained his glass, "will you be leaving on Saturday morning?"

"After breakfast, I was hoping to catch the eight-ten train back to St Erth."

"I am leaving Friday evening. I have an appointment on Saturday morning that I don't want to miss."

Caroline felt a sudden, overwhelming sense of disappointment. One of the ginger cats sauntered across the sitting room floor and jumped on to the sofa between them.

Dora had decided to spend the morning painting on the beach rather than looking at any unclothed aspect of Ed. Ben carried an easel down for her and left her with a basket of lemonade and shortbread.

Sarah had been smiling to herself all through breakfast, almost annoyingly so, thought Caroline. As they went up to their rooms to collect their straw hats, Caroline asked if Sarah was looking forward to the morning's session.

"I've had a preview," Sarah replied with a broad smile.

Caroline stopped on the stairs, "What?"

"I've seen it, him, already."

"What do you mean?"

"Last night. He came to my room. It wasn't entirely a surprise; he is such a flirt," she giggled and carried on to her room.

Caroline shook her head. She didn't understand how people behaved, she decided. Phyl had stayed mostly in the kitchen with Emily over breakfast and Caroline wondered if Sarah was the first or just one of a long line of affairs. She felt it was probably the latter.

Caroline found it difficult to put thoughts of Sarah and Ed together out of her mind in order to concentrate on her drawing. As a model, Ed was angular where Phyl had been rounded. Caroline tried to concentrate on the material aspects of his body rather than what he might have done with them, and after an hour she had managed to produce an acceptable likeness. Ed's next pose was a standing full-frontal, a challenge to the men as well as the women it seemed. And why not, thought Caroline; he is in his own home after all. He was confident in his own body, and she respected that even if she still felt a twinge of discomfort.

When they took a break mid-morning, Caroline went to look at Max's easel. To her surprise, along with the two timed sketches of Ed, there was a third drawing that was not of the man at all.

"That's me! I thought you were drawing Ed like the rest of us."

He was standing so close to her, their arms almost touching. He was wearing a shirt with the sleeves rolled up to the elbows and the scars on his left arm stood out white and red on his skin.

"I wanted something nicer to look at."

"Max..." they were interrupted by the others returning and Max reached up to remove the paper from the easel. Caroline went back to her own easel thoughtfully.

As they all rose from the dinner table that evening, Max said quietly to Caroline, "I am going to the beach. Would you come with me?"

They slipped out of the house and followed the winding path past the workshop. On a steep section Max held out his right hand to Caroline and she took it to steady herself as well as him. She did not let go. The tide was in. They walked along the small bank of dune grass so that they were away from the path, should anyone else follow them down. Max eventually said they'd walked far enough, and he shrugged out of his jacket so that Caroline could sit on it, retrieving his cigarettes and lighter first.

They sat in silence for a while, watching the sun sink towards the horizon. The weather all week had been warm and sunny, and Caroline's arms and face were turning from pink to brown after liberal amounts of moisture lotion had been applied on Phyl's advice.

"It's hard to believe it's our last day tomorrow, this week has passed so quickly," Caroline said, still looking at the sea.

"It's been good to get out of the city in this heat."

"Is Bath like Bristol?"

Max lit another cigarette, "Not at all. Bath is regal, sedate, suffocating sometimes. Bristol is industrious, busy, brash. Do you know Bristol?"

"My friend's mother lives there; I have been twice."

"Which is Cheltenham more like?"

"From your description, Bath, certainly."

"And how do you stand it? The suffocation?"

Caroline thought for a moment, "I have been looking elsewhere. Running away I suppose. I ran away to here."

"What were you running from?"

Caroline turned her head to look at Max as he smoked, "Men," she said quietly.

He pushed the end of his cigarette into the sand and looked at her.

"Plural?"

"My father has been asked twice recently for my hand in marriage. Oh, he's been very diplomatic about it all, he knows I do not want to marry anyone just yet, but I felt as if I was being pushed into a corner and I just had to get away for a while."

"But they will still be there when you return."

"I needed to put some space between me and them, to think. Were you running away too?"

"My doctor suggested this to help with my rehabilitation. I don't know if it has. It's not as if my ear will grow back or my arm suddenly be able to hold anything."

"Does it hurt still?"

"Sometimes I think I can feel my ear itch. I reach up to scratch it before I remember it's gone. My arm and leg feel tight where the scars are, and sometimes I get stabbing pains. It's mostly nerve damage."

He lifted his own left hand with his right and then dropped it again into his lap.

"I have very little feeling in my arm but thank God my leg came back enough to walk again."

Caroline turned to face him.

"Lift your arm again."

Max did as she asked, and this time she held her hand out and he let his left hand rest on hers.

"You can't feel my hand at all?"

"In patches. I can feel the warmth of you, but my doctor says it's because I can see my hand. If I can't see it, I feel less sensation."

They were very close. The light was fading but Caroline could still see the amber flecks in Max's eyes and smell the tobacco on his breath. She wanted him to kiss her, not the brief brush of lips against her cheek as other men had done, or on her hand as Luke had once. She wanted to be kissed with purpose. And when Max did kiss her, it was as if her mind went blank. She was no longer thinking, but simply feeling. Max kissed her slowly; she let his left hand fall and reached up to his shoulder. He gently pushed her down to lay on the dune grass, and she held on to his neck as they continued to kiss, his right hand gradually exploring her body.

She had a moment of memory where she was back in Milton Abbot with Harry on top of her, but it passed as quickly as it had arrived. This was different. She wanted this. Max's hand was under her skirt, he was rubbing himself against her thigh, and she instinctively knew how this would end. She was aware enough to pause for a moment.

"Max.... precautions."

He stopped kissing her neck and looked down at her, "In my room."

A distant church bell rang two chimes, and Caroline opened her eyes. She needed the bathroom but didn't want to move. She was laying on her side, Max behind her, his right arm across her hip.

"Are you awake?" he whispered into her hair.

"Yes."

"Your breathing changed."

"I need the toilet. I should go back to my room Max."

He moved his arm and she sat up, swinging her legs over the side of the bed. Her clothes were on the floor, and she hurriedly put on her vest and knickers, gathering the rest of her clothes and picking up her shoes. She turned, bent and kissed Max once more, lingering until she really did need the bathroom. He let her go.

Caroline dropped her clothes just inside her bedroom door and went into the bathroom. Sitting on the toilet, she reflected on the hours before. Max had told her he was married, had asked her once if she was sure she wanted him. In that moment he could have admitted to anything, and it wouldn't have mattered to her. It was not rushed or uncomfortable as Sarah had described. It was not disgusting as Florence had told her. It had been a slow and deliberate exploration by both of them. Caroline put her head in her hands, elbows on her knees and sighed, then yawned. Did she feel different? There was something, but she couldn't put words to it. She went back to her own room and dozed until the sun came up.

At breakfast Caroline felt everyone was watching everyone else. It unnerved her, she felt self-conscious and spilled the milk as she poured some into her glass. Did anyone know she had gone to Max's room last night? She would never see these people again, and she decided she didn't care if they did know.

That morning's painting class was taken on the beach. A picnic lunch was provided, with Emily gallantly using a wheelbarrow to transport the food and drink down from the house. The afternoon was spent sorting through their own work, deciding what was to be kept or discarded, and packing up their craft projects ready for dispatch to their various homes. Caroline was pleased with her embroidery and had made a shallow basket on Thursday afternoon finding she could pick up the technique quickly and easily. Everything she wanted to keep was packed and Edgar was summoned after dinner to take the various parcels and Max down to the station to be sent on their way.

As Max was taking a final cigarette on the patio, Caroline went out to say goodbye. They walked a little way through the garden, so they were not in the line of sight of anyone coming out through the garden room. There were two cats laying on the flagstones in the evening sun and bees lazily bumped from flower to flower in the border. Max finished his cigarette. He stopped and turned to Caroline; the sun was golden on the side of her face.

"I think my doctor was right after all."

"You feel rehabilitated?"

"I feel whole again. Thank you, Caroline, for helping me feel like a man again."

She frowned, "But your wife…"

"For her it is duty. I know that. The vows we made she intends to stick to. You are not bound by duty. You are not bound at all."

"It felt right," she frowned, "we won't see each other again, will we."

"No."

"No. Thank you Max," she kissed his mouth. Then she took his right arm and they walked back to the house.

10

THE ARROW

*S*aturday lunchtime and Minehead was busy with the inhabitants shopping and promenading in the gardens and along the seafront. Children ran with hoops and kites, little girls pushed prams with hairless dolls inside, small boys pushed boats out onto the ornamental lake. Some fed the ducks, others fought off the seagulls. Tommy stood at the bay window of his bedroom and surveyed the newly laid out Blenheim Gardens across the road. It would be colourful and lively in a couple of years once the trees had begun to grow and the flower borders filled out. Now it was more of a skeleton; a mannequin waiting to be clothed and put on show.

Tommy sighed. He could hear Helen downstairs showing the new housekeeper where the broom cupboard and polish was. Mrs Rich had been recommended by the house agent and Helen had wasted no time in bringing her in for an interview. Unfortunately, Mrs Rich was already engaged at a position across town, but Helen was determined both to woo Mrs Rich and to avoid doing her own housework and cooking, and so the wage offer had been increased.

It had worked, and Mrs Rich would be starting with them on Monday. Tommy cared very little for housekeepers, gardeners, milkmen or window cleaners. He cared for Christopher. Had cared for, he told himself. Christopher must be past tense.

He leaned on the windowsill and looked up the road. A taxi pulled up in front of the house and a familiar figure stepped out. The figure handed the driver the fare and waited while her case was deposited on the pavement. The taxi pulled away, the figure picked up her case and turned towards the house. She looked up and waved at Tommy. Caroline had arrived.

Caroline had felt as if she were in a dream since Max had left St Ives the evening before. She had begun to replay the night they spent together over and over in her head, grasping on to every detail, wanting to savour it all. She told herself, it was not love. It was experience. At breakfast she had felt particularly guilty when Phyl spoke kindly to her. Caroline's previous judgement of Sarah's behaviour with Ed lay in her stomach like a contaminated meal, threatening to resurface at any moment. Sarah had asked her, away from the rest of the group, if anything had happened between her and Max. Caroline's silence elicited a squeal of delight from Sarah, who hugged her and said she was proud of her for being an independent woman.

On the train to Minehead, Caroline had thought only of Max. She knew so little about him and was aware she was in danger of building him up to be some kind of gallant hero when in reality he was an adulterer. And she had been his mistress. She blushed, with shame and pleasure together. She must try to forget him; she would never see him again. She did not want to forget him yet. She would tell Helen, get Max out of her system before she went home. She had gazed out of the carriage window and saw only the amber in his eyes.

When Mrs Rich opened the door, Caroline thought for a moment that she might have the wrong address. "Is Miss Postgate, I mean is Mrs Gersen-Fisch at home?"

"Won't you come in and I shall enquire." Mrs Rich stepped back from the door allowing Caroline to enter the hallway. "Who shall I say is calling?"

"No need Mrs Rich!" Tommy trotted down the stairs. "Caro, so good to see you, Helen is playing the lady again. Is she in the sitting room Mrs Rich? Could you bring us some tea?"

"Yes, sir."

"Leave your case there for now, come into the sitting room." He opened a door on the right and as Caroline peered in Helen turned away from the fireplace having just lit a cigarette.

"Caro darling! How absolutely perfect! Come in, sit down, you must be famished, Tommy have you sent Mrs Rich for tea?"

"Of course."

"Run after her, ask for sandwiches and whatever fruit we have."

Tommy winked at Caroline and left them.

Caroline took off her hat and gloves. "This is a lovely house Helen, I liked your Budleigh one, but this is bigger, isn't it?"

"It is, with the added bonus of not getting one's feet wet if one slips off the front path! Are you sure you can only stay one night with us darling?"

"Yes, Bob is coming to tea tomorrow, so I have to be home."

"Bob?" Helen raised a quizzical eyebrow.

Caroline looked at her with a serious expression. "Helen, I have so much to tell you."

After the tea tray was brought in, Helen concluded her business with Mrs Rich and sent Tommy up to Caroline's room with the case and carpet bag while Caroline consumed the refreshments. She was then given a brief tour of the house, which had five bedrooms all larger than the Budleigh house and a different layout on the ground floor with the entrance hall on one side of the house and three rooms downstairs that looked out on to the street. The kitchen and scullery were at the rear and another bright garden room that opened on to a smaller but just as established garden.

More tea was brought out to the garden by Mrs Rich who was then told that would be all by Helen a little more forcefully than Tommy thought necessary. He was about to make his excuses and leave the two women to talk when Caroline insisted that she wanted to tell both of them together what had transpired over the recent weeks. Tommy was intrigued, and though he thought he would be able to offer no informed comment, he sank into a deck chair next to Caroline in the garden to listen. Caroline talked for over an hour. Her friends only interrupted to clarify a point here and there, but for the most part she gave her monologue as they sipped their tea. When she came to Max, she looked up at the sky rather than at Helen or Tommy. She smiled as she described him, and although she didn't go into lurid detail of their time together, she left Helen and Tommy in no doubt what had occurred.

When she finished, there was silence for a moment as her friends digested all she had told them. Tommy was first to speak.

"So where does this leave you with the dashing knights back in Cheltenham, and indeed the errant knight in Italy?"

"I rather think," said Helen, "that none of them could possibly live up to Max. Isn't that so, Caro?" She was somewhat amused at her friend's apparent infatuation, yet at the same time understood what a momentous shift had occurred in Caroline's life over the past few days and did not want to make light of it.

"They are all so different, that's the thing. Dependable Bob, Luke who I have decided does not have a particularly high opinion of women who think independently, Vaughan who I think I terrify and enthral in equal measure, and James..."

"James who is not husband material. He says it often enough, but I'm not sure he completely believes it you know." Tommy went to refill his teacup only to find the pot empty. "Drat. Does anyone want more tea? I can go and get more hot water."

The women nodded and Tommy left with the tea pot.

"Caro, with Max, you were careful, weren't you?"

"Oh gosh yes. We almost got carried away on the beach, but I remembered just in time."

"Thank goodness. No need to complicate things further. Darling, do you want my opinion?"

"Yes, please Helen, I do. You and Tommy were the only people I would want to tell all of it to, I knew you'd understand without getting cross or being offended, but I rather think I have just made my life more difficult, haven't I?"

"Not necessarily. First thing first, and I am not trying to preach virtue here, but no more experiences with married men. I mean it Caro, it's just too much of a mess for everyone. Only sleep with men who you would consider marrying if you had to. Now, it sounds to me as though you have dismissed Luke, and really, I'm sure Midge won't think any less of you for that. I wouldn't be surprised if he has a young nurse in his sights by the time you get back to Cheltenham. This Vaughan fellow, you say he lives in the same building as you and your father. That could be more difficult, you will of course keep bumping into each other which could become frightfully inconvenient."

"I could find somewhere else to live."

"Well, yes, but could you really afford it by yourself darling? And Dependable Bob seems to be the kind of man who will be perfectly alright by himself, at least for a while longer. I think our question most pressing is what about James. He is due back in England at the end of this month, isn't he?"

"Yes, he wrote to say he would be leaving Florence on the 30th and should be in London by the second of September."

"Lina and Albert's wedding is on the eleventh, are you to meet him in Worcester or somewhere else?"

"In Worcester on Friday the tenth."

"Tommy and I will be driving up on the Wednesday and will stay for a week, I have reserved you a room for the Saturday, but I will telephone and arrange the Friday and Sunday as well. The trains are unreliable on Sundays as you found out. Better to go home on a weekday. But that will provide you and James with time to sort things out between you."

"Do you think we should?"

"Absolutely. You are dancing around each other and neither of you will be happy until you do something about it, one way or another. Trust me Caro."

"I do, Helen."

"And I know it will be difficult, but you really must put all thoughts of Max at the very back of your mind. Keep the memories for those dark days that will undoubtedly come, when you need the warmth of your feelings on that night to sustain you. But Max must not become a yardstick to measure all others by. No one will live up to his impression on you. As you say, he has a wife, and you have no means - and no need – to contact him again."

Caroline nodded and Tommy returned with the tea pot.

"So, Mrs Rich won't be starting until Monday? Then we shall need to dine out tonight, ladies. Let's have one more cup, and then why don't we take a stroll into town, and I'll book us a table at the Plume of Feathers for dinner. Did you know we have a pier here in Minehead, Caroline?"

The afternoon and evening passed very enjoyably for the three friends. They walked out along the pier and watched a steamboat pull alongside to take on and discard passengers. They returned to the house to change for dinner, and Tommy drove them back into town to the Plume of Feathers Hotel where they dined on asparagus soup, seafood salad and ice cream pavlova for dessert. Caroline slept particularly well that night; she breakfasted on toast and marmalade the next morning before Tommy drove her to the railway station and she continued her journey back to Cheltenham. She felt restored and ready to face the predicament of the gathering suitors again.

The first was Bob, who arrived at four o'clock, an hour after Caroline herself had reached home. George had left her a note to say he was visiting some friends from church and would be home around six. Caroline's art and craft items had preceded her, and after taking Bob's jacket and hat, she carefully showed him each piece in turn in the sitting room. When they came to the life drawings of Phyl, Bob was taken aback. He looked quickly away and muttered, "Oh my."

Caroline chuckled. "It's only a woman's body. It's Phyl, the lady who runs the course with her husband Ed. He's here too."

Bob glanced at the full-frontal drawing Caroline had made of Ed, and then glanced away again, blushing furiously.

"That's indecent!"

"It's artistic. It's no different to the classical statues in museums."

"But those are statues. What you've got there, you saw, in the flesh!"

"Yes, I did." She was not thinking of the drawings. She shook her head. "Bob, lots of artists paint, and sculpt, the human form. It's the most natural thing in the world. One can see beauty without being corrupted, surely. You don't know these people, you'll probably never meet them face to face, can you not observe my drawings as artistic pieces?" She spoke gently, trying to coax him with her voice.

Bob was in conflict. He had not expected to be presented with what he considered to be pornographic images, and worse, created by the woman he would do practically anything for. He took a deep breath and turned his head back to the drawings. He tried to look at individual lines, feet, hands, a shoulder, anything except the intimate regions on full display. Gradually he could understand that Caroline did have a talent, the drawings were well proportioned, the muscle tone and shadows were keenly picked out. It still felt embarrassing to him, but he would not upset Caroline by making her feel his disgust was aimed at her.

"You've drawn them well." He managed.

"Do you really think so? Of course, they can't go up on the wall like the landscape or still life pieces can, but I was rather pleased with how these turned out. Bob, I was embarrassed at first too, we all were in the group, but we all just got on with it. Some of the other's drawings were much better than mine."

They finished looking at her portfolio, Bob relieved to see other subjects again. Then Caroline fetched her embroidery, which Bob really didn't understand, but all the same he liked the colour and texture of the piece. Finally, Caroline presented him with the shallow wicker basket she had made.

"I never did have a go at pottery, maybe I'll do that some other time, but I made this, and I'd like you to have it. You could put apples in it perhaps."

Bob was more comfortable with something so practical. He was very interested in how Caroline had finished the top edge of the basket and turned it over and over in his hands for some moments before declaring it a good piece of craftsmanship.

They took tea and cake at the dining table, and Bob told Caroline of the papers he had signed to make the house in Blacksmith Lane his. He would stay at his parents while the repair work was carried out over evenings and weekends and move in when it was weather-tight.

"No point in getting good rugs and linen to have them all get damp is there?" He smiled one of his very rare smiles, and Caroline suddenly felt like kissing him, to share in his joy. It surprised her; she had not felt physically attracted to Bob in such a strong way before. She smiled back with what she hoped was a genuinely joyful expression and passed him the plate of jam tarts Annie had made for them.

That evening, when Bob had gone home and her father had returned and looked at her portfolio, with less shock and upset than Bob had displayed much to Caroline's own surprise, she retired to her room to read the letters that had arrived for her while she had been away. There was one from Lina, several pages of very small handwriting that

Caroline had difficulty deciphering in places. From what she could understand, it seemed that Lina was very pleased that Caroline would be able to attend her wedding as most of the guests would be from Albert's family. Caroline hadn't realised she had made such an impression on the young woman and was touched that she genuinely wanted Caroline to be there on her special day.

The next envelope was from Midge.

7 August 1926
Pangbourne, Berkshire
Dear Caroline

The best news! I have been accepted by the Mission to go to Africa and join Mark. I really thought I'd messed it all up at the last interview, they asked me about scripture and how I might deal with natives who were reluctant to hear the word of God. One never knows if a strict or compassionate stance is required, but it seems compassion was the order of the day, and I shall be leaving from Southampton in three weeks' time. It would be lovely to see you and Helen again before I go, but I doubt we can arrange it all in such a short space of time. I shall write to you regularly when I get to Tanganyika, I'm sure I will have so much to learn and describe to you.

I will be gone for two years rather than the one I'd expected. They said it is better for the natives not to see too many changes of staff, which I can see would make sense when you are trying to win people over. That does mean though that I shall miss the birth of Matthew and Kate's baby! Yes, Kate is pregnant and very happy about it, as is Matty. She will make a wonderful mother I am sure, and Matthew has already started making a crib for the little one.

Mother says you are welcome to visit again just before Christmas if you would like to. She enjoys having you to stay, and Luke would like it too I think. You must know by now he has taken a position in Cheltenham. It sounded as though you had put in a good word for him, which was very kind of you. He has become very ambitious and often talks of spending a few years in hospitals before setting up in Harley Street.

I shall end this here, there is so much to arrange, and I have to have several injections for tropical fevers and the like. As soon as I have an address I will send you the details.

Au revoir my dear friend
Midge

As Caroline put the letter back into its envelope, she could hear music faintly from Mrs Bassett's apartment. She considered knocking on Galina's door to see if she might want to look at her paintings but decided not that evening. There was one other letter, postmarked from London but with familiar handwriting.

9 August 1926
Chelsea, London
Dear Caroline,

I must start with an apology. Peter tells me that you have called twice at the shop now and found me absent. My dear, I am sorry. I am spending more and more time here in the city at the moment, there are so many people to meet, and I have been helping Bobby set up a gallery. It's mostly to display her art, but we are using some of my prints as well, and some of her artist friends have asked her to show their work too. I think you would love to see it all, we painted the walls are a dramatic navy blue to show off each piece.

I shall be back in Cheltenham briefly on the 18th for a few days. Could you come to the shop? Or we could

take tea somewhere? I'm really thinking of getting out of
Cheltenham for good, though I know it would be a shame
for Peter. I just feel I will never be truly able to make a go
of the business in such a small town. London is so vibrant,
there are so many things to capture. Bobby refuses to leave,
so I have to be the one to up sticks.

Write to me at the shop if you can meet me. I truly do
want to see you before I leave again.

All the best
E. A. House

Caroline went back into the sitting room.

"Father, do you remember Elsa House?"

"I could hardly forget."

"She is thinking of moving to London permanently. I would like to have her here before she goes, to show her the apartment and my artwork. Would that be acceptable to you?"

George put down his newspaper and took off his spectacles. "You don't need to ask my permission Caroline but thank you for doing so. I see no reason not to have Miss House here to tea. When were you thinking of?"

"She says she will be here on the eighteenth for a few days. Perhaps the nineteenth?"

"Would you like me to be here, or should I absent myself?"

"Oh Father, you mustn't feel you have to go out!"

"I could perhaps see if Vaughan would like to play chess."

Caroline had an idea. It was wicked, and she didn't know if her father would entertain it, but she tried anyway. "Father, could you make sure you tell Vaughan that I am entertaining Elsa? I expect he knows of her reputation; everyone seems to. Could you make sure he understands that she and I will be alone?"

George looked steadily at his daughter. He knew exactly what she meant and wasn't at all sure he liked it. "You wish me to fabricate a story on your behalf?"

Caroline sat on a chair. "Vaughan really is not the man for me, I think you know that. But he is a nice man, and I don't see how I could tell him without hurting his feelings. I just thought it might be easier if... if he thought I was not interested in him that way."

"Caroline, I have said nothing in objection to your travels and the people you are staying with when you are not here. I have not pried into your habits, and I hope that my trust is not being abused by lurid or scandalous activities that could come to haunt you in the future."

"There is nothing lurid about my habits, Father!"

"I am glad to hear it. I know times have changed, young people are more open and less tied to tradition than my generation, but all the same, if you are getting yourself entangled with more suitors than you can cope with, you really will have to sort that out yourself my dear."

Caroline was crestfallen. It had been a risky suggestion and she regretted it now. "I understand. I will find a way to explain to Vaughan. I'm sorry for putting you in that position."

"Let's say no more about it. Just be aware that not everyone is as indulgent as I am with you."

Elsa arrived at four o'clock the following Thursday afternoon, after Caroline had spent the whole day cleaning and getting in Annie's way in the kitchen as they both vied for the oven. George had been asked by Captain McTimony to help him with his accounts and instead of burdening Vaughan Rickard, George used the bookkeeping to excuse himself from the apartment. He arrived home as the women

were drinking tea in the dining area and briefly said hello
to Elsa before going out again.

After the sandwiches had been eaten, and the fruit
cake pronounced moist and delicious by Elsa, Caroline
asked if she would like to see her paintings from Cornwall.
They went through to the sitting room where the canvas
and sketches had been temporarily stored to the side of
George's writing desk. Elsa went through them all critically
appraising each one.

"These are really rather good you know."

"Do you think so?"

"I think Bobby might even be able to find space for
one or two if you'd be willing to let me take them up to
London when I go."

"You mean in the gallery? But they are just sketches."

"People like that sort of thing. Particularly the female
nude here. It's rather similar to Degas, don't you think?"

"It hadn't occurred to me, but I suppose it is a little. With
Phyl's hair pulled back like it is, she does look a little like a
dancer or a bather."

"You see, they are very tasteful. I'm sure someone would
want to snap them up. Will you let me try for you?"

"Of course, if you really think they might sell. But won't
they need a frame?"

"We can see to that in London. All it needs at the moment
is something sturdy to keep it flat, some plywood or the like."

"Ferris, our doorman, might have something. Shall we
go and ask him now?"

Ferris said he had just the thing, but it was at his house,
and could they wait until tomorrow? Elsa agreed to return
the next day to collect the sketches and bid Caroline farewell
with an embrace that was bold and defiant and full of care
for her younger friend.

It was Sunday afternoon when Caroline next had the opportunity to tackle Vaughan. She had gone to call on Florence again, thinking that Josiah would be at chapel. She had been right, and Florence had welcomed her into the front parlour with a little more colour to her cheeks.

"You look well, are you feeling better now?"

"I feel more positive yes."

"And the baby?"

Florence, looked down at her hands in her lap. "I was mistaken."

"Oh. Well perhaps that's for the best. I was thinking you might like to take a walk if you are feeling up to it, perhaps come and see the apartment with me?"

"I would like that. Let me get my coat."

Caroline thought, as Florence stood up, that a coat would not be necessary. It was still warm and sunny, though the wind had been steadily rising and there were a few billowy clouds scurrying across the sky.

They walked at a sedate pace, Florence with her arm through Caroline's in case she felt faint. They talked about the weather, about servants, clothes, and Florence appeared to be drawing strength from her friend. Caroline described her week in Cornwall and Florence was keen to see her art. As they arrived at Norwood Court, Florence stopped and gazed up at the building from the entrance to the semi-circular drive.

"It's so modern," she breathed. "So clean. And you have a doorman, you say?"

"Yes, Ferris. He's a Godsend. We manage quite well with him and Annie. Come and see the garden first."

They entered through the front glass doors and went straight through the hall to the rear doors. Ferris had planted a few lobelias and pelargoniums at the front of the borders, and they were putting on a patriotic show of red, white and blue.

"It's such a nice place to sit, and so quiet. Oh, Mr Rickard, I didn't realise you were here. We can leave you in peace if we're intruding."

Vaughan stood up hurriedly. "No, please don't go on my account. Do sit down, you and your friend can have the bench, I will take the chair here." He stepped over to the chair that was in the sun and moved it into the shade.

"If you are sure. This is my friend Mrs Curzon. Florence, this is Vaughan Rickard, he lives in one of the apartments here."

"Pleased to meet you, Mr Rickard." Florence held out her hand. Vaughan looked into her eyes and gently shook her hand with a smile.

"Call me Vaughan, please. Do sit down."

"Vaughan is an optician. He has his own office in town."

It was as if she were not there, thought Caroline. Florence and Vaughan were gazing at each other, smiling. A slight thorn of irritation pricked Caroline; for the second time Florence was flirting with a man who was meant to be interested in Caroline. Then the idea came to her that if Vaughan was so easily swayed by a pretty face, perhaps he would not be so distraught to find Caroline was not willing to commit her future to him. That cheered her somewhat and she waited patiently for the two young people to remember her presence. After a moment, they both slowly turned their heads towards Caroline, and the conversation resumed. It was almost comical, Caroline thought afterwards, that their attraction had come so suddenly and obviously.

Eventually Caroline tempted Florence up to the apartment with the promise of a cool drink and they left Vaughan in the garden.

"Such a delightful man," sighed Florence. "My eyesight has been a little blurry recently, I should pay him a visit."

"I'm sure he will be pleased to see you."

Florence was impressed with the minimal elegance of how George and Caroline had furnished the apartment and agreed the view from the sitting room window was charming. She asked to sit while Caroline passed her the drawings and sketches one at a time, and said she had a headache starting as they got to the end. The nudes that Elsa had not taken with her had been tactfully stowed underneath Caroline's bed, and only the respectable still-life and landscapes remained. As they stood up to walk back to Florence's house, Caroline noticed her friend briefly hold her stomach. How mistaken, she wondered.

Caroline got her bicycle out of the garage and pushed it along as they walked back through the Suffolks and on to Tivoli. When they reached the front steps of the Curzon's house, Florence glanced at her wristwatch and asked if Caroline would go inside.

"I think I should be getting back. I have to make a start on lunch."

"I forgot you do the housework these days."

"Not all of it, Annie is still with us for now, but I try to help on Sundays so I can keep learning how to cook. Florence, are you sure you are quite alright?"

Florence looked directly at her. "Yes. I am perfectly well, thank you. It was lovely to see you. Do call again soon."

As Caroline rode away, Florence did not take off her coat. She stood in the doorway until Caroline was out of sight, and then went back down the steps and headed off in the opposite direction towards Montpellier. She had an appointment at the far western end of the High Street that she had been waiting all week for. It had been difficult for a woman such as

Florence, with no close female friends in the town, to find the information she needed. More difficult still with Josiah almost constantly at her side. But she had found an opportunity to visit a chemist on the pretext of indigestion and quietly, asking on behalf of a friend, discovered the information she required.

Not knowing that end of town well, it took her some time to find the house she was looking for. She had half expected it to be some kind of hovel, with a black cat at the door and cobwebs decorating the windows. Instead, it was a neat, terraced home with a scrubbed front doorstep and a bright brass letter box. She took one last look around her and knocked on the door. It opened after a moment; she heard the security chain being withdrawn on the other side.

"I was told to come at midday, I'm afraid I'm a little late."

The door was opened fully so that Florence could enter. Once she was inside, Gwen closed the door behind her.

Caroline was eating her lunchtime sandwich the following day at the dining table when there was a loud knock on the apartment door. When she opened it, Vaughan Rickard was standing in front of her, as white as a sheet and looking as if he might collapse at any moment. Caroline invited him in, insisted he have a glass of water and sit down at the dining table with her and tell her what was wrong.

Vaughan's hand shook as he took a sip. "Your friend, Mrs Curzon. Came to my office this morning for a sight examination. I thought she looked flushed, but she said it was the heat. As she stood up to leave, oh my. Caroline, she was bleeding. Heavily. Her dress was ruined of course, and the chair will require a thorough clean. I thought she was going to faint. I made her sit back down. I called for an ambulance. I held her hand, she was clutching her stomach. It was simply awful. The poor woman was in such pain."

"What on earth…?"

"They took her away to the hospital. She didn't want to let go of my hand, but then she passed out as they carried her to the ambulance."

Caroline noticed Vaughan's hands had smears of blood on them and were trembling. He was clearly traumatised. She got up and covered her sandwich with a second plate.

"Vaughan, you should wash your hands. The bathroom is just along the hall on the right. I shall get my hat and shoes while you do that and then we will go to the hospital and see if we can find out how Florence is. I assume someone has told Mr Curzon?"

"I really couldn't say."

"You gave the ambulance men Florence's details?"

"Yes, yes I did, sorry."

"No need to apologise, you've had a shock. Clean your hands and then we'll go."

She wrote a note for her father, left it on the dining table, and went to put on her shoes.

At the hospital, Josiah was sat at the side of Florence's bed. She was on a ward with nine other beds, six of which were filled. One woman two beds down had a distressing cough, and Josiah wondered how his wife could sleep through the noise. He had hurried to the hospital after a messenger had been sent to inform him of his wife's admission, parking his car at the front of the main building. She had looked so small in the bed when he arrived, her hair a mess, her face ghostly pale. Immediately he had been reminded of his first wife, who had died of the influenza only a couple of years after they had married. Taking Florence's hand, Josiah had muttered a prayer to God to bring his wife through whatever ailed her.

Caroline and Vaughan found him there. He shook Vaughan's hand vigorously, thanking him for saving his wife's life. Vaughan blushed bright red and said he had done no more than any man would, asking if there had been a diagnosis. Josiah, suddenly galvanised in the presence of another man, said indeed there had not, and he would find a doctor that minute. Caroline suggested Vaughan go with him, and when both men had noisily left the ward, Caroline sat in the seat Josiah had vacated, took Florence's hand and said her name quietly. Florence stirred.

"It's alright my dear, they have gone for a moment."

Florence opened her eyes; they did not focus fully. She was sweating yet her hand felt cold to Caroline.

"So much blood." Florence whispered.

Caroline had been piecing together what she knew on the way to the hospital without saying anything to Vaughan. She felt she could not be cross with Florence, seeing as she had had what Caroline thought was the same idea on her behalf only a few days before. She was simply sad that Florence felt she must risk her own life in order to not bring another into the world.

"You were not mistaken, were you?" She said gently.

"No."

"Do the doctors know?"

"Not what I did. But what resulted."

Caroline presumed Florence had been sworn to secrecy, just as Lottie had insisted that she tell no one herself.

"Can't go back." Florence with great effort turned her head to Caroline, who was surprised to see genuine fear in her friend's face. "Won't go back."

"There, there, dear, calm yourself. No need to think of any of that now. You need to rest. Come on, close your eyes again. That's it."

Florence drifted back into what Caroline hoped was sleep. Vaughan returned alone.

"He's arguing with the doctor. Has she, has she said anything?"

"No. Nothing."

Vaughan looked down at the young girl in the bed and wished he could pick her up and carry her away from the hospital, away somewhere safe. The few minutes he had spent in Josiah's company were enough to convince him that Josiah was a brute; a bully and Florence would be better off without him. Vaughan knew he was a romantic, he couldn't help his sensitive nature, but what he thought he had felt for Caroline paled into insignificance to the emotions Florence Curzon provoked in him.

"I think we should go, Vaughan." Caroline touched his sleeve. Vaughan reached down and laid his hand on top of Florence's for a moment and then turned away from her bed.

They found Josiah in a corridor near the hospital entrance. To Caroline's annoyance, Luke was the doctor he was berating. She could see by his body language that Luke was not intimidated by Josiah at all.

"Dr Frampton, is there a problem?" She asked.

"Caroline! Good gracious. Do you know this gentleman?"

"Josiah, perhaps you would go and say goodbye – for now – to Florence?"

Curzon glared at Luke, turned on his heel and stomped back to the ward. Vaughan said he would wait outside, and Caroline nodded her agreement. When they were on their own, she explained to Luke that she had known Florence all her life as a neighbour. She wanted to know exactly what was wrong with her, so she could help Josiah come to terms with it.

Luke shook his head. "Damned foolish woman is what's wrong with her. Did you know she was pregnant? Well, she was but she is no more. Some kind of instrument was used, and goodness only knows what potion, or should I say poison, was consumed."

Caroline nodded slowly. "Will she recover?"

"Impossible to say without knowing what she has taken, but my immediate concern is the haemorrhage and infection. And having her husband blundering around accusing me of neglecting her will not help matters at all." He was calming down, but Josiah had touched a nerve. A young nurse came trotting along the corridor.

"Nurse! The man that is in my ward with his wife in bed seven, give him no more than five minutes then have him removed. The patient needs to rest." He barked.

She nodded and carried on her way. Caroline had noticed the awe with which the nurse had looked at Luke, hanging on his every word. She sighed.

"I'll wait outside with Vaughan. Take care of her Luke, please."

"As I do all my patients."

They waited for Josiah. It had started to rain, and they tucked themselves underneath the entrance porch, behind a stone column. There was a distant rumble of thunder and the wind scurried across the front of the hospital whipping dried leaves into swirls around the tyres of the cars and bicycles.

"She looked so delicate." Vaughan was looking out at the rain as large lazy drops fell onto the surfaces.

"She is quite ill, the doctor says."

"Was it something her husband did?"

Caroline frowned. "No, no I'm sure it was not. Josiah is a good man Vaughan, I think he is as upset, probably more so than you or I by this. He lost his first wife early in their marriage. I imagine he is afraid of losing Florence too."

Josiah eventually reappeared, mopping his face with is handkerchief. He offered to take them back to Norwood Court as the weather had broken and Caroline persuaded Vaughan to get in the car. Vaughan was very quiet all the way home. Caroline put it down to his delayed shock. Josiah drove aggressively and they were home within a few minutes. He rambled on about incompetent young doctors and said he would demand to see Dr Riley later that evening when visiting time was officially sanctioned. Caroline thanked him for the ride and hurried into the entrance of the apartment building.

Caroline knew that Miss Kettle would be watching from her sitting room window. She thought she had also seen Galina at her window on the third floor looking out at the car and the rain. She practically led Vaughan to his door, and then decided to go inside with him and make sure he was alright. He fumbled with his key, dropped it, and in the end Caroline took it from him and opened his door. Once inside, she told him to sit in the leather buttoned chair by the window and poured him two fingers of whiskey in a glass. Looking around, she spotted a blanket draped over another chair. She gathered it up and insisted on tucking it around Vaughan. It was not cold, but she thought it was the right thing to do. She left him in the chair and closed his front door behind her.

As Caroline reached her own door, Galina opened hers.

"Are you alright? Come in for a moment."

They sat opposite each other as they had done while listening to Galina's gramophone. Caroline told Galina almost everything; the only part she withheld was her conversation with Lottie and her suspicion that Florence had come by the same information.

"And you say she has been unhappy in her marriage?"

"I don't think she is unhappy with her husband, but she appeared to have an aversion to conjugal relations."

Galina shook her head slowly. "I have heard of such a thing, but thankfully have never experienced it myself. You think she will recover?"

"I don't know. I do hope so. I think she was delirious, she said she couldn't, wouldn't go back. I think she meant to Josiah, but she will have to once she is well again."

Caroline waited a couple of days before taking her bicycle and riding to the hospital to check on her friend. She had decided to go for the hour after lunch when visitors were permitted, thinking that Josiah would want to spend the evening visiting hour with his wife alone. She propped her bicycle against the stone column at the main entrance and went inside. First, she went in search of Luke, and found him at a desk in a small office with the door open. She knocked and went in when he barked, "Come in!" without looking up.

"Good afternoon, Luke."

He stood up as soon as he realised it was Caroline, indicated for her to sit on the chair to the side of the desk, and shut the office door.

"I presume you are here to see Mrs Curzon? Yes, well she has a visitor at the moment. He has been quite the Labrador."

"I thought Josiah would come in the evenings."

"It's not her husband, it's that young man you came with the day she was admitted."

"Vaughan?"

"I believe it was his office Mrs Curzon collapsed in. Yes, he has visited every lunch time. Quite devoted to her."

"How is she?"

"I believe we have the infection under control. She lost a great deal of blood, but that appears to be stopped now.

Of course, she hasn't been moving about, so the proof will be in the pudding as it were when she does. Should be tomorrow I think, just a few steps. I'm more concerned with her mental state. She becomes rather agitated when her husband visits. The ward Sister had to ask him to leave early last night."

"Is it alright if I speak with her? I won't tire her, I promise."

"Well, yes, she might prefer to see another woman for a change. He's a friend of yours, this Vaughan?"

"My neighbour."

Luke nodded his head and opened the office door.

Caroline stood in the ward entrance for a moment before approaching Florence's bed. She could see Vaughan sitting in the chair, his hand holding Florence's on the bed. He was leaning towards her, as if to hear her better, and slowly nodding his head.

The ward Sister looked up from her desk at Caroline.

"Can I help you?"

"I've come to see my friend Mrs Curzon, but I can see she has a visitor."

"Yes, Mr Rickard. I'm sure he will vacate his seat for you, he has been here for twenty minutes already." She stood up and walked with Caroline to Florence's bed. "Mr Rickard, would you mind cutting short your visit today, Mrs Curzon has another friend to see her."

The ward Sister went back to her desk as Caroline and Vaughan exchanged greetings. He picked up his hat and whispered something to Florence that Caroline couldn't hear before bidding them both a good afternoon.

"You are looking brighter," Caroline pronounced, hoping that she was more convincing than she felt. Florence was still very pale, and a light sheen of sweat glistened across her upper lip and brow.

"Vaughan has been very kind. He brought me some fruit, but I haven't felt like eating it just yet."

"He is a nice man. And Josiah has been visiting you as well?"

Florence turned her head away from Caroline.

"Florence, he is your husband. He must be so worried about you."

Caroline waited until Florence turned back towards her again. "I am not going back Caroline. Vaughan has said I can stay with him. I cannot live with... what I described to you before."

Caroline was shocked. "But you are married to Josiah. You can't go to Vaughan's apartment. Josiah will be furious."

"I don't care. I need quiet. I need to be left alone." She raised her voice and the nurse at the other end of the ward looked in their direction.

"Well, you'll be here for a few days more I expect. Perhaps things will change again."

Caroline's attention was diverted to Annie and her wedding as it approached. She received a telegram, much to Ferris' excitement, from James to say he was back in London and would meet her in Worcester the following week. Caroline was looking forward to seeing him again, but at the same time she felt something had changed for her about James. She wondered if things would be the same between them when they met again.

Mary noticed that Caroline was distracted as they arranged the flowers in St Mark's the day before Annie and Jacob's wedding. Angelica was crawling up and down the aisles dragging a small wooden horse on wheels by a string behind her.

"Some more greenery on this side perhaps, Miss Caroline?"

Caroline stopped trimming the carnation in her hand and looked at the arrangement. It was not at all up to her usual standard, with all of the flower stems on one side of the vase and all of the greenery on the other.

"I'd better start again." She said, pulling the carnations out of the water.

"Is your mind not on your work?"

"No, my mind is on my old neighbour, Florence."

"The one who married the flower man? Did you read the newspaper last night? Let me see, I have it here." Mary thumbed through the small pile of newspapers they had brought across from the vicarage. "Yes, here, look at this."

Caroline wiped her hands on her apron and took the newspaper from Mary. Her eyes grew wide as she read.

FRACAS AT HOSPITAL
MAN EJECTED AFTER ARGUMENT –
POLICE CALLED TO THE SCENE
(Reporter: Arthur Shaw)

A man was escorted from the Hospital yesterday evening by two police officers after an argument broke out on the women's ward. Local businessmen, Josiah Curzon of Curzon's Exotic Plant Nursery, allegedly became loud and boisterous towards doctors who have been treating his young wife. A witness to the outburst informed this reporter that Mrs Curzon has been receiving visits from another gentleman of the town, which caused Mr Curzon much distress. We understand that no charges have been brought against Mr Curzon, on the understanding that he refrains from attending on his wife for the rest of her recovery. Mrs Curzon could not be reached for comment.

"Oh dear. I do hope Florence is alright. She has quite captured Vaughan Rickard's heart, and said she was going to stay with him when she left hospital. It rather seems that she means to do just that. Poor Josiah."

"She is leaving her husband for your neighbour?! But she has only been married to him for a few months! I do not know what the world is coming to, really I don't."

Caroline chuckled. "You sound more like Celestine every day, Mary."

Annie and Jacob were married in a joyous ceremony. Despite only officially inviting close family, the congregation of St Mark's were not to be prevented from joining in and filling the wooden pews to bursting. There were lustily sung hymns, resounding 'Amen's to the prayers, and a round of applause as the new bride and groom turned and walked out of the little church and into the sunshine. Caroline and her father walked with the others to the field behind Annie's father's cottage that had been donated after all for the wedding party. A large canvas tent had been found and erected so that the bride and groom could remain dry in case it rained, and everything was decorated with wildflowers that Annie's sisters had been out early that morning to collect from the lanes and hedgerows. Annie's bouquet was of a similar frothy mix of cow parsley and sweet peas; the men wore no buttonholes, but each had a bright red handkerchief tied around their necks.

Annie's father brought out his fiddle once everyone was assembled and began the musical entertainment. Another guest had a tin whistle, and one more found a wooden crate to use as a drum. The children danced first while the adults milled around the refreshments. Then after a brief quiet for speeches of thanks from the groom and bride's father, the tea and beer had lubricated the adults sufficiently to get them dancing as well. Caroline and George stayed for an hour, conscious that they were better dressed than almost every other guest there. Annie and Jacob made sure to stop and talk with them for a few minutes just as they were thinking of leaving, which made their exit less awkward. Annie couldn't stop the tears of joy and gratefulness as she thanked them for the beer glasses, and Caroline gave her a firm hug and told her she looked beautiful, which she did. George reminded her that she was not required to return to work until the following Wednesday and shook Jacob's hand warmly.

11

THE FIGHT

They were at the dining table eating Sunday lunch when the shouting began. Caroline had roasted a chicken following Annie's scratchy written instructions to the letter but had decided on boiled potatoes and carrots to be sure everything was cooked properly. George had been telling her of someone at Christ Church who had just opened a dress shop and was looking for an assistant. The first voice they heard was Josiah's demanding to know which apartment belonged to Vaughan Rickard. Ferris was valiantly trying to prevent him from climbing the stairs. Miss Kettle had come to her front door and mercifully the Monks were away for the weekend; Josiah had received no response to his knocking on their door.

Captain McTimony came out of his apartment dressed in khaki shirt and trousers, looking every inch the African soldier, his moustache waxed and his hair, such as it was, slicked back over his scalp. Now it was his turn to demand what on earth was going on. Ferris called up that the gentleman was looking for Mr Rickard, to which McTimony replied that no gentleman would cause such a commotion. This inflamed Josiah further, who had now reached the first landing and was standing toe to toe with McTimony.

Ferris, prudently, retreated to his room and telephoned for the police. George, having been Josiah's best man only seven months before, felt he should try to establish some decorum. He went down to the first landing to reason with Josiah and prevent McTimony taking further offence. Caroline had told him of the newspaper report, and he had wondered if some kind of incident might occur. Josiah, now red in the face and with spittle flying from his mouth, lunged past George towards McTimony having been accused of behaving like a common hooligan, and on a Sunday too. McTimony, a boxer in his youth, side-stepped neatly and punched out at Josiah but only connected with his shoulder. George was no pugilist; he stepped back and up two stairs out of the way, while Josiah and Captain McTimony wrestled on the floor of the first landing. Neither landed any damaging punches, they were holding on to each other too closely, but neither would release their grip on the other.

Caroline sat on the top step of the second-floor landing hugging her knees. Galina quietly came out of her apartment, a worried look on her face, and sat next to Caroline. She had seen brawls such as this in locations across Europe, often involving her husband, and she did not like the sound of the violence below. She drew deeply on her cigarette, and the women exchanged glances uneasily. The distant sound of a police car bell grew closer but did not appear to be heard by the men on the floor of the first landing. Heavy boots on the stairs, shouting, more scuffles, George's voice trying to explain, trying to calm the situation, McTimony gruffly returning to his apartment and slamming the door. After a few moments, Ferris' face appeared looking up the stairs at the women.

"Miss Caroline, your father has agreed to accompany the gentleman home and asks that you keep his lunch on a hot plate for him."

Galina returned to her apartment, and shortly afterwards the Rachmaninoff third piano concerto could be heard from its sitting room.

Caroline covered her father's plate and set it on top of a pan of water on a low heat. Then she went down to the first-floor landing and knocked gently on Vaughan Rickard's front door. She heard movement on the other side, but the door did not open.

"Vaughan, it's me, Caroline."

The bolt was drawn back, and Vaughan's face appeared as the door opened a little way.

"I'm on my own, let me in for a moment."

He did so. Caroline noticed he was sporting a black eye and the arm of his spectacles was held in place by a piece of copper wire twisted and bent around the joint. She stood in the middle of his sitting room.

"Vaughan, what on earth is going on?"

He cleared his throat and motioned for her to sit down.

"I am sorry for the disturbance. I had not considered that Curzon would find out my address. I shall apologise to all of the residents."

"That's not what I meant, and I think you know it. I saw the newspaper article. That's how you came by that black eye isn't it? Did you fight with Josiah at the hospital?"

"I had gone to visit Florence on Wednesday evening after closing the office. She had begged me, and I could not refuse. I took her some flowers. Oh, I know you've said you are not disposed to a bunch as a gift, but Florence loves flowers so. I wasn't going to stay very long, but he arrived just as I was saying goodbye. He saw the flowers, demanded to know who

I thought I was attending to his wife and what the meaning of my presence was. Caused quite a scene. A young doctor came running in just as Curzon swung for me. I was lucky, that doctor surely saved me from a thrashing. But it would have been worth it all the same."

He stopped and looked past Caroline to the doorway that led to the bedrooms and bathroom. Caroline turned, and Florence was standing in a loose light blue dressing gown, bare foot and just as pale as she had been in hospital.

Caroline crossed the room and gave her friend a hug, which eventually Florence returned. She began to sob into Caroline's shoulder. Vaughan suggested that the women go through to Florence's bedroom, and he would bring a pot of tea for them.

With Florence safely back in bed and Caroline on a chair by her side, Florence explained the situation fully. She left nothing out, not even the visit to Gwen's mother this time, though she would not name the chemist who had told her where to go. She stopped when Vaughan came in with the tea things on a tray, but he left them to it and closed the door behind him, understanding that they needed to talk alone. Caroline listened carefully. She nodded as the information she had suspected fell into place. As Florence's voice grew dry and brittle, Caroline poured the tea and handed her a cup.

"I have been humiliated. I have been inspected intimately, by the woman, by doctors, by nurses. I have been drenched in my own blood in public. And now I am to be talked about, whispered about, known as the woman who left her husband. I no longer care." She finished. Tears rolled down her face again, and Caroline passed her a handkerchief that was folded up on the dresser.

"Were the doctors in agreement that you could leave the hospital?"

"Doctor Frampton said I could as long as the bleeding was no heavier after a walk up and down the ward. I managed that yesterday morning. Dr Riley agreed that I could leave as long as I had someone to look after me. Vaughan said he would."

"I understand that you don't want to, but you really should have gone to your own home Florence. I could have come to look after you. I still could."

There was a flicker of fire in Florence's eyes. "I will not go back to him."

"He is very angry about it. I don't think he could be blamed for that."

"His pride is hurt. It will mend. My body is hurt. It may not mend."

"Florence, was he, did he, I don't know how to say what I want to say."

Florence sighed. She knew that she would be thought of as being in the wrong by most people who learned the truth. She was so very tired, having lost so much blood and the infection had not been completely dismissed. The tablets on her bedside table were meant to keep fighting it on her behalf.

"He was never rough. He is, in all other aspects a good man. But his belief in what is his right, nightly, has been too much for me to bear."

"Did you ever love him?"

She shook her head. "I don't care if I never have children, Caroline. I don't care if I never have sexual intercourse again. I can't bare it."

Caroline took the cup from her friend's hands and put the tray on the dresser. She helped her settle down in the bed and pulled the covers up over her. Then she sat on the edge of the bed for a few moments stroking Florence's hair as the girl went back to sleep.

Back in the sitting room Caroline put the tea tray down on the coffee table and sat on the leather chair.

"You can't hide here forever. I don't know what my father can say to Josiah to calm him, but you must know you have behaved irresponsibly in encouraging Florence to come here."

"She did not want to return home. There was no other option."

"Of course there was! She could have gone to a hotel, or a convalescent home. She could have gone back to her parents. What have they said about all of this?"

"I don't think she has spoken to them since the wedding."

"And what about you, Vaughan? This will damage your reputation in Cheltenham as well."

He took off his spectacles and rubbed his face with his hand. He looked closer to forty now, a little more grey in his hair and the stubble just showing on his chin.

"I have written to my parents. As soon as Florence is well enough to make the journey we will travel to Norfolk. It will do her good to be by the sea for a while, the air is better. If I can find a suitable premises, I will take my practice there."

"But you've only just moved in here! And Florence is a married woman. Vaughan, have you really thought all of this through?"

"I love her Caroline. I can't explain it. I can only try to look after her and make her happy however I can."

There seemed no more to be said. Caroline went back to her apartment and topped up the pan of water that had almost boiled dry beneath her father's plate.

It was the evening of Thursday September nineth. Caroline, Helen and Tommy were in the small lounge bar of the London Hotel in Worcester, with a number of other guests who were to attend the wedding of Emelina Cantor to Albert Robert Rouse in Worcester Cathedral the following Saturday. Helen and Tommy had listened to Caroline's retelling of the events since her return to Cheltenham over dinner, completely entranced. They had gasped, laughed, and sighed, drawing looks of interest from the other diners.

Caroline finished her glass of port and retired to her room early. The journey from Cheltenham had not been a long one, but she was tired and also excited to be seeing James the next day. The first telegram from him had been followed by a letter with more details of where he would be staying in the city and when and where she was to meet him. Before leaving Cheltenham Caroline had arranged for the cocktail set she had reserved in Cavendish House to be carefully packaged and sent to Lina's address. It meant she travelled relatively lightly to Worcester, although she had included her sketchbook and a box of charcoal in her luggage, in case she had the opportunity to draw before she went back home.

The hotel was noisy, her room looked out over an inner courtyard where men were playing skittles. It was too warm to close the small window, and she leaned on the windowsill for a while watching the game below. As the cathedral and the churches across the city began to chime ten o'clock the game ended, and Caroline climbed into bed. She slept poorly, not because of the bed, but because of the dreams that had begun to haunt her sleep since the altercation on the stairwell between Josiah Curzon and Captain McTimony. In them she was in her nightdress, barefoot as Florence had been, and running along a beach at night. Something was behind her, and something further up the beach prevented her from seeking help. Her only option was to wade into the water, and as the waves closed over her head each night, she woke up gasping for breath.

A fine rain was falling as Caroline walked to the Guildhall to meet James the next day. The wedding reception
would be held there in the upstairs rooms, as it was a short
walk from the cathedral precinct. James was waiting for her,
standing in the shelter of a shop canopy, hatless as usual.
She stopped a little way from him, before he noticed her.
She wanted to see how she felt seeing him again after so
long, and after what had happened between her and Max.
Then she crossed the High Street and called his name
in greeting.

They found a coffee house and spent the morning talking
about the film James had worked on in Italy, about his friend
Pavel who had promised to visit England as soon as he and
Marta were married, and about the Italian way of life that
James had so enjoyed. He was sun-browned, relaxed, and
very good company. As always, Caroline felt at ease with
him, and they talked as equals.

Helen and Tommy had set out to find a wedding present.
Partly due to their hasty removal to Minehead, and partly
because Helen refused to purchase such an important gift
from a provincial store, they had left it to the last minute.
James was to dine with them later that evening, but the
day had been left unplanned for him and Caroline to fill as
they chose.

After lunch in the coffee shop, they walked down to the
river and strolled along with the town's people of leisure.
It had stopped raining, but the sky was still heavy with
grey clouds, and everything felt damp. They reached a stone
bridge and stopped to lean on the parapet and watch a pair
of racing boats being rowed by two sets of six young men
pass underneath.

"Caroline, I have thought about you often while I was in Italy."

"I have thought of you too."

"I have thought about what kind of life I want, what kind I will have if I continue in the film business. It will be one of constantly moving from place to place, wherever the work is. Perhaps more overseas travel, certainly within Britain. The pay is hardly more than pin money, and there may be times when I have no money at all. There will be many late nights, particularly if I am working in a theatre. It is not a life that lends itself readily to intimate relationships."

"You do mean to continue with it."

"I do, yes. I can't imagine doing anything else. But as I say, it's not..."

"Not a life of stability. It sounds as if you are trying to dissuade me from considering it."

"On the contrary. I am telling you in case you would be willing to consider it. Caroline, I have told you many times, I am not husband material. I do not believe many women would be content to be my wife, given all I have described. It would take a great amount of trust and would mean many lonely times if the woman did not or could not travel with me."

"A man only needs one wife. At least, in England that is usually the case."

"Pavel said I am married to my work."

"He sounds a jolly fellow. I should like to meet him one day."

"Caroline..."

"James. Are you trying to ask me if I would be willing to share the life you have just described?"

"Yes. Yes, I am. I have no ring. I don't even know if this is a real proposal. But I've reached a point where I need to know. A fork in the road if you like."

"Do you require an answer right now?"

"No. It's something I would be grateful if you would consider. Perhaps give me your answer before we leave Worcester? Or if that's too soon, write to me when you return home? I don't know how long it might take someone to consider it all, but I do know it is not something I would want you, or anyone, to agree to on a whim."

Caroline looked at him. "Do I strike you as someone who acts on a whim?"

He smiled, a gentle, relaxed, somewhat cheeky smile. "The more I know of you, my dear Caroline, the less I know of you. And I think that is why I am asking you in this way."

"Then I shall give it the weighty consideration it deserves. Shall we walk back now?"

Of the four weddings Caroline attended in 1926, she later mused, Annie and Jacob's was by far the one she most enjoyed. Florence and Josiah's was stressful, Lottie and Eric's was more of a formality. For Lina and Albert, Worcester cathedral was decorated with streamers and flowers, and wooden chairs were arranged in rows for the guests of which there were almost two hundred. Helen, Tommy, Caroline and James sat towards the rear on the bride's side after some discussion with an usher in a grey morning suit. They were passed by several lords, ladies, a duchess, a baron and three members of parliament who strolled across the stone floor and found their seats closer to the raised area before the choir stalls. Caroline commented that there were no children present, and Helen said it was not considered appropriate for a society wedding. Of the four, Helen was most at ease in the company of such high social dignitaries. James was fidgety, and Tommy seemed only partially to be paying attention. The cathedral itself was impressive and Caroline resolved to return the following morning and explore the side aisles and chapels.

Lina looked much smaller than Caroline remembered, dwarfed by the long white dress and lace veil she wore. She was walked up the centre of the rows of chairs by her father, also a short man. Albert waited at the altar in his morning suit with his brother in his naval uniform as Best Man. He stammered through the vows, though only the first row of guests could hear him, his voice was so quiet. The service dragged on, lasting well over an hour. Caroline grew bored of the droning voice of the Reverend Canon Benson, and wished he had more animation like Philip had at St Mark's. She found herself thinking of James's words on the bridge.

Would she be happy with the life he had described? It was odd, she thought, that he had not asked if she would be happy with him. Had he taken that for granted? Or was he really more concerned that circumstances might disrupt an otherwise potentially successful union? She knew he had confidence in himself as an individual, yet he lacked the confidence to make a clear proposal.

Max's face came to her mind. He had been similarly confident in himself as an individual, she recognised. Suddenly she understood that it was a quality which she found attractive in a man. Yet Luke was also confident, and he was not within her consideration. Because he did not treat her as an equal, she realised. She, or whoever became Luke's wife, would be an adornment to his career. He would want someone at home, raising his children. James was not proposing that, James was asking if she wanted to go wherever he went. But what if there were something she wanted to do, somewhere she wanted to go, would she have to sacrifice that for his career? She thought the answer would probably, always, be yes.

At the reception in the Guildhall Assembly rooms, there were refreshments and dancing. Another rain shower had caught many of the guests as they walked from the cathedral to the Guildhall, and they were now gently steaming as the sun poured through the long Georgian windows. Caroline had spotted Harry Gregory and his brother with a group of other young men. She had turned away, and then a moment later turned back holding her head high. Harry had looked in her direction; had looked straight through her without registering who she was. Helen had noticed, and asked Caroline a few minutes afterwards if she was alright. Caroline assured her that she was and allowed Tommy to lead her on to the dance floor.

Lina and Albert were gradually making their way around their guests, trying to speak to everyone before they started to drift away. They reached Helen and James just as Tommy and Caroline were finishing their dance. They all exchanged friendly hugs, kisses and handshakes, and Lina thanked Caroline for the cocktail set which had arrived the day before.

"We will be in Scotland for the rest of September before we take up residence in Great Malvern. You must all come and visit once we are settled."

"That's really not very far from Cheltenham, is it?"

"No, I believe the railway connects the two. Although James, do you still have your car?"

"Sadly, no. Had to sell it when I went to Italy. Tommy does though, don't you?"

"Indeed, going like a dream at the moment, though goodness knows how long for. We could certainly collect Caroline on our way to you if that's acceptable?"

It was agreed that there would be a small house party sometime in November, with golf at the Worcestershire course at Poolbrook Common a little way south of the town.

When Lina and Albert had moved on, Caroline asked why Helen and Tommy hadn't moved to the house in Tavistock that Helen's father had bought the year before.

"Papa is using it for some army chums. Jolyon is having some of his friends there for Christmas and William stays often. I believe he has some interest in a girl in Tavistock at the moment. Really, it was rather inconvenient, but there we are."

"Is it Minehead you are staying at now?" Asked James.

"Yes, a little house overlooking a new public garden. I think we might stay for a while, don't you Tommy?"

"I rather think so. We've been exploring Exmoor, there are some wonderful spots to paint. Caroline you should come back down as soon as you like, and we'll take a day out on the moor."

They stayed until around half the guests had left, and then made their way back to the hotel where James joined them for dinner. He had decided to return to London taking the slow train the following day and was happy to spend his remaining time with his friends. They asked for a set of dominos after dinner and played for pennies until the landlord rang the bell to close the bar.

"The train leaves at ten. Would you meet me at Foregate Station at nine-thirty to say goodbye?"

Caroline was caught mid-yawn. She nodded and eventually agreed.

James bought Caroline a platform ticket and they climbed the steep flight of steps to wait for his train. It had rained heavily in the night, but the morning was clear and cool with a little mist obscuring the Malvern Hills to the southwest. They sat on a bench and were alone except for a young man smoking at the other end of the platform and the porter changing an advertising poster.

Caroline felt the silence hanging between them and knew she had to give James her answer. She had thought about it long into the night having enjoyed their evening together and had made her decision. It would not be fair on James to make him wait unnecessarily.

"James, the proposal on Friday that you wished me to consider. I have done so. I am very fond of you. In fact, I could love you. But I would always be in competition with your work, and I don't think I could endure that for very long."

James crushed the end of his cigarette into the platform and blew out the smoke. "Even if you were to travel with me?"

"Dear James. Your mind will always be on your next film or production. Always. It is now, isn't it, that's why you are going back to London today."

"There is a company that need a director for a short run in Ipswich, I'm lunching with the chap funding the production tomorrow. I have to go back today."

"That's good news, I'm sure you'll get the position. You know, in some ways I envy you. I wish I knew as you do exactly what you want from life and had the drive to pursue it."

"It sounded as though you might have found art to be your calling. Didn't you say your friend has taken some of your paintings to show in London as well?"

"Yes, though I have no idea if they will sell. Elsa seemed to think they might, but I don't know. I can't imagine they would make enough retire on." She smiled.

"Write to me with the name of the gallery, and when I am rich, I shall buy them all."

"Oh James, that is exactly what I don't want! Don't you see, if I lived with you, I would always have to rely on whatever income you could make. We would have to chase each production, and I would never have the chance to pursue any career of my own. I don't want to be reliant on a man's income to support me. And even if we had a home and I stayed there while you were off working, it would be as if we were not together. You were right, it is a difficult situation to reconcile and even if I do love you, I don't think that would be enough."

James looked at her, and then looked away down the railway tracks. The signal at the end of the platform changed and the Porter went into his office to collect his flag and whistle.

"You have grown while I have been away. I should have asked you to marry me last year before we left Dorset, I believe you would have agreed then."

Caroline blushed. He could not know how she had changed. "I would like to keep you as a friend, rather than loose that because of your first love."

James stood up and held out his hand to her. She took it and stood also.

"Then friends we shall remain. I value that. I'm not sorry that I asked you, but I'm also not disappointed that you've said no. Write to me? And if not before, we'll see each other at Lina and Albert's in November, yes?"

"Yes, we will."

On her way back to the hotel, Caroline slipped into the church of St Nicholas on The Cross in the city. She sat in the pew nearest the door, despite the church being only half full. She listened to the end of the service and took in the simple beauty of the church interior. The vicar mentioned in his sermon how the saint was patron of unmarried people, and Caroline smiled to herself. It had been some time since she had listened to a sermon that was not related to a wedding.

She had fallen out of the habit of attending either St Marks or Christ Church every Sunday and had not felt a need to commune with a congregation. Sitting in the cool, dim pew, she felt she had made the right decision about James. She believed that somewhere there would be a man with whom she would feel the passion she had shared with Max, and the intelligence and understanding she had found in James, with the stability of Bob. Any of those things by themselves would not be enough.

Caroline found Helen in the hotel lounge. Tommy had gone to sketch the cathedral and would not be back for lunch. Caroline thought she might join him after she and Helen had eaten.

"James is safely on his way back to the capital?"

"Yes. Our issue is resolved."

Helen tilted her head and blew the smoke from her cigarette to the side away from Caroline. "How did he take the news?"

"He said he was disappointed, but I think, no, I know, he understands."

"I fear he will end up a lonely old man."

"He lives for his work; it is everything to him. I think he has been right all along; he is not husband material."

"So, with what you have told me of Mr Rickard, he too is now out of the running. Midge's brother has been discarded. Currently that leaves Dependable Bob, does it not?"

"Helen, are you taking notes?"

"Darling, I simply like to understand the situation. One could make a terrible faux pas by saying the wrong name at the wrong time."

They chuckled together. "I don't think there will be any chance of that. With Bob, the shoe would be on the

other foot; he would be the one to stay at home and tend
his chickens while I would crave the freedom that I am
becoming used to. If I am to have a husband, I want to be
able to share my adventures as well as his."

"There is something to be said for staying out of one's
husband's adventures."

"I'm sorry, it must have been so difficult for you recently
with Tommy and Christopher and having to move house."

"Tommy has taken to writing letters, and then tearing
them up and putting them in the wastepaper basket. I fear
Mrs Rich will find one and then we shall have to make up
some fantastical story to cover it all up. It is tiresome, but
I do love the old duffer in my own way, and we shall see
this through."

"Letters to Christopher? You don't think he would
actually send one, do you?"

"I really don't know. I had hoped with some distance
that he could put it all behind him. Christopher appears to
have made a larger impression on Tommy than either of us
realised at the time."

Arriving back at Norwood Court at lunchtime on
Monday, Caroline was about to climb the stairs to the
apartment when Miss Kettle called out to her from the
older lady's front door.

"I was just about to take luncheon; would you care to
join me? I am sure I have enough for two and it would save
you from having to prepare your own after your journey."

Caroline could hardly refuse. She was hungry and knew
Miss Kettle would enjoy hearing about the big wedding. Over
tinned tomato soup and fishpaste and cucumber sandwiches,
Caroline described the bride's dress, the decorations, the
Guildhall and the dancing to Miss Kettle's satisfaction.

"Have I missed anything exciting here while I've been away?" Caroline asked as she took another small triangle sandwich.

"There have been comings and goings. The business with Mr Rickard appears to have been concluded, he left with his young lady friend yesterday. They had several suitcases with them, I assume they will be staying away for some time. More tea?"

"No, thank you. Has Mr Curzon been back at all? The man who was shouting on the stairs the other night."

"Yes! He came one evening and your father was with him. I heard raised voices again but nothing like the rumpus previously. He left again soon afterwards. I gather you and your father know him well?"

"We were neighbours. Miss Kettle, Agatha, you've been very kind to provide me with lunch, but I really should go and see if I have any letters and catch Annie before she leaves for the day."

"Of course, my dear. It's always pleasant to have your company."

Having exchanged news with Annie, and agreed the week's menu, Caroline unpacked her case and opened the letters that had arrived for her.

6 September 1926
Chelsea, London
Dear Caroline

Your art has gone down a storm here! Bobby had only hung the male nude on Thursday morning and by the afternoon he had been sold. It was just as well, as we then had a visit from the local police after someone had complained the gallery was showing indecent images. Of course, by the

time they arrived there was no evidence of such. Isn't it
absurd that the female form is acceptable, but the male is
not? In any case, Bobby has been taking details of those
who would be interested in any other similar pieces if you
can produce them. The seascapes have also sold. I shall be
back in Cheltenham on the 15th and will bring your profits.

   Yours affectionately
   E. A House

I am an artist, Caroline thought to herself, but with such
a controversial subject. She couldn't see how it would be
possible to produce more of the same without access to a
male model. It was not something a young woman could
simply ask a stranger in the street to do. Indeed, she wasn't
convinced that there would be a large number of art lovers
who were just waiting for sketches of naked bodies to appear
on the market. Elsa had said the seascapes had also sold, so
perhaps that would be an avenue to explore further. It would
be a reason to return to the sea at least. Caroline thought
back to the art exhibition she had visited with Lady Victoria
in London the year before. There had been nudes included
there, but they had all been women. She wondered if that
was because most artists were men, and they did not want
to paint the male form. Perhaps they felt intimidated or
uncomfortable, as Dora Fisher had done.

   It's all down to confidence.

   Caroline heard her brother Freddie's voice in her mind
as clear as if he had been standing next to her. It had been
a while since she had thought of Freddie, and it caught her
by surprise. Freddie would have been interested in her art.
He would have taken her to the sea, or to climb mountains
or cross the moors. They would have travelled in a fast car,
the canvas roof down and the wind whipping at their faces.

Freddie would have talked through her selection of potential suitors and helped her come to a decision, she was sure of it. They say women marry their fathers, she mused. Perhaps I am looking for my brother instead.

12

THE PLAN

When Elsa arrived at Norwood Court the following week, she handed Caroline an envelope containing seventeen pounds and six shillings.

"Your wages of sin," she said with a grin.

"Please don't make it any more sordid than it already feels, Elsa. Did the police really turn up at the gallery or were you pulling my leg?"

"Honestly, they did! It's not unusual, Bobby quite regularly has busy bodies complaining about the art she displays, so don't think yours was particularly unusual. It was very good though and she has a list of at least ten people who want to know the very minute she has anything more from you, of the same subject matter of course."

Caroline squirmed in her seat. "I really don't know if that is possible. It was a spur of the moment thing."

"Well, Bobby is happy to take anything you'd like her to show for you. You have the gallery address, just parcel it all up and send it to us there."

"Us?"

Now it was Elsa's turn to fidget in her seat. "Yes. I've decided, I can't keep the studio going here when everything is happening for me now in London. I've found a space I can use quite close to Bobby's gallery, and would you believe it, Peter is going to come with me?"

"The boy who took over from me?"

"Yes! Stroke of luck really, he is keen to relocate and has a relative who is willing to give him bed and board in Shoreditch. And he's not really a boy, he's come on very well and is almost as organised as you. It means I can still have him taking bookings and seeing to all the paperwork, while I can work. There is so much movement in London, well, you know that too. But it's so vibrant, and so different to Cheltenham. I feel energised just being there."

Elsa's eyes sparkled as she spoke. Caroline could see how enthusiastic she was about this new direction in her life.

"I am very happy for you Elsa, truly."

"You must come and visit once we're settled."

"I would love to. Although it feels as if I should be settling somewhere myself and inviting everyone to me, rather than always going to everyone else!"

"Is that on the cards? Do you have an idea of where you want to be?"

"The more I think about it, the more I want to be near the sea, or open spaces. I could never settle in London, or Bristol. The entertainment is wonderful of course, but I feel I need to be surrounded by the elements rather than people and tall buildings."

"Well, if you can keep producing those paintings and sketches, you should be able to take a place very soon."

"I'm not going to rush. It has to be the right place."

At the end of September, a large truck pulled into the gravel drive of Norwood Court. Ferris had been expecting it and went out to speak to the driver and his two assistants before showing them into the building. Agatha Kettle watched from her sitting room window as the men began to emerge again through the glass doors which Ferris had wedged open with blocks of wood, carrying furniture and boxes. Vaughan Rickard's apartment was emptied that afternoon and an advertisement placed in the *Chronicle* stating the apartment was again available to rent or purchase.

Caroline briefly toyed with the idea of taking it herself for a few months. She could be independent, while still being close to her father and in familiar surroundings. Eventually she decided not to. She had come to feel slightly annoyed by the closeness of her neighbours, the all-knowing Ferris and the feeling that she was being watched whenever she stepped out of her own front door. She mentioned it to Galina one evening as they sat listening to Borodin's Symphony number two, the two table lamps giving the only illumination in Galina's sitting room.

"I did warn you about old women." Galina sipped her drink. She had taken delivery of a case of vodka from London and had opened a new bottle for Caroline to try.

"I am happy that Father has people around him, but I don't think I will stay here for very much longer."

"Your friends in the west country, could they not help you find accommodation near them?"

"I was thinking I might ask them if they knew of somewhere small. I've only spent one day at Minehead, not long enough to know if I'd like to live there, but I did like Budleigh Salterton where they were before."

"I think it will do you good to live on your own for a while. But not for too long; I think you will eventually want to share with a man. Have you given that any more thought?"

"It seems easier to know what I do not want."

"That is often the case. But come now, you must have some idea?"

"You'll think me foolish, but if I could find a man who resembled my brother Freddie, I would be satisfied. So far, I have only found elements of him in men. I want someone with his drive, his passion for life, his humour, his understanding, his encouragement."

"That does not sound at all foolish, unless you are romanticising the idea of who your brother was, instead of who he really was."

"I don't think I am. I suppose I looked up to him, he was older by nearly seven years."

"A thing to consider is that many men of that age now have been damaged by the War. If you are searching for a perfect specimen of manhood, I fear you will be disappointed. Can you look past a physical infirmity if the man has everything else you wish for?"

Caroline finished her vodka. Galina could not possibly know about Max, yet it was as if she did. Colour came to Caroline's cheeks, and she hoped Galina couldn't see in the dimly lit room.

"Yes, I could look past physical war damage."

"You sound very definite."

"I know I can Galina. Mental damage would be more difficult, but physical is not always as limiting as some people believe."

Galina nodded slowly. She studied Caroline from across the room. She had detected a change in the young woman and understood her need for independence. Since Marius' death Galina could not entertain the thought of sharing her personal space with another man, though she had spent nights in Oxford hotels with one or two acquaintances recently. She liked Caroline's company, mainly because it was not filled with insubstantial chatter.

"I think it would be appropriate to ask your friends to help you. That is what friends are for."

It would be a big step to take. Caroline was not in any immediate need of her own home, and she decided to wait until she saw Helen and Tommy again in Worcestershire before she asked them face to face. It would give them time to settle into the area as well, she thought.

Caroline discussed her ideas with Mary the following Wednesday, who was concerned about Caroline being on her own and lonely. Mary had gone directly from her home with Celestine to a small house that Philip had been provided with by the Diocese. She had never lived on her own and even with Angelica she still disliked Philip staying away anywhere overnight.

"But if I find a nice house by the sea, you and Philip and Angelica can come for holidays."

"All that sand, getting everywhere."

"We could swim too."

"I do not swim. If God had meant me to swim, he would have provided flippers instead of feet, don't you see?" Mary was straight faced, but Caroline couldn't help laughing.

"Very well, you stay on dry land. But I could teach Angelica to swim. She might find it useful when she gets older. Why, a woman swam across the whole English Channel a few weeks ago, did you see it in the newspaper?"

Angelica was at that moment pulling herself up to stand by Caroline's chair, a big grin on her face showing her perfect little teeth.

"And why on earth would a woman want to do such a thing?"

"I suppose because she could. Or perhaps someone told her she couldn't."

Lottie was rather more enthusiastic when Caroline broached the subject with her. They had not seen each other since the wedding, and Caroline had only seen Bob once now that he was working his spare hours on the house and the football season had begun again. They had gone to the cinema as they had many times before and Caroline had felt Bob had accepted her stance on their relationship. For his part, Bob felt he had put his case and would be content to spend the rest of his days waiting if that's what he had to do.

Caroline met Lottie on a Saturday morning, and they walked through the orange leaf-coated town streets to a coffee shop where they could sit and talk. Caroline was curious to know how Lottie was adapting to married life, particularly after Florence's near hysterical reaction to it. Annie, Caroline knew, did not yet feel properly married as she and Jacob were still living apart until they could secure one of the new houses built on what had been Arle Farm.

They ordered coffee and apple turnovers, and Lottie gazed out of the window at the shoppers passing by. "It will be Christmas before we know it."

"This year has felt slower than last year to me."

"The first part, yes. But since the strike and Eric's change of job, time has flown."

"Is he enjoying the training still?"

"Oh yes. He says the writing is hard, and remembering all the laws, but he has a big book, and he spends most nights reading and making his notes on it all. I'm so proud of him. He would never have got far at the gas works, but when he passes his exam and gets a posting, I shan't have to work in the sewing room anymore and we can start a family."

Caroline didn't have to ask if that was what Lottie really wanted, her smile was genuinely broad at the thought of it all. "Where do you think they will send him?"

"Might be Gloucester, Stroud, Cirencester. Could be anywhere in the county. That strike was a Godsend Caroline, I know the miners are still out down in the Forest, but it gave Eric and the other men something useful to do."

"Looking after the gas is useful too."

"Yes, but being a Police Constable is respectable. The uniform and everything. I know the works have done Father and Bob alright, but I'm glad that Eric isn't there anymore. By the way, Eric said there was a bit of a to do over your way a few weeks ago, I meant to ask you about it."

Caroline's stomach fell. Josiah's temper was clearly the town gossip. She explained as simply as she could, trying to make it sound much less violent than it had actually been.

Lottie didn't believe her. "They don't call out the police for a disagreement Caroline, I know that much!"

"There was a bit of a scuffle."

"I heard your friend ran off with an optician."

Caroline had forgotten how connected Lottie's family was to the town grapevine. There was no point in denying it. "Florence and Vaughan have gone away, yes. There was no convincing either of them to stay. Who can say if it will last any longer for them than it did for Florence and Josiah."

"Sounds scandalous!" Lottie said with a grin as the coffee arrived.

"It was certainly unexpected. Particularly as only a few days before Vaughan had asked Father for my hand in marriage."

"Lummy! You had a narrow escape there then! Don't worry, I won't breathe a word of it to Bob."

"Bob and I understand each other, Lottie."

"Yes, he said the same thing. So, tell me about these paintings."

Caroline retold her stay in St Ives, mentioned drawing her hosts but not that they were naked, and said nothing about Max at all. "It has made me think that I would very much like to live near the sea." She finished.

"In Cornwall?"

"I haven't decided yet, but my friends live in Minehead so I may start near there if I can find a house."

"I went to the seaside once, down to Weston for the day. It was all mud; the tide was so far out we couldn't even see it. I was sick from too much ice cream on the way home again."

"It wouldn't be a holiday; it would be my home. I would need to find some employment I expect as well."

"You could join one of those cabaret shows that put on performances at the end of the pier." Lottie chuckled, but Caroline was struck by the possibility. "You will write, won't you, and come and visit us when Eric gets his posting?"

"Only if you promise to visit me in my little bathing hut on the shore."

Annie ran up the stairs at Norwood Court and let herself in to the apartment with the key she kept on a string around her neck. She was so excited she could hardly breathe; she certainly hadn't slept for more than an hour the night before. She held in her hand the letter that would officially start her married life with Jacob.

"Miss Caroline! It's here, it's come!" She called as she changed her outdoor shoes for the softer house shoes George had provided her with.

Caroline came to the door of the sitting room. "What is?"

"This letter! From the Town Council Housing Committee. We've got a house! We can move in on the first of

November!" She was starting to hyperventilate and clutched the envelope to her chest.

"Annie that is wonderful news! Let me see?"

They went into the sitting room and Caroline read the letter out loud. She knew Philip had vouched for Annie and Jacob to the Housing Committee, and George would have if necessary. Along with the confirmation letter was a simple map with the outline of a plot marked in red ink. Number fifty-three Milton Road on the development now known in the town as the Poet's Estate had two bedrooms. It was listed as a 'non-parlour' house, meaning it had a sitting room but no separate dining room. It did however have a bathroom with an indoor toilet and a gas supply for cooking and heating. It was built from red brick, with a curious sloping portion of roof over the front door. The whole estate had been planned with a 'garden city' layout and houses built in an Arts and Crafts style with ample front and rear gardens and new tree-lined roads. Annie would finally be able to take the furniture from the garage at Norwood Court and the sheds at the coal yard and have use of it herself.

Caroline had not yet seen the new houses, so when Annie had finished her work both young women took their bicycles and rode beyond St Mark's church to where the new estate began. They found Milton Road, where some of the houses were already occupied. Caroline was impressed with the sense of space, and how new young trees had been planted at regular intervals along the paths. The roads curved gently, creating rear gardens of varying lengths, and at junctions there were terraces of four or six houses with longer shared front gardens. A row of small shops had been thoughtfully provided for the residents; a butcher, baker, hardware and sundries, tobacconist selling newspapers and confectionary, and a hair salon which would also cater for men. Annie was very excited; she chattered on about the things she would need for the house and how they would like to have fruit trees. Jacob was keen to grow vegetables in the back garden, with the front garden devoted to flower borders and a small lawn.

All the while Caroline was conscious that Annie would be leaving them before too long. She knew how much Annie wanted her own family, and for Jacob to have some respite from the coal dust that found its way into every part of their home no matter how much his mother cleaned. The coal strike had caused Jacob and his father to evaluate the viability of their business, with Jacob's two younger brothers finding employment elsewhere. They had discussed the possibility of diversifying, branching out into other items that required yard storage such as timber and paraffin. Being reliant on just one product had cost them and while they decided to continue with the coal round, Matthew Jenks would do so alone for as long as his health permitted while Jacob would start to look for new suppliers. He would start cautiously, they had only a small amount spare to invest in the new venture, but Jacob was convinced it was the right thing to do.

Annie told Caroline all of this while they stood in the front garden of number fifty-three Milton Road. The builders were doing their final fixes inside.

"It sounds a very sensible thing to do. Father was of a similar opinion when he reviewed our shares portfolio, he invested in something called National Benzole on my behalf and said only the other day that the share price was higher than when he bought them."

"What does that mean?"

"I think it means I might get a slightly larger dividend at the end of the year than Father was expecting."

They turned their bicycles around and wheeled them back down Milton Road towards St Mark's church. "If the price can go up, then can it go down as well?" Annie asked.

"Father says so, yes, which is why he went for low-risk shares. They don't make as much income, but they also don't go up and down as much."

"I would be worried that they would go right down, and I'd have no money at all."

"I'd never thought of it like that, but I suppose it is perfectly possible. You are right, I shouldn't like to rely completely on that kind of income. If I can sell some more of my paintings, then that will help with my day-to-day needs."

Annie thought for a moment. "To be safe, you need to find something that other people can't do without. We thought that about coal, but all of these houses have gas and electricity installed so people won't need as much coal as they used to. Your paintings are nice, but people don't need them, they just want them if they have the money. Things like clothes, shoes, food, building and fixing things, those are the safe jobs."

"I have been lucky haven't I, to not have had to worry about such things."

"Yes, but that's how the world is. You are unusual Caroline. You've worked when you really didn't have to, and you're still not married so you have the freedom to do as you please. All I've ever wanted was a husband and family and a nice home."

"Am I wrong not to want those things? Or at least, not want them yet."

"Not wrong, just unusual. Times are changing, and perhaps there are more women out there like you, but I don't know any."

As the evenings began to draw in, the leaves left the trees and carpeted the streets around Cheltenham, and thoughts began to turn towards Christmas for many people. For George and Caroline Munhead, November once more brought the anniversary of Freddie's death. Caroline had begun to attend meetings of the Women's Section of the Royal British Legion after seeing a poster in a shop window. She had explained to the committee that she might not be able to help for very long, but that she would like to be of use to them while she remained in Cheltenham. It was a relatively young movement, having only been formed in 1921, but the women were enthusiastic in their endeavours to raise funds to support the families of servicemen. Many of them, like Caroline had experienced the loss personally.

It was at a meeting of the Section on a damp and chilly Tuesday afternoon at the end of October, that Caroline made an interesting discovery. She had been helping to sort through some donations to be distributed by the members and sat next to a woman who had also only recently joined the Section. Joyce Frobisher was a widow whose only son had returned from the War after sustaining extensive damage to his face in an explosion. He had been treated at a hospital in Sidcup, Kent, where although the sight in one eye could not be saved, his nose had been rebuilt and the side of his face that had been lost was reconstructed by the pioneering surgeons there. The mental damage had been as, if not more, traumatic for the young Private William Frobisher. Joyce spent much of her time taking care of him and the young man refused to leave the house. He suffered flashbacks, tremors and nightmares, and was revolted with his own appearance.

As the women assembled the small parcels of aid, Joyce mentioned that her sister had also recently joined a Women's Section in the village of Dunster on the north Somerset coast. Caroline recognised the name, having passed through the railway station on the edge of the village as she travelled home from Minehead. She asked Joyce if she had been there and what it was like.

"It is rather a romantic place. It has a castle built halfway up the hill and the village spills downwards from it. Of course, it has been several years since I visited my sister there, she comes to us for Christmas now."

"A castle?"

"Yes, still occupied. Not at all a ruin. They occasionally open the gardens to the public for charity."

When she returned home, Caroline searched her father's books for any mention of Dunster and its castle. She didn't remember seeing one from the train but thought she could have been looking out of the sea-ward side of the carriage at the opportune moment. The Bradshaw Guide mentioned the castle only in passing, focusing more on the coastguard station at the small port of Watchet and the Exmoor Forest further inland. To Caroline it sounded as if it had everything she was looking for; proximity to the sea and the open expanse of the moor, a small community with a larger urban neighbour nearby. It was also close enough to Helen and Tommy without being on their doorstep.

Caroline did not feel particularly superstitious, but she did begin to feel as if the universe was conspiring to lure her to the west country. Freddie would have approved, she decided. Her father was also not against the idea but suggested she might spend a little more time in the area before making her final decision. After the Remembrance Service, held in the pouring rain at the memorial on the Promenade, Caroline walked back to the British Legion headquarters with Joyce Frobisher.

"You mentioned the other day about the castle at Dunster. I have been thinking of taking a house in the area next year."

"Exmoor certainly has a stark beauty. Have you read Blackmore's *Lorna Doone*? It is set on Exmoor. I have a copy you can borrow if you would like."

"Thank you that would be very kind. I admit, I have not been able to find much information about the area."

"My sister is somewhat of a local historian, she would be able to tell you all about the castle, and the archaeology of Dunster. She owns a small guest house, no residents, strictly those spending a few days touring the moor. She would no doubt be able to put you in touch with an agent if you are looking for a more permanent base there."

Caroline couldn't believe her luck; it would be the perfect way to test the waters before diving in. When they reached the headquarters, Joyce wrote down her sister's address and telephone number, and insisted that Caroline contact her directly to arrange her stay.

The following day, a letter arrived from Tanganyika.

14 October 1926
Dear Caroline,

I hope you and your father are well. There has hardly been a minute since I arrived here that I have had to myself, but this evening I have finished my duties and have some time to write to you.

It is a beautiful evening, the sun is so much larger here and the sunsets are exceptional. The whole horizon shimmers in the heat as the enormous ball of fire sinks into the west. I am sitting at a small table outside our hut. I am sharing with a French girl who speaks only a little English. Her name is Marie-Claire, and she is a year younger than me.

It is just as well I paid attention in Miss Devereau's lessons and my French is coming back to me. We are in a small compound with eight such huts, a larger one for our group activities and a latrine block which is the most disgusting thing I have ever experienced, but one must grin and bear it as there is no alternative.

Mark is not here, he is at a compound about thirty miles away, but we did see each other a couple of weeks ago at a group prayer day. The mission is making good use of his mechanical skills and appear to have wanted me for my ability to cook and clean. It is not exactly what I had expected, and from what I can understand, Marie-Claire is not impressed either. We thought we would be teaching, yet there is no school here. The closest is at Mark's compound, and we can only hope they move us there soon.

We exist chiefly on goat meat, goat cheese, fish, a sort of porridge made with maize and bananas that people here call plantains. Vegetables arrive in large tins that are difficult and dangerous to open with the equipment we have. I have several cuts on my hands from attempting it. We try to only drink boiled water after an unfortunate incident just after I arrived when almost the entire compound suffered for a stomach complaint that was attributed to some ice that was brought in from the coast.

There is an abundance of wildlife. Of course, the exotic species we see regularly outside the compound such as giraffe, lions, hyena and a herd of elephants. You might think that at night all is quiet so far from civilisation, but you'd be wrong. The noises from the animals continue well into the night, with yips and snorts that keep one awake. Not so welcome are the insects. I have been bitten numerous times, despite my mosquito net, but thankfully the spiders and snakes have not wanted to make my acquaintance just yet.

As we are not nuns, Marie-Claire and I have taken to wearing the cotton shorts that the men favour, and shirts with sleeves that we roll up. She arrived here with beautiful long black hair, but after three days she begged me to cut it short for her. I did my best, she kept asking for more and more to be removed I did wonder if it might be easier to borrow a shaving kit and make her completely bald! She now resembles the film actress Louise Brooks who I am sure you have heard of.

Our days are all very much the same. We rise early to prepare breakfast for the compound. We clear up afterwards and set about the laundry with the help of some local women. The idea being that we talk to them about God as we work together. After lunch we either help with the compound crops or we type up scripture leaflets to be distributed to the local communities. After dinner there are prayers and then we set about mending any clothes or equipment that require it. As I say, it is not exactly what I had expected but the Reverend Canon says there are plans to build a new school nearer to our compound and then Marie-Claire and I should begin teaching. If I am not devoured by mosquitos first of course.

I must write to mother, so I will close here. The lamp light only attracts more insects. If I have made this sound like a difficult life, forgive me. It is quite the most amazing experience already and I am so very pleased that I have the opportunity to be here.

Letters will find me at the address above, despite the strange appearance.

Much love to you
Midge

Caroline stayed at home for the few days either side of the anniversary of Freddie's death, only venturing out to the Remembrance services. There was an unspoken understanding that she should be home that year. George could sense that it might be the last anniversary they spent together. He was trying not to become selfish in wanting Caroline to stay in the apartment. He had always known the day would come when she would leave and have her own home, though he had hoped it would be with an upstanding young man who would keep her in the manner to which George had tried to do.

He had been encouraged by the two requests for her hand, despite being surprised by Vaughan's evidently infatuated proposition. A lucky escape there for Caroline, he decided. As for Bob, he was not as well advanced socially as George would have liked, but he was clearly a trustworthy and reliable fellow, and George had no objections if Caroline did eventually decide that he was the man for her. Yet, he doubted that she would. She had grown into herself over the past two years, and he had watched her with wonder and pride. He applauded her efforts to try out new things, including manual work for which her position in society had not prepared her. He had worried privately when she had been away in Dorset. He had argued on her behalf with Elizabeth to ensure her wings were not prematurely clipped.

Elizabeth. He tried not to think of her too often, not because he did not care but because he cared a great deal. He wished they had had a photograph taken together before she had become ill. The only image he had of her was one taken just after their wedding, when she was a beautiful young woman and he a proud if bewildered younger man. It was a small portrait of the two of them in a classic pose; she seated and he to one side with his hand on her shoulder. He kept it by his bedside rather than on display in the sitting room. His grief was private.

George hoped that Caroline would wait until after Christmas before striking out by herself. He kept an eye on her shares and was satisfied that they would return somewhere near forty pounds in January. He did not think it would be enough for Caroline to live on by itself and had tried to encourage her to take up the offer of a position as an assistant in the women's outfitter in town that his acquaintance at Christ Church had recently opened. Caroline had not been interested.

She had continued with her art. There were now two sketchbooks full of drawings from around the Park area of Cheltenham. Caroline drew street scenes, churches and chapels, the shops along the Bath Road, the pavilion and lake in the Park itself. She had bought a set of charcoal pencils to save her fingers from smudging the paper, and a small pen knife which she used to sharpen them. Some of the sketches she had filled in with her watercolours, the black lines standing out starkly against the pale pigments. It was becoming her style and George liked them immensely. He offered to have one or two framed for her, but Caroline refused, saying they were merely practice works. Still, he hoped she would leave some behind for him, perhaps his favourite, of the church of St Philip and St James on Grafton Road.

It was at the end of November that Helen and Tommy arrived at Norwood Court to collect Caroline on their way to Great Malvern. She waved to Miss Kettle as she got into the car, having told her over tea and crumpets a few days earlier about her upcoming trip. Annie had agreed to adjust her hours so that George would have his evening meal ready for him after work. The weather was glorious, an early frost melted by weak but bright sunshine. Caroline had packed for all eventualities, though at the last minute had removed her bathing costume from her case as an over optimistic and unnecessary item.

They sped through the countryside to Tewkesbury, then branched off at Upton on Severn and onwards with the Malvern Hills looming in front of them. James had written to say he would join them for two nights at the end of the week once the Ipswich play had finished. Caroline knew she would not feel she was playing the gooseberry and had been a little relieved not to be thrown in with James straight away no matter how much she enjoyed his company.

Lina and Albert had taken up residence at Oakbourne House, Abbey Road, Malvern. Caroline had imagined a house somewhat like Helen's parent's villa in Plymouth. When they arrived as the sun was setting and the air fast becoming cold, Oakbourne House was impressively lit in almost every window. It was twice the size of the Postgate's home, having eight bedrooms and three bathrooms on the first floor, servant's rooms on the second floor, formal and servant's staircases, three reception rooms and a grand dining room on the ground floor, with the kitchens, scullery, cellar and cold room beneath. Large bay windows looked out across the Severn valley and the grounds swept down from a small terrace to the side of the property. There was a small ornamental lake, and woodland to the rear.

The front door opened as they climbed out of the car, and servants in black uniforms descended on their luggage like a disturbed nest of ants each carrying off an item into the depths of the house. Caroline started to explain whose luggage was whose, but Helen placed her hand on Caroline's arm to stop her.

"Leave them to sort it all out darling. It's what they are paid to do, remember."

Lina and Albert came to the door to welcome their guests inside. Lina and Tommy were distant cousins, Lina from the branch of the family who had not had to turn to industry to make their fortune. Yet she was open and warm towards everyone she met, and Caroline liked her. A pair of spaniels yapped and chased around the newcomers until Albert shut them away, and the party went into one of the reception rooms for refreshments and to give the servants time to arrange the contents of the various travel cases inside wardrobes and dressers.

Caroline learned there were more staff than guests and residents at Oakbourne House. A butler had jurisdiction over the household, with Albert's personal valet answering to Albert alone. The Housekeeper oversaw the chambermaid, the two housemaids, the scullery maid and the maid of all work. The chef and under-chef held sway in the kitchen, and the groundsman lived in a small two-room apartment at the rear of the house with its own entrance, taking his meals in the servant's dining room with the others. While they sat and talked, the maids brought in trays of tea, dainty sandwiches and tiny cakes balanced on elaborate tiered serving stands.

It dawned on Caroline that Lina and Albert were behaving the way they thought was expected of them. They were both still so young, at 20 and 22 respectively, yet they were trying to fill such a huge house and make it feel homely by doing the things their parents had also done at home. Caroline had to stifle a giggle at the ridiculousness of it all, which turned into a coughing fit as she inhaled a crumb of cake.

After tea everyone was shown to their rooms and left to amuse themselves until dinner at seven. Caroline was surprised to find her clothes neatly hung and folded and congratulated herself on bringing a book to read to pass the time. She took off her shoes and put her feet up on the bed which creaked as she moved on it but was otherwise comfortable. The room itself was cosy, decorated in a faded burgundy flowered wallpaper and with a small fire glowing in the grate. The coal scuttle was full, and Caroline wondered how cold the room might become if the fire were to go out.

They dressed for dinner and gathered in the library before being summoned by the butler to take their seats in the dining room. The spaniels were allowed in and sat at Albert's feet waiting for scraps. They were evidently his dogs and Lina had no say over whether they stayed or were banished. Later, after coffee in the drawing room, Albert brought out a new board game that the couple had been given as a wedding present. It was called *Pegity* and consisted of a board drilled with 16 rows of 16 holes with four sets of coloured pegs. The aim of the game was for each player to take turns to place their pegs in a row of five, without being prevented by the other players with their pegs. Albert apologised that there were only four sets of pegs, but Lina said she would watch so the others could all play. After several games, with Tommy having won the most, Caroline glanced at the mantle clock and saw it was just after eleven. She thanked her hosts and made her way up to her bedroom and slept contentedly until seven the next morning.

They spent the next day on the golf course. Albert had joined as soon as they returned from Scotland and played two or three times a week. Lina usually did not accompany him but was happy to attempt to hit the golf balls alongside her friends. Caroline soon rediscovered her skill at putting, and Helen and Albert became very competitive on the afternoon's round. Tommy gave much encouragement to them both while being greatly over par himself, while Caroline and Lina tagged along behind.

"Albie so enjoys his golf. It's nice for him to have someone of accomplishment to play against. Helen is rather good, isn't she?"

"Yes, she enjoys playing the men. Will Albert be taking up an occupation now that you are settled here?"

"He rather hopes to go into politics. My father says there is a seat soon to be available in Hereford and Albie will be put forward as a candidate."

"But this is Worcestershire."

"We won't have to live there. Albie will simply represent the constituency. It will mean he spends some time in London, but that's not too much of a cross to bear and I shall have the children for company." Lina smiled brightly.

"But you don't, you mean..."

"Yes, I think I am. Keep it under your hat of course, I do need to visit the doctor and Albie doesn't know yet, but yes."

"Congratulations."

"Thank you. It's such a wonderful house and I should like to fill it with children."

"I suppose it is much easier to travel with young children these days, with the motor car being so convenient."

"We shall have a Nanny of course, and if I do ever need to accompany Albie anywhere, they will naturally stay with her."

"Naturally." Echoed Caroline.

"And you? Any wedding bells on the horizon? I did wonder if you and James would be announcing something soon."

"No." Caroline said abruptly. Then more gently she continued, "James is far too devoted to his work to give any woman the equal devotion she deserves. James and I are good friends, nothing more. I don't think I have met a man yet whom I should agree to marry at the moment."

"Being married is simply delightful! I am so lucky to have Albie as my husband, and Helen and Tommy seem equally well suited to each other."

Caroline wasn't sure if Lina knew the exact details of their friend's marriage arrangement, but she smiled as she agreed that they were indeed very well suited.

That evening after dinner, Lina returned to the subject. "So, Caroline, if you are not going to marry James, what are you going to do with yourself?"

The drawing room was quiet with only the crackling of the logs in the fireplace and the ticking of the mantle clock to be heard. Caroline put down her glass of port and looked at her friends.

"I have been thinking of taking a house near the sea. Perhaps near to Minehead, unless you two object terribly?"

"Not at all! That's wonderful news!" Tommy was on his third pink gin.

"Of course not darling!" Helen had coffee rather than alcohol.

"I have the name of a guest house owner, a sister of someone I know at home, and I thought I might stay for a month there and see how things are."

"On your own?" asked Lina.

"Yes, on my own."

"But what will you do with yourself?"

"Perhaps nothing in that first month, until I know my way around. But after that, if I decide to stay, I hoped I might be able to keep painting or find a position somewhere for a few hours a week. It really will depend on what's available, but I feel I need to be near to the sea."

"I completely understand darling," said Helen. "One loves to visit other places, but one always feels the pull of the sea after a while."

"Golly, we'll need to teach you to drive! It's rather remote in our part of the country. We can find you a little car, not an old battle-axe like mine."

"I hadn't thought of that, but it sounds exciting if you really think I could learn."

"I'm not sure that I could." Lina turned up her nose, "I don't think I should want to."

"Not quite the thing for a young lady," commented Albert and the young couple smiled indulgently at each other.

"Nonsense!" replied Helen. "It's the very thing for a modern young woman to do. So much more convenient than relying on trains all the time."

"Exactly! And then you have the freedom of the open road. We can go off to the moor and paint all day with no one else around." Tommy was becoming animated, sitting forward in his chair.

"Caro, I rather fear I might lose my husband to you, how will you cope with Tommy tagging along behind you like a puppy?"

"It sounds more like I'll be racing to keep up with him!"

"What does your father say about it all?" Lina was still struggling with the whole concept.

"He is a little sad that he'll be on his own, but we talked about it the other day and he is very happy for me to be spreading my wings as he called it. Which makes me sound like a seagull, but I know I can always go back to him if things don't work out. I am very lucky in that respect. He was insistent that I should not feel as though I had to stay to look after him, like I did Mother."

Helen nodded. "I always did think that it was unfair for you to take those duties on almost straight after we finished school. I often thought of you when I was in Europe or at parties."

"I didn't mind at the time, but it started to feel as if Freddie's death would not have been worth anything if I didn't make good the freedoms he had been fighting for."

"I'm so sorry, Caroline, I didn't know," Lina reached across and patted Caroline's hand in sympathy.

"It's quite alright, it was years ago. But Freddie was so full of life, I simply couldn't sit around doing nothing any longer."

"And now look at you!" beamed Tommy, "A true adventuress!"

"Hardly! Midge is the true adventurer of us three from school. She is our other friend, Lina, she has gone to Africa with a Christian Mission."

"Africa? To work with the natives? My goodness. I am rather comforted that you will be staying in England at least!"

James was due to arrive the following day. Lina appeared at breakfast but explained she was feeling a little off colour and returned apologetically to bed. Caroline and Helen decided to explore the town, leaving Tommy and Albert to talk politics, cars and money. They had realised the day before that the town of Great Malvern was draped precariously over the side of a large hill, with spring water that emerged from the rocks at the top and at several other points around the town. There were a number of large hotels and curative establishments offering a range of water treatments, not dissimilar to Cheltenham before the turn of the century. Malvern had held on to its prestige, partly down to the excellent views across the

Severn valley and the clean air, as a destination whereas Cheltenham was a town of empty buildings on the way to somewhere else.

The women were wrapped up against the cold, their breath steaming from their mouths as they talked. They wandered down and then back up the main vertical street, and then along the horizontal terrace of shops at the top of the hill overlooking the Abbey Hotel. On a whim Caroline purchased some yarn, knitting needles and a pattern for a scarf, thinking she might make her father a gift for Christmas. As they walked back to Oakbourne House, Helen stopped by a bench near the Abbey Gate and sat down. She patted the bench next to her for Caroline to sit.

"My dear, are you quite sure you are ready to strike out on your own?"

"Not entirely, that's why I thought a month would show me one way or the other."

"Yes, an infinitely sensible approach. Tommy and I will support you in any way we can, you know that. Only I sense that you are perhaps not running to but running from something. Am I right?"

"If you had asked me that at the start of the summer, I would have had to agree with you. I was feeling crowded, as if everyone were expecting me to behave one way and I could not meet their expectations. But those ... problems, have resolved themselves. It was really only James that I had to make a decision about in the end, and that became clear to me when I saw him in Worcester. I like James a great deal. In any other situation, I should probably agree to marry him and follow him wherever his work took us."

"And yet you turned him down."

Caroline bit her lip. "I don't feel passionately about James." She said at last.

"That man in Cornwall. Oh, Caro, didn't I warn you not to measure everyone else against him?" Helen was not angry, but she was concerned for her friend.

"You did, and I have tried not to. It's simply made it clear to me that while I cannot be with Max, ever, I also cannot settle for mere comfort. Galina knew it before I did, she said I needed to find someone who I could share my passions with."

"Galina?"

"She lives in the apartment opposite ours, she is Russian although you would never guess, and a widow. Her life has been extraordinary, but she and her husband shared a passion for whatever they did and wherever they went together. She could see I would not be happy with just anyone who asked, even before Max. And she is right, I know that now."

Helen sighed and took out her cigarette case. She lit one and blew the smoke out away from both their faces.

"You may never find a man who has the same passions as you."

"I shall be content with myself until I do. I want to live by myself, to prove that I can. Everyone else is getting married, with varying degrees of happiness. I'm not ready for that yet, and certainly not children."

"It certainly suits Lina, though I do wish she would stop simpering after Albert."

"She said married life suits you and Tommy too."

The women looked at each other for a moment before breaking into giggles as if they were back at school.

The End